THE SERPENT'S COILS

A Tale of Blades and Darkness

BOOK ONE

K N TIMOFEEV

ISBN: 978-1-0878-5771-8
ISBN-13: 978-1-0878-5771-8

For my lovely writing club students. You guys inspire me!

ALSO WRITTEN BY K N TIMOFEEV

Lost Guardian Trilogy:
The Lost Guardian
Souls in the Dark
Time of Prophecy

Bardon
Dorage
Stalmar
Istton
Storm's Pass
Cemont
Toe
Nealet
K'aski
God's Gate
The Dead Lands
U
Verance

N
Paddniq
Vilnia
The Gray Seas
Lorcea
Eddany
Black Marsh
The River Lands
Zallino
Three Kings Bay
Xhu'Rozo
os
The Keep
The Holy Isle

CHAPTER ONE

IT WAS HOT, SO UNBEARABLY HOT. TAKA WAS ALREADY sweating under his summer furs. He should have listened to his brother and purchased a linen garment from the Nealetian traders at the last port. Well, it was too late now.

A small breeze teased Taka, cooling his brow but bringing a horrid stench with it. Taka fought the urge to cover his nose with his sleeve. It wouldn't help his sales for these southerners to see weakness, even if their city smelled like an archon's backside.

Taka chose the least intrusive corner of the ship, watching the sailors bring the massive trade ship into the docks. Ships were fascinating. The seas around Cemont were too dangerous for anything larger than a sturdy canoe, and even then, it was a risk. He wondered if the waters around his homeland were as calm as the seas surrounding him if his people could trade more than furs taken from the great beasts of the ice fields.

"All ashore, that's goin' ashore!"

The cry shook Taka from his thoughts. He picked up his satchel, slinging it over his shoulder. "Trade time."

His footsteps echoed against the gangplank. He stood to the side with the other merchants, waiting for his goods to be unloaded. Luckily, he was the first off the boat. A massive pile of furs of varying shades and sizes was lowered to the docks by an enormous wrench.

"Will ya be needin' a cart?"

Taka turned. The ship's captain stood behind him, shadowed by a sickly-looking man with a ledger. "No, I have a contact in the city."

The captain nodded, stepping off to inspect the other goods being unloaded. The sickly man walked up to Taka and coughed pointedly. Taka rolled his eyes and tossed him a small purse filled with coins—payment for safe arrival.

The sickly man took the purse, scribbling into his ledger. "Return passage? We sail again in two days."

Again, Taka shook his head. The sickly man scurried off to retrieve payment from the others. Taka checked the straps securing the furs together. The last thing he needed was for the bundle to fall apart, ruining the pelts.

"Taka! Quanuippit!"

Taka turned, beaming. "Quanuinngittunga, Nukilik! How's that pretty wife of yours? Is she missing me yet?"

Nukilik threw his head back, laughing.

Though the pair had grown up in the same village, their yurts a stone's throw away from each other, they couldn't look more different. Nukilik left to join the priesthood when he turned thirteen, the age of manhood, while Taka stayed, becoming a trader. Nukilik wore robes of their god, although altered to accommodate the southern heat. His hair hung loosely around his shoulders, black and shining. Taka's furs were worn and sea-stained. His hair was in a long plait down his back. Though they were a part of two different worlds, once together, they quickly fell into old habits, conversing in their native tongue rather than the commonly used in Undros.

"It's always good to see you, my friend," Nukilik said, clasping Taka on the shoulder. "Let's load the cart, and you can fill me in on everything from home."

"How much longer is your indenture?"

A careless shrug. "A few more years, I think. They don't really give you a concrete answer. One priestess was only here for a season before they released her."

"But you've been here for three years already? And two years before that, you were at the Holy Isle."

Again, Nukilik shrugged. "I think it's because I studied under The Smelter. There's a lot of things that need to be fixed in the temple."

Taka made a noncommittal noise in the back of his throat. Gods and priesthoods were things he knew very little about. Give him the physical world with problems he could solve with his hands any day.

As Taka filled Nukilik in on the comings and goings of a tiny village an entire world away, their little wagon wove its way through the spiraling streets of Verance. He always admired the old kings and queens who looked at a massive hill rising up from the shoreline and ending in a cliff and thought, *Why not build a city here.*

Their destination was the temple of Etunis in the Divine District, but to get there, they had to wind their way through the lower Merchant District, a short trip from the docks. Taka would come back tomorrow and sell the furs the temple didn't take.

His stomach rumbled as they trudged past taverns, restaurants, and street vendors. Meals on the ship had been tasteless and tough; Taka looked forward to having a decent meal and a comfortable bed for once.

As they rounded a sharp corner, Taka spied a castle at the very top of the hill. Even from his position, the castle was massive, looming like an ice eagle searching for its prey.

"Never fails to inspire, does it?"

"I prefer home."

Nukilik laughed again. "For someone whose life demands he travel, you're rather sentimental."

A small pack of street urchins ran across the street, yelling and laughing. To Taka, they were no different than the packs of wild dogs that scavenged at the village border. "At least at home, people are civilized."

One of the urchins paused as if it had heard what Taka said. The urchin scowled behind a tangled mass of hair the color of pitch. Taka gasped. The urchin's eyes were the same color as the floating ice mountains of the Northern Sea, and behind them, power simmered.

Mirra watched the cart roll by with a sneer on her face. *What you know, fur head!* She bet he'd be a bit rough if he grew up the way she did. *It don't matter. I ain't got a family or a real home, but I got my gang, and they're better than any old fur head!*

"Hey, Mirra, hurry up!"

Mirra spat at the retreating cart before dashing off to join her gang. The sun was setting, and they still had many things to steal.

THE SUN SLOWLY CREPT OVER THE TOPS OF THE BUILDINGS, casting beams of light into the dark alley below. Orphan Alley, where untethered children slept together for protection against the elements, slavers, and child lovers. As the shadows retreated, huddled forms stirred. Here and there, a blanket or burlap sack was thrown aside, revealing children huddled together for warmth. Some were more fortunate, sleeping in makeshift shelters made up of discarded sail, broken crates, or barrels.

A band of light landed on one such crate, working its way through gaps in the boarding, shining a light on the sleeping forms below.

One band fell across Mirra's eyes, waking her from her slumber. She rubbed the sleep and dirt from her eyes, landing on the empty crumpled blanket on the other end. She scowled at the blanket.

The vacant spot belonged to Bao, the leader of their gang, and the closest thing Mirra had to a friend. Her frown deepened. It wasn't like him to be gone already. He must be up to something already. Groaning at the thought, she stretched, releasing some of the tightness in her back. She wiggled the top off the crate and crawled out.

She gazed about the alley, numbly taking in the dozens of other makeshift shelters like hers and scattered lumps of those less fortunate.

A few of the other orphans gave Mirra a short nod in greeting before quickly casting their eyes to the ground.

Mirra returned the gesture. She was a member of a notorious gang in service to Bossman Jax, the crime lord of the Merchant's District. Which meant any disrespect toward her was disrespect toward him. And those who disrespected the bossman ended up dead.

Mirra never threw that backing around. All it would take is one extremely pissed off person with nothing to lose, and it could be her that ended up with a blade to the belly.

Show respect. That was the first rule to surviving the underworld. Actually, the first rule was, never betray your people. No matter who you were waring against, never squeal to the lawmen. Two rules may not seem like too much trouble, but Mirra had witnessed the gutters running red with the blood of those who couldn't follow them.

Mirra made her way to the closest public fountain to wash up. Even this early in the morning, the fountain was crowded. Most people took what they needed and rushed back to the safety of their homes. But for those like Mirra, with no home of their own, they were left using the communal buckets.

Mirra picked up a bucket, turning it upside down. Sometimes drunkards left unpleasant gifts behind. Seeing and smelling nothing out of the ordinary, she dunked the small, rickety bucket into the ice-cold bubbling water. Without stopping to think, she withdrew the bucket and dumped the contents over her head. She gritted her teeth against the cold water, quickly sloshing off the dirty water. She shook her hair like a dog before wringing it out. Marginally cleaner, she placed the bucket back with the other communal buckets and walked away.

If she lingered, a well-to-do housewife with too much time on her hands would approach, asking Mirra about her family. It was apparent she didn't have one, but asking would give the housewife an excuse, not that she needed one, to set the city guard on Mirra. If caught, they would throw her in the nearest orphanage. Her early years had been spent in one of those crown sanctioned hellholes. The moment she turned five, she ran away, swearing to never enter one again.

Mirra wiped the dirty water away from her eyes, spitting whenever it ran over her lips. She looked about the square, hoping to see Bao or the other members of the Shadow Guild, their little gang. They only numbered six in total, but what they lacked in size, they made up for with skill.

There was Bao, their leader, even though he was twelve. The same age as Mirra. Unlike the rest of the gang, he actually had a formal education. His family hailed from the merchant class in Zallino. His formative years were spent safe and secure, learning things like reading, writing, philosophy, and math. He often tried to teach Mirra, but she refused. What use were books to her? They couldn't feed you. They couldn't protect you. The only thing they were good for was stuffing into your close to keep the chill away and burning. Now, if you're wondering how a merchant's son from Zallino ended up running a gang in Undros, it's nothing complicated. His parents were killed in a marketplace riot during the Summer of no rain. Mirra found him unconscious but alive under the wreckage, blood matted in his black hair. She took him home and treated him as best she could, fearful that his almond eyes would never open again. When he did, Mirra took him under her wing until he fully regained his strength. That was two years ago.

The road is not safe. Especially for a child with no protector. Too many children were lost to slavers or worse, who disguised themselves as a helpful hand. So, Bao stayed in Verance and learned the way of the underworld. His past turned out to be a mixed blessing. He was smart enough to pull off elaborate but lucrative schemes, but his morally right upbringing sometimes clashed with the harsh truths of his new world. The other members had similar stories with varying degrees of malaise.

Krill, ranked just under Mirra, had initially been from Lorcea—one of the Stone Clans whose name he refused to speak of. He was thirteen when his parents were killed during a Horse Lord raid. The war chief took him as a slave and sold him to a man that used Krill in ways that no child should be used. Luckily, his master caught a blade to the belly during a dispute over a card game. During the chaos, Krill filled a small sack with provisions and coin and stole away on a caravan heading south. Sometimes his dark eyes would grow darker as he thought about the past. It was on those days that his temper was short, and blood was spilled from his hidden daggers.

Sorro was from Nealet. His ebony skin stood out in stark contrast to the rest of the gang. He was a full head and shoulders taller than most of them, being the oldest, a hearty fifteen. He ran away from his village to pursue his dream of becoming a dancer. He actually did well, dancing with a traveling troupe, but when he got to Verance, there was something about the capital city that made him stay behind. Mirra suspected the what was actually a who, a moon-faced girl from the Night Jasmine, a brothel. His den was set up somewhere near there. It worked out well for him all the same. That area was thick with shops and restaurants. Street performers often gathered there, and he would dance to their music, earning some extra coin. Being a dancer meant that he was also a great acrobat, perfect for thieving.

The next two members of the gang looked like siblings, but they weren't. Em and Tul were both Undrosen natives, born and raised in the slums. They both had blonde hair with gray eyes. But that's where their similarities ended. Tul's entire family died from the Sweating Sickness. He survived the sickness, but it stunted his growth, leaving him wiry and small with long delicate fingers, perfect for pickpocketing. Em's mother and father were still alive, as were her seven other siblings. She ran away when her father drunkenly mentioned that he was going to sell her to a brothel. She had a fair face and used that to con her victims so convincingly that they weren't even aware they had been robbed until much later.

Mirra was the only member who didn't have an actual past. The only thing she knew about her parents was that they dropped her off at the orphanage when she was barely a moon old and never looked back. At night, Mirra bragged about her accomplishments to them. In her imaginings, they were ashamed that they gave her up and begged for Mirra to forgive them.

But even as much as she hated them, she couldn't stop herself from looking for them in every strange face she saw. The capital brought in people from all over the world, yet none of them bore any resemblance to Mirra's face. Beneath a thick layer of grime and filth, pale white skin streaked through on a narrow face. That pale skin was a stark contrast to her raven's wing hair that she used to hide her most striking feature; ice blue eyes that held more sorrow and steel than they should at the tender age of twelve.

The madams of the pleasure houses clamored after her and her strange eyes for as long as she could remember. She'd like to think that it was her ruthless nature that kept her out of the madam's clutches, but that wasn't true. As an active member of a gang, her life belonged to Bossman Jax.

It was him that turned madams down because he valued Mirra more as a thief than a painted lady. But his favoritism wouldn't last forever. One day he would sell her to the pleasure houses and pocket the coin without sparing her another thought.

Mirra closed her eyes and shook away the thought. She would plunge a blade into her own heart before she ever became a whore. There were painted ladies younger than her, not many but enough for her to worry. Whenever she came across one, a shudder ran down her spine at the sight of their soulless, empty eyes.

A shadow crept over her shoulder, breaking Mirra out of her thoughts. Her hand going to the blade strapped to her side. She spun around, pulling the knife loose.

Bao laughed, stepping back with his hands raised.

"Did I getcha?" he teased. Mirra scowled up at his smiling face, fighting the urge to smile back.

"Nah, knew you was there," she said, sheathing her knife.

Bao just smiled wider and said, "Sure, you did."

Mirra stuck out her tongue.

"If you're done lookin' at yourself, I got us some breakfast." Bao held out two pastries. Mirra recognized the wrappers and smiled. Who could be mad when presented with fresh pastries from the most famous bakery in all the districts?

"I'll forgive ya for runnin out on me this morning," Mirra said, taking a pastry. Bao gave her a mocking bow before sitting on the ledge next to her.

Staring up at her friend, Mirra felt a wave of warmth crash over her that she never had a name for. Whatever god pushed Bao her way, she was grateful for it. Never in her life had she known someone with so much light in them. The streets usually beat it out of you at a young age, but Bao seemed immune.

His round face was always quick to smile, and his tilted eyes were always filled with laughter. Mirra liked to think that she kept him grounded, but Bao kept her tethered to the light. He held the darkness of their world from seeping into her soul, forever numbing it to the pain that surrounded them.

She bit into the pastry. Her mouth flooded with sweet cream filling. The pastry's outer layer practically dissolved on her tongue, leaving only the barest hint of bread behind.

"Mmmm."

Bao smiled briefly before reaching into his pocket, withdrawing a single black feather with a red ribbon around it. Mirra took note of it, the pastry turning to ash in her mouth.

"The tithe."

Every bossman enacted a tithe for their turf. If you were a gang that worked on that turf, you had to give a portion of your hauls to the bossman. Refusal to do so usually ended with your entire gang "missing." For the small businesses that couldn't afford hired guards or bribe the city watch, paying tribute to the bossman kept his goons from burning your business, along with your family, to the ground.

"I wanna do a run before tonight," Bao announced.

Mirra licked the sugar residue off her fingers. "Of course, you do."

Bao rolled his eyes. "I heard that there's a fresh shipment of Nealetian wool on Toffery Street. The Thread Guilds are trying to get 'em. I even heard some new colors are being shown."

"New colors," Mirra said blandly, nodding like she cared. Bao narrowed his eyes.

"Laugh all you want, but dyed wool from Nealet is something that even the nobles will come down here for."

"And other things."

Bao's frown turned into a full scowl. "Cut it out."

"Make me," she teased. Bao groaned.

They washed their sticky hands in the fountain, strolling quickly by each other's side. "There'll be plenty of marks, ripe for the pickin'," Bao said.

"Lots of guards too," Mirra countered.

"Hard to keep an eye on every pocket."

"I heard that the farmers have come to sell their stuff too," Mirra mentioned, switching topics. "We could split up and hit both?"

Bao paused, tapping his finger to his mouth like he always did when he was deep in thought. "You and Tull go to Toffery Street and lift what you can. Me, Em, 'n Sorro will hit the farmers."

Mirra stretched both arms overhead, loosening her muscles. She smirked at Bao, who smiled back, catching her mood. Without a word, the pair tore down the street. They raced onward, bare feet pounding against the cobblestone streets. Ducking and weaving, they moved through the crowded streets. Yells and curses trailed after them.

Mirra and Bao laughed like crazy people and continued their race, although neither one gained much ground over the other. But that was the point. They weren't trying to be better than the other. They were trying to be better together. To move and think as one person.

Bao went left. Mirra went right. They came back together for a moment before a cart pulled out in front of them. Bao instantly cupped his hands, vaulting Mirra over a breath before he spun out of the way. They met up on the other side, flashing identical wild grins.

A rope from a broken clothesline hung against a building. Mirra grabbed the line, reaching back for Bao at the same time. Using his momentum, he flew through the air. With his free hand, Bao latched onto an open window. Mirra released her hold on the rope, trusting Bao to not let her fall.

They scrambled up the building, running along the gently sloping roofs until they used another set of clotheslines to reach the street again. They slowed their frantic pace to a jog and then to a walk, smiling like madmen. This is what put a gang of kids at the top. Alone, they had some skills, but they worked best as a team, as one.

Around another public fountain, the rest of the Shadow Guild lingered. They weren't together but milling around the square, watching for the city watch and rival gangs. When they spired their leader and his intrepid second, they left their posts to meet them down a narrow alley.

"What's the word, hummingbirds?" Bao asked in his way of greeting. His greeting was met with numerous eye rolls.

"The bossman's got a secret, special job for who brings in the best haul tonight," Krill said, shaking his head with a half-smile on his face.

Bao's head perked up, and the overall mood darkened.

"But I don't like it," added Em, quickly looking to Mirra for support.

Mirra gave her a small shrug. She could try, but the tithe was tonight. Bao would be infuriatingly single-minded until it was over. "Why?"

Em and Kril shared a glance before the former shrugged.

Kril sighed. "No one knows anything 'bout it. Not even a rumor. Whatever it is, Bossman got it all wrapped up. He only does that when it's somethin' big and dangerous."

Bao's brow furrowed as he processed Kril's input. Mirra ground her teeth to remain silent. She had a strong inclination what his response would be, but she hoped she was wrong. Her gut twisted, usually a sign of trouble. She tried to brush the feeling off as nerves.

Tithe night was always stressful. No one knew how the evening would go. Sometimes it got bloody, primarily when there was a top job on the line. Mirra chewed her lip.

She would have liked to have stayed in the middle. Not enough to put them in the spotlight but enough to keep them alive. If she was in charge, she would do whatever it took to not get the job. But she wasn't the leader.

"We'll worry about that later," Bao told the others. "We got things to do."

The others perked up, eyes sparkling with excitement. "Tull, you're with Mirra. She'll fill you in. The rest of you are with me. Let's go. Happy hunting."

"Happy hunting," they murmured back. They clasped each other around the forearm before scattering through the streets.

THERE WAS BARELY ANY ROOM TO MOVE ABOUT TOFFERY Street. Merchants, nobles, and the common masses jostled each other in a pickpocket's wet dream. With people bumping into one another every few steps, they would hardly notice the hand that relieved them of their valuables.

Mirra and Tull shared equally wicked grins. Mirra made a spiraling motion with her finger, indicating that they would circle the crowd in opposite directions until they met up in the middle. From there, they would decide whether or not to make another round or get out while the getting was good. Tull nodded, understanding the meaning.

Tull was the first to slide into the crowd. Mirra soon lost sight of his shaggy head, but she knew that he could handle himself if there were any trouble. Mirra studied the gathering merchants a moment longer, trying to get a feel for the temperament of the crowd. She opened her mouth and inhaled. Spices and smoke coated her tongue, creating a heady mixture that mingled with the excitement in the air from the ever-growing crowd. Dyed wool could be found in every market around the world, but wool from Nealet was worth a king's ransom.

Nealet was one of Undros' closest neighbors, but it lacked many of the similar resources that allowed Undros to thrive. Vast grassy savannas and rugged mountain ranges provided little substance for its people. But deep within the mountains that ringed the plains grew one of the rarest herbs that, when mixed with other colors, produced a vibrancy and shade utterly unique. Each tribe had its signature color whose recipe was kept hidden by the tip of a blade. Anyone who sought to steal a clan's secret recipe found their head pitted on a stake as a warning for other would-be thieves.

When Nealetian dyers came to market, everyone stopped to see their wares, no matter their station. It could be their only time to see the famed dye masters and to see if the rumors they've heard held any merit.

Mirra's eyes locked on a haggard-looking woman. Her dress was simple but finely made. As the woman turned, Mirra spied a crest embroidered on the right-side shoulder, a merchant's wife. Mirra could see the frustration on her reddened face from clear across the square. The merchant's wife kicked one of her servants, who she probably treated like a slave, sending him careening down the sandstone square. Mirra clenched her jaw. She hated the way people with money and power looked down on those without. It went against every tenet their bright sun god, Yrdris, commanded them to do. She didn't believe in the gods, not really. Still, at least she could say that she lived honestly by the tenets of the Dark Mother, Yulla, and her son the Night Prince who ruled over those who made their way through the world by their wits and their moral compass.

She slid into the crowd, heart pounding. She tilted her head down, letting her dark hair obscure her face, masking her tell-tell eyes from being marked, and keeping her hunter's gaze hidden. Moving through the crowd without unintentionally bumping into the other patrons required the skill of a dancer, and thankfully, she had an excellent teacher who was also a good friend.

With each deliberate step, Mirra made her way toward her target. It wasn't a straight line. That would have been too obvious. So, her path was a twisting, winding trail, and along the way, she pulled in as many details of her surroundings as possible. She would need a new mark after the merchant's wife.

Her blood filled with electric energy making her bones hum with excitement. She always felt this way before. Carefully, she narrowed in on her prey, the woman completely unaware of any out of the ordinary. Mirra smiled wickedly. Why should the merchant's wife suspect that she was about to be a target? Her life was one of ease. She would never have to worry about an empty belly, not having enough loot, or of being killed in the night over a scrap of a blanket.

The warm hum of excitement in her veins was replaced with cold fire. It was time for her to earn a bit back from the people at the top. Time to teach them a small lesson in loss. Fast as a swooping hawk, Mirra deftly cut the ties to the merchant wife's purse strings. She caught it in her other hand and was already off to her next target before the merchant's wife even realized her purse was missing. Mirra couldn't help but smile when a shrill screech filled the air. She lived for days like this.

Bao watched the farmers as they unloaded their crops for inspection—dusky apples, golden grains, bright gourds, and piles and piles of green vegetables. That, coupled with the hundreds of animals slated for the butchers, was a wealth of food that Bao had not been able to sample since his parents died.

He wondered what they would think of him now, not an honorable merchant like they had planned but a leader of a gang that stole from honest, hardworking people like they were. He'd like to think that they were proud of him for learning how to survive their deaths and finding a way to provide for himself. They always stressed resourcefulness; it was one of the few things he still remembered about them. Though he could no longer recall his mother's smile, or how his father sounded when he sang the songs of their homeland. He could barely speak what used to be his native tongue, and reading it—forget about it. Bao shook his head. If he were honest with himself, they were probably suffering in the afterlife. When they had been killed, Bao didn't have the means to give them a proper burial. He couldn't burn their bodies or sing the Songs of the Dead.

Shaking his head, Bao pushed all other thoughts but what laid out in front of him out of his head. He needed to keep a level head to pull the heist off. If Mirra were with him, she would have smacked him upside the head and called him soft-hearted. He smiled at the thought.

As far as he was concerned, Mirra was a walking, talking contradiction. She always claimed that she was better off alone, yet he took him under her wing and helped him learn the rules of this new hard world he found himself in. She brought in the others as well. She had a knack for drawing in the weakest and making them resilient. He owed everything to her, and that's why he needed their gang to be the best. The more notorious they were, the better jobs they would get, and the more they could squirrel away for a better tomorrow. Perhaps even a chance to do some good in the world.

The farmers finished with their unloading, headed off to some of the local taverns scattered throughout the market place. There they would eat and drink until the inspectors came to determine just how much of their products they could sell inside the city. The inspectors were wrapped up in examining the permits the farmers were required to produce to even bring their products into the capital.

It was time.

Bao removed a small fragment of a broken mirror wrapped in a spare scrap of fabric from his pocket. Holding it just right, he flashed twice. From their hiding spots around the marketplace, Em, Krill, and Sorro flashed their fragments, confirming that they were in place and ready. Carefully, rewrapping the broken mirror, Bao slid it back into his pocket and sent a silent prayer to Onear, the god of his people, and to his ancestors for everything to go off without any complications.

In a mad dash, Bao tore off toward the unprotected pile of goods. The others did the same. They each snatched a different bag of products before speeding down the nearest alleyway. Shouts and the thundering of iron nailed shoes followed soon after. Em sped past Kril and tossed him her bag of apples; he threw his sack of grain to her before they both changed directions. The farmers who chased them paused, confused as to which thief had their property. That pause allowed Em and Krill to disappear into the lower streets where the farmers dare not go. Bao and Sorro did the same before disappearing themselves.

Several blocks away from the marketplace, Bao and the others laughed as they shouldered their haul. It was a good day. More than once before, they've had to drop their hauls or risk capture. They all agreed when they first formed their little gang that no haul was worth their lives. Live to steal another day; that was their motto.

"All right, all right," Bao said, calling order even though he laughed breathlessly as the others, "Let's head to the Lair and wait for Mirra and Tull. Remember …"

"No celebrating until everyone is back," the others finished in unison.

LAUGHING, MIRRA AND TULL SPED THROUGH THE STREETS, their pockets heavy with the spoils of victory. Mirra silently thanked the Nealet traders for creating the best distraction she could have ever hoped for. They paused a few blocks away, catching their breath and waiting to see if they had been made. A few people watched them warily, but no cries of "thief," no clank of the city guard armor. Tull flashed a wide grin, already giddy. Mirra held in her smile for later; there was still plenty of time for everything to go tits up.

They walked calmly down a few streets until they came to a building that was partially collapsed because of a fire. The building was abandoned, and the city builders had yet to repair it. But this low in the city, that would probably never happen. Most of the coin went to keeping the upper levels in pristine order. The lower levels had to make do with what they already had. The only time any serious coin was spent on the lower streets was when there was an epidemic that threatened to overtake the city. The illnesses usually started in the lowest levels of the capital, where there were fewer doctors, and most buildings were condemned and filthy. The city officials often did whatever it took to keep whatever sickness it was from spreading to the higher sections of the city.

Most of the honest citizens of the lower sectors avoided the derelict buildings, fearful of injury due to the compromised structures or the hordes of homeless that had nowhere else to go. But for the members of the Shadow Guild, the crumbling buildings of the low streets were a godsend.

The uneven stones made scaling the walls as easy as walking. And while a fair amount of the walls was gone, the main support beams were still sound and the best secret highway through the city for those with the surest feet.

Mirra and Tull dashed along the crumbling rooftops like the sure-footed goats from the Cemont mountain ranges. Occasionally their foot would slip because of some rotting piece of wood, but it only slowed them down for a breath. They stopped when they reached the last roof before their hideout. Gasping slightly, they survey the distance. One small misstep would leave them in a bloody heap on the cobblestone street below. Tull placed a foot on the edge of the building and peered over the edge.

"Looks clear," he said. "We'd best get on before a patrol comes by."

Mirra nodded, turned, and walked to the opposite side of the building. Tull joined her. They quickly clasped each other's forearms in both luck and farewell. With determined faces, they sped toward the edge of the building. Everything in their world narrowed down to the pounding of their feet and the upcoming edge. As they neared the point of no return, they sped up, pouring every last ounce of their strength and raw determination into gaining every ounce of momentum they would need to clear the massive gap. In unison, they reached the edge and sprung into the sky, limbs outstretched and breath held as for the briefest of moments; they became like birds in the air flying free.

THE APPLES WERE AS DELICIOUS AS THEY LOOKED. THEIR pink flesh was tender, yet still crisp enough to give a satisfying crunch when bitten into. The white meat underneath quickly gave way, filling their mouths with sweetness. While the others savored the spoils of their labors, Bao's gaze was fixated on the two uneaten apples sitting off to the side. Two of their members still unaccounted for. He knew that Mirra and Tull could look after themselves, but he hated the wait. Hated, not knowing. To occupy his mind, Bao went over their haul from the market. One sack of apples, two bags of grain, and salted ham. Not too bad but not good enough. The other gangs would have hit the markets as well. He hoped Mirra and Tull were able to use the Nealetian wool merchants to their advantage. If they wanted to make an impression on the bossman, they would need coins and shinnies.

Two loud, distinct thuds shook the rafters, sending bits of debris showering down on the children below. Bao and the others are instantly on the alert, their hands going to whatever weapon they carry.

A whistle comprised five quick notes.

They all relaxed. Bao whistled the two-note reply. Mirra and Tull sliding through the open window.

"How'd it go?"

Mirra and Tull emptied their pockets with wide grins. Coins, rings, necklaces, and bracelets cascaded to the floor, followed by various thuds from stolen purses.

Em picked up a gaudy ring that had rolled in her direction. She slid it onto her finger. "Nice."

"Same to you," Tull said, his mouth full of apple.

Bao tossed the other apple to Mirra. "Eat."

Mirra bit into the rosy flesh of the apple. Her eyes rolled as sweetness coated her tongue.

Bao flashed a half-smile before becoming severe. "Hey, we'll be all right."

He shook his head. "I hope so."

Mirra bit into her apple, not knowing what else to say. Either they would have enough for the tithe tonight, or they wouldn't.

While the others dozed, piled on one another like puppies, Mirra watched Bao as he counted, sorted, and calculated. He muttered sums and thoughts under his breath.

Regret tightened her chest. Even without parents, Bao could have lived a better life, an honest living, if he hadn't met her. To this day, Mirra still didn't know why she offered to help an orphan from Zallino. Perhaps she never would. But for better or worse, she was stuck with him now, and that was a comforting thought. When she had finished the apple, core and all, Mirra stretched out across a sunny patch of flooring and settled down for a long and tedious afternoon.

Bao and Mirra laughed and jostled each other as they walked back to their home in Orphan Alley. The final jobs they pulled that morning ensured that their tithe would be met and then some with enough left over to put a little coin into the Shadow Guild's tattered pockets, along with the currency they earned from selling the pilfered produce at a reduced rate.

Bao kept half of the remaining apples, claiming that he wanted to enjoy eating them while they lasted. Mirra knew better. She knew that Bao would spread them around the most desperate in Orphan Alley.

Sure enough, as soon as they walked into the alley, Bao started handing out the remaining apples to the hungriest looking children, who all looked at him, confused. In their world, no one gave anything without wanting something in return. Mirra swallowed back a sigh before walking up to a small boy with a scar running down his face. He eyed her with suspicion, reaching for a hidden weapon. Mirra said nothing as she reached into her bag and removed an apple and the loaf of bread she had planned on making her dinner and held them out to him.

"What's the catch?" a little boy with the scar demanded.

"No catch; just take it."

The boy watched her for a heartbeat longer before snatching the food she offered and scampering away without a thank you. Mirra didn't expect one. She knew what it was like. Plus, cheap bread and stolen apples weren't much to gush praises over. But it could mean the difference between a kid surviving another day or ending up dead or worse.

What's worse than death for an orphan? Ending up a plaything for a twisted noble.

They come down from their ivory towers from time to time, decked out in riches, and offering the world on a platter for any child willing to enter their carriage. Those that did were seldom seen again, and those who did come back ended up in brothels with vacant, soulless eyes.

Neither Mirra nor Bao liked to see the other orphans disappear into those carriages. They hated that there wasn't anything they could do to stop it. No one cared about the children that made their homes in the various alleyways of the capital. Neither crime lord nor city guard was willing to step up and say no more. So, Bao and Mirra gave what they could when they could. If that kept a child from ending up a plaything to a wealthy noble, then so be it.

"Bao! Mirra!"

A gangly teenage boy waved to them in greeting from his makeshift tent. The teenager was gangly but was well known in the fighting pits. His look often caused his opponents to underestimate him. When not fighting, he doted on his little sister, a sweet girl with a voice fit for the halls of the gods. Mirra noted the girl's absence, and her stomach clenched.

"How's your sister?

The boy's face dropped. "Not good. She needs to go to the doctor, but I don't have the coin. The only way to get it is to go back into the fighting rings, but I'm afraid to leave her alone."

Mirra and Bao shared a glance. Bao handed over what's left of the grain sale. The boy's eyes widened.

"I can't take that!"

Mirra took the bag and shoved it into his hands. "You will if you want your sister to live. You can pay us back later when she's well enough to sing again."

The boy stared at the small bag of coins in his hand. Tears lined his eyes but didn't fall. You never let someone see you cry. "I will pay you back for this."

Mirra nodded and walked off, leaving Bao to catch up to her.

"Even if he makes it up, you won't take it."

Mirra scoffed.

Bao chuckled and shook his head. "And you call me soft-hearted." Mirra punched him in the shoulder. Bao laughed. It jarred against the poverty and desperation all around them and yet made it a bit more bearable.

A THOUSAND GLITTERING LIGHTS SHIMMERED FROM windows and street lamps. Their glow gave off the impression of warmth and safety, but it's all a lie. Neither could it protect you from the darkness in the world nor could it drive away the forces that work within the dark.

The members of the Shadow Guild walked up to a brightly lit tavern. Music and laughter poured from the windows and doorway a pretty mask to keep careless eyes from witnessing the black deals brokered in shadowy corners.

The Gilded Lily, the seat of power for the bossman of the Merchant's District.

Mirra hated it. She hated the way good, honest, hard-working people mingled with the worst of the worst without even realizing it. She hated the way eyes of certain people marked and followed her gang the moment they got within a block of The Gilded Lily.

All day, thieves, a murderer for hire, prostitutes, and even the honest working business owner had made their way down to the inn to pay tribute to the crime lord of their district. For the former, it was a tax for operating on "his turf," while for the latter, to keep the criminal elements out of their homes and places of business.

"Better fix that face of yours," Em whispered as she sidled next to Mirra. "Before it gets us into trouble."

Mirra raised a brow. "This is my face."

Em chuckled, shaking her head. "I hate coming here too. Anything can happen on tithe days. We could end up scattered to the four winds, slaves forever to some new cruel master or dead or both."

"I won't let that happen," Mirra swore, her voice as hard as steel.

"And that's why I'm scared. The bossman knows that we are more loyal to each other than to him." Em sighed and squared her shoulders. "Blank face, blank eyes."

All light, emotion, and thought fell from Em's face, leaving it bland and bleak. The look of someone who has nothing in the world and couldn't care less.

Seeing that expression on her friend's face caused a heavyweight to settle in the pit of Mirra's stomach, yet she didn't reach out to comfort Em. She knew that it was a mask that her friend had to wear whenever they had to come face to face with the man who held their lives in his greasy hands. Mirra did not attempt to mirror Em's blank expression; instead, she settled for a scowl that hinted that she was bursting for a good fight.

"Oh, look, street rats."

"How original," Bao drawled to the guard that barred their way inside. "But you're not too smart, so I guess that's the best you can do."

The man's expression hardened, his hand going for the hidden blades in his sleeves. "Stop baiting him," ordered a tall, thin man dressed all in black.

Bao bowed to the tall, thin man. The others quickly followed suit.

"He should dish it if he can't take it," Sorro muttered under his breath. Everyone tensed when the thin man arched a brow. Sorro grimaced and bowed deeper. "Apologies."

The thin man sighed and lazily waved his hand. The guards stepped back and allowed the young thieves to pass over the threshold.

Inside, they were swallowed up by shadows barely held at bay by a dozen weak candle flames and smoke from dozens of glowing pipes.

As the young thieves passed by a few of those pipes, their sickeningly sweet smoke snaked their way through Mirra's senses, making her feel like she was underwater. She cursed Bonedust, a popular drug in both the lower and upper districts. It looked innocuous as a dull, odorless powder. But when burnt, it produced a sickly-sweet smoke that slowed the senses and, in large enough quantities, produced waking dreams.

They would need to finish their business quickly or risk becoming pliable because of the smoke. Mirra clenched her jaw and wondered if the smoke in the air was intentional — a way to make supplicants unsteady — or merely bad luck.

"The infamous Shadow Guild! My favorite little thieves!"

Trying to not breathe too deeply, Mirra turned her full attention to the man sitting in an ornate chair in front of a large fireplace. The summer heat meant that it was too hot for any type of fire. Instead, hundreds of candles flickered in the space behind the ornate chair. Their light cast dancing shadows across the walls and shrouded Bossman Jax's face in shadows, no doubt exactly how he wanted it. With his face hidden in the shadows, it would make it ten times harder to gauge his reaction to their tithe. Another trick to keep them unsteady.

Jax Harrow, the bossman of the Merchant's District, stood from his throne and threw his arms wide. The Shadow Guild quickly bent their knees and head. Mirra hated exposing the back of her neck to a room full of strangers. She would have preferred to keep her head held high, but to do so would be to invite death.

"Do you know why you're my favorite?"

"It's obvious, isn't it?" Boa said as he lifted his head to smirk at their master. "We're clearly smarter than anyone here, except you."

Mirra heard Tull and Sorro snickering behind her. She fought to hide a snicker of her own. From under her hair, Mirra watched Bossman Jax descend upon the still kneeling group. Try as she might, without lifting her head, she couldn't get a good look at his face to judge his reaction to Bao's jest.

Jax's unhurried gait and the fact that he hadn't ordered their deaths meant that, at least for now, they were safe. He stopped just in front of them. He was so close that Mirra could make out the stitching of his excellent leather boots.

The air between Jax and the Shadow Guild suddenly became tense and heated. Mirra held her breath, hand ever so slightly shifting to the blade at her side, ready to fight her way out. But then, Jax threw his head back and gave a hearty laugh.

"That you may be. Definitely the ballsiest of all my minions. Now arise, my little pickpockets, and show me what you've brought me tonight." He turned his back on them and swaggered back to his throne to watch them from the shadows.

Bao stood and stepped forward first. Mirra came up next, standing just off to his right. Behind her, Tull and Sorro flanked Em, who stood just behind Boa and Mirra. Each of them held out their sacks, which were taken by slaves that had been waiting in the wings. The slaves walked over to a small table just to the left of the throne and emptied the contents of the sacks. Gold and silver coins clanked against each other, creating small glittering mountains peppered with gems of all sizes, colors, and shapes. Pearls snaked around the piles, glowing like stars in the soft candlelight.

Mirra never once took her eyes off the bossman. She saw the way he slightly shifted in his seat at the wealth that laid out on the table. She knew that his eyes gleamed with wicked delight and greed, but also a twinge of misgiving.

"You never cease to amaze," Jax crooned. "I have spent my entire day accepting small gifts of grain and beans. My coffers a filled with copper coins stolen from the weak and cowardly."

A low rumbling came from the surrounding criminals. Sorro and Tull shifted closer, not liking where the conversation was heading. "Yet your children bring me tribute that is worthy enough to please the warlords of the Losceain plains. How in the world do you manage that?"

Mirra and the others shifted on their feet. The air around them buzzed with prickly energy. Other gangs and criminals, none too pleased at being insulted or one-upped by children, pressed in closer. Tull tried to get Bao's attention, but he was already speaking, unaware of the growing danger surrounding them.

"We can steal a lash between the blink of an eye. You won't find a better crew than us."

Jax grinned at the young, proud thief in front of him. But where Bao saw approval, Mirra saw something else, something darker and far deadlier than anything else in the smoky room.

Bao knew that he was playing a dangerous game. He could feel the rising tension in the room, could feel the unease from his friends at his back. He knew they wanted him to back down, but he couldn't, not now. Risk nothing, gain nothing. That's what his father always told him, and Bao continued to live by those words. The more favor he could curry with the bossman, the better jobs they could pull off. Better jobs meant more for everyone, even the other orphans that Bao lived with in the alley. Mirra could call him soft-hearted all she wanted, but he knew that he was doing the right thing for everyone.

"Perhaps you're right," Jax mused. "Well done."

A serving girl refilled Bossman Jax's wine glass. He completely ignored the children he had heaped praises on just moments before—an apparent dismissal. The Shadow Guild bowed once more before making their way out of the tavern as fast as they could without looking like they were running away. Just before crossing the threshold, Mirra spared one last glance over her shoulder toward Bossman Jax. The smile on his face as he watched them leave chilled her to the bone.

They split up shortly after that, worn out more from the ordeal of paying their dues than from the day itself. They all promised to lay low for a while and meet up in a few days at their usual spot.

Mirra and Bao walked in tense silence for several blocks before he broke and spoke first.

"Say what you want to say, Mirra. You won't let me sleep otherwise, and I wanna take it easy for a bit."

Mirra rolled her eyes. He'd be up at dawn already scoping out potential scores. "What the hell were you playing back there? Do you want the other gangs to come after us?"

"They'd have to find us first."

"We're not that hard to find," she pointed out.

Bao made a noncommittal grunt.

"You're still thinking like a merchant's kid. The only thing people are loyal to around here is to coin." Bao laughed and stretched his hands overhead, clasping them behind his head.

"So, are you gonna sell me out?"

Mirra scowled. "I might. You're starting to be more trouble than you're worth."

"True, but then who would get you pastries for breakfast?"

A smile tugged at the corners of Mirra's mouth. "That's all you're good for, but I think I could find some quickly."

The two friends bickered and teased all the way back to Orphan's Way. The tithe had worn them out, leaving them too tired to engage with the children who called out to them as they passed. Instead, Bao and Mirra gave them small waves in greeting before continuing to their home. They crawled into their makeshift house and bundled up against the cold as best they could.

With full bellies and no debts hanging over their head, sleep was quick to ensnare the two thieves. But just before Mirra drifted off, the bossman's smile echoed in her mind.

"I think the bossman's planning something nasty for us."

Bao groaned. "Don't be daft. We gave him a literal mountain of gold and jewels. We're his favorites. We're safe. Now go to sleep."

Mirra twirled a strand of hair around her finger. "But are we too good? You know how he gets."

Bao sat up. "I know what I'm doing, and you just gotta trust me. There's a reason I'm in charge."

"Just what are you trying to do, Bao?"

He frowned at Mirra before plopping back down. "I'm too tired for this. We'll talk in the morning."

Mirra let the matter drop. They've had the same argument a hundred times before, and not once had he given her a straight answer. Mirra wondered if she made a mistake taking him in all those years ago, if his decent upbringing was going to come back and bite her in the butt one day. No, she made the right choice. He was a good friend and a good leader. She'll talk to him again in the morning.

The streetlights had burned out, leaving the alley in complete darkness. Just the sort of thing Bao hoped for. Rising before Mirra once wasn't much of a challenge, but twice, especially when she had something on her mind, was a real test of skill.

As quiet as an alley cat, he sped off down the alleys, trying to put as much distance between him and his second as possible before she woke. He knew that she'd be pissed, but honestly, he didn't want to get into an argument with her again. Why couldn't she understand what he was trying to do? The reason why men like Jax Harrow were able to keep the power they stole was that everyone kept playing the same game, schemed the same schemes, round and round in circles with nothing ever changing. But he was going to change all that. Crime would always exist in the shadows, and sometimes bad things had to be done to survive; he knew that well enough. Yet that didn't mean that some good couldn't come out of it. Why couldn't bad people do good things?

His fellow street urchins waved to Bao as they either headed in for the night or out for the day. He raised his hand in greeting. See, this is what he was talking about. The other gangs and criminals were hated and feared because of their ruthless nature and bloody tactics, but the Shadow Guild was different. They weren't just a gang. They didn't work together because it made jobs easier. They were a family. They looked out for each other. They protected one another and had each other's back, and that was a rare commodity on the streets. Mirra was worrying over nothing. He'd make her see. But first, he'd help her work off some of her nervous energy.

CHAPTER TWO

Mirra groaned and stretched her body, arching. She touched both sides of the overturned crate that served as her and Bao's home. They would have to rethink their housing situation soon. They were still growing. Mirra sat up with a start, banging her head on the top of the crate. Wood. She should have jabbed Bao with her toes. She gritted her teeth at the space in front of her.

"Rat bastard coward," she cursed.

Mirra threw herself out into the alley. "Gone already." The few lingering residents of the alley watched her with wary eyes. They'd seen her anger before and knew to stay well away from her. Mirra kicked the top of the crate back into place and marched into the center of the alley. She closed her eyes and reached out with her senses, taking deep, calming breaths. A tug to the left. Mirra opened her eyes and ran off in search of her wayward leader that she was going to throttle thoroughly when she caught up with him.

YOU KNOW SHE'S GONNA BE ILLER THAN A HORNET WHEN she finds you," Tull said, sprawled out across a low wall, tossing an apple up in the air.

Bao waved a careless hand. "By the time she finds me, she'll be too tired to fight. I'm not worried."

"Is that so?" Mirra snapped, emerging from the shadows. Tull fell off the wall with the thud while Bao smiled up at his furious second.

"Took you long enough."

"Well … I'm going to … bye," Tull vaulted over the wall, leaving his leader at the mercy of his second.

Bao stood, still smiling. "Wanna grab lunch?"

Mirra pressed her lips into a thin, white line. She clenched her fist, her blood boiling. The sight of Bao's smirking face sent a roar crashing through her head. She reared her arm back and lashed out, connecting her fist to Bao's face. The blow snapped his head back and sent him stumbling into the same wall that Tull had escaped over a few moments before.

"Do you think everything is a game? We're making enemies, painting targets on our backs, and you have the balls to sit there and act like it's nothing!"

Bao spat blood onto the sun-bleached stones at his feet. "Come off it already, Mir. You can't walk through this life without making enemies. There's always going to be someone who wants what you have. And don't you dare accuse me of not caring. Everything I do is for the gang, for our family."

"We're not family!"

The words hung in the air. Bao's body went ramrod straight, and his eyes narrowed. The fire that swirled inside Mirra sputtered and died. Her shoulders rolled forward, sending her hair cascading into her face.

"I didn't mean it like that," she whispered.

"No, you did," Bao said, his voice clipped. He closed his eyes and sighed. "I get that you've never had a family but ..."

A small ember of her anger flared back to life. She raised her head, eyes simmering. "Be careful, Bao. Try to reach too high, and you'll fall."

"With each tithe, we earn more of the bossman's favor. That favor protects us. It's what keeps the others from circling around us like vultures. Why can't you get that? We can't be touched."

"And when that favor ends, what then?" Mirra asked, suddenly tired. "Nothing lasts forever."

Before Bao could open his mouth, Mirra stepped back into the shadows and seemed to completely merge into the darkness until there was nothing left.

Bao cursed. He raised his eyes skyward. "Ancestors, give me strength."

No matter what time of day it was, the docs were always a hive of energy and action. All manner of ships come from every corner of the known world to unload their cargo to only disappear once again over a crimson horizon to destinations unknown. Sailors and traveling merchants scurried to and fro, shouting words too faint for Mirra to make out from her perch on top a warehouse roof. She rested her chin on her knee, watching the controlled chaos below. She ached to be on one of those ships, to cross that horizon and leave everything behind.

"Mind if I sit?"

Bao settled down next to her without waiting for her response. He knew he wouldn't get one anyway. He gazed out at the water. The pair sat in comfortable silence.

"I know that my life was pretty easy back then. I had parents with strong morals. The same morals that I'm trying to live up to. It's a way to keep my parents alive; to not be alone."

"You're not alone," Mirra said, not taking her eyes off the ships.

Bao turned to look at her. He had a shy smile on his face. "But you have to realize that for most of us, we don't care about reputations, don't care about gaining favors. We only care about living another day."

"There has to be more to life?" Mirra rolled her eyes and sighed. "What do you want out of life?" Bao asked her.

Mirra finally tore her eyes away from the ships setting sail. Bao's face was earnest and open. Not one that she was familiar with dealing with. Once again, the differences in their upbringing struck her. He truly wanted to know so he could help her. What was it like being that good? She looked out across the water.

"I don't know."

"Mirra ..."

She sighed. "I guess ... if I had to choose something ... I want to be free. I want my life to belong to no one but me. I want to get on one of those ships and sail away. I want to see the world … to learn who …" She shook her head. "It doesn't matter. It'll never happen anyway."

She could feel Bao studying her. Mirra stood, turned her back on the docks. "I guess I just don't want any demands or responsibilities. A chance to just be me."

"Sounds a little lonely."

Mirra shrugged. "It will never happen, so why waste time dreaming?"

"We have to keep dreaming, or we're no different than the dead."

HUNDREDS OF PEOPLE FILLED THE STREETS. THEY scurried from place to place in a frantic attempt to complete whatever businesses they had to finish before the festivities started. Colorful banners of gold, white, and crimson crisscrossed between the buildings and over the streets. Small blue and gold flags bearing the symbol of Yrdris, the sun god and ruler of the heaves, fluttered in the breeze over doorways and in the hands of the children that ran amuck underfoot.

It was the eve of Zedi Sorear, the longest day of the year when Yrdris' eye lingered on the mortal world, observing man's true nature. It was when the whole city treated each other with civility and kindness. Gifts are given among friends and family, and special treats are handed out to those less fortunate.

All the urchins lived for Zedi Sorear. Not that any of them were especially religious; most didn't believe in the gods. They loved the holiday because it was the one day that they were welcomed everywhere they went. Clothes, food, money, medicine was made available to them because no one wanted Yrdris to see them ignoring his central tenet that demanded that those who have been blessed with good fortune care for those who have not been as fortunate and lose his favor for the year.

But the best part of Zedi Sorear happened at sunset. At that time, all the poor children would gather at the bottom of the steps of the Great Temple to see if they would be chosen by the High Priest of Yrd for a once-in-a-lifetime feast within the temple. Those selected were marked by the people who milled around to witness the choosing and were often taken in as good luck charms for the year.

It was one of the best ways to get off the streets, if only for a year, but that could mean the difference between life and death.

Mirra could have cared less about the choosing; she just wanted all the free stuff. She loved not having to steal to eat. Mirra also planned on hitting a bathhouse and tailor for her yearly hot bath and new clothes. Time willing, she might even stop by the cobbler's. The thin leather shoes currently on her feet would be hard-pressed to survive another winter. She'd love to have a pair of good sturdy boots. Either way, she was going to treat herself.

Her predictions came true—well, most of them. Jealous of the attention from the bossman the Shadow Guild received at the last tithe, several street urchin gangs sought to claim notoriety by pressing in on the Guild's territory. The Guild, in turn, squashed the encroaching crews with precise, well-calculated strokes. They also worked their fingers to the bone attempting to top last tithe's amount. If they didn't get the job that had all the gangs frantically stealing anything that wasn't bolted down at each other's throats, then everything would be for naught.

The tithe could not happen fast enough for her liking. Mirra groaned and stretched her arms over her head, arching her back. Several spots along her spine popped and crackled, releasing a good portion of the pent-up tension in her body. There were more ships docked in the harbor than usual. But that's to be expected for the Zedi Sorear. Mirra rested her chin on her knee while her other leg swung freely over the warehouse roof's edge. Just a few more hours, and then she'd be free to enjoy the one good thing about being an orphan living on the streets of the capital.

"Have you seen any dignitaries yet?"

Mirra peered over her shoulder to see Bao approach, bearing a small, colorful, and slightly beat-up box under his arm. She smiled when she recognized the logo of a well-known chocolatier.

So that's where he had been all afternoon.

"No, they already arrived weeks ago. Although I did see a few ships from Zallino arrive today."

Bao made a face. "I've told you once; I've told you a hundred times; I'm not going back."

Mirra shrugged and held her hand out for the chocolate.

Bao smirks. "And what makes you think these are for you?"

"Because I'm your second and best friend." Bao went to tuck the box behind him. Mirra narrowed her eyes and said, "And if you don't, something nasty will end up in your bed."

"Wouldn't that mess up your bed?" Bao asked, handing the brightly colored box over with a laugh.

Mirra ripped open the box and glowed over the sight of the neat rows of chocolaty goodness inside. "I live with you, so I'm used to it."

Bao laughed and gave her a playful shove. She deftly dodged him, tossing a chocolate square into her mouth. Sweet and bitter flavors battled for dominance in her mouth. She closed her eyes and enjoyed the ride. Bao took a piece for himself before laying back with his hands under his head.

Since the day he found her watching the ships, they ended their day at the harbor. Both knew that it wasn't a good idea to continually go to one place at a specific time, too easy for a rival to mark them and lay a trap, but they didn't care. They needed one thing in their miserable lives that had no other purpose than pure enjoyment.

"You ready for tonight?" Bao asked as he popped another chocolate square into his mouth.

Mirra could have killed him for ruining the mood. "I don't have another choice?"

Bao seemed to chew on something more than chocolate. "If we don't get this job, then we'll back down. Take it easy for a while."

Mirra raised a brow.

"You were right. I'm making things difficult for us. We survived a few tithes, but we can't keep going … not until …"

"Until what?"

"Never mind." Bao stood and brushed off the back of his pants. "Let's go meet the others and save some sweets for them."

Mirra stood and tucked the box into her shirt. "Can't promise a thing."

Like the last time, light, music, and laughter poured out of every crevice of the Gilded Lily. But unlike last time, there was an undercurrent running through the building that left a sour taste in the back of Mirra's mouth. Something was off, and she wasn't the only one to notice it. Bao's eyes darted back and forth as he took in everything, the only sign of his nervousness. Sorro slid closer to Em while Tull and Krill put their hands near their weapons.

The hairs on the back of Mirra's neck stood on end as she picked up on the cruel glee on many of the older thieves' faces. This was not good. The urge to drop her tribute and run warred with her conviction to her crew. She gritted her teeth and shifted ever so slightly to guard Bao's back. They would definitely be taking a back seat when they made it out tonight … if they made it out tonight.

"The infamous Shadow Guild at last!" Jax Harrow spread his arms wide in greeting but didn't rise from his throne. More warning bells went off in Mirra's head. He always stood when he greeted them.

The Guild knelt, each one tense and ready to flee. Just a few moments; that's all that it would take. They just needed to get through the next few moments, and then they could step back to keep the heat off of them.

"Time and time again, you have demonstrated your skill in thievery, loyalty, and ruthlessness." He delicately grasped the stem of his wine glass and took a long sip.   Mirra glared at him from behind her hair. The bastard knew they were uneasy and was enjoying every minute of it. "If I were a lesser boss, I would think that you were making a move for my position."

Ice water filled Mirra's veins. She saw Bao shift uncomfortably in front of her.

"We would never …"

Jax cut Bao off with a raise of his hand. "I do not doubt your loyalty, though some within my court do. You have put me in a precarious position, and now I must find a way to remedy it. But how?"

The kneeling children shifted closer to each other. It would appear that their greatest fears were about to be realized. Bao reached a hand slowly back toward Mirra. A silent apology.

Jax Harlow laughed. "Don't look nervous, children. I'm not going to do anything to you … yet." He took another sip of wine. "In fact, I want to bring you in on this job I've been working on for some time."

Mirra and the others lift their heads, struggling to keep their emotions off their face.

"How can we be of service?" Bao asked, bowing his head once more. Mirra didn't know if he did it to show gratefulness for sparing their lives or to hide whatever emotion was on his face.

Her money was on the latter.

"There is this priest who has been making it … difficult for my agents to conduct their business. He's getting the local business owners all worked up and has them thinking that they don't have to pay their dues for my services." Jax set down his wine glass and folded his hands neatly under his chin.

"This priest is the new High Priest of the Yrd. I want the Shadow Guild to help me send a message to this overstuffed good-doer."

"And just how can the Guild help you?" Bao asked with a sickening feeling in his stomach.

"I need you to infiltrate the Grand Temple tomorrow night and steal the sun god's face."

Bao's composure finally cracked. His head snapped up. He ignored protocol and stood before the bossman, dropping his portion of the tithe to the ground.

"You can't be serious!" he exclaimed.

The bossman of the Merchant's District only smiled a viper's smile. "If you think that I'm asking too much, just say so."

Bao swallowed in an attempt to regain his composure but didn't back down. "It's not that," he said. "It's just that to steal the earthly face of Yrdris is a crime punishable by death."

"Only if you get caught," Jax said calmly.

Bao continued to stand his ground and frowned. "And do so during a high holy day."

Jax Harrow laughed again. "Relax, little one; you aren't actually going to steal it. Just simply cause a little diversion so that my true messenger can carry out his task."

Mirra could taste Bao's indecision in the air. She rose to stand beside him, a silent show of support and hopefully enough to help him figure out a way to get them out of this mess with their lives still intact. She sensed the others standing up behind her. The Shadow Guild stood together in support of their leader and in solidarity against the people who took delight in their precarious predicament.

Seeing no other way out, Bao reluctantly agreed. They unceremoniously dropped their tribute and left with the promise to return in the morning for their assignments.

In shocked silence, they made their way toward the burnt-out building that served as their hiding place. They didn't care who saw them because, depending on the outcome of tomorrow, they'd either be dead or pull it off and become gods among the other crews. Either way, it would all be over tomorrow.

Safely gathered in the top portion of the building, they sat in a circle, unsure of what to do next. Bao rubbed his face and said with a voice thick with emotion, "I'm sorry. This is all because I kept pushing us, kept trying to do whatever it was that I was trying to do. If I could have gotten out of this job, I would … but I …" He placed his face in his hands.

"It's all right," Krill said. "Look at it this way: if everything goes according to plan, we'll each have enough money to make a new life somewhere else."

Em reached out and grasped Bao's arm. "He's right. No one really wanted to stay and make a living out of this."

Bao raised his head and looked out over his crew. The kids had become more than his underlings, more than his friends. He smiled weakly, lowering his hands. "Just for tonight and maybe tomorrow; let's all sleep here tonight."

No one argued the point.

They huddled together like dogs seeking warmth and comfort from being able to touch those who meant the most to them. As the rest of the city readied itself for the oncoming celebration, the Shadow Guild dreamed of blood, loss, and terrible screams of their friends.

THE GILDED LILY LOOKED DIFFERENT IN THE LIGHT OF the sun. Under the gentle glow of the moon and street lamps, it was far easier to hide the crumbling façade of the building, the rickety roof, or missing shutters. It looked even more decrepit and seedy to Bao this morning than before. Perhaps Yrdris or even Onear, the god of his people, would strike the building down, taking all the criminals who dwell within with it so he and his friends wouldn't have to sacrifice their souls. Mirra was with him. He hadn't asked her to come but grateful that she was there with him. She stood like a stout, calming wall, guarding his back. He was thankful for that. He owed her, and the others, a considerable apology once all this was said and done.

Perhaps Em had the right idea. Maybe it was time to leave this cesspool of a city and head back out to the broader world. He could return to Zallino and maybe find the rest of his family, but the others … Bao mentally shook his head. *Focus*, he told himself. *Get through the job first.*

Back at the safe house, Bao and Mirra filled the rest of their crew in on the plan. They still weren't too thrilled to take part, but at least their role wasn't as bad as they feared. The priest in charge of the choosing had already been bribed, ensuring that all the members of the Guild were in the group chosen for the feast. Once inside, they would drop small black glass balls onto the stone floor, sending a harmless black smoke into the air. From there, one of them would grab the golden mask that served as the sun god's face on earth and pass it around to each other before dropping it near the priest. That way, it would look like the High Priest had been killed by someone who had tried to steal the mask. Nothing that would lead back to the bossman or anyone else involved, just another senseless crime in a dangerous part of the capital.

A few hours to sunset, and dozens of ragamuffins clustered near the Grand Temple. Mirra shifted in her spot, still unhappy and uneasy. Every ounce of her intuition screamed for her to run as far away from the temple as possible, but she couldn't, not when the rest of her crew was already in position. She scanned in the crowed area, looking for them, but couldn't see them amongst the hoard of children. The sheer number of them milling around the temple steps alarmed her. How so many children could be left on their own? Her stomach clenched as she thought about the other chosen children's fate. Usually, being chosen meant comfortable living for a year, but when you're chosen, and the High Priest is killed … she shuttered at the thought of how the other children would be treated because of what transpired today.

She pushed all other thoughts aside. They were only distractions that would get her or one of friends killed. All she had to do was play her part and then get out as fast as she could. The crowd began to cheer as the priest exited the temple to greet them with arms wide open. The children shifted on their feet in anticipation, silently offering up prayers to their various gods that they would be chosen for the feast and the life of ease that would undoubtedly follow it.

One of the priests came forward to address the crowd. Mirra was taken aback by just how young the High Priest of Yrd was. Barely into his thirties, his warm eyes and bright smile surveyed the mass of people beneath his feet.

"Greetings, my children!" His voice carried out across the square warm and welcoming. "As Zedi Sorear comes to a close, we open our doors to those who need our help the most. These children before you should never know hunger, never know pain, and yet they do." His face became stern. "You have failed these children. You have allowed yourself to become callous and indifferent. You let criminals rise to seats of power that they should only glimpse at through bars of iron."

The crowd began to murmur uncomfortably. They had come for a party, not to be lectured by the High Priest. The High Priest's stern face softened once more.

"But you can change. I have faith in you, and so does our Lord. Tonight is the last chance for you to show the sun god that mankind has not lost its capacity for caring. After the selection, look to those who remain. Welcome these children into your home like we welcome them into our temple."

The High Priest folded his hands in front of his robe and nodded to one of the older priests standing off to the side. The waiting children straightened and watched the approaching priest with hungry eyes. It was time. Mirra partly hoped that none of the Guild were chosen, that the priest had a change of heart. That way, they wouldn't have to go through with stealing the sun god's face. But it was not to be.

When the priest pointed to Mirra, her heart sank. She silently cursed the crooked priest and made the long trek up the stairs where the other children awaited. Each time one of the Guild was chosen, the sickening feeling in her throat grew. Phase one of the bossman's plan went off without a hitch.

Twelve children were chosen, one for each month of the year. The rest shuffled back to whatever hole they crawled out of. A few were taken in by a person moved by the High Priest's words, but not enough. That's why the bossman wanted him gone. If left unchecked, the new High Priest of Yid could sway enough minds to make criminal activity a bit more challenging than they preferred.

In a single row, the children were led into the temple. Some of the pews were already filled by the nobility and their guests. Some of the crowd from outside filed in behind the children and took the remaining seats.

Incense burned Mirra's nose, making her sneeze. The priest walking next to her offered a small kerchief. She accepted it, feeling guilty. These were good people who only wanted to help the people in their community. This was wrong. The priest led the children up to the altar. Mirra tried to catch the eye of her conspirators, but they were too busy staring at their mark.

The priests encircle the children and begin to chant in the ancient language of the gods. Only they know in truth what they're saying since no one outside the priesthood is taught the language. The strange lilting sing-song words added to the overall tension and apprehension in Mirra's heart. Her eyes are drawn to the golden mask as if Yrdris himself commanded her to look at what she was about to sully with her unworthy hands and intentions.

Sitting center stage on the altar, the golden mask wasn't much to look at. It was a vague humanoid mask with holes for the eyes and mouth. Yet, despite its ordinary appearance, Mirra could feel the power radiating off the mask. Mirra's blood chilled. She had always thought that Yrdris' earthly face was nothing more than a prop the priesthood used as a stand-in for the god. Well, apparently, she was mistaken. Her trepidation only grew, leaving a cold sweat in its wake.

A flash of movement brought her out of her blind panic. It was Em who had reached into her pocket and pulled something out. Mirra nodded her head to her friend's silent question. Mirra reached into her own pocket and pulled out a small glass ball the size of an apricot. Without looking, she knew that the rest of the Shadow Guild was doing the same. The chanting of the priest grew frantic and feverish reaching a crescendo. The spectators in the pews leaned forward as if under a spell. The High Priest took over the chanting and raised his arms overhead. From where he stood, the last light of the sun bathed him in a fiery glow. Mirra's breath caught in her throat, even though she knew it was a clever trick of placement and timing.

Three more words. All hell would break loose after three more words.

"Nilatha. Crats. Ha'jar!"

Six glass orbs shattered in the silence that fell after the final three words of the invocation. Thick, acrid black smoke irrupted from the children gathered at the base of the altar. The black smoke quickly spread throughout the temple, causing the crowd to scream and flee, tripping over pews and people. It was chaos.

Mirra lunged forward, reaching for the golden mask that had chilled her to the bone only moments before. She had calculated the number of steps between her position amongst the other children and the altar during the chanting. In her head, Mirra counted her steps, holding her breath against the smoke that caused the others around to fall to the hard-stone floor in coughing fits. The altar banged against Mirra's chest when she ran full force into it. The other items clattered to the floor as she lunged for the mask.

Pain erupted in her fingers the moment she touched the surprisingly warm metal. She bit the inside of her mouth to keep herself from crying out. Ignoring the pain, she spun to the left and held the mask out for the next member of her crew. They would run the mask the same way they ran stolen goods. They would pass it off to one another until the last person got it and dropped it outside a window, letting the mask fall to the street. Hopefully, someone would find and return the mask to the temple soon after. Krill took the mask from her. She heard a hiss when he touched the metal face. He sped off after handing Mirra a cloth to tie around her face to help protect her from the smoke. She took a few shaky breaths. Her throat burned as a little of the smoke filtered through the cloth mask, but it was better than nothing. It wouldn't be much longer now. The smoke was already starting to dissipate, bringing a few large forms into focus and brought to light a significant problem.

The guards reacted much faster than the plan had anticipated. Of course, they would, as some of the visiting nobles from other countries were some of those in attendance for the festival. Half the guard kept order, leading the civilians out of danger, while the other half zeroed in on the epicenter of the smoke, making it difficult for Em to pass the golden mask off to Bao who was supposed to be the one to dump it in the alley. Frantic, she tried to hide the mask within the folds of her clothing, but the mask shone like a beacon in the smoke as if Yrdris himself had set himself against the Guild and their plan.

Drawn in by the shine, the guards closed the distance with swords drawn. Pure terror contorted Em's pretty face.

Mirra scanned the near-empty space, her eyes meeting Em's. The latter began to cry because she knew what fate awaited her once the guards got their hands on her. She knew that she didn't have the skill to avoid men three times her size; yet, there was someone who was. Mirra rushed toward her friend, dashing through the guards, surprising them if only for a moment. They chased after Mirra, but she reached Em first. Mirra tore the mask from her friend's white-knuckled grasp, barely noticing the pain when her fingers touched the sacred metal. She waved it over her head, drawing their attention to her. The guards paused for a second, unsure of whom to follow. That was all that Em needed to disappear into the crowd. Mirra didn't know if her other friends made it out. She now had to find a way to dump the mask and go without getting caught in the process. She could lay low for a few weeks until the heat died down, but first, she had to get away.

She spied a small narrow doorway just off to the left. She raced toward that doorway for all she was worth, but it wasn't enough. A man dressed in the uniform of the city watch cut her off. His eyes locked on hers and the mask in her hands. He shouted and drew his sword. Mirra made a sharp right turn, hoping to make it to the door that the priest used to enter and exit the main temple. Her whole world narrowed down to that one door, the key to her salvation. She stretched her hand out. A sharp pain erupted from the back of her head. Warm sticky liquid poured down her back as her world faded to black. Her body gave out, crumbling to the unforgiving stone floor. Her fingers were still stretched out to the door. So close. She was so close. As the darkness swallowed her whole, Mirra hoped that her friends made it out. She hoped they got away.

CHAPTER THREE

HER WORLD CONSISTED OF NOTHING BUT DARK, ROLLING waters; cold, hard stones; and pain. Pain that burned like a flaming flower somewhere at the place where her skull and her spine met. Slowly, the darkness ebbed away to a muted, gray light twinged with red. As the darkness receded, other things came into focus. The stench of human refuse, unwashed bodies, and the unmistakable scent of blood. The acrid burn of lamp smoke at that back of her throat. The sharp jabs from matted straw under her body. The cold kiss of iron on her skin.

Mirra opened her eyes and sat up quickly. That proved to be a bad idea as her world rolled violently beneath her, and darkness crept back around the edges of her vision. The sore spot on the back of her head pulsated with each heartbeat, sending fresh new waves of pain cascading through her body. Her stomach heaved and rolled, attempting to expel food that she hadn't eaten. Bile rose, burning her throat, adding to the overall sickness in her mouth. She smacked her tongue around in her mouth, trying to work up some saliva to no avail.

When her world ceased rolling and spinning, she took in her soundings. Her cell was tiny. If she stood up and stretched out her arms, she could probably touch both walls. The wall to her back had a narrow slit for a window that let in the minuscule sliver of light. Every so often a wisp of fresh air found its way through the narrow window, but it did nothing to cool the growing sweat breaking across Mirra's brow. Nor did it ease the tepid air.

She would glean no more information from her cell. She would have to, as quietly as she could, saddle up to the iron bars that marked the front of her cell. The iron manacles around her wrists and ankles would most definitely hinder her movements. It was painstaking and nauseating work gathering the chains so they wouldn't make any noise when she moved. Mirra eased up onto her knees and shuffled toward the sparsely lit hallway. When she had stretched the chain as far as it would go, she would release a tiny bit more until the chains were their full length. Mirra groaned. She was still an arm's length away from the bars.

Mirra was no stranger to cells and their chains. Most prisons didn't bother shackling their prisoners; too much of a hassle. The few prisons that insisted on shackling their inmates at least made sure that the chains extended all the way to the door so the inmates could get their meals. The only place that she could remember that had short chains was the …

"No," Mirra whispered, falling to the ground once again. *No. No. No. It couldn't be.* But where else would they put her? She had been seen attempting to steal the sun god's earthly face on a Zedi Sorear, a high holy day, in front of half the nobility in the world. The Undros royal family would have to move swiftly and harshly if they wanted to save face. She probably was taken directly from the temple and thrown into a criminal's worst nightmare—the palace dungeon.

Only the worst of the worst made it to the dark cells beneath the palace. The nobility delighted in watching the dregs of society meet their, often bloody, end. She heard that the nobles even threw parties where they danced as the condemned dangled from the gallows.

No longer caring who heard the clinking of her chains, Mirra scooted away from the bars as fast she could. She didn't stop her awkward backward crawl until her back met the impenetrable back wall of her cell. She pulled her knees into her chest, buried her head, and sobbed. What was the point of being brave now?

She was only twelve years old. Sure, she lived a life that didn't adhere to what could be called "the right path," but it was the only life she had. The only life that she had been able to carve out for herself, and it took her sitting in a dark cell facing her emanate death to realize that she liked it. She liked living in Orphan's Way with Bao in their little crate. She liked laughing with Em over how ridiculous the boys were. She liked working and teasing with Tull, Krill, and Sorro. And it was all over now. Her only consolation was that it was her in the cell instead of Em. But that thought did little to quell the tears that flowed from her eyes.

The first day, no one stopped by her cell. No one came on the second or the third. By the fourth day, she wondered if they were going to let her die from starvation or dehydration. Both ways sounded terrible, and it was only a matter of time before one of them won out.

By the fifth day, she had begun seeing things that were not real. The tiny slit in her cell only marginally let in light, and yet, the shadows in her cell seemed to writhe and dance, whispering terrible things in the dark. Pale faces with black fire eyes—cold fires licking at the stones. Mirra no longer had the strength to battle these apparitions. She only curled up tighter and watched it all play out with dull eyes.

Sometime later, she couldn't be sure if it was minutes, days, or weeks, a man appeared in her cell. Mirra didn't have the strength to push herself up from the floor. Just cracking her eye to peer at him from behind her hair stripped what little energy she still possessed.

The man was undoubtedly a noble. His clothes were of the finest quality and tastefully done. He wore somber colors of gray and black. Mirra pondered if he had dressed for her execution. The only jewelry that the man appeared to wear was a silver chain with a black stone pendant. But the more she stared at the man, the stranger he became. His face was shrouded in writhing shadows. Not just his face, all around his body, darkness coiled around him like hundreds of smoky serpents. A tendril of that writhing darkness slithered toward her. She watched it indifferently. Perhaps this man wasn't a man at all but one of the dark gods here to exact holy retribution upon her.

Good, let him, Mirra thought. She closed her eyes, accepting her fate. *Get it over with already.*

Nothing happened. The black tendrils never reached her. Instead, she heard the man bark an order down the corridor. There came a muffled reply, and the man turned and walked out of her cell.

Some old part of Mirra wondered what the whole incident was about, but not for long. Her addled mind only held onto the question for a half a heartbeat before dropping into the abyss that the dark, cold, and hunger had created inside of her.

When she regained consciousness, there was another visitor in her cell. *Two in one day ... or at least I think it's one day. I must be special.*

This visitor was a middle-aged woman in a simple dress with a green apron. Her hair was wrapped up in a blue head covering—the marking of a healer. The healer frowned down at Mirra and muttered something over her shoulder. Two palace servants entered. One carried a pot of slightly steaming water, while the other carried a small tray. They set down their loads and quickly scurried back to the upper levels of the castle. The healer woman sighed and pulled a small clay vial from the pocket of her apron. She poured the vial into the steaming pot of water, stirring it with her hand. The pungent odor of medicine filled the air. Mirra breathed deeply, desperate to smell something other than the filth of the other prisoners and herself.

The healer woman gently picked up one of Mirra's ankles, causing her to hiss as the chain rubbed against the raw skin beneath. When the healer woman applied the medicinal water, pain flared. Mirra tried to pull her ankle free, but her efforts were futile. The healer woman's hold was firm but gentle. When the pain faded, the skin beneath the chains felt marginally better.

After the rest of her extremities had gone through the same treatment, the healer woman poured the rest of the water over Mirra, sloshing off a few layers of sweat, dirt, and other bits of filth. Slightly cleaner than before, Mirra felt a bit more like her old self. She was able to push herself up to a sitting position.

"What's this?" Her voice crackled and croaked from nonuse.

The healer woman said nothing. She slid the second tray over to Mirra. On it sat a small bowl of thin broth and a small cup of water.

Mirra stared at the items. After days of being ignored, she wondered what brought about this sudden change. She wondered if the food in front of her was laced with something to end her life. She looked up at the healer woman who silently urged her to eat and drink.

Cautiously, Mirra picked up the bowl of broth. "Slowly!" the healer woman commanded. Mirra jumped at the sound of the healer woman's granite-like voice. Not what she expected; no wonder the healer hardly spoke.

Slowly, Mirra brought the bowl to her lips and, even more slowly, tipped the contents into her mouth. The broth was oily and bland, yet her body screamed for more. She fought against the urge to gulp it down. Once the oily broth hit her stomach, she was glad she did. Her stomach rolled in protest, threatening to rise against the unfamiliar substance. Mirra clamped her hand over her mouth to try and keep everything down. The healer motioned for her to breathe deeply. She did, and it helped. Once her stomach stopped threatening to revolt, she picked up the small cup of water and took small sips.

After she finished, the healer woman collected the dishes from Mirra, set them back on the tray and left, taking everything with her.

She had no other visitors that day.

Every day, the healer woman would come and visit Mirra. For each visit, she would wash the skin beneath her shackles and bring a little bit of food and water. It was never much, just enough to keep her alive. Mirra figured it would be much fun to watch a living skeleton swinging from the gallows.

With the regular visits from the healer woman and from what she tracked in the beginning, Mirra figured she'd been in prison for roughly a week—give or take, a day. She began to pace about her cell, gnawing on her filthy nails, wondering why she was still alive. Perhaps that snake man had something to do with it. Mirra shook her head. That man was too strange and unnatural to be anything other than a hallucination. The only person she ever saw was the healer who was occasionally accompanied by a servant woman or two. So, when she heard the creaking of her cell door opening, she hadn't bothered to open her eyes. A good night's sleep was hard to come by when sleeping on a stone floor shackled.

"I must say you look marginally better than the last time I visited."

That was not the voice of the healer woman. Mirra spun to her feet, balling the excess chains in her fist. Not much of weapon but better than nothing. Haloed in light instead of darkness stood the nobleman from before. Only, this time, he looked like an ordinary mortal, not some demon from the night lands.

The man smiled coldly and took two pointed steps forwards. His movements were smooth yet powerful, reminding Mirra of a cat slowly stalking its prey. She gripped her chains tighter. She was tired of always being the prey. She straightened and stood tall. If this is her end, then she will face it on her feet instead of cowering in her filth. She met the man's gaze head-on. The excess chains drop from her slack fingers.

The man's eyes; one as black as a raven's wing, while the other was as icy blue as Mirra's own.

"Attempting to steal the earthly face of Yrdris on Zedi Sorear. You have balls; I'll give you that."

His voice was low and slightly melodic. It helped to bring Mirra back to the matter at hand. She scowled and crossed her arms. If he wanted information out of her, he had another thing coming. Speaking ensured the death of her friends. She would rather die than betray them.

The man's smile took on an oily texture. "Loyalty, quite a noble trait for a mere thief. And a trait I require for those who work for me."

Mirra bit back her surprise. Just what was this man's angle? "Why would you want a thief who got caught?"

The man gave a deep chuckle. "You let yourself get caught."

A muscle in Mirra's jaw feathered. The man smiled like a man who'd already won.

"I was there, you know? The black smoke was a nice touch, very startling. People are still hiding in their homes, afraid that the gods are going to come down at any moment and destroy the world." He laughed cruelly at the antics of the devout. "Of course, I know that the mask wasn't the *true* target. The High Priest of Yrd is dead. Slain by a knife across his throat."

A cold sweat slithered down Mirra's spine.

The man's two-toned eyes bored into her, almost down to her shattered soul. "Your former boss should have picked his targets more carefully. The High Priest who has openly condemned men like him and his practices suddenly ending up dead; not too hard to put it all together."

Mirra swallowed the bile rising in the back of her throat. "You want something, or are you gonna talk me to death?"

Another low chuckle.

"You have a fiery spirit. I admire that. But if you were to work for me, you'd have to temper it. I have no use for defiant servants."

Mirra mused over his words. "The way I see it," the man went on, "you only have two real choices available to you. You know as well as I do that there's no rescue coming for you. You can either accept my offer or meet the gallows. Think fast because when I walk out this cell, your choices boil down to one."

He hadn't told her what he did or what he wanted Mirra to do. She knew that he withheld that information for a reason. But a chance, that's what he offered her. She could always run away later once she was strong enough. A little voice in her head told her to tread carefully with the nobleman standing in front of her. He had an agenda and owed no loyalty to her.

With a shrug, the man turned and strode toward the opened door of the cell. Mirra then noticed the guard ready to seal it and her fate once more.

"And what do I call you?" Mirra called out just as the man crossed the threshold of her cell.

He turned around and gave her a smile that chilled her to the core. "My name is Lord Julian, but people most often refer to me as The King's Viper, Master of Spies."

MIRRA HATED BEING OUT ON THE OPEN ROAD. THERE WAS no place for her to hide, nothing she could use to defend herself. Plus, her teeth were about to rattle out of her head, thanks to the wagon she rode in, bouncing through every divet in the road. She scanned the wide-open farmlands framing both sides of the road, groaned again before slumping back against the hardwood that served as the seat.

It was almost like a whole other world outside the capital's walls. Here, people weren't pressed in on each other, and they generally appeared happy. The few people that she did come across smiled and waved. Though they seemed to be more directed toward the man sitting next to her driving the wagon instead of her.

She studied him from the corner of her eyes. When Lord Julian dumped her into the wagon, he hadn't bothered explaining anything to her or the farmer. Although the farmer didn't seem surprised at all.

Mirra had tried for hours to get the man to talk to her, but he remained firmly silent, staring ahead at the road.

He wasn't too old, probably still in throws of his prime, but a hard life of cultivating the land had already given his tanned face a few deep wrinkles, mostly along his brow, and a few strands of gray hair mixed in with his muddy brown hair. *Brown*, Mirra snorted. That was the man's defining feature. His hair, skin, eyes, and even his clothes were all various shades of brown as if the earth itself had given birth to him instead of a woman.

The man's eyes cut sharply toward Mirra when she snorted before snapping back to the road.

"You know I'm not going to bite or anything," Mirra said, shifting on the bench. "I'm not dangerous."

This time, it was the man who snorted, his eyes shifting to rest on Mirra's wrist. Her eyes fell to the same spot. She knew his snort had less to do with the raw flesh around her wrists but from the healing tattoo that encircled her left wrist— the brand of one who worked for the deadliest man in the kingdom, The King's Viper. She traced the delicate, ink-marked skin gently with her finger.

MIRRA STUMBLED AFTER LORD JULIAN, WHO PAID HER NO mind as he led her through the labyrinth of hallways that took her further from the dungeons. Her eyes began to burn as they made their way back to the light. Oddly enough, she didn't see another living soul the entire time. *This must be a secret passage or at least not widely used. Good to know.*

They soon came to a small staircase that led to a single door, most likely in a tower somewhere. Mirra frowned. If this was where he was going to keep her, escaping would be slightly more challenging than she would have liked.

Lord Julian pulled a set of keys from his pocket and unlocked the door. He opened it and walked through without a backward glance. Mirra thought about turning and running back down the stairs but quickly brushed that aside. She had no idea where she was, and if she was completely honest with herself, she was a wreck and most likely wouldn't make it two floors before dying. She crossed the threshold, silently praying that she wasn't about to walk into another dungeon.

The room was either a small study or a really small office. Most of the walls had been taken up by large bookcases that were near bursting with books, scrolls, and other artifacts. A brazier provided enough heat to make the room warm with minimal smoke. A single, triangular window sat behind the moderately sized desk that the lord sat behind. While the bookcases were a mess, not a single scrap of paper was out of place on the desk.

Lord Julian folded his hands under his chin and surveyed Mirra with a calculating gleam in his eye.

Mirra remained where she stood.

"Take a seat."

Mirra stepped forward on cautious feet to the only other chair in the room, a hard, uncomfortable-looking seat no doubt used to put the occupant at unease. She fought not to snort—childish tactics. After a week in the palace dungeons, the chair felt like a throne.

"Just out of curiosity, what were you and your little friends going to do with the sun god's face?"

Mirra stared straight ahead, choosing to focus on the window behind him. She could see his smile.

"You'll be happy to know that all your little friends got away and that no one has been brought in on charges of murder yet."

Silence. Say nothing. Show nothing. He'll get to the point soon enough.

His smile grew. It was cold and calculating. Mirra could barely suppress the shiver that ran down her spine at the sight of that frosty smile.

"Again, I must commend your silence. So few people could spend a week in the palace dungeon, nearly die, and *still* retain their loyalty." He rose from his desk, walking around to lean up against the front of it. He crossed his arms and studied her more.

"Stand."

Mirra complied. Lord Julian closed the space between them, leaving an arm's length between them.

"I'm glad you've chosen to work for me. It would be a shame to waste such a talent." He brushed her hair out of her face and tilted her chin, making her look him straight in the face. "And to waste such a pretty face."

Mirra jerked her chin out of his grasp and stepped around the chair, putting it between them.

"If you think I would ever become a painted woman, you are crazier than a bonedust addict. If that's what you want me to do, take me back to my cell. I'd rather die."

Much to her surprise, Lord Julian threw his head back and roared with laughter. He continued to laugh until he doubled over, wiping tears from his eyes.

"No, no." He laughed. "I wouldn't dream of wasting your talents on something as trivial as that."

Mirra's already weakened knees nearly gave out from under her. The only thing that kept her upright was the white-knuckled grip on the chair. She let out the breath she had been holding when the lord returned to his original spot behind the desk. She remained standing, still needing to put as much space between her and him as possible. Plus, having the door right to her back increased her chances of escaping if she decided to make a run for it after all.

Lord Julian stopped laughing. "You wouldn't make it very far."

Mirra swallowed. More and more, she regretted thinking that she could somehow outmaneuver Lord Julian. She should have stayed in her cell, silently awaiting her death.

"Sit."

She did.

He began to play with the black stone pendant. "Undoubtedly, you know who I am and what it is that I do?" She nodded. "Good. You have skills that I find immensely useful. Sign this, and we can begin."

From an unseen drawer, Lord Julian pulled a long slip of parchment. He slid it over to Mirra, who took it obligingly. She stared at the page, unable to decipher the words written on it. There's no school on the streets. A stone settled into the pit of her stomach. It looked like a long and complicated document. Did she want to take it on good faith that the man who lied for a living didn't add anything that she wouldn't want to do? *Fat chance*, but what other choice did she have? She closed her eyes and pushed away her unease.

"Fine," she said, her voice barely above a whisper.

His smile would have made devils shiver in their shoes. He motioned for Mirra to come closer to the desk and took out a quill.

Mirra stared at it. "I don't know how to write."

"Of course, what was I thinking," he said with mock sincerity. He put the quill back and took out a small knife, probably a letter opener. Mirra swallowed. "Give me your hand."

She reluctantly complied. Fast as a snake, Lord Julian pricked Mirra's thumb with the letter opener, leaving a single red bead of blood in its wake. Mirra stared at her bleeding thumb, then back to Lord Julian.

"Press it here," he said, pointing to blank space near the end of the document. Mirra pressed her thumb to the parchment for a moment, then pulled it back. She sucked on her thumb, hoping to stop the bleeding. The mark she left shimmered against the dull-colored parchment, but she thought that it shone a little too much for what it was. "Excellent."

Lord Julian quickly withdrew the document and rang a small bell that Mirra hadn't noticed before. A small, dark woman came in from the door behind Mirra, bearing a wooden box.

"See to the girl, will you? And put her in one of the small cells until I gather her."

The small woman bowed and placed her box on the desk. Mirra watched as she opened it and gasped recognizing a tattooist kit. She took a closer look at the woman and saw small, intricate tattoos running over nearly every inch of her skin, which identified her as a woman of the Horse Clans of Lorscea. The woman gave Mirra no encouraging words as she went to work, grinding and mixing the ink that she would hammer somewhere onto Mirra's body.

"I am Xoi," the woman said.

"Mirra."

Xoi extended her hand, her many bracelets clinking against each other. "Give me your hand."

Not knowing what she intended to do, Mirra gave Xoi her left hand, tucking her right under her thigh. Xoi frowned at the scaring and bruising that encircled Mirra's wrist. "This will hurt."

"What will?" Mirra asked, dread filling her chest.

The blow came without warning. The first of many as Xoi inked the Viper's brand into Mirra's skin.

MIRRA TRACED THE SERPENT SPIRALING AROUND HER wrist and sighed. Now the whole world would know what she was and who she worked for as long as she knew where to look. Even if she were to escape and disappear into some other country, The Viper had agents all over the world. All it would take would be one of them to see this mark, and she'd be caught — again.

Well, there's nothing she could do for now. Perhaps she could find someone to remove the ink from her skin. Until then, she would go along with whatever Lord Julian wanted her to do until she had a plan.

Two more days on the road brought Mirra and the farmer to a small village in the heart of the continent. The locals called out in greeting as the wagon approached. They stopped short when they took notice of Mirra. They asked questions, but the farmer shook his head, indicating that he couldn't explain it right now.

The village wasn't much to look at, nothing more than a collection of simple buildings and muddy streets. Mirra clasped her hands in front of her and stared straight ahead. She was in a new world now. She would have to keep her wits about her to figure out the rules and how she was supposed to fit into it.

They rode through the village. The landscape changed again, becoming a mixture of farmland and wild spaces.

"Where are we going?"

The man sighed. "To my home."

Mirra perked up. "How long?"

"Dunno."

Mirra frowned. That wasn't the answer she expected. Maybe the man knew about as much as she did.

"I'm hungry."

"Ya eat at the house."

"Your house? Just us?"

The man groaned and fell silent. Mirra cursed herself. She pushed him too fast. But at least she knew that they had a destination and weren't going to be trapped on the wagon forever, rattling from one end of the kingdom to the other.

The sky had shifted from blue to shades of yellow and red. Mirra dozed slightly, letting her head bounce where it will. She heard the sounds of chickens squawking and a woman's voice shouting in greeting. The wagon came to a halt, and the man slid out without a word. Mirra sat up and rubbed the sleep from her eyes.

The man was talking urgently to a pretty woman in a green dress. *Must be his wife,* Mirra thought. *And she doesn't look happy to see me.*

The farmer's wife's face flushed with strong emotion; anger or fear, Mirra wasn't sure. She muttered softly to herself before returning to a small thatched house.

The man's shoulders fell. Mirra felt sorry for him. He didn't ask for The Viper to dump a half-starved thief on him.

"I like your farm."

The man turned around. Mirra made a show of nodding appreciatively. He seemed to battle with himself over something for a moment before his body relaxed.

"It's not much, but it's mine." He rubbed the back of his neck. "I know ya've been tryin' to get information outta me. I canna give ya what I dunno. The name's Brian, and my wife's Yanna."

"Mirra."

Brian strode toward the wagon, grabbed two sacks and threw them over his shoulder. "Well, Mirra, head on into the house. Yanna will fix ya somethin' to eat."

Mirra walked slowly toward the house. Brian seemed to have accepted the change to his world with only sulking for three days. She got the feeling that Yanna would sulk a bit longer than that.

The inside of the house was cozy and well worn. All the furniture was simple but sturdy. Off the right was a staircase that led to where the bedroom must have been because the main area was taken up by a large stone hearth and a well-worn table.

Yanna stood next to the hearth, stirring what smelled like stew in a large pot. She was still muttering under her breath, unaware that Mirra had joined her. She finished her stirring and turned. Seeing Mirra standing in the doorway, she jumped, placing her hand over her heart.

"Don't do that," she said. "You scared me 'alf to death."

Mirra looked down at her feet. "Sorry."

Yanna harrumphed. "I don't know why my husband agreed to take ya in, but I won't 'ave ya mucking things up. Ya 'ear. You'll follow the rules we give ya, or there'll be trouble."

Mirra looked up from her feet, scowling. Though Yanna's eyes were the same color as her husband's, they lacked his warmth, especially as she narrowed them at Mirra.

"Around the way is a well. Go get water for ya bath."

Yanna turned her back to Mirra and went back to her cooking. Too road-weary to argue, Mirra went back outside. She blinked against the bright light of the sun and the tears that threatened to fall. Yanna was no different than some of the people who worked in the orphanages, always looking down on the people they were supposed to help. Only, this time, Mirra couldn't run away, or could she?

Rubbing the tears from her eyes, she took a better look at the farm and the surrounding countryside. She walked toward where Brian had lumbered off, figuring it a good place to start.

The only other building beside the house that she could see was a medium-sized barn. The well sat in between the house and the barn, no doubt to make watering the animals and humans easier. Attached to either side of the barn were two small paddocks. One held a mother sow and her piglets, and the other held a dairy cow. Chickens had free range, pecking and scratching at the dirt.

Mirra walked past the well, heading toward the bar. Behind the house stood a small dairy and the chicken coop, and beyond that, a decent-sized garden. Even further out were fields full of green crops. Mirra sighed. Where could she run away to?

Far in the distance, a dark forest bordered the farm. Mirra smiled. She could figure out how to live in the woods.

"I'd stay outta there if I were ya," Brian said, coming up behind her.

Mirra jumped and spun. "Why?"

"That's the Mystic Woods. No one goes in there unless they gotta."

Mirra laughed. "The Mystics died forever ago."

Brian leveled a cool gaze at her. "Not all. Ya aren't to go near dem woods until yer stronger."

Mirra nodded. He had a good point. She turned to the well and gathered two buckets worth of water before heading back to the house.

There was a small room under the stairs that served as a washing room. Yanna took Mirra's buckets and emptied them into a vat and lit a small fire under it. Soon, steam filled the small room. She ordered Mirra to strip and sit in a smaller tub. The bath Mirra received was short but efficient, if not a little bit rough. Freshly scrubbed and cleaner than she had been in ages, Mirra let Yanna drag a comb through her tangled locks, knowing that it was better to let Yanna do with Mirra what she willed.

Yanna pointed to a pile of clothes on a stool. "Those should fit ya. Get dressed and come out to eat."

Mirra made a face at Yanna's retreating backside before stepping out of the tub. She put on the simple under things then frowned. She didn't wear dresses. She pinched the cream-colored homespun dress and held it up with a look of disgust. Dresses made girls targets, and they kept girls from being able to climb, run, or fight. But she had no other choice. The fabric was rough and a little stiff. It hung loosely around her body, and a tad too long. Mirra kicked her feet about, trying not to trip herself up. She held her arms out and twisted from side to side and shrugged. It would do for now.

Brian and Yanna were already seated at the table. They both studied Mirra as she shyly walked toward them. Brian gave a grunt that Mirra took for approval. Yanna's cold eyes gave nothing away.

"Come sit and eat."

Mirra chose to sit next to Brian. He was the only familiar thing in the room. Yanna sniffed but chose to remain silent. The adults bowed their heads before Brian offered up a prayer.

"We give our thanks to Yrdris for sharin' with us his bounty. We give thanks to de Dark Mother for sparin' us from her children for another day. We welcome Mirra into our home and hope that she finds a measure of peace here with us."

Mirra shifted uncomfortably in her seat. "Uh … thanks." she said weakly, earning her another pointed glare from Yanna. Brian patted her on the head, then dug into the food on the table.

Compared to the meals she used to get, the fare laid out on the table as a feast. Mirra's mouth watered at the sight of fresh rolls, bright green beans, and the savory smell of stew. Yanna served out the foods to Brian and Mirra before serving herself. There was no conversation around the table. Whether by habit or because of her, she didn't care. The only thing she cared about was to stuff as much of the food down her throat as possible. She would most likely throw a fair bit of it up later, but she couldn't stop herself. Brian chuckled over Mirra's enthusiasm. And surprisingly, even Yanna managed to look pleased.

Fortunately, she managed to keep the food down. Yanna cleared off the table and set to washing up the dishes. Brian walked over to the hearth and plucked a wooden flute from the mantle.

"Come and sit by the fire, Mirra," he said, sitting down himself. "It's been a long few days."

Mirra yawned as she sat down on a low stool. Brian smiled and brought the flute to his mouth. A simple melody filled the quiet spaces in the house. Mirra caught herself rocking gently to the melody while she stared into the flames of the hearth. Warm, well-fed, and clean, her body relaxed for the first time since Jax pulled her gang into that damned job. Since then, she'd been arrested, nearly starved, and almost executed. She had signed her life away, been branded and thrust onto a long journey with a stranger. She wondered what Bao and the others thought happened to her. Her throat tightened, and tears rimmed her eyes.

Brian stopped playing. "Ya been through a lot for such a wee thing. Yanna love, take the girl to bed."

Mirra stood and followed Yanna up the stairs. At the top of the stairs was another open space, slightly smaller than downstairs.

"We're through there," Yanna said, pointing to a door at the far end of space. "You'll sleep 'ere." She led Mirra to a small room just off the stairs. There wasn't anything in the room but a small pallet and a couple of apple crates.

"Setup 'owever ya like." Yanna turned to leave but stopped. "We lock our doors, so don't get any ideas now."

Mirra gritted her teeth. *I'm too tired for this mess.* "You do know that I'm not a killer or anything like that."

"For now," Yanna replied, closing the door behind her with a firm click.

CHAPTER FOUR

MIRRA WOKE THE NEXT MORNING FEELING ALMOST LIKE her old self again. She stretched; enjoying the free range of movement after so many days locked in a cell and trapped in a wagon. She heard movement down below, most likely Yanna. *Joy*, Mirra grumbled. *I wonder how she'll be mean to me today.* Mirra pulled the dress from the day before over her head and headed downstairs.

Yanna stood at the table, covered up to her elbows in flour, kneading the day's bread. She took one look at Mirra and froze.

"Ya look a mess, child. Did yak even run year fingers through that 'air of yers??"

Mirra reached up and awkwardly ran her fingers through the tangled mess that was her hair. Yanna sighed and dusted off her hands. "Come 'ere." She made Mirra sit at the same low stool from the night before. She quickly washed her hands before fetching the comb from the other day. "If yer not gonna look after yerself, then we might as well keep year hair in a braid."

Mirra winced as Yanna yanked out the knots in her hair. After that assault was over, Yanna continued to pull and yank on Mirra's hair. Mirra gritted her teeth and endured. Yanna wouldn't go easier on her if she complained.

Finally, Yanna finished letting Mirra's hair fall to her back. Mirra moved her head, feeling the weight of the braid. Without her hair to hide behind, she felt as exposed as she had on the open road. She reached out to touch the braid, only to have her hand slapped away.

"If ya canna keep yerself neat, then I'll 'ave no choice but to cut it."

Mirra leaped from the stool, spinning to face Yanna. "Like hell, you will."

Another slap, this time across Mirra's face. "Watch yer mouth. Now sit an' eat."

"Where's Brian?"

"Gone off for the day. Yer to eat and rest. Yer no good to us 'alf starved the way ya are."

What good was she? Just what was she going to be doing on the farm? Her old sense of defiance reared its head, rising like a serpent in the grass. She squashed it down. She had no allies, and her time in the dungeons only served to steal away what little strength she had. Already, exhaustion caused her limbs to shake and her head to hurt.

Yanna smirked as she turned her back on Mirra.

Mirra stuck her tongue out at the older woman's back. The only thing that kept her from bolting back up the stairs was the aroma wafting off the hearty breakfast sitting on the table. She arranged herself so that she could keep an eye on Yanna, who seemed content pretending that Mirra wasn't there.

Fair enough. Mirra dug in with relish. Bacon, eggs, warm yeasty bread, and frothy milk disappeared in record time. Once she cleaned her plate, she leaned back in her chair, marveling at the roundness of her stomach, thanks to the two solid meals she consumed. Yawning, Mirra got up from the table, leaving her dishes where they lay, her only form of defiance, and trudged back up the stairs. Yanna's hiss followed after her. Mirra smiled. She fell onto her pallet, not bothering to undress, falling asleep almost instantly.

Dark shapes writhed and danced to music that she couldn't hear. The dancers were as graceful as they were terrifying. Mirra stood in the middle of the swirling darkness, transfixed. A few of the dancers beckoned for her to join them, but she couldn't move. It made her sad. Her heart ached, tears falling down her face as she struggled to move even a finger. Slowly, the dancers moved on, leaving Mirra alone in the dark.

Come back! Don't leave me!

Over and over she silently pleaded, but they couldn't hear nor did they seem to care. Darkness pressed in all around her, but it was different from the dancers. While their darkness had been warm and welcoming, this new darkness was cold and hungry. Terror snaked its way through her body. The new darkness laughed and swallowed her whole.

THE LAST OF THE SUN'S LIGHT FADED, LEAVING THE SKY A rich purple. Dozens of lights already twinkled from homes, shop fronts, and lanterns. People milled about, laughing amongst themselves or walking linked arm to arm. They hadn't a care in the world. They got to go home to their loved ones safe and warm. Bao hated them; hated them for what they had, hated them for what he couldn't. More importantly, he hated himself. Hated himself because his desire for power, for recognition had cost him the person closest to him. Would he ever learn from his mistakes? It was like the day he lost his parents all over again.

Em sniffled behind him. He pushed all other thoughts aside. He needed to be strong for the others, for himself. Bao turned to face the remaining members of the Shadow Guild.

Krill and Tull stood silent. Both their eyes simmering with raw emotions. Sorro, stoic as always, held Em close, letting her cry on his shoulder. Bao's throat tightened.

"Mirra was the best of us. She was a good thief, a good fighter, and a good friend. She gave herself up because she knew that she could take it." A hoarse laugh. "She was always like that. She always thought that she was expendable, nothing special. But she was wrong."

Bao turned and faced the docks. How many times over the past weeks had he and Mirra sat here laughing and scheming? He wished he knew back then just how much those moments would mean to him.

"Let's do this."

Five candles sparked to life, illuminating the simple, unadorned paper lanterns. The members of the Shadow Guild lined up along the edge of the building and released the lanterns into the air.

A strong sea breeze caught the lanterns and carried them out to sea. They stood on the roof until the lanterns had faded from view. Then, one by one, they disappeared to mourn the loss of their friend in whatever way they saw fit.

Bao lingered on the rooftop and vowed to set things right so Mirra's spirit could rest in peace in the afterlife.

Mirra woke up only to eat her first day on the farm. When she shuffled down the stairs for the evening meal, Brian smiled up at her.

"Good day?"

Yanna set the dishes down with more force than necessary. "Course she 'ad a good day. All she did was sleep and eat."

Brian made a noncommittal noise, shooting an apologetic smile Mirra's way. "Well, ya look better than the day his lordship put ya in my care. On the morrow, ye'll help Yanna around the house."

Both women looked stunned over the declaration. But after a pointed look from Brian, neither argued the point.

Dinner was quiet and tense. Brian, tired from the day's labor, retired right after eating. As much as she didn't want to admit it, Mirra was disappointed that there wasn't to be music tonight.

Realizing that she was alone with Yanna, Mirra slowly turned to look at the older woman. Yanna sighed and waved Mirra on to sleep.

She scrambled up the steps before Yanna could change her mind. Taking her time to undress this time, Mirra wondered about what the morning would bring and just how soon she and Yanna would be at each other's throats.

At first light, Brian woke Mirra up. "Yan's already up. Yer to help her for now."

Mirra smoothed the strands of hair that had escaped her braid during the night. She rubbed the sleep from her eyes and pulled her dress over her head. She walked down the stairs, yawning.

"Put these on and go fetch some water."

Mirra stared at the wooden clogs handed to her. She hadn't needed them the other day. Yanna arched a brow over Mirra's hesitation. *Whatever.*

The wooden clogs were too big for her feet, but she managed to make it to the well without tripping. So, she figured it a success. She drew two buckets from the well and brought them back to the house. Yanna took them without thanks before sending Mirra back out for more.

Grumbling, Mirra shuffled out, playing scenarios in her head that involved Yanna screaming over something squirmy ending up in her bed.

It took three more trips to the well for Yanna to be satisfied. "We're workin' in the dairy today. I take it ye've never done it before."

Mirra shook her head. Yanna closed her eyes and muttered a prayer to the gods for patience.

"Listen well and do as I tell ya."

Mirra's life took on a new routine. She would wake in the morning and work with Yanna until it was time for breakfast. After eating, the pair would dive into whatever chores awaited them that day. Mirra learned how to make cheese, cream, and all kinds of butter. She kneaded bread and learned to cook simple dishes. She assisted in the washing and cleaning. It was hard work. Most nights after the evening meal, she would sit by the fire and fall asleep next to its warmth to only find herself tucked into her bed the next morning.

Brian opened up more and more each day, teaching Mirra how to whittle and telling her stories. Even Yanna eventually softened toward her, sharing a laugh now and again. But there was always the undercurrent of tension throughout the house. They couldn't forget what Mirra was, not when the truth was branded on her skin.

Mirra also changed as the days progressed. She could feel herself becoming strong or even stronger than before. The dress that used to hang off her body now fitted reasonably well, although she would have preferred britches. But it was less of an issue now. She'd gotten used to wearing dresses and to her new life. However, from time to time, she would look across the horizon and wonder about her friends and what they were doing, if they missed her. Luckily, there was too much to be done on the farm for her to wonder long about her old life.

One night, at dinner, she caught Brian watching her closely. "Ye've filled out nicely this past month."

Mirra nearly choked on her drink. *Had it been a month already?*

Brian patted her on the back. "There now. Well, now that yer a bit bigger, ye can start helping out with the other chores."

"What other chores?"

"Come to the barn after ya help clean up breakfast, and I'll show ya."

The next morning, Mirra trekked across the farm to the barn, a place she hadn't been yet. Inside was dim and dusty, smelling strongly of hay and manure. She wrinkled her nose.

"There ya are. Thought ya got lost along the way." Brian chuckled as he walked out of a stall. "As I'm sure ya can guess there's quite a bit of work that has to be done around here."

Mirra nodded slowly.

"It's just been me and Yan for years, and we manage, but now yer are here to help us."

She couldn't stop the question that bubbled to the surface. "Is that why Lord Julian gave me to you?"

Brain rubbed the back of his neck, something he only did when he was uncomfortable. "I canna say for sure. He just told me to make sure that ya dinna die."

"Oh."

Not one to linger on the awkward, Brian dove into a long-winded speech about the tasks that she was to help him with when not assisting Yanna in the house. She heard none of it. *Just keep her alive? That was it?* It drove her crazy not knowing what Lord Julian had planned for her.

Instead of taking up the remaining free thoughts, the extra chores only caused Mirra to chafe under the yoke of farm life. More and more she let her mind wander, dreaming of new ways to escape from Brian and subsequently, the King's Viper. For the first time since her arrival, Mirra felt the woods that surrounded the farm beckoning call. It might be time to see just how long of a leash Lord Julian let her have.

Later that evening, as Mirra collected the night's water for the animals, she felt the presence of the forest in the distance. She looked across the darkening fields to the black tree line in the distance. The tops of the trees swayed in the breeze against the purple sky. Mirra pulled her braid over her shoulder and played with the end. Could she do it? Could she make a run for it? She had put weight on, but was it enough to keep her going while she learned the ways of the forest? She shook her head. She'd only been on the farm a month. That wasn't enough to erase the years of near-starvation from the streets, nor her most recent stay in the dungeons. She knew no woodcraft. She didn't know how to hunt, find water, or build a shelter. She still had plenty to learn before she dared to make a break for it. As for Lord Julian, he would come back for her eventually. He didn't seem like the sort to haul someone out of a cell to only forget about them in the end.

For the next few weeks, Mirra continued working as if nothing had changed. In the morning, she milked the cows and gathered eggs from the hen house. She helped Yanna make cheese and butter and cook the meals. With Brian, she learned how to build simple structures and repair damages made by the animals and time. She learned how to tend and care for both animals and crops. She toiled from sun up to sun down, never once complaining. She knew that it could be much worse and was much worse for some.

From Brian, she earned warm smiles and praise that filled a hole inside herself that she hadn't been aware of until it had started to fill. With Yanna, things were different. The two came to a begrudged truce. Yanna stopped trying to dig at Mirra for things that were beyond her control so long as all the chores were done to her satisfaction.

For Mirra, the farm became a time of peace, the first-ever in her life. She didn't have to worry where her next meal came from—she received three a day—or worry about someone attempting to kill her in her sleep for the things she possessed.

Another month went by.

Brian had gone into the village to trade some of the goods for supplies they needed on the farm. Mirra spent most of the day tending to the animals, leaving Yanna to tend to the house. Neither complained. A few hours before the sun would start to set, the animals started to kick up a ruckus, a sign of someone coming up the path. Mirra dumped the rest of the slop into the pig's troth before running to see who was coming up the lane. She spied Yanna standing in the doorway, wiping her hands on her apron. Mirra's face broke into a smile when she spied a familiar wagon bouncing up the path. Brian had returned. Mirra rushed to greet him but slowed to a stop when she noted his grim expression.

What had happened in the village?

Brian rode up to the house and dismounted without a word. Yanna pressed her lips into a tight white line when she, too, noticed his expression.

"Bad day?" She bunched her apron in her hands in apprehension. Brain shook his head. Yanna's sharp eyes cut to Mirra. Mirra's stomach clenched, though her face continued to remain void of any emotion.

Brian pulled a weathered piece of parchment from his pocket and handed it to Mirra. She took it with trembling fingers and frowned at the words that she couldn't read.

"I don't know how to read." She held the paper back out.

Brain gave Yanna a pleading glance. The latter muttered a prayer and snatched the paper from Mirra.

"Three weeks ago, an unnamed thief attempted to steal a relic from the temple of Yrdris. The theft led to da death of the "'igh Priest. Justice and retribution 'as been served with da death of da thief."

Yanna looked at Mirra with ice in her eyes and spat at the dirt at Mirra's feet. Mirra stood still, too stunned even to register the action.

Who'd they killed in my place? Guilt settled around her shoulders like a colossal weight. She spun on her heels and made a mad dash toward the woods. She needed to get away. She needed space. Brian called after her, but she didn't slow. Past the livestock and through the fields, she ran, not stopping until she was underneath the comforting darkness of the Mystic Woods.

She didn't go far into the woods, just enough to where she couldn't see the farm. Mirra sat on a fallen tree and cried. She didn't hold anything back. Great wracking sobs shook her body. She tore at her hair and screamed to the heavens. She mourned for the poor soul who had the misfortune of taking her place at the gallows and for her friends who thought she was dead. Any hope she had of quietly returning was now gone. If she returned, there would be too many questions asked, which would most definitely end up with more innocent blood on her hands. Mirra was no stranger to death; life on the streets often ended up bloody, but every drop of blood she spilled had always been in defense of the Shadow Guild and its territories. She cried until there was nothing left in her. She felt hollowed out and numb.

The setting sun had given strength to the shadows under the canopy. Mirra closed her eyes and listened to the darkening woods. Nothing. The shadows held nothing for her. Sighing, she rose from the log. She might as well return. She didn't want to get into any more trouble than she already was. The walk back felt like an eternity. With each step, the weight around her shoulders grew. Her shoulders curved inwards, and her gaze fell blankly to her feet as she trudged along, feeling older than twelve.

Light streamed out of the windows of the house, but they lacked the warmth that Mirra had become accustomed to feeling when she saw them. She walked up to the door and paused when she heard the raised voices on the other side.

"She's a killer, Brain! A priest killer! Who knows what she'll do ta us? She might slit our throats in our bed and not lose any sleep! I won't 'ave her under dis roof anymore. Ya 'ear me! NO MORE!"

Brain sighed, undoubtedly rubbing the back of his neck. "She didn't kill da priest, Yan."

"Dat's not what da paper said."

Another sigh. "They never found the guy who'd done it. They had to punish someone, so they put it all on the girl. She did try an' steal the god's face, but it was a distraction. That's what he told me."

"An you believe everything he tells ya, is that it?"

"What choice do I have, Yan? An what do ya think he'll do to us when he finds out the girl's gone?"

Sniffling.

Mirra pushed the door open and walked in. Yanna was slumped in her chair, a handkerchief under her eyes. Brian leaped from his seat and crossed the space in a few long strides.

"There ya are, girl. Donna scare me like that again."

Mirra lowered her gaze. "I'm sorry."

Brian huffed awkwardly, and Mirra heard the rustling of parchment. "He sent a message to ya. I found it in my things after I unpacked."

Mirra stared at the slip of parchment in Brian's hand. Her cry in the woods left her empty, unable to feel anything at all. With dull eyes, she looked to Yanna, waiting for the woman to tell her what was written on the paper. Yanna glared at her husband who pleaded with her silently to read the note. Yanna sighed and snatched the paper from her husband.

Her voice was hard and chipped. "I trust year findin' yer new life an improvement on yer old one. Grow strong and await my summons."

Yanna threw the paper into the fire. With her back turned, Mirra had no idea what her face was like, but her body stood tall and straight, defiant.

"Thank you." Mirra turned and trudged up the stairs. She had no appetite. All she wanted to do was to curl up beneath her blankets and sleep. Perhaps in the morning, things would look better.

She finally understood why The Viper had sent her to the farm. She was meant to fatten up like a solstice hog until he came to claim her for the next leg of her journey. Whatever that might be. She played with the end of her braid, lost in thought. She never once thought about what would happen to Brain and

Yanna if she were to disappear. Would he kill them as punishment for losing her? Mirra shuddered and wrapped her blankets tightly around her body. Yanna was a pain, but Brian was nice to her. Her thoughts went back to the kid they had killed in her stead. Another shiver. She couldn't bear to have another innocent death caused because of her. She would stay and do as told.

Her dreams were blissfully absent that night. When she woke the next morning, she walked downstairs, only to find that all the morning's chores had already finished. Yanna ignored her completely, vehemently pretending that she couldn't see Mirra standing meekly at the foot of the stairs.

Mirra shrugged. Point taken. She slipped into her outside shoes and set off to work on her other chores. Like the house ones, her outside chores were also completed, and Brian was nowhere to be seen.

Mirra blinked back tears, her throat tight. She figured Yanna would avoid her, but Brian; his rejection stung more than she cared to admit. She lifted her gaze, scanning for the man who had come to mean the world to her, and she heard the call; not one that could be heard by mortal ears but one that wormed its way past her pain and the lingering numbness from the day before. The Mystic Woods called out for her. "Come and hide," it seemed to say in her mind. Mirra's feet carried her toward the woods as if compelled. Perhaps Brian was right, and the woods were haunted by hungry monsters. Perhaps by going into them yesterday, she fell under a spell and was now on the way to her death. Good if she died; then maybe no one else would suffer because of her.

Nothing leaped to eat her when she crossed over into the woods. She made her way to the fallen tree she sat at yesterday and waited. Birds chirped overhead, and squirrels or chipmunks rustled in the underbrush. The longer she sat, the more at peace Mirra felt, and that peace cleared away the haze of the previous day, leaving anger in its wake.

It wasn't her fault. She never wanted to steal that stupid mask in the first place. She didn't care about the High Priest or his stupid war against the crime lords of the capital. She never wanted to be sent off to live at a farm while they killed some poor unlucky soul in her place. She didn't want to be here, sitting in the woods. She was tired of not having any control over her own life.

A wild and crazy thought snaked its way into the back of Mirra's mind. Why did she stay? She didn't owe Brian or his wife anything. They weren't as innocent as they appeared if they were tangled up with the King's Viper. Why should she care what happened to them? They didn't care about her; not really.

Mirra looked over her shoulder, studying the vast forest around her. She was clever. She could figure out how to live in the woods long enough to reach another village or a port town. Then she could find a way on a ship and disappear into the unknown; contract and tattoo be damned. She leaped to her feet, her heart thundering wildly inside her chest. All she had to do was take a single step toward her freedom and never stop running.

Pain exploded from her wrist, sending waves of fire up her arm and throughout her body. Mirra fell to the forest floor with a strangled cry, convulsing. As she rolled about on the ground, unable to cry out for help, she caught a glimpse of the farm. She reached out in vain for Brian and farm, even for Yanna, wishing she was there instead of slowly dying alone in the woods.

As suddenly as the pain started, it stopped. Mirra took several moments, gasping for breath, before she pushed herself up to her knees. There were no marks on her body. No signs of anyone or anything around her. There was nothing that could have caused the pain. Small waves of pain fluttered at her wrist. Her eyes fell to the serpent tattoo around her wrist. The pain was emanating from the tattoo. Mirra's mouth went dry. For two months now, she had that tattoo. It only hurt while getting it and as it healed—until … until she decided to run away. But how?

Magic, whispered a part of her.

Mirra balked against the idea, but what other explanation could there be? Her first meeting with Lord Julian played back in her mind. At the time, she chalked up the dark aura around him as a hallucination, but now …

Magic.

Mirra sat back hard on her bottom, drawing her knees into her chest. She was bound to a man by magic. A force that shouldn't exist anymore. Suddenly the forest didn't feel as welcoming as before.

She pushed herself to her feet, not wanting to spend another second within the borders of the woods. Her steps were stiff and shaking. She stumbled from tree to tree, making her agonizingly slow trek out from under the wide-spreading branches. She kept her eyes locked on the distant buildings of the farm. She let everything else fade away until the only things that existed for her were the farm in the distance.

Five more trees. Four. Two. One.

Mirra clung to the last tree, gasping deeply. She would have nothing to lean against once she let go. She would make it back, even if she had to crawl across every field between here and the farm. She took several deep breaths, trying to draw on as much of her strength as possible. She would have to move quickly if she wanted to put as much distance between her and the woods and the horrible truth she just learned.

"Let go." She dug her nails into the bark and then music.

Haunting and sweet music filled the air around her. It filled her senses and consumed her every thought. It flowed in her veins, carrying ice to quell the lingering flames dancing along her blood. It soothed the shakiness in her legs and straightened her spine. It chased away her fears, regret, and sorrow.

She turned back to the woods, releasing her grip to stand tall and sure. The music coated her tongue, as sweet as anything she tasted in the capital. She gulped the air, eager and hungry for more. She leaned against the beckoning call of the music. Once again, her feet moved of their own accord.

"Mirra!'

Brian shouted her name, near frantic. "There ya are, girl. Where have you been all day? Let's head back."

Mirra didn't move. The music was gone. She strained her ears, desperate for more.

"Mirra?"

Gone. The music was gone, and with it, her desire to run off into the woods. A great ache settled over her. She turned and stumbled. Brian caught her and set her on top of the farm's donkey.

"Thought ye might want a day to think on things," Brian said. "I know year a good person. No matter what they say. I can see it in year eyes. Ya just got to take things one day at a time."

I'm not. Mirra thought, too tired to argue; *I'm not good. Not at all. A priest and another child are dead because of me. All I want to do is run away, even though it means you'll die.*

Brian continued to talk, unaware of Mirra's silent rebuttals. "A good night's sleep. That what ya need. Things will look better in the morn. You'll see."

Mirra glanced over her shoulder at the retreating woods. In the last light of the day, she could have sworn she saw a flash of silver in the dark.

CHAPTER FIVE

For three years, Mirra lived peacefully on the farm with Brian and Yanna. Mirra tried to forget that day in the woods, but the memory of the pain she endured lingered like a ghost. She spent many a night tracing the serpent coiling around her wrist, speculating and regretting. She would often sigh because there was nothing she could do to change the past. It happened, no matter how much she wished otherwise. There was nothing she could do about it now.

While Mirra couldn't change the past, there were a few things that had changed over the years. Steady meals and hard labor had taken Mirra from a waif of a girl into a strong and lean young woman. Whenever she went into town with Brian or Yanna, she noted how the village boys would stop and stare at her. The village girls, however, were a different story. Their eyes would narrow, and they would whisper vicious things behind their hands. Mirra paid no mind to either group. She didn't care what they thought of her. One day, Lord Julian would send word, and she would leave, becoming nothing more than a distant memory. She would leave no mark on this place, and that was exactly how she liked it.

A rooster crowed in the pale morning light, rousing Mirra from her sleep. She groaned, throwing her arm over her eyes. She lay in bed for a few more precious seconds before throwing the covers back and placing her feet on the thin, worn rug that barely protected her bare feet from the cold floor. She quickly pulled on her socks and threw on her clothes. She frowned at the simple gray dress. Yanna insisted that Mirra continue to wear dresses, even though she still preferred britches.

"'Ave to look like ya belong," Yanna always said. "Nice girls don't wear men's clothes."

I'm not exactly a nice girl. Mirra quickly ran a brush through her hair and braided it back. She took the long braid and coiled it around her head, pinning it in place, before heading out to handle the day's work.

The downstairs was dark and quiet. Yanna and Brian were still in bed. Brian would be up soon enough. Yanna, now pregnant, would sleep a little longer. That left the brunt of the housework to Mirra.

The sky was still dark, though the stars had already returned to their daytime homes. A few of the animals stirred, their sleepy noises adding to the calm of the farm. Mirra drew a deep breath, savoring the chilly air. As she walked to the well to draw the morning's water, her eyes fell, as they often did, to the Mystic Woods. The trees loomed along the border like dark giants swaying gently from side to side.

She would visit them later.

It didn't take her long to get over her fear of the woods. Life with Yanna and Brian had been peppered with fights; always about her. The only place where she could snatch a few moments of peace was underneath the limbs of the great trees in Mystic Woods. The trees whispered to her, taught her secret things and lessons of the forest. She heeded those imposing, silent master more than any teacher that the tiny village provided.

Brian lumbered out of the house and began his trek to the barn where he spent most of his morning. Instead of passing by with a grunt, he slowed. Mirra tightened her grip on the water pail. She braced herself for what she knew was coming.

Brian halted and rubbed the back of his neck. "Yanna's not doin' too well this mornin'. She's awantin' her meal a bed."

Mirra only nodded because she could barely keep the words building in her mouth from spilling out. It wasn't Brian's fault that his wife had become a tyrant during her pregnancy. They'd already been through six months of it. They just had to hold on for a few more, and then it would be over.

Brain shuffled quickly off to the barn, his sole refuge, leaving Mirra to face the queen of the farmyard on her own.

Yanna was seated by the cold, empty hearth when Mirra entered. She sat in her chair with a pile of sewing at her feet.

Mirra wordlessly dumped the morning's water before turning to attend to the hearth. Yanna remained silent, watching Mirra through narrowed eyes, lips pursed. It took only a few breaths to light the kindling and set up the smaller sticks to get the fire going. Mirra then removed the shutters from the windows, letting in the fresh air and the growing morning light. Next, she filled a kettle with the water she brought in and set in on its hook near the stove.

Yanna huffed and picked up her sewing. Mirra noted the dark circles under her eyes; another hard night for her. Mirra felt a twinge of guilt. Even though the older woman made her life miserable more often than not, Mirra couldn't help but feel sympathetic over her condition. Pregnancy was hard enough on its own. She was sure that having her living with them caused additional stress that Yanna truly didn't need.

"No matter what Brian or that Lord have said, I want ya gone when da baby comes." Mirra turned, mouth pressed tight against the retort building in her mouth. "I don't want my child growing up with a priest killer and thief. It's been three years, an' he ain't come back for ya. I don't know why ya haven't run away yet. I can see ya wanna. Go, I won't say a word."

Mirra clenched her fists. It would do her no good to argue, not when she agreed with Yanna. "I'm going out. There's some cheese and bread if you get hungry."

She walked out of the house, blinking fiercely. She strode past the well, past the barn where Brian still hid, past the garden and the chickens already clucking. On and on, she walked, Yanna's words swirling in her head. If she could leave, she would have done so already. She didn't dare to try and explain the magic tattoo that kept her bound to the farm until the day Lord Julian came for her. Yanna would no doubt kill Mirra herself if she ever knew.

Mirra paused just along the border to the forest, scanning the horizon. As usual, no one. She ducked under the branches and followed the well-worn trail to the only place in the world that she could call her own. Nothing more than a small alcove of trees; Mirra had turned it into a small hideaway, near indistinguishable from the landscape around it.

She paused once again, listening to the sounds of the birds and other creatures of the woods. They went about their daily lives unbothered. Mirra pulled open the small door and walked inside.

Only a few beams of weak sunlight filtered through the gaps in the brush, but Mirra didn't need light. She knew where everything in the little hut was. She immediately removed her dress and tucked it into a small, waterproof bag that held what she wore when she went into the woods. The dark green tunic had once belonged to Brian. She had nicked it from the rag pile and used the sewing skills that Yanna taught her to refashion it to a loose-fitting tunic that came down to her knees. The britches she nicked from a washing line the day Brian had sent her to the village by herself. The boots, she was particularly proud of. They had taken her the longest to steal. If it weren't for the questions they would undoubtedly bring, Mirra would have worn them all the time. The leather was pliable and fit around her feet and legs as if they had been made for her. A small leather belt cinched the tunic around her narrow waist, finishing her transformation from farm girl to a hunter. The last piece of her transformation sat in another waterproof wrapping. Her bow. It was the only thing that she spent the coin on. Bows were highly prized and fiercely guarded. She traded fabric scraps, baked goods, and whatever she could squirrel away to earn the coin she required. It was worth it.

The bow gave her a reason to be in the woods that had become her sanctuary. She brought home game often enough that her excursions were tolerated. The meat fed the family while the pelts brought in extra coin or were refashioned into something useful. When Mirra brought home her first kill, it was the only time that she had seen Brain mad. He had bellowed and gotten red in the face as he lectured Mirra on how she was his responsibility and how she was putting her life in danger every time she went into those woods. Surprising for all, it was Yanna who calmed her husband and helped him see the benefit of letting Mirra continue to hunt in the Mystic Woods. Mirra thought that Yanna secretly hoped that one day Mirra would get hurt or die in the woods, absolving them of having to deal with Lord Julian.

After slinging her quiver over her shoulder, Mirra exited the makeshift shelter and trekked out into the woods to see what they had to show her today. With each step, she left her worries behind. She dropped Yanna and her biting remarks. She left Brian and his kind eyes filled with pity. She left Lord Julian and his contract behind. The only thing that she couldn't forget was the serpent tattooed around her wrist. The further she moved away from the farm, the more it pulsated, a small reminder that no matter how free she felt in the woods, she still had a leash still firmly tethered to her.

She spent the whole day in the woods. She set up snares for small game while looking for signs of larger game. She managed to bring down a pair of pheasants, a good meal for tonight.

Tonight.

Mirra sighed glancing at the serpent coiling around her wrist. "If not for you, I'd be gone." No point pining over things that could never be. She turned to start the arduous journey back, but she heard a noise that stopped her cold—a melody. One that she was fairly certain that she'd heard before. The pheasants dropped from her stunned fingers as she turned to look behind her. She couldn't see another person, but the melody is clear in her head. A cold sweat ran down her back. She hadn't heard that melody for years, not since that day she tried to run and learned the terrible truth about the tattoo around her wrist. What new horrors did it bringing with it this time?

She took an involuntary step toward the sound. And then another. She stepped on a twig. The snap jarred her free from the song's hold. Shaking her head, she stepped back to pick up the drooped pheasants. She started to run. Her heart pounded in her chest, wild and frantic like a deer running from a pack of wolves. She didn't stop until she reached her hut, painfully gasping for air. She paused, straining her ears for any sounds of pursuit or the beckoning melody. Nothing. She breathed a sigh of relief. Changing as fast as she could, Mirra kept one ear strained toward the world beyond the door. She still took time to make sure that her bow was properly protected from the elements before hurling herself out the door and running the entire way back to the safety of the farm.

For two days, Mirra avoided the woods. She never went to check her traps. She even refused to look in their direction. She went about her chores as usual, but Brian still noted a change in her.

"Did somethin' happen to ya lass in the woods? I know ya can handle yerself, but the woods aren't a place for a young woman."

Mirra shook her head. "Nothing happened; just laid out some snares. I'm heading back tomorrow to check them." She mentally flinched, cursing herself. Now she had to go. She prayed that whoever or whatever played the music had moved on.

Mirra checked her snares with her bow drawn. If something came after her, she'd be ready for it. But nothing did. She bagged a brace of rabbits and a raccoon. Not a bad haul.

The familiarity of the woods and routine of cleaning her kill lulled her into a false sense of security. Then she heard the song again. She gripped the handle of her knife so tight that her knuckles turned white. For some reason, hearing the song this time filled her with anger. She was tired of being scared of a song played by a being that she has never seen. She abandoned her kills and followed the song.

Every so often she would pause to make sure that she remained on the right path. It was no different from stalking a deer. After some time, she came across a moderately-sized river. She knelt by the bank and dipped her hands into the cool water, washing the blood of her kills off her hands. She cleaned her knife as well.

The rushing water drowned out the soft melody. Mirra stood along the bank, closed her eyes, and pushed away all other sounds to pick up the music again. Silence.

She looked about her, trying to spot the source of the music. The only thing that drew her eye was the small bit of land in the middle of the river. It was more of an island than a sandbar. A grove of small trees filled every inch of land; a good place to hide. The river ran swift and clear. She spied several large stones that could serve as stepping stones to the island. Mirra contemplated leaping when she heard a different sound, one just as familiar to her as the song that she followed, the creaking of a bowstring drawing back.

She spun, drawing her bow.

A man stood behind her with his bow aimed at her heart. His garb was drab and ragged, perfectly blending into the foliage around him. A huge scar ran down the left side of his face in a jagged line that dominated all other features of his face.

Mirra forced herself to focus on the rest of him and not just his scar. His face bore the signs of someone who has lived a hard and haggard life for years. Deep lines creased his brow and framed his sensitive mouth. His eyes reminded her of Bao, with the exception that they were vibrant green, not warm brown. The man's eyes also carried a deep pain that gave them a mournful appearance.

The two archers kept their bows pointed at one another, neither one willing to be the first to lower their weapons.

The man's eyes dropped to the tattoo on Mirra's wrist. To her surprise, his eyes widened and his muddy skin turned pale. He closed his eyes and lowered his bow with a sigh. "Go ahead and get it over with." His voice was softer than Mirra expected it to be. It was a voice better suited for telling stories in grand halls than living deep within the woods.

She gripped her bow tighter. "Get what over with?"

He looked pointedly at her wrist. "You're one of his. A bit younger than I would have imagined, but neither the less, one of his."

"Just who do you think I belong to?"

The hunter's face broke out in confusion. "The King's Viper. You are one of his, aren't you? You have his mark."

Mirra lowered her bow. "Not really," she conceded. "He snatched me from a dungeon and dropped me here. But that was three years ago. He's probably forgotten about me by now."

The hunter shook his head. "He hasn't; trust me."

Curiosity blossomed inside of Mirra. "Just how do you know him?"

The hunter narrowed his eyes, studying Mirra. He turned and started to walk away. Mirra called out after him.

"Wait! Don't go!"

But he had already disappeared into the woods. Mirra raced off after him but found no trace. The hunter left no signs at all. If Mirra hadn't seen him with her own eyes, she could have doubted that he existed at all. But no person could travel without leaving a trail in some shape or form.

She searched and searched along the river bed, finding nothing. She peered over her shoulder at the small island in the middle of the river. She thought it could make a good hiding place; perhaps the hunter thought the same.

Mirra walked to the edge of the river, studying the gap between the shore and the first stone. The muscles in her leg tightened in preparation for the leap when a shadow fell across the river. She glanced at the sky. Night approached. She didn't like to stay in the forest at night; harder to see the path and predators. She looked out at the island one last time and then turned her back on it. With each step, she knew that the man would return and pack up his camp. She would lose her chance to meet him, but then he might leave a trail that she could follow.

The forest is even quieter in the early morning hours before the sun has fully risen. Mirra crouched in the bush along the riverbank, eagerly watching the island nestled in the middle of the river. She had already been sitting there for hours, watching for any sign of movement, but saw nothing. She wrestled between remaining where she was and making the perilous trek across the river to see what lay on the island. In the end, her curiosity won out. Slowly, she rose from her hiding place and stalked toward the river's edge. It took on a few steps at a running start to propel her over the raging water to the first stone.

She crouched low, fingers grazing the icy water, to keep from falling headfirst into the frigid water. The distance was slightly greater to the next stone. She took a deep breath and crouched lower. A mighty leap carried her across the water. Her right foot slipped, causing her to teeter precariously before she righted herself, gripping the rock tightly. Gasping, Mirra ignored the cold water that splashed her face and soaked her clothes. Thankfully, the next few stones were close enough that Mirra made it across without any further mishaps.

The island wasn't much, but there was enough ground to set up a small camp. In the middle of the island was the remnant of a small fire. Eager, Mirra held her hand over the charred remains. *Cold, blast it.* She swallowed her disappointment. The man no doubt packed up the moment he realized that she was pursuing him. She would have done the same if she were him. With a pout, she sat on the slightly damp ground, stretching her feet out in front of her, pondering what to do next. A quick scan of the campsite gave her no clues, but she would find them eventually. A man on the run would most definitely leave a trail, no matter how cautious he was.

Mirra smiled. Hunting this man would be no different than hunting a deer. She leaped to her feet and gathered what she needed to make trip snares. If two game trails had similar signs of activity or no activity at all, she would set them up and see which one currently had animals on it. She would hunt for the man with the scar to get the answers that raged in her mind, and these trip snares would let her know if he came back to his island. She may not be the best hunter, but this was her forest, and she knew it better than he did.

The man with the scar watched the young woman setting up her snares. She was clever, he'd give her that, but what else would you expect from an agent of The Viper? How could one so young be desperate enough to let herself be branded by a man who lived in shadows and spoke lies as easy as breathing? He turned to head deeper into the woods. It wasn't safe for him to linger, not with her around. He put his hands into the pockets of his coat and turned but found that he couldn't take a single step away from the young woman who was now making her way back to the shore.

A soft, sad melody, one meant for his ears only, caressed his skin like a lover. He closed his eyes and groaned. *Great, just what I needed. Fine, I'll play your little game—for now.*

CHAPTER SIX

As the days turned to weeks, it became clear Mirra had underestimated the man's ability to evade her. Every day, before dawn, she made her way to the woods filled with determination. That determination often gave way to frustration by mid-morning as she went on one wild goose chase after another. At first, she was surprised to find signs that the man still lingered in Mystic Woods—a footmark, a bit of cloth, smoldering campfires—but it became painfully clear that he was jerking her around. *But why?* That question stoked the flames of her ire and drove her to neglect all else but the hunt. She ignored Yanna's attempts to bully and belittle her as she ignored her chores. She pretended that she didn't see the worried glances Brian shot her way when she came home at dark, scratched and fuming.

The man with the scar had answers for her. She could feel it in her bones. She couldn't stop, not until she found him and got the answers to the questions he stirred up inside her.

Though the sun had begun to rise, its light was not strong enough to penetrate the canopy above, and the forest was quiet. The nocturnal creatures had already settled down in their homes for the day, while the creatures that lived under the sun had yet to stir from their slumber.

The trail to the island was still cloaked in shadows. Not that it mattered to Mirra. She'd walked that trail hundreds of times to the point where she could have found her way there in total darkness.

None of the trip snares had been triggered. Mirra hadn't expected them to be, but she still checked them every day. Mirra built a small, smokeless fire and sat down. From her pocket, she pulled out a weathered slip of paper; a map of all her traps and trails, of every place she'd discovered a sign that the man with the scar still lingered in Mystic Woods. She studied in the light of the fire, glaring.

The man had always made sure that he stayed well within her comfort zone. That meant that he watched her, hunted her just like she was attempting to do with him. *Bastard.* Mirra crumpled the map and shoved it back into her pocket. For weeks, she'd chased him all over the woods with nothing to show for it. He was making a fool of her. She ground her teeth as she made the precarious leaps across the river. Back on the shores of the forest, she clenched her fists. Living a simple life had made her soft. When she lived in the capital, she would have found the man in a matter of hours, with the help of her friends. Weeks of frustration finally caught up with her.

Mirra found it difficult to swallow the tears that welled in her eyes. Her friends. Her old life. Her new life. This man. Everything came crashing on her like a summer's storm.

"Coward! You bloody coward! What kind of man runs from a girl?"

"One that knows the master she serves."

Mirra spun. The man with the scar down his face leaned casually against a tree with a serious look on his face.

"I serve no master," she spat.

A pointed glance to her wrist. She didn't bother to hide it. Instead, she pulled her sleeve back, fully exposing the twining serpent.

"You know this tattoo?"

The man nodded.

"How?"

He sighed, pushing off the tree. Mirra tensed; ready to take off after him should he run. "That's a long story and is not fit for a young girl such as you."

"You have no idea what life I had before coming here."

"That is true, but I still won't tell it to you."

Mirra crossed her arms, arching her brow. "Then why show yourself now? You can't have gotten bored messing with me already."

The man chuckled. His face softened, showing that at one time in his life, he could have been considered handsome.

"That is the question, isn't it? Honestly, I can't explain that either." He ran his hand through his hair. "Look, I know you have questions. I can't answer them, not all of them. And I know we got off to a rocky start, with you pulling your bow on me and everything."

"You had yours out too!"

The corners of the man's mouth twitched. Mirra found hers threatening to rise as well. She held firm, not wanting him to think that his charm was working on her. He'd play her for a fool again if that happened.

The man must have sensed her distrust in him. What little of a smile he had on his face fell. His eyes became serious once more. "My name is Shiro." He bowed slightly toward her.

"Mirra."

Shiro straightened and opened his mouth to say something but stopped. He cocked his head to the side as if to hear something better. Mirra strained her ears but heard nothing outside the river at her back and the birds waking up in the trees. Whatever Shiro heard was enough to turn his expression sour.

"Meet me here in two days, and I promise that I'll answer what I can."

Mirra nodded. Shiro turned to disappear into the woods like before. "Why the sudden change in heart?" Shiro only shrugged and disappeared into the fading darkness beneath the trees.

Mirra stared after Shiro for several long minutes. The sun rose higher, pushing back the shadows. The daytime creatures of the forest went about their usual routine, paying the young woman standing still as a stone by the river no mind.

Should she meet him? What if it was all a trap, a ruse to test her loyalty? She glanced down at the serpent encircling her wrist. Not once did it cause her pain, not even a twinge. What did it all mean? Mirra groaned, dragging her hands down her face. It was too much, too soon, and too early. She huffed and strode toward her hut where she stashed her hunting gear. He wasn't expecting her for two days; no need to make a decision now.

Back at the farm, Mirra buried herself under all the work she neglected during her search for Shiro. Brian watched her with outright worry. Yanna made one snide remark after another, but they all failed to reach their mark. She might have physically been with them, but in her mind, she went over every scenario that could arise if she chose to meet Shiro or not.

That night, after she had retired to bed, Brian and Yanna sat by the fire, whispering furiously to each other.

"For weeks, she's gone from one end of 'dem cursed woods to the other. She says not one word to us the entire time. Just what do ya think she's been doin' in there, Brian? What fresh 'ell is she 'bout to bring on us?"

Brian wrung his hands, staring into the fire.

"O'course you ain't gonna say nothin' to her. Yer just as 'appy to let her run wild. Well, that's well enough for her, but what 'bout our babe? Just what kinda influence is Mirra gonna be?"

Yanna scowled at her husband's continued silence. In a huff, she threw down her needlework and waddled off to bed, muttering under her breath. Brian lingered by the fire, staring at it without really seeing it. Above, he heard the door to his bedroom close with more force than necessary. Silence settled around him. The whole house seemed to settle down for the night.

He slid from his seat and pried up a loose floorboard. From the hidden space, he carefully pulled out a stack of parchment and a charcoal pencil. He scribbled a short message by the firelight, after which he folded up and sealed it with a black wax seal bearing the symbol of a serpent coiling around itself. After replacing everything to its proper place, Brian stood before the fire, staring at the cooling seal. A rare flare of irritation flashed in his usually calm eyes. He crumpled the letter into a ball before throwing it into the fire. He glanced up at the ceiling that separated him from Mirra's bedroom. For three years, he had cared for that girl. He had seen her grow from a living shell of a child to a strong-willed young woman that any father would be proud to call his. He knew that by not sending the letter, he'd put his family in danger. He would, eventually, but if she found a way to free herself from The Viper's clutches, then he would do all he could to help her by giving her a little more time.

THE RIVER LOOKED COMPLETELY UNCHANGED SINCE HER last visit, not a single leaf out of place. She kept to the shadows, straining her senses for any signs of a trap. In the end, her desire to escape Yanna's incessant nagging and nit-picking drove her to keep her meeting with Shiro. Death would be better than listening to that woman's grating voice.

Mirra's legs started to cramp from their crouched position. She shifted slightly, not wanting to give away her position.

"You might as well stand up and give your legs a break."

Mirra scowled at Shiro's controlled voice and stood. Her legs groaned and sighed. "How'd you know where I was?"

Shiro stood just a bit further down the bank from her. She hadn't spotted him when she arrived nor heard him arrive. "When you live in the woods for as long as I have, you learn a thing or two about moving about unseen." He gestured to the island. Mirra nodded. "A bit of privacy while we talk."

Safely hidden by the brush and trees, Shiro and Mirra settle down on opposite sides of a small fire. Once again, Shiro had set up camp on the island. His attention was not on Mirra, who was busy taking in the rough campsite but on the small, simmering pot hanging over the fire. When he stirred, the aromatic scent of tea filled the air.

"In my culture, when entertaining guests, refreshments must be served first."

Mirra brought her attention back to the man she had come to see. "Where are you from?"

A sad smile. "Zaliano. My family had a bit of land not too far from Three Kings Bay."

He poured a portion of tea into a small clay cup. Mirra accepted the cup, wrapping her cold fingers around the cup, soaking up its warmth. Cautiously, she smelled the tea but didn't detect anything outside of the ordinary. She pressed the cup to her lips and pretended to take a sip. Shiro laughed.

"I'm not going to drug you. It would be a breach in tradition and dishonor my ancestors."

Mirra made a noise, unsure of what else to say. Shiro smiled again and poured a portion of tea for himself and drank it with great relish. Mirra narrowed her eyes and set the tea aside.

"No offense to your ancestors or anything, but I don't know you. I may look like a country girl, but I grew up in the slums in the capital. And there, you trust no one."

"So young, yet already so hardened." Shiro shook his head. Heat flooded Mirra's face.

"You said you had some answers for me."

The light faded from Shiro's eyes. "Some."

Mirra motioned with her hand for him to speak. Shiro's face took on a pained expression as if the words burned him from the inside.

"I knew your master a long time ago. We were once friends."

"What happened?"

"A long, complicated story that I'm not ready to get into right now. I'm more interested in your story."

Mirra cocked her head, eyes narrowing down to slits. She pointed her finger angrily toward Shiro. "That's not what we agreed to."

It was Shiro's turn to scowl. "Don't be naive. I don't know anything about you than that you are one of Julian's people. He wants me dead, so until I figure out who you are, I'm not going to tell you anything."

Lord Julian wanted this vagrant dead? Mirra kept her face neutral but filed that morsel of information away to chew on later. She pressed her lips together, deciding just how much she should reveal.

"As I said, I grew up in the low streets of the capital. I was a thief and got caught. He pulled me from the gallows and gave me a chance to keep living. I was twelve at the time, so I took it."

"What did you try to steal that carried a death warrant?"

Mirra gave him a pointed look that said she'll tell more if he did. Shiro's face hardened. He took another sip of tea.

Mirra shrugged. "He dumped me here three years ago. I haven't heard anything since. He's probably forgotten about me."

Shiro scoffed. "I highly doubt that."

Mirra leaned back on her arms and muttered, "What do you know."

Dark fury transformed Shiro's face. Mirra swallowed.

"What do *I* know? What do *you* know! You let yourself be carried on the currents of life without any thought as to where it takes you. You're as listless as the leaf on the wind."

"I had no choice!" Mirra shouted back, jumping to her feet. "I'm an orphan. I have no family, except the one I made, and I've lost them forever! You think I wanted this! I had no choice!"

The darkness receded from Shiro's face. It softened until he looked at least a decade older and exhausted. "We always have a choice," he whispered. "It may not be easy. It may go against everything we believe, but we always have a choice."

"So, I should have just let them kill me? At twelve!"

Shiro sipped his tea.

Rage blinded her. Mirra spread her feet wider, her fists white-knuckled at her sides. "To hell with you! I bet you lived a good life before you crossed paths with The Viper. I bet you grew up with a full belly and a warm bed. Well, I didn't. Life's never given me a scrap of anything. What I had, I fought for—viciously. I earn what I have. It may not always be 'the right way,' but it's the only way I know how, and I'll be damned if anyone look down on me for that."

She took great gulping breaths. Her face flushed, and her eyes were bright. If Shiro said the wrong thing now, Mirra would launch herself over the small fire and pummel him to a bloody pulp. She flashed him a wolfish grin and silently dared him to be that stupid.

Much to her dismay, Shiro only finished his tea before packing up. Lacking fuel, her fire sputtered, taking her rage with it.

"Where are you going?"

Shiro clinched his bag and stood, kicking dirt onto the fire to put it out. "I learned what I needed to and not; it's time for me to leave."

Mirra blanched. "What?"

"I know that you weren't sent after me, and that's all I needed to know." Mirra stared at him, mouth wide agape. "You're just one of his many underlings, and a green one to boot." He turned to leave when Mirra called out after him.

"Wait! You promised me answers!"

"There's nothing that I can tell you that you don't already know. You just have to face it." His face was incredibly sad as he looked at her over his shoulder. He chewed the inside of his jaw and then said, "The only thing I can offer you is a small bit of wisdom. Everyone's life comes to a point where they have to make a choice that will alter the way their life will head. Have the courage to make the right choice." And with that, he made his way across the river and disappeared into the woods.

Mirra remained where she stood, transfixed. The parting words Shiro spoke filled her mind until nothing else remained. They flowed in her and through her, coiling unseen in the air. They coiled tighter and tighter like a serpent crushing its prey.

Something deep within Mirra stirred and uncoiled. It rose its head and snarled at the invading words. Black fire rippled through her body, incinerating Shiro's words until they were nothing more than glittering specks on the wind.

Mirra shook her head and took a deep breath. Typical she thought darkly, unaware of what just occurred inside her. She shouldered her bag and headed back to the farm. She had chores to do.

ONE MORNING, MIRRA WOKE TO FIND A SMALL BROWN package sitting at the foot of her bed. A smile broke out across her face. Every year, without fail, she would wake one morning and find a package at the foot of her bed; a gift from Brian. Each gift marked another year of living and working on the farm. The first gift, wrist guards, had taken her completely by surprise. When she asked Brian what he wanted in exchange for them, he said nothing. Mirra cried later, clutching the guards to her chest. She had never received a gift before. The second year, she received her hunter's bag. Mirra reached across the bed and picked up the small package. She wondered what it could be.

Brimming with excitement, she tore into the gift. "Oh," she breathed.

Nestled within the brown wrappings sat a dozen metal arrowheads. Mirra could only stare at the small fortune in her hands. Most hunters used flint arrowheads. They were cheaper to make and worked just as good as the metal ones. The metal ones, however, could be used for numerous things, including bringing down an armored attacker. They also lasted longer than flint heads.

Why would Brian buy such a gift for her? She was a decent enough hunter with the flint heads. Why would he gift her with arrowheads that could bring down armored opponents?

From below, she heard the sound of a wagon approaching. She bolted from her bed, still clutching her gift and went down the stairs as fast as she could. She ran past an anxious Yanna, throwing the door wide open.

A black carriage stood in front of the farmhouse. A team of stark white horses pranced on an eager hoof, ready to be going again. A man in dark livery sat in the driver's seat with a vacant expression. The door to the carriage swung open.

"She's grown quite nicely."

Ice filled Mirra's veins. She knew that voice. It was the same voice that haunted her nightmares. Lord Julian, the King's Viper, exited the carriage. Sharp pain brought her back to her senses. She relaxed her white-knuckled grip on her incredibly sharp arrowheads.

Lord Julian gave her an oily smile. "What a fine young woman you've grown up to be. No doubt the jewel of this dusty little place."

Brian shifted on his feet, his face reddening. A fierce wave of protection washed over her.

"Why are you here?"

Julian placed his hand over his heart and bowed slightly. "To collect you, of course. It's time for you to meet your new teacher."

Mirra took an involuntary step back. She suddenly found that she didn't want to go. The farm had become her home. She would miss the quiet mornings working with Brian, taking care of the land and the animals, hunting in the woods. She would even miss Yanna. Julian's eyes narrowed.

"You belong to me and will obey."

His voice resounded in the air around them. Pain flared at her wrist. Mirra hissed and grabbed it, dropping her gift in the dirt. The pain intensified, bringing her to her knees in agony.

"Stop it," cried a voice outside the pain. "She'll be ready in but a moment."

The pain receded. Brain helped Mirra to her feet and corralled her back inside the house. Much to Yanna's dismay, Lord Julian followed. She quickly set the kettle on and set a platter of hard cheese and bread on the table. Julian touched neither. He watched Brian usher Mirra up the stairs with his unnerving two-toned eyes.

Back within the safety of her room, although it was feeling more unsafe by the minute, Mirra finally was able to shake off her feelings of dread and confusion.

"Did you know?" she snarled, rounding on Brian. "Did you know he was coming?"

Brian rubbed the back of his neck. "One day but not today. I'm sorry lass."

Her anger fizzled out. Brian would never betray her like that. "I don't have a choice, do I?"

"I'm afraid not. He owns ya until he decides that he doesn't. Best go along and not make a fuss." He turned to leave the room. "I'll leave ya ta pack yer things. Take as long as ya need."

Mirra nodded. The click from the door closing sounded like the sound of a cell to her ears. She should know. Mirra sat down hard at the foot of the bed and wondered at how fast her day changed. Her throat burned. She swallowed, but it did nothing to stop the tears that welled up in her eyes. They fell in hot, silent streams.

It wasn't right. It wasn't fair. She didn't want to go now. She wanted to keep pretending that Lord Julian had forgotten about her. She wanted to live out the rest of her life in peace.

Muffled voices carried up through the floorboards. Those dreams weren't an option anymore. Mirra quickly pulled one of her dresses over her head and tied her boots before heading downstairs.

Lord Julian was the first to spot her. He raised a brow at her lack of baggage.

"I need to get the rest of my stuff."

A small smirk. "And just pray tell, where is the rest of 'your stuff'?"

"In a hunter's shack in the woods."

"The Mystic Woods? I thought that it was filled with monsters and evil spirits?"

Mirra shrugged. "I never saw any. But my bow and hunting bag are there."

"And your real clothes, no doubt." Mirra bit back a retort. Lord Julian brought his hands together and tapped his mouth with a finger. "Very well," he said after several tense moments. "But know that if you don't return, I will slaughter this farmer and his wife and burn everything to the ground."

Yanna gasped, one hand going to her round belly and the other reaching out to her husband. Bile burned the back of Mirra's throat.

"No need to be so dramatic," Mirra said with false bravado as she walked out the door.

Once she was out of sight of the farmhouse, she took off running. Her lungs burned as she sped faster and faster across the fields. It took only a few moments to rip off her dress and pull on her hunting clothes. She grabbed her bag, bow, and quiver and raced back toward the house. Who knew how long he would wait for her before he burned all that she had come to love to the ground!

She nearly fell to her knees when she saw that the farm still stood. She slowed to a brisk walk, gasping and face flushed. There would be no way to hide that she ran the whole way.

The black carriage still sat in front of the house. Mirra tried not to shutter when she walked past it. When she walked through the door to the house, her heart leaped to her throat. Yanna and Brian were still alive. She gave them a quick nod of her head before rushing back upstairs to finish packing. She ignored Lord Julian completely.

If truth be told, she didn't have that much to pack, just a few basic toiletries and a few underthings. Everything fitted into her hunter's bag, and for some reason, that made her sad. Noise from below brought her back to her current situation. She shouldered her bag and quivered and picked up her bow. The familiar weight and feel gave her a morsel of calm in a sea of confusion and pain. She could do this. She had survived much worse. She would survive what came next.

Lord Julian seemed pleased over her change in attire, and the bow gripped tightly in her hand. He rose from his seat and reached into his cloak. From a pocket, he withdrew a decent sized pouch and dropped it on the table next to the untouched food. Even from her position at the foot of the stairs, Mirra heard the unmistakable sound of coins clinking together. She willed her face to remain neutral. Had everything been a lie?

"For your troubles," Lord Julian drawled. "This won't count against your debt. Consider it a bonus. Until next time."

Lord Julian exited the house without another word. Mirra spared one last glance at the people who took her in, fed her, and clothed her. "I'm sorry for any trouble I caused. I hope you both have a happy and peaceful life."

"Take care," Brian said, stoic as ever.

Mirra nodded and turned to leave, but Yanna called out for her to stop. Much to her surprise and Brian's, Yanna crossed the floor and embraced Mirra tightly.

"Be safe," she whispered, the first and only kind words ever spoken by the older woman.

Too stunned to do anything, Mirra could only nod and walk out the door to face her fate.

"Make yourself comfortable," Lord Julian said when Mirra entered the carriage. "We have quite a way to go."

CHAPTER SEVEN

EVEN THOUGH THEY HAD BEEN ON THE ROAD FOR THREE weeks since leaving Brian and Yanna's farm, Mirra hadn't seen much of the surrounding countryside. During the whole trip, the windows on the carriage remained closed, leaving her in near darkness with Lord Julian for hours on end. When they came across a tavern or inn, Lord Julian and his manservant would get to stay inside and have a hot meal with warm beds; Mirra had to remain in the carriage to "remain hidden on pain of death."

She groaned, shifting on the bench seat in the carriage, trying in vain to find a comfortable position to sleep in. *This is stupid. Why do I have to stay hidden?* Mirra moaned, pushing herself into a seated position. She cut her eyes toward the door. She knew that it wasn't locked, because there was no way *to* lock it. With Lord Julian and his always silent manservant inside the main building, they would have no way of knowing whether she obeyed or not. A spark of her old, mischievous soul sparkled to life a half-smile. She reached her hand out toward the handle.

Pain flared around her wrist, quickly traveling up the length of her arm.

. Mirra hissed, drawing her hand back. The pain subsided. She cradled her tattooed wrist against her chest, eyes watering and silently cursing the day Lord Julian entered her cell.

MIRRA DOZED, HER HEAD ROLLING AROUND LISTLESSLY. She heard a rustling of papers broken up by the occasional pen scratch from Lord Julian. The days had grown warmer, making the inside of the carriage stuffy and unbearably hot. Summer was upon them at last.

The carriage slowly came to a halt.

"Hold! State your name and intention!"

"Lord Julian for the Lady Nora," replied the manservant in his deadpan voice. "His business is his own."

The exchange brought Mirra out of her daze. She peered at Lord Julian from under her lashes. He looked as nonplussed as always, completely unbothered by the heat and the exchange happening just outside.

She wanted to pull the curtains back a little further and see just where they were but knew better. Instead, she ground her teeth and sat back, pretending to not care, even though she was dying to know where they were and who Lady Nora was.

The door of the carriage opened, temporarily blinding Mirra with the bright, warm sunlight. She closed her eyes against the burn and wildly stepped out into the sun, eager to be free of the carriage and its owner.

Blinking rapidly, Mirra stood adjacent to the carriage, awaiting instructions. She glanced about, trying to get her bearings. They stood in a small courtyard, fully surrounded by tall stone walls. Atop the walls, she spied a few men at arms patrolling the garrets. The courtyard, while small, was filled with colorful flowers, gentle trees swaying in the summer breeze, and resting benches. Nothing that screamed, "Here lives the most twisted person in all the kingdom." She allowed her body to relax a fraction of an inch but still remained alert and wary.

A sound of a great door opening drew Mirra's attention toward the main house. A youthful-looking man in gold and green livery, most likely a footman, descended and quickly strode toward them.

When he reached Lord Julian, he bowed deeply. "Greetings, my lord. We have your rooms prepared for you." He cut his eyes to Mirra. "Your companion's room will need some more time, I'm afraid. Perhaps the young lady would like to visit the baths while she waits?"

Mirra was taken back by the man's question. She wasn't sure if he was asking her or Lord Julian. After weeks on the road, she knew that she was a sight and in dire need of a bath. She turned with a questioning glance at her master. He seemed to smile at her deference to his power over her. With a slight nod of his head, Lord Julian urged her to follow the man in gold and green.

The inside of the manor house was just as feminine as the outside. Rich tapestries displaying images of spring and summer graced the walls, and nearly every table had a bouquet of flowers. Maids and footmen went about their tasks with bright smiles on their faces. Everyone looked well-fed without a care in the world. The more she looked about, the more confused Mirra grew. Just what was her role to be in this new place? Would she become a chambermaid or a scullery maid?

The footman led Mirra down a set of winding stairs. The further down they went, the warmer and more humid the air became.

"The house was built on top of an underground hot spring. It supplies all the hot water you could ever need."

"That's nice ... I guess," Mirra responded. While it would be nice not having to heat up water for a bath, she was not looking forward to hauling buckets up the winding staircase. Her arms and legs were already aching just imagining it.

They came to a door, and the footman stopped. "I leave you here. Aira will attend to you."

"Thank you."

He bowed to her, spun on his heels, and began the long climb back up the stairs. Mirra turned to face the door. At first glance, there was nothing special about the door. But as she got closer, she noted the delicate vines of silver inlaid into the wood. The handle was silver as well, molded into the shape of a blooming rose. It looked so real that Mirra could have sworn that she caught a whiff of the heady perfume of roses wafting through the cracks of the door. She shook her head. She was just tired after a month on the road. She unquestionably looked forward to sleeping in a real bed tonight.

A cloud of rose-scented warmth enveloped Mirra as she opened the door. "Oh."

"Come on in," called a voice beyond the heavenly steam that coiled out of the open doorway. "I will be but a moment."

Tentatively, Mirra entered the room. Steam and the fragrance of roses were infinitely stronger inside. It was almost too much, almost. Mirra took a few more steps and gasped.

The narrow entryway opened up to a room twice the size that the main room of Brian's farmhouse. The entire expanse of the room was filled with large tubs faintly steaming in the soft light that came from dozens, if not hundreds, of lanterns hanging from nearly every available space. It was a wonder to behold.

"I had the same look when I first saw the bathing room," said a girl that looked to be only a few years older than Mirra. Her face was as lovely as a spring morning. She wore a simple light-green dress that swayed slightly with each step. Her hair was bound up in a white wrap. Although, as she got closer, Mirra noticed a few stray strands as red as wine that had escaped and curled in the heat.

"I am called Aira," the girl said with a bright smile. "I am the Head Bath Assistant." She curtsied. "Do you require help undressing?"

"No," Mirra said quickly clutching her collar. Horrified at the thought of stripping in front of a stranger. It wasn't that she was ashamed of her body—living on the streets of Verance had quickly erased that. She didn't want to put herself into a vulnerable position if she could help it.

Aira smiled as if she knew what Mirra had thought. "Very well. If you'll please follow me, I have a bath ready."

Mirra followed, still clutching the collar of her shirt. Aira led her to a tub near the back of the room. Mirra saw no other ways to enter or leave the room other than the door that she went through. She would not want to face an enemy down here.

Aira halted in front of a tub. "This bath is ready. Please let me know if there's anything else you require." She bowed once more to Mirra before leaving her to undress in private.

Mirra strained her ears, listening to Aira's retreating footsteps. She waited for a few more breaths for any signs that the woman doubled back. Hearing nothing, she slowly peeled off her road-worn clothing. She had to slowly unwrap her undergarments that had adhered themselves to her skin because of sweat. Mirra left her filthy clothes in a pile on the floor. She carefully climbed the stairs to the tub and dipped a toe into the steaming water.

A groan escaped Mirra's mouth before she could stop it. The water was perfect. Without a second thought, she quickly vaulted over the edge of the tub and submerge her road-weary body into the soothing water. Every inch of her tired, achy body breathed a sigh of relief as heat encircled around her. A week's worth of filth flaked off and drifted along the top of the water. Mirra made a face and looked for the soap. She spied a small shelf on the inner wall of the tub. On it sat several colorful jars. When she pried the tops off, the scent of lavender filled the air.

She lathered herself up with the sweet-smelling substance, and soon the water was filled with slightly purple foam. She scrubbed until her arms ached and her skin was raw; then she went under the water. She repeated the process three more times until she finally felt clean enough.

A towel and a clean set of clothes had been left for her on a bench. Mirra stared at them and swallowed. She hadn't heard Aira or anyone come up during her bath. She'd never met someone who could move so silently.

She quickly dried off and dressed. She slid the thin shift over her head. It flowed around her softer than anything she'd ever felt. The slippers weren't much but better than walking barefoot. Lastly, she wrapped up in a thin robe, knotting the belt firmly. After running a brush quickly through the tangled knots in her hair, Mirra braided her hair back.

Now that she was clean, her stomach demanded her attention by growling loudly. Lord Julian hadn't let her starve during their trip, but he hadn't kept her well-fed either.

Mirra heard the sound of footsteps coming toward her. Through the steam, she spied a different woman walking toward her. The newcomer wore a simple gray dress with a crisp white apron. Her hair, too, was covered under a head-wrap, although hers was gray like her dress.

"His Lordship demands that you be properly dressed before joining him and my lady for supper."

Mirra suppressed a groan. *Of course, he does.* She motioned for the girl to lead the way. Up, up, up, they went. Down one corridor after another. Mirra was soon completely lost. The only thing she wanted was a hot meal and a soft bed. Her stomach rolled and clenched at what Lord Julian had planned for her.

The servant girl stopped in front of a door next to a tapestry of a young huntress. "Here is your room. You'll find your maid already waiting inside for you." She bowed to Mirra before turning to walk away.

"Thank you," Mirra called out after the girl. "Thank you for everything."

The servant girl turned; a small smile splayed across her mouth. "You are most welcome, my lady."

"I'm not a lady."

The girl's eyes crinkled as if Mirra had told a joke. She bowed once more before leaving Mirra alone.

Shaking her head, Mirra pushed open the door. Her mouth fell open at the sight of the massive, well-furnished room. It was not fit for the likes of her. This was a room of a noblewoman. Mirra took a step back, about to shout out for the servant girl when she heard a small noise from inside the room.

Curious, she peaked back inside. A maidservant dressed in a simple gray homespun dress curtsied low.

"Evening, my lady. I'm Shara, and I'm to be your maidservant while you are staying here at Rosmanor."

"I'm no lady," Mirra protested.

Shara shrugged. "Not yet. Now, if you would, please sit so I can get started."

Mirra shuffled into the room and sat dutifully at the mirrored vanity. Shara undid Mirra's braid and started to brush her hair out again. She piled Mirra's raven locks atop her head one way, then another. It all looked the same to Mirra, but clearly, for Shara, there was a marked difference.

As she began to braid and coil Mirra's hair, a small knock came at the door. "Refreshments for the Lady."

Mirra perked up at the word "refreshment," too aware of the growing ache in her stomach to argue against being called "Lady."

A serving girl set a small silver serving tray on a small table near the vanity where Shara was busy taming Mirra's locks. The serving girl presented Mirra with a plate of small, delicately frosted cookies. Mirra grabbed a cookie that was frosted with the same color as spring leaves and popped it into her mouth without a thought.

It was heavenly. The cookie disintegrated the moment it touched her tongue, filling her mouth with sweet sugar, mild nuttiness, and vanilla. She hadn't tasted something this good since the capital.

"Would you like some tea as well, my lady?"

Mirra stuffed another cookie into her mouth and nodded. She knew her manners were terrible, but she didn't care. The sugar from the cookies filled her blood with glittering goodness, chasing away the weariness of the road. It would be a short-lived burst of energy but one sorely needed if she was to keep her wits about her while she dined with Lord Julian and the lady of the house.

After pinning up her hair, Shara then tried to apply cosmetics to Mirra's face.

"If you value the use of your hands, you won't."

Shara sighed but complied. "If I'm not to apply your face, then we might as well get you into your dress."

Mirra groaned but allowed Shara to slip her into a bulky dove gray dress with a tight bodice. On her feet, she wore a delicate pair of slippers a shade or two darker than her dress. To top her ensemble off, Shara fastened a silver necklace with a pendant around Mirra's neck.

Shara stood back, impressed with her handiwork. Mirra fought to keep her emotions in check as she stared at the stranger in the mirror. Gone was the thief from the capital. Gone was the young huntress. She didn't know if she liked this noblewoman standing in front of her.

A different maid led Mirra through the winding corridors until they reached the main hall. Much of the hall was taken up by the large table that nearly ran the length of the room. At the far end of the hall, a great hearth blazed merrily, despite it being the onset of summer.

Seated at the head of the table, elegant in black velvet, was Lord Julian. To his right sat a breathtakingly beautiful woman with golden hair dressed in an emerald green dress. The table could have seated a dozen more people and still have room to spare.

"My, my! You do clean up rather well." Lord Julian scoffed. "If I hadn't traveled with your all the way here, I wouldn't know who you truly are."

Mirra swallowed. "And just who am I meant to be?"

Lord Julian smiled his serpentine smile, turning to his dining companion. "Mirra, may I introduce you to Lady Nora of Rosmanor, the finest courtesan in the land."

CHAPTER EIGHT

I am not going to be your Painted Woman!"

Magic branding or not, there was no way that Mirra would ever let herself be used in that capacity. She'd rather die. She took a step back from the grand table, fist clenched. She bared her teeth in a silent snarl.

Much to her surprise, Lord Julian laughed. "I'm pleased to see all those years living on that farm hasn't made you soft, but that is not why I have brought you here."

"Why have you brought me here?"

Lord Julian took a sip of wine, smirking over the rim of the glass. "All in due time. *Now, sit.*"

The last two words wrapped around Mirra like an iron band. Her feet moved of their own accord, though her movements were jerky and unbalanced. Her eyes were wide as she made that terrible long walk toward the table to sit at Lord Julian's left. Like a rabbit caught in a snare, she looked anywhere and everywhere for something to break this unnatural control over her body. She thought that she caught a flash of pity from Lady Nora, but it was gone too quickly for her to be sure.

Like a puppet on a string, Mirra pulled out the chair and sat down. Lord Julian's command still held her strong. She cut her eyes at him, glaring, not caring that the full force of her hatred burned in her eyes. He seemed nonplussed by her anger and, with a slight twitch of his finger, released Mirra from his hold.

"How do you know magic?"

"I know a great many things," Lord Julian said with a laugh. "But now is not the time to discuss them." His eyes turned toward Mirra, filled with power that shouldn't exist anymore. "Need I remind you that *you belong to me.* You signed the contract, and if I want to whore you out to the entire continent, I will, and there is nothing that you can say about it. Have I made myself clear?"

Under the table, Mirra bunched her fist into her dress. Her jaw ached from how tightly she clenched her teeth. Lord Julian looked at her, expecting an answer. "Yes, my lord," she spat.

"Good. Now let's eat."

Servants filed in, carrying platter after platter of steaming food. The first course was a simple summer salad full of dark-green leaves, fruits, and sweet dressing. The second course was the main meal of roasted pigeon stuffed with tart apples and a honey glaze. For dessert, they had delicate cakes with candied rose petals. The food was probably delicious, but it tasted like ash in Mirra's mouth. She ate only because her body demanded it, and she didn't want to be forced by her unnatural master. The longer she sat at that table, the more she wished she had died back in the capital.

"Excellent meal, as always, my dear," Lord Julian said as he wiped his mouth with a napkin.

"You are too kind, my lord."

"Not at all. You may retire for the evening, Mirra. The lady and I have much to discuss."

Mirra quickly pushed her chair back and walked as fast as she could without actually running. She spied a footman waiting quietly in the hallway.

"Yes, my lady," he said with a bow as Mirra approached.

"Can you take me to my room?"

The footman bowed again and led Mirra to her room. This time, she paid attention to the turns and the decorations on the walls. She didn't want to be dependent on the servants forever.

Shara was waiting for her when she walked through the door.

"Are you ready for bed, my lady?"

Suddenly bone-weary, Mirra let Shara prepare her for bed. She yawned as Shara unpinned and brushed her hair, re-braiding it for sleep. She numbly took the warm washcloth and dutifully wiped her face, even though she didn't think she needed to. She was glad to get out of the tight dress and into a soft, warm sleeping gown.

The bed was to die for. A sigh escaped her lips as she crawled into bed. The plush feather mattress cocooned around her like a glove. Sleep claimed her quickly. She did not hear Shara wish her a goodnight nor the sound of the door when it closed and the lock was turned.

A RATHER LOUD KNOCK AT HER DOOR WOKE MIRRA THE
next morning. "Yes," she called out, rubbing the sleep from her
eyes.

"It's Shara, my lady. May I come in?"

Mirra threw her covers back and got out of bed. She
flinched as her bare feet touched the ice-cold stone floor. She
quickly crossed the span of her room and opened the door. She
had to jump back quickly as a small army of women barreled into
her room.

Many carried bolts of brightly colored fabrics. Those
women were followed closely by young women carrying baskets
spilling over with bits of lace and ribbons. Mirra remained
where she stood, not sure how to react to the chattering horde of
women that had descended upon her.

"It's a bit off-putting the first few times, but you'll
become accustomed to it soon enough." Lady Nora entered into
the crowded room as regal as a queen.

The sight of the kingdom's most renowned courtesan
brought Mirra back to reality. "Get used to what exactly?"

Instead of answering, Lady Nora just smiled, linking
arms with Mirra. "I'll explain everything down in the baths
while they set up here. I'm afraid it's going to be a long and
uncomfortable day for you, my darling."

"I took a bath yesterday."

"Yes, and a lady must bath as often as she can.
Cleanliness is close to godliness."

"And I should care because …"

Another tight-lipped smile. "Our master wishes for it."

Mirra stopped short. "*Our* master?"

"Yes, I belong to him as surely as you do. I also know the price of refusing to comply with his commands." Mirra remained rooted where she stood. Lady Nora sighed tiredly. "If I tell you my story, you will come along without a fuss."

"I don't want to be a whore," Mirra said, barely above a whisper. She quickly looked down at her feet to hide the burning in her eyes. She wouldn't show weakness.

A delicate pair of fingers entered Mirra's vision. Lady Nora gently but firmly made Mirra lift her gaze and meet her eyes. "You won't be. A courtesan is different from being a whore."

Mirra snorted. "Men buy your time?"

"Yes."

"Do you have sex with them?"

"Sometimes."

"Then there's no difference."

Lady Nora laughed. "There's a world of difference. But I understand your unease. I was not born a noblewoman. I was born in the slums of Eddany, the capital of Lorcea and Hearth City of the Stone Clans; a bit like you. Unlike you, I grew up with my family, for a time. We were quite poor, you see. We rarely had any money because my father often drank or gambled it all away. My mother had five of us to care for. I was the only girl and the oldest. I tried to help however I could, but it was never enough." Lady Nora's face transformed into something unyielding. Mirra recognized for her own when she lived wild on the streets. As quickly as it came, Lady Nora's true face disappeared behind the courtesan's mask.

"Unable or unwilling to care for me any longer, my mother sold me to a pleasure house when I was six. I cried and pleaded with her to let me stay. I would do the washing, cooking, look after my younger brothers so she could find work, but she didn't listen. She shoved me into the Matron's meaty claws, saying that it was either the brothel or the streets. She said that I might live longer in the brothel than on the streets. She accepted a sack of coins and walked away, not looking back once."

"What happened to her?"

Lady Nora looked off into the distance. Her eyes glazed over, lost to the past. "Now is not the time for that story. You need to be bathed and refashioned into your new identity."

Mirra tilted her head but allowed Lady Nora to lead her down to the baths. Down there, Lady Nora handed Mirra off to a trio of stern-looking old women that roughly stripped Mirra bare, ignoring her attempts to cover her body. Those rough old women manhandled Mirra into a tub of milky white water. Unprepared, some of the liquid ended up inside of Mirra's mouth. It tasted like milk and soap.

"Ug! What is this?'

"Milk bath," replied one of the crones.

"And why am I having a *milk bath*!"

Lady Nora chuckled. "To remove dead skin. It will help to keep your skin pale and smooth. Although any paler, and people would think you're a ghost."

Mirra stuck her tongue out at Lady Nora and received a smart whack on the back of her head from one of the old women. She muttered a curse that earned her another whack and retreated into the strange bath, rubbing the newly tendered parts of her body.

The old women went about their work with a sort of cruel efficiency. With their hard-bristled brushes, they took layer after layer of dirt, grime, and skin until there was nothing left but pink raw skin. After the milk bath, they poured cold water over Mirra's head. The shock from going from warm to ice-cold caused her to gasp, but she was to earn no sympathy from these harpies of cleanliness. They threw a thin cotton robe around her still stinging skin and forcefully plopped Mirra into a chair. They then took her hands and feet and put them into individual bowls of sweet-smelling steaming water. It was then that they retreated no doubt to get new tools for torture.

Mirra looked to Lady Nora who had remained by her side throughout the whole ordeal. She didn't know why, but she felt like she could trust the older woman. But that couldn't be wise because she was an agent of Lord Julian. *So are you*, a nasty corner of her mind reminded her.

"So, you gonna tell me the rest of your story or what?"

Lady Nora sighed and gracefully took a seat across from Mirra. A serving girl appeared out of the shadows, bearing a tray with a rose-colored liquid and two chalices. "This rosé was brewed on this very estate." She poured two glasses. "It's light and sweet with just a hint of tartness. Perfect for telling ugly stories."

Mirra furrowed her brow, not knowing what the Lady Nora was going on about. All the same, she accepted the chalice and took a long sip. Light and summer winds danced along her tongue, down her throat, to settle in a glorious warmth in the pit of her stomach.

"By the gods!"

"I told you it was good. Hopefully, the sweetness of the wine will temper the sourness of my tale."

Lady Nora refilled both their chalices before speaking again.

"So, after my mother sold me to the pleasure house, I cried two days straight. I refused to eat or drink anything. I simply lay on my sleeping pad and cried. The Matron grew weary of my cries and hauled me from my sleeping pad and threw me into the courtyard. She beat me with a cane until my body was black and blue. 'I paid good money for you,' she told me. 'You belong to me now, and I will not suffer girls who laze about and whimper over a life that is over. Honestly, you don't have much to lament over anyways. You were only a few short years away from walking the streets as a two-bit whore.'

"She left me there in the courtyard, too sore to move. No one came to my aid until after the evening meal. Another young girl, Kuhlan, picked me up without saying a word and helped me back to my sleeping pad. She set a bowl of soup and a heal of bread next to me and left.

"I realized then that I had only two choices: die or keep fighting. I chose to keep fighting. I ate, I healed and made myself forget my old life. I studied and slaved until after my first bleeding which marked me as a woman. By then, my looks had improved greatly, and I was already considered a beauty. So, when the time came to auction off my maidenhood, it was sold for the largest price at the time.

"I soon became the highest-paid whore in the entire city. I always knew what my patrons wanted, even if they didn't fully know it themselves. Then one day, a group of Undrosian nobles had come for a visit. And you can guess who was among them?"

Mirra took a large swallow of wine. "Lord Julian."

Lady Nora nodded. "He had heard of this whore who knew men's minds better than they did. He came to see for himself whether or not the rumors were true. When I first laid eyes on him, I knew that he was not there to enjoy the pleasures of the flesh. He looked at no girls, boys, anyone. He only sipped slowly from his glass and watched the room, noting everything. When he saw me studying him, he smiled. To this day, the memory of that smile causes me to shudder.

"He bought me that night and whisked me south to his estate. There he honed my skills as a courtesan among other things. He turned me into his spy."

"So that's what you're going to teach me?"

"In a way. I am to teach you the ways of the court. I am to show you how to see the truth behind a person's eyes and to use all the weapons in your arsenal."

"I have a bow, and I can wield a blade," Mirra quickly said.

"Those aren't your only weapons, child," Lady Nora countered.

Mirra opened her mouth to ask what other weapons she had, but the harpies had returned. Each woman took a bowl and removed an extremity. Then they attacked with all the callousness of a tanner. Mirra wanted to smash her chalice against the closest woman's head as she took a rough stone to her foot, but a sharp look from Lady Nora stilled her hand. Mirra gritted her teeth as the old women removed decades of calluses and dirt from her feet, hands, and nails.

It took a few more baths before Mirra was finally allowed to leave the torture chamber of the evil cleanliness crones. But the rest of her day wasn't much better. A prissy looking man took a pair of shears and cut a good portion of her hair off, saying that he was framing her face better and removing the dead ends. After that, she was forced to stand on a pedestal for hours while yards and yards of fabric were wrapped around her body, and she was stuck with pins.

She wasn't even allowed to eat during it all. The most that were provided was a bit of cheese and more of the rosé. But even that sparkling drink lost its appeal after time. The sun had set, and the lanterns and candles were lit by the time that Mirra was finally free. She sat at the foot of her bed with her knees pulled tightly to her chest. Glass after glass of wine had made her head feel overly large, the room to sway like trees in a strong breeze. She didn't trust herself right now to find her way to the chamber pot, let alone the kitchens.

"Yes," Mirra called out, answering the sharp knock at her door.

Shara entered, bearing a tray of food and a crystal pitcher of clear, clean water. "The first few days are always the hardest. I imagine the only thing you want to do is eat something and go to bed."

Mirra could have kissed the girl for having a bit of common sense. A bit of roasted chicken, freshly baked bread with rosemary butter, and garlic green beans; a simple meal, but a welcomed one. Mirra dug into the food, ravenous after not eating all day. She only stopped to drink water that was cold and sweet as a mountain stream after the snows melt. With each bite, the haze from the wine receded, but in its place, exhaustion grew. After her meal, it was all she could do to crawl under her blankets before sleep took over her.

"Thank you, Shara," Mirra managed to mumble out before succumbing to sleep.

"Goodnight, my lady," Shara said as she gently closed the door.

CHAPTER NINE

THE NEXT MORNING, MIRRA WOKE TO THE SOUND OF someone knocking at her door. "Yes," she called out, not completely ready to face another day like yesterday. She let out the breath she had been holding when only Shara walked through the door. In her arms, she carried a sky-blue dress trimmed in cream with matching slippers.

"The Mistress wishes that you wear this today and meet her in the greenhouse for breakfast."

Mirra threw back the covers and walked over the vanity. With a better idea of what was expected of her, she sat down and let Shara style her hair and help her dress. The dress was made of a soft material that she couldn't identify, but it moved freely around her body without making her feel overly warm. The shoes were another matter entirely. While pretty to look at, they pinched at the toes and heels. Mirra knew that she would have blisters by lunchtime. She sighed, not relishing the prospect.

"Is something wrong?"

"The shoes are a bit too tight."

Shara waved a dismissive hand. "They will stretch."

Mirra glowered at her maid. Shara pretended that she didn't notice. Once dressed, Shara led Mirra through another set of unfamiliar corridors.

"You should be able to find your way from here," Shara said when they reached a door covered in gilded flowers and vines.

Mirra watched Shara's retreating and stuck her tongue out. Some moments she liked the maid, but other times—not so much. Mirra pushed the door open and smiled. She walked into an inner garden. On one side were pretty flowers like roses, lilies, and chrysanthemums. On the other side were herbs that the kitchens used. In the warm Summer morning light, the entire space was filled with scents of flowers and the spicy aroma of rosemary. Rich green grass grew alongside a pretty little garden path. Mirra's feet ached to be free from their constraint to feel the ground beneath them. At the far end of the garden was a small hut made out of glass. She stared at it in wonder and confusion. She had never seen anything like that before. The things noble people spent their money on. She shook her head and walked along the path heading toward what could only be the glass garden.

The glass that made up the garden was not like normal glass. Instead of being clear, it had a greenish tinge to it. Mirra wasn't sure if it was made that way or tinted because of the numerous plants on the inside. As she got closer, she could just make out a white form sitting in the middle of the room.

Inside the glass garden, the air was heavy and moist. Mirra felt it settle around her like a warm blanket. Strange flowers and plants bloomed in every available space, filling the air with exotic perfumes. Lady Nora, dressed in a simple white dress, sat at a small ironwork table.

"Good Morning, Mirra. I hope you slept well?"

"I did."

"Come and share a meal with me and let us talk awhile, just us girls."

Mirra held back for a few breaths, unsure of what to do. So far, Lady Nora had been kind to her. The lady's story of how she came to be an agent of The Viper was similar to hers. She came from the streets just like Mirra had. She knew what it was like to go without for so long that you stopped realizing it. Lady Nora had also suffered in ways that Mirra could never fully fathom, and yet, she still was able to smile, still had light in her eyes—or was it all a mask?

The table boasted several bowls of fresh fruit, sweet rolls, and a steaming pot of something darker than tea with a strong bitter smell.

Lady Nora answered the unasked question. "Coffee."

Mirra regarded the nearly black liquid with trepidation. "Does it taste good?"

"I think so, but only with a lot of cream and sugar. I can have some juice brought up for you instead."

Mirra thought about it for a moment. She figured that it would be best to stick with what she knew, at least for the time being. "Juice would be fine, Lady Nora."

Lady Nora smiled and gestured to an unseen servant. While they waited for the juice to be brought out, the two women filled their plates and started their breakfast.

A servant quietly entered and placed a small pitcher of fruit juice on the table before backing out with a short bow.

Mirra filled her glass, aware of the mild tension around the table. Even though Lady Nora told Mirra an abridged version of her history, that didn't mean that Mirra trusted her at all.

"So, just how often are you going to send letters about me to him, Lady Nora?"

Lady Nora smiled into her cup of coffee. "Every few weeks, or unless you do something worth reporting." She put her cup down. She dropped her courtesan mask and studied Mirra with intelligent eyes and a studious face. No doubt what made her into a formidable agent. Mirra fought the urge to squirm in her seat and met Lady Nora's gaze head-on. "You might actually last a bit longer than the girls he normally sends me."

Mirra's brow furrowed. "What do you mean by that?"

"Most of the girls he sends me are pretty but empty-headed," Lady Nora said with a dismissive shrug. "Good for nothing more than collecting information. But you, you seem to have a mind behind that pretty face of yours."

Mirra leaned back as far as her chair allowed. She needed space between herself and those piercing green eyes that stripped her down to her soul.

As if sensing her discomfort, Lady Nora put her courtesan face in place once more, looking very much like the cat that ate the canary.

"When it's just the two of us, I want you to just call me Nora. I hate standing on circumstance if I can avoid it."

"All right, Lady … I mean Nora."

Lady Nora toasted Mirra with her coffee, and the two enjoyed the rest of their breakfast in comfortable silence.

"Take the rest of the day to orientate yourself with the manor. There is no place that is restricted to you. Explore to your heart's content."

"Why are you being so nice to me?"

Lady Nora frowned. "I imagine that you have not been shown much kindness in your life. And given the path that you are following, I doubt it'll get much better. I hope that one day you will count me as an ally."

Ally. That word seared through her heart like a flaming arrow. "I had allies once. They're the reason why I'm here in the first place. Allies make you weaker, not stronger. They can be used against you. I'm better off alone."

Lady Nora's face turned sorrowful. She bowed her golden head and left Mirra standing alone in the garden.

Mirra never had free range of a place before. Even when she lived in the city, there were certain places that she couldn't go. She stood where Lady Nora left her, uncertain. Where should she start? The inner corridors? Along the turrets? Was there a library, the stables? With a thousand choices available to her, Mirra felt the dark serpent of panic uncoil deep in her gut. As its head started to rise, she closed her eyes and took several calming breaths. Panic did nothing but slow you down and get you killed. She needed to think about her next steps carefully. While Lady Nora talked about friendship, she was still Mirra's jailer, much as Brian had been. She wouldn't make the same mistake she had made with him. She wouldn't forget and let someone get close like that again. She would need to bury her heart deep and rely on her mind.

A shout from above drew her out of her inner conflict. A pair of guards clasped arms, laughing about something. As she watched them, the corner of Mirra's mouth curled up. Studying a building's defenses and searching for weak points was something that she was familiar with, if not a little bit rusty. Everyone around the manor carried on without a care in the world, even the guards; no one would notice her walking throughout the grounds, and if they did, they wouldn't pay her any mind. If anyone questioned her, she would simply state that Lady Nora bade her to familiarize herself with her new home, which was completely true.

As the sun reached its zenith, hunger pains drove Mirra to abandon her systematic inquiry of the manor's defensive capabilities. To find the kitchens, all she had to do was simply follow her nose. A hive of busy men and women and steaming pots on top of roaring fires, the kitchens were a sight to behold. With everyone rushing about, Mirra knew that her presence would not be welcomed, no matter what Lady Nora claimed.

She was just about to turn away when a familiar voice called out to her.

"Do you need something, my lady?"

Aira rose from her seat at a long table. The other servants looked up from their plates to look at Mirra. She shuffled her feet and clasped her hands behind her so that they couldn't see her fingers fidget.

"No, I'm fine. I just smelled the kitchens, and it was so delicious that I felt like I had to come."

Aira smiled. "Lunch will be served shortly if you don't mind waiting?"

"That's fine. Don't let me keep you."

Mirra put her back toward the mouth-watering aroma, ignoring the rumbling in her stomach. Walking as fast as she could without breaking into a trot, she let her feet carry her where they willed. After a time, she halted in front of a pair of great doors, but unlike every other door in Rosmanor, this one didn't have a flower motif. It was plain and unassuming. Mirra cocked her head, pondering why this set of doors would be plain while the rest of the manor was painstakingly decorated to always remind you of being in a garden.

Well, she did say that no room was forbidden. A wicked smile broke out across her face as she pushed the great doors open and crossed the threshold.

Two large windows let in giant beams of buttery sunlight illuminating several overstuffed chairs, perfect for curling up in on dreary days. On one side of the room was a modest fireplace framed on either side by rosewood bookcases that went from floor to ceiling. The remaining walls were also taken up by bookcases. Mirra walked in as if entering a dream, running her hand absentmindedly down row after row of books. The markings on their spines and covers meant nothing to her. It had never bothered her before, but now seeing this room full of hidden things, she realized that not being able to read put her at a disadvantage.

Swallowing down bitter anger, she left the library as fast as she could. She had started to make her way back to her room when a maidservant came upon her.

"Here you are? Lunch is served in the Great Hall."

Mirra nodded and followed the maidservant.

Lady Nora was already seated at the table. She had changed her dress from the morning. Her new dress was a rich green velvet trimmed with copper accents. The bodice was bound tightly to her chest, and it was cut low enough to accent her breasts. Around her neck, she wore a collar of pearls. Her face was painted, but unlike the women from the brothels, her makeup accented her already becoming features instead of masking years of abuse and pain. Mirra had to admit, Lady Nora looked stunning.

"I will be away this evening," Lady Nora said as Mirra took her seat. "A patron, sweet man, really." Mirra poured a glass of sparkling juice to give herself something to do. She didn't know what to say. "Have you enjoyed searching for weaknesses around my home?"

Mirra choked on her juice.

"You might have a brain, but you are predictable. It's all right. I would have been quite disappointed if you hadn't. I *do* want you to trust me. You don't have to think of me as a friend or ally," Mirra bristled again at the word, "but I do want you to know that I will never intentionally lead you astray. I've been charged with getting you ready for the next stage of your training."

"To what end?"

"I can't tell you because I don't know myself. I only know that I am to teach you the ways of court ... and other things."

An ice-cold hand gripped Mirra's heart. "Like what?" she asked, her voice small.

"Nothing like that. Part of being a successful courtesan is knowing how to read people, to read a situation. To be a courtesan, you have to change yourself, become someone new.

And speaking of which, we need to give you a name to use while you're here."

Lady Nora tapped her crimson lips, contemplative. "Misha. It's close enough to your real name that you won't get too confused. That's your first lesson; stick as close to the truth as you possibly can. The more elaborate the lie, the harder it is keeping it straight."

A man in a simple brown robe entered the dining hall. When he reached the table, he bowed.

"Ah, Father Soren, right on time." Lady Nora stood, walked around the table to embrace the priest.

He stiffly returned her hug, barely managing to keep the look of disgust from his face. He spotted Mirra, and his eyes narrowed. "Is this the girl?" His voice was as hard as his face.

"Yes, my ward, Misha. Quite a lovely thing, isn't she?"

The priest mumbled a reply.

"Well, I leave you to it." With a conspiratory smirk, Lady Nora winked at Mirra before disappearing around the corner, leaving Mirra and the priest alone.

"If you're done with your meal, then we'll start."

The priest looked at Mirra with the same look of disgust as he gave Lady Nora. Despite what she was, Lady Nora was a good person. She didn't like what Lady Nora did for a living, but that didn't mean that she deserved that look, and neither did Mirra.

"I've just sat down; I'm afraid. You don't mind waiting, do you?"

Father Soren pursed his lips and clasped his hands in front of him, unable to say anything. Suppressing a smirk of her own, Mirra deliberately took her time, finishing her lunch. She cut her broiled fish into small bites before slowly putting them in her mouth. After every bite, she patted her mouth with the linen napkin. She then would pick up her goblet, study it, then take a sip.

At the end of the table, Father Soren's jaw feathered as he shifted side to side on his feet. His eyes, however, were full of ire that grew with her every movement. A servant appeared at a side door, ready to clear away the table but hesitated because Mirra was still eating. The young servant looked back over her shoulder, uneasy and unsure. That sucked all the fun out of torturing the priest. She picked her goblet up one more time, downing the contents in three large gulps. Father Soren's face flushed scarlet with barely contained rage. He would dole out his revenge on her when they were alone, no doubt about that, but two could play at this game.

CHAPTER TEN

Father Soren led Mirra to the library she found earlier that day. The afternoon sun filled the room, making it warm and cozy.

"You sit here," Father Soren commanded, pointing to an empty chair. Mirra briefly contemplated toying with the priest some more, but she figured it would be best to play along to see what his purpose was.

He returned sometime later, carrying a stack of books, parchment, and a quill. Mirra watched him place the items on the table next to her with growing apprehension. And from the cruel smirk on his face, Father Soren knew what she was thinking.

Father Soren grabbed the first book on top of the stack and thrust it at Mirra. "Read this, if you can."

Mirra held the book in her hands, running her fingers over the gilded letters.

"Well?"

Mirra looked up, her eyes burned with ice-cold fire. "I can't."

Father Soren smiled cruelly. "I'm not surprised. I doubt they saw fit to teach whores how to read wherever you came from."

In a flash of movement, Mirra had leaped from her seat, book falling forgotten on the floor. Her hand wrapped around the priest's throat before he could register the movement. Using her momentum, she pushed the priest to the floor, digging her knees into his gut. He clawed at her hands, gasping for air, eyes wide with fear.

"Never call me or Lady Nora that again," she growled. "I've known men like you my whole life. I wonder what secret sin you hide."

"Nothing."

Mirra's laugh was cold and cruel. "You hate being here; your face told me as much. The only way that a man like you would ever subject yourself to be in the service of a woman like Lady Nora is because she has something on you. I wonder what it is? Do you like little boys, little girls?"

Father Soren tried and failed to spit in Mirra's face. "Demon spawn, let me up, or it will be your head. Priests are protected by the gods and the crown."

"You're a long way from both." Father Soren blanched. "I'll leave you be because I don't want to tarnish Lady Nora's reputation, and she has been kind to me. So, do you think that we can learn to tolerate each other? Because, trust me, I don't like you either."

Father Soren opened his mouth to speak. Mirra pressed harder on his windpipe, strangling the spiteful words he no doubt was about to spew at her. His face turned a blotchy red. Mirra felt his spirit cave a second before he sputtered a bitter yes.

Mirra stood and straightened her dress before retaking her seat. Coughing and gasping for air, Father Soren picked himself up with as much dignity that he could muster. He rubbed his throat, glaring daggers in Mirra's direction. She arched a brow and looked pointedly at the stack of books. She let him see her smirk when his shoulders sagged, and he reached for a small book near the bottom.

"There are twenty-seven letters in our alphabet, and each one has a sound that it makes. We will start with A, apple, ah."

"A, apple, ah."

With a head swimming with letters and sounds, Mirra ate her dinner in a haze. Instead of eating alone in the dining hall, she took her meal in the garden. Her dinner was a simple but hearty summer vegetable soup with several loaves of dense black bread. She was sure that it was tasty and filling, but her mind was elsewhere. Why had she defended Lady Nora? The more she thought about it, the more confused she became. Her head already hurt from her lessons with that bastard of a priest, so she dropped it. She would try to figure it out later—maybe.

After dinner, she returned to the library. Father Soren had left as soon as their lesson was complete. A servant had come at some point and lit the lanterns to illuminate the darkening room. She walked over to a small table where her solitary practice sat waiting for her. She frowned at the book she was supposed to read and the writing she was supposed to complete before tomorrow. The throbbing in her head increased the longer she looked at them. She would have rather gone to bed, but she knew that if she didn't complete her tasks, Father Soren would use it as an excuse to get back at her for threatening his life. With a weary sigh, she pulled out a chair and sat down to tackle, unraveling the mystery of the alphabet.

Lady Nora returned three days later. Mirra practically ran to meet her at the gate, desperate for some company other than Father Soren and herself.

"I think you may have actually grown since I saw you last, Misha."

Mirra felt a smile break out across her face. "I'm surprised that I'm not rounder the way your people feed me."

Lady Nora's face held the amused smile, but behind her eyes, Mirra could see an inkling of surprise. Mirra beamed, knowing that she had surprised the courtesan who had no doubt seen it all.

"I trust things went well with Father Soren?"

Mirra's smile took on a wicked edge. "More or less."

Pride shone through Lady Nora's eyes, and at that moment, Mirra knew why she had come to her defense. Lady Nora was the first person to actually see and wanted to foster Mirra's full potential. She saw the *real* Mirra and what she could be with a little bit of help. The wall that Mirra had built around her heart to protect herself from being hurt started to fracture.

As it had on Brian's farm, in Rosmanor, Mirra quickly adapted to her new life. She had breakfast with Nora in the glass garden most mornings. Soon thereafter, Father Soren would show up and fill her head with words, numbers, and stories from the far reaches of the continent. In the afternoon, Nora instructed Mirra on the intricacies of court and ways to wield her femininity as a weapon. In the evenings after dinner, Mirra would retreat to the baths and soak away the day before delving back into her academic and courtly assignments.

The days quickly turned into weeks, months, and a year had passed before Mirra realized it. Though she would never admit it aloud, she found that she was happy, truly happy. But it was not to last. Nothing ever does.

Mirra was curled up in a window seat, reading a book about a pirate that had numerous adventures, when she heard the sound of a carriage pulling into the courtyard. She quickly closed the book and hurried to her room. It took her only a moment to twist her hair into a knot before slipping a blonde wig over her raven locks. Next, she grabbed a cobalt blue bottle. She applied two burning drops of a special liquid that darkened her icy blue eyes to a natural shade of blue. All this was her typical disguise for when visitors stayed at the manor. Nora insisted on it to help keep her identity a secret until Lord Julian was ready to reveal her.

Blinking against the burn, Mirra gave her reflection one final go over before heading out to meet their guest. She saw the black coach with matching horses and stopped short. Her heart stopped beating, and her bowels turned to water. *Lord Julian.*

He couldn't have come to collect her already. She had only been with Nora for a year and couldn't have possibly learned everything that she needed to. Mirra heard Nora's steady footsteps come up behind her.

"Watch your face," she warned. "He wants you to be off-balanced. That's why he didn't send word that he was coming."

Mirra took comfort in her teacher's words and swallowed her rising panic. She schooled her face into a pleasantly neutral mask she dubbed her "Misha face" and went to meet the man who owned her body and soul like he was a stranger to her.

A footman opened the door to the carriage. Mirra took comfort from Nora's steady presence at her side. Lord Julian exited the carriage with the same smirk that haunted Mirra's dreams. She fixated on that smirk, feeling her confidence face with each passing second.

"Welcome, my lord," Nora said smoothly. She curtsied, and Mirra followed a fraction of a second later. She lowered her eyes to the ground, choosing to focus on the small stones in the courtyard. She felt Misha's personality settle on her like a warm cloak in winter. When she rose, her mask was firmly in place as she smiled absentmindedly at the most dangerous man in Undros.

"My lord." Her voice was high and sweet as a bird's song in the morning. She looked upon Lord Julian with a mild interest and assessing eyes. His smirk turned into a wide grin.

"And who is this little dove?"

"Misha, my lord."

"Misha? What a lovely name for a lovely young girl."

"My lord is too kind," Misha said, blushing slightly.

Lord Julian held his arm out for Nora. "Charming as always."

"I aim to please. You must be tired from your journey. Shall I have some refreshments brought up for you? The gardens are lovely this time of day."

"That won't be necessary, my dear. I've come from the capital. It's only a half a day's ride."

"Dinner then?"

"That will suffice."

Mirra followed dutifully behind her two masters, grateful that neither could see her face. She struggled to maintain her composure. She was only a half a day's ride from Verance. A half a day's ride from her old life, her old friends. Her chest tightened. She tried to not think about her past too often; it hurt too much. She couldn't stop her mind from wondering how the Shadow Guild was doing. Were they even still alive? Did they split after her "death"? Did they miss her as much as she did them? Was Bao beating himself up over what happened?

"Misha, my dear," Nora called over her shoulder. "You have studies that still require attention."

"Is she a studious young woman?" Lord Julian asked, peering over his shoulder as well. He dropped his courtier mask and silently warned Mirra that she would be punished greatly if he found her not fully applying herself to her studies.

"Oh, she is, my lord," Nora said with a laugh.

Mirra bowed, turned on her heel, and put as much distance between her and Lord Julian as possible. Back in the sanctity of her own room, she pressed her back against the door before sliding down to the floor. She brought her knees in tight to her chest in a feeble attempt to quell the quivering of her limbs.

Why after so many years was he still able to affect her like this? Would she ever lose her fear of him, or would it always linger? Her mind drifted to a conversation deep within the woods that she hadn't thought about for some time now.

You always have a choice.

No, I don't. Mirra thought vehemently. *I don't have a choice at all.*

So, HOW LONG HAVE YOU BEEN STUDYING UNDER LADY Nora? I do not think I have had the pleasure of seeing you in court." He smiled blandly at Mirra from across the table. He was testing her ability to maintain her cover as Misha.

Mirra took a sip from her glass. She thought it was ridiculous since they all knew who she was in truth, but if Lord Julian wanted to play this game, then she had no choice but to play along. "I have yet to go to the capital city, let alone the royal courts. As to your question, my lord, I have been in Lady Nora's care for nearly a year."

"Interesting, where do you hail from? What are your parents like?"

"From the east. I doubt your lordship would even know my village's name. It's a small farming community." She looked down at her lap. "As for my parents ... they're dead, two winters past."

"I am sorry to hear that. The loss of one's family can be world-altering. But at least you've found a new benefactor." His voice dripped with false concern, but only those sitting around the table would recognize it for what it was—cruel spite.

Mirra kept her face blank, but underneath the table, she twisted her napkin into knots. She clenched her teeth together, not trusting the words building in her mouth to stay inside.

Fortunately, Lord Julian turned his attention to Nora, completely ignoring Mirra the rest of the evening. She didn't know whether to be insulted or relieved. He always seemed to know how to get under her skin, how to push her just to the breaking point and then stop. It left her feeling raw and unsettled. All the same, she was grateful when the servants came to clear away the table. Bad manners or not, she wasn't about to spend another second in his presence.

"My Lord, my lady," she said with a small curtsy. "I am off to bed."

Lord Julian arched a brow. "So soon after supper?"

Mirra clasped her hands in front and looked demure at the floor, not fully trusting her composure to last much longer. "I have to rise early on the morn to meet with my teacher."

Nora crossed the empty space and lightly embraced Mirra, kissing her on the forehead. "Sleep well, my darling. I will see you in the morning for breakfast."

With a short nod of the head, Mirra turned her back on Lord Julian, the King's Viper, and walked out of the dining hall. She felt his piercing gaze boring into the center of her back. Thankfully, Nora captured his attention so Mirra could quicken her steps and be free from his burning gaze.

She slept fitfully that night. Every sound woke her from her sleep. She tossed and turned in her bed, unable to find a comfortable position or the right amount of covers. As the moon rose higher in the sky, it cast a soft silver light across her floor.

Mirra watched the light chase away the shadows of her room with mild interest. She wondered at what point should she abandon any hopes of sleep and rise from bed. Then she remembered that The Viper was still present inside the halls of Rosmanor. She shuddered at the thought of running into him in the dark corridors.

Soft footsteps echoed outside her door. Mirra bolted up in her bed, reaching for the stiletto blade she kept under her pillow. The blade was a gift from Nora when Mirra passed the first round of testing Father Soren put her through. At first, Mirra had scoffed at the thin, delicate-looking blade. But now, she welcomed its weight in her hand.

The footsteps came closer to her room. While there were guards who guarded the house during the night, they remained upon the walls and *never* came near her room. There was only one person, one *man*, who would be stalking the halls near her room this late at night.

The footsteps halted right in front of her door, and thanks to the light from the moon pouring through all the windows on the western halls, she could see a small shadow lingering by her door. She held her breath and adjusted her grip on the hilt.

She nearly lost her grip on her stiletto when the shadow slithered under her door and collected in a pool of unnatural darkness. This time, there would be no denying it. She was not half-starved and delirious. The dark thing rose in the middle, slowly until there was a small knob on top of a slender shaft. It writhed and wiggled like a serpent as it scanned the room with unseen eyes. Mirra, frozen in fear, stayed as still as stone, only taking in the smallest of breaths. The dark thing had not spied her yet. However, if she were to move, even an inch, she knew that it would spot her and pounce. She silently cursed the moon for its light that illuminated her, especially when it didn't seem to have an effect on the dark thing.

The seconds ticked by like centuries until the dark thing sank back into a pool of darkness and slithered back under the door. The footsteps retreated, but Mirra didn't release the breath she had been holding for a few moments longer.

She thought that seeing the dark thing would have kept her awake for a week, but it proved to be otherwise. Worn out emotionally, Mirra fell asleep, propped up in bed, clutching the stiletto tight in her hand.

"My lady?" Shara's inquisitive voice woke Mirra from her sleep. Thankfully she had been too exhausted to have nightmares. "My lady?"

"I'm fine, Shara," Mirra snipped, slipping the stiletto back into its resting place. "Just a rough night."

Shara pursed her lips together and looked like she wanted to say more, but Nora entered Mirra's room before she got the chance.

"I'll see to Misha this morning, Shara. I need a private conversation with my charge."

Shara bowed and quickly left the room, not looking back once.

"Lord Julian left this morning before the sun rose."

Mirra exhaled, her body relaxing for the first time since she laid eyes on Lord Julian's black carriage.

"He ... did, however, have some words about my tutelage of you."

"What do you mean?"

"While he applauds your scholarly growth and your mastery of the courtly arts, he fears that you are growing soft under my care. To put it as he did, I am 'fattening you up like a spring hog.'"

Mirra grimaced. "So, what are you going to do now?"

Nora gestured for Mirra to take a seat in front of her vanity. She positioned herself behind Mirra, took up a brush and dragged it through her hair. Her touch was soothing and gentle. Mirra closed her eyes and leaned back into the brushing.

"He is right, in a fashion. There are many lords *and* ladies in the court that pursue more active hobbies. We shall add those to your list of studies. Starting tomorrow, you will meet your new instructor in the large courtyard. After working with him for an hour or so, you will continue to meet me for your courtly studies."

Mirra said nothing. She only grunted to let Nora know that she had heard what she had said. Nora smiled in the mirror. "I shall tell Father Soren that you are unwell this morning. No doubt last night was hard for you."

Mirra stilled, remembering the dark thing that had entered her room. Did Nora know what it was, or did she simply mean see Lord Julian?

"It was," she replied.

Nora nodded. "I figured as much. Get some rest, Mirra. I will have Shara come up in a bit with something to help you sleep."

Mirra yawned and crawled back into bed. She let Nora tuck the covers around her. Nora pulled the drapery of the canopy bed free, shielding Mirra from the growing light of the coming day. Safely cocooned in warm blankets and sheltered in shadows with the knowledge that Lord Julian was gone, Mirra fell into a deep sleep before Nora could gently close the door behind her.

Her new instructor turned out to be a grisly looking man dressed in muted browns and greens. "This is Gregory Archer, the finest woodsman in three kingdoms."

"Your ladyship is too kind," Gregory said, inclining his head. Nora waved off his words and left Mirra in the strange man's charge.

He was a full head and shoulders taller than Mirra. His face was deeply tanned and lined from decades of living out under the sun. His clothing was simple but well cared for. Around his waist, he wore a multitude of blades and a small hatchet. A full quiver was slung at his back. Mirra didn't see his bow and figured that it was somewhere nearby. She still had her bow stored safely in the armory. She hadn't drawn it once since coming to Rosmanor, and for once, she agreed with Lord Julian. She was growing soft.

"Well, I'll leave you two to it," Nora said, gathering her skirts. "Let me know if there's anything else you require."

Gregory and Mirra stood in the courtyard, looking at one another in total silence. Though he had a soft smile on his face, his eyes hardened as they assessed Mirra. No doubt he saw a pampered princess who knew nothing and would complain the moment she experiences the slightest bit of discomfort.

"Well, miss, we might as well get started."

"I have a bow," Mirra blurted out. Gregory cocked his head, clearly surprised. "I haven't used it in a while, but I used to hunt."

Gregory rubbed his stubbly chin. "Why don't we start with that, then?"

Mirra gathered her skirts and dashed off to retrieve her bow. She would not let new skills erase the skills she already had.

Thwak! Thwak! Thwak!

Mirra fired three arrows in rapid succession. Not a single one hit the back spot in the center to the target. She gritted her teeth and flexed her sore fingers.

"You're aiming with your eyes."

"That's what you're supposed to use," Mirra snapped back.

Gregory shook his head. "If you're just shooting at targets with some lord, then that's fine. But if you want to shoot faster, better, you need to see the target in your mind. Trust your arrow. It knows where you want it to go."

Mirra scoffed. Gregory motioned for her to go again. She rolled her shoulders to loosen and rolled her head around on her neck. With quick, determined steps, she strode back to the firing line. Gregory handed her three more arrows.

"Aim in your mind."

Mirra took an arrow and notched it. The bow creaked as she drew back. Her eyes zeroed in on the target the far end of the field. She took a deep breath, drawing her bow all the way back. *Trust your arrow.* She closed her eyes and pictured the target in her mind's eye. She exhaled and loosened her arrow at the same time.

Thwak! Thwak! Thwak!

"Nice shooting, young miss."

Mirra opened her eyes and beamed at the three arrows neatly clustered in the center of the black.

Another year went by. She learned that she rather enjoyed the subtle crooked workings of the nobility. In all honesty, it wasn't that much different from her earlier life, with the exception that any killings were done quietly. Father Soren continued to be a prick, but Mirra was grateful to him. Without his tutelage, she never would have learned how to read, and in reading, she found her first taste of freedom. All she had to do was pick up a book, and instantly, she was transported to new and unseen worlds with a thousand adventures at her feet. Her favorite by far was a series about a dashing pirate lord. He battled against the crown and pirates alike, occasionally scraping with magical entities.

Gregory taught her how to wield swords, short blades, and knives. His lessons were a mix of what was expected of a person of noble birth and that of a commoner. He even put her up on a horse. Mirra could ride, not well but well enough to stay in her seat. Riding terrified her. She didn't like the rolling stride precariously perched on top of a half-wild beast. But she didn't let her fear of falling keep her from learning something that might save her life one day.

Mirra woke and burrowed deeper into her blankets. Fall was in full swing, bringing the cold with it. She heard her bedroom door open.

"Good morning, my lady," said the chambermaid. "It won't take but a moment to get the fire going."

Mirra sat up, pulling her head out from under the covers. "Thanks."

The chambermaid smiled and bowed her head before kneeling by the cold hearth. Mirra grimace at the cold, dark void across from her bed. She now regretted not taking the time to bank the fire. If she had, then it would have made the chambermaid's task a little easier. There was no helping it now. With an inward groan, Mirra threw back her deliciously warm covers, bracing for the cold.

The stone floor was colder than ice, even with her fleece-lined slippers. Mirra walked over to her wardrobe and selected one of her new dresses made for the cooler weather. It was a deep gray color with bits of white lace along the bodice and sleeves. She pulled on a pair of matching thick stockings and laced up her new leather boots. By the time she was fully dressed, the chambermaid had left, leaving a roaring fire in the hearth. Mirra sat in front of her vanity and brushed her hair. She was not looking forward to her afternoon training with Gregory. She braided her hair before wrapping it around her head. She used a few pins to secure it in place. Then she added a few pins that were sharper than the rest. With a steady hand, she strategically placed them in her braided crown. She added a faint hint of rouge to her cheeks, just enough to bring some color to her pallid face.

As she walked through the halls, her stomach tightened, and her senses heightened. Something was off about the manor this morning. She couldn't quite figure out exactly what was happening, but her feelings of dread grew the closer she got to the dining hall.

She crossed the threshold, and her innards turned to ice.

Lord Julian had returned.

CHAPTER ELEVEN

Mirra paused for only a single breath. She willed her face into an empty smile and continued forward. She made sure that her footsteps could be heard by Lord Julian and Nora who sat at the far end of the room, closest to the hearth.

"My lord, my lady." Mirra sank into a deep curtsy. She rose and took her seat to the left of Lord Julian who sat at the head of the table.

Lord Julian's piercing two-toned eyes caused her spine to crawl, but Mirra would never give him the satisfaction of knowing it. She had learned to completely hide her emotions by now.

Lord Julian turned to Nora and toasted her. "You've done it again, my dear. I hardly recognize her. You've managed to take a thieving guttersnipe and turn it into a respectable lady."

Nora smiled as if his praise pleased her, but Mirra saw the tightness around her eyes and how tightly she gripped her glass. Her mentor was not pleased one bit.

"I'm almost tempted to let you keep her and see just how truly magnificent she would become under your tutelage." Mirra took a sip from her own glass to mask her excitement. Would she really be allowed to stay?

"But of course, that would be a complete waste of her talents, and she still has more to learn."

Why did I even get my hopes up?

"The usual procedure, then?"

Lord Julian nodded and then switched the topic.

Mirra had sensed being able to hear. She was to be moved again. Where would she end up this time? How many more times was she going to have to learn the rules of a new world, a new way of life? Would she ever find out what he wanted with her, or did he just enjoy reshuffling her life every few years?

After diner, Mirra tossed and turned in her bed. No matter how hard she tried, she couldn't shut her mind off. She ran every possible place he might drop her next, what else he thought she needed to learn. Part of her was excited; she had come to enjoy learning new things, but the larger part of herself was filled with dread. Nothing Lord Julian wanted could ever be good for her.

On the night of the new moon when the only light came from the lanterns mounted on either side of the black carriage, Mirra stood in the outer courtyard of Rosmanor for what was probably the last time. Two footmen loaded her trunks onto the back of the carriage.

She stood awkwardly off to the side, dressed in a charcoal gray traveling gown. In her hands, she toyed with a pair of kidskin gloves. Her eyes darted around, taking in every last detail she could.

"Until we reach our destination, I want you to remain inconspicuous. Do not speak to anyone; do not go anywhere without my express approval first."

"And just where are we going?" Her voice sounded tired to her own ears.

Lord Julian answered by smiling his usual serpentine smile. Mirra sighed and turned her attention back to the laboring footmen.

"This will be the final stage of your training before I place you."

"Where?"

"All in due time, my dear, depending on how you do over the next year."

"Only a year this time?"

"It's much more intensive than your other training."

Mirra scoffed. "What other training. I spent three years on a farm before coming here. This is the only place where I received any form of training."

"With Brian, you learned how to tend to crops and animals. You learned domestic skills and how people live outside of cities. You learned to hunt and how to test your boundaries. You have had the unique experience to see how the low, the common, and the nobility live. With that, if you aren't completely useless, you'll be able to blend in anywhere."

Mirra starred at Lord Julian, unable to deny the truth of his words.

"All done, my lord, my lady."

Lord Julian held out his hand. "Shall we?"

Mirra slid her hands into the kidskin gloves before placing her hand in his. As he led her toward the carriage, her eyes were drawn to a flash of gold in a window. Nora had not joined them in the courtyard. Mirra suspected that she didn't want to say goodbye. Mirra lifted her free hand to adjust a nonexistent strand of errant hair. Nora disappeared from the window with another flash of gold. It was as much a goodbye that the two women were ever going to get.

The carriage ride lasted through the night until the sun started to rise. Bleary-eyed and stiff limbed, Mirra stumbled after Lord Julian. They stood on a dark street, surrounded by quiet houses with gaping black windows. A shiver ran down Mirra's spine. It was too quiet and too dark. It was unnatural. When she lived on the streets back in the capital, even in the lower streets, there was always some form of activity going on and lights, especially street lamps. But here, there was nothing, the street lamps had been doused or perhaps never lit as to avoid raising too much suspicion.

"This way."

Despite not having any light to see from, Lord Julian stalked the dark streets without any hesitation or impression of uncertainty. Mirra struggled to keep up. She didn't trust her feet to safely navigate the unfamiliar terrain without mishap. The scents of brine, sewage, and fish grew stronger with each alley they turned down. Finally, Lord Julian's cloak disappeared around the corner of a tavern. Mirra scurried after and stopped short when she saw their destination—the docks.

How long had it been since she had seen ships? Smelled the brine of the sea? She closed her eyes and took a deep breath, filling her lungs with salty air. Filled her body, driving away the day's pains and troubles.

Lord Julian talked in a low whisper to a man that had emerged from the shadows. Mirra heard the shuffling of papers as the man handed something over to Lord Julian. The man disappeared as quickly as he appeared. Mirra marveled at the man's ability to move so silently.

"Let's go."

Lord Julian led Mirra down the docs. The ships loomed over Mirra like slumbering giants. She couldn't keep the look of wonder and longing on her face as she walked past ship after ship; each one could have been her ticket to freedom.

They stopped in front of the only ship that had a burning lantern swinging from a post. A sailor slumbered nearby, snoring with his feet propped on top of a crate. Lord Julian cleared his throat. The sailor leaped from his seat, swearing. Mirra caught the glint of a knife in the golden candlelight.

"I booked passage two weeks ago for two." He held out a folded piece of paper. The sailor took and tucked it into a pocket without looking at it. Mirra realized that he most likely didn't know how to read. There could have been nothing on that piece of paper, and the sailor would have never known because, why would he bother to look at something that he couldn't figure out? She felt a twinge of pity for the sailor but squashed it down.

If she could, she would have traded the ability to read with being free, sailing to places unknown.

"Right this way, me lord," the sailor said with an awkward bow. He led them up to the gangplank and straight to a set of doors that undoubtedly were the captain's quarters. The sailor rapped sharply on the door, leaving when a gruff voice answered.

Lord Julian walked into the captain's private quarters as if he owned them. Unsure of what to do, Mirra remained outside. She wanted to enjoy the fresh air before being shut up again below decks.

There was hardly anyone else on deck. Only a few sailors serving as a night watch. They watched Mirra from the corners of their eyes but made no move to speak to her. She made her way toward the back of the ship, walking up a short series of steps. She spied the steering wheel and smiled. She ran her hand over the spokes, worn smooth by years of use.   She stood behind the wheel and stared out over the ship. What would she give to never leave with Lord Julian and remain on this ship?

"Mirra!"

She let go of the wheel and spun. Lord Julian had yelled out her true name. Why? She hastily made her way back to the lower deck. His handsome face glowered up at her, ire simmered in his two-tone eyes.

"Do not wander around."

"My lord," Mirra said demurely, looking down at her feet.

"Our cabin is this way."

Cabin! They were to share a room! Mirra's body felt as if it had been dunked into icy water. Her mind flitted from one thought to another like a bird captured in a cage. She was *not* going to sleep in the same room as the King's Viper. That would be signing her own death warrant.

To say that the cabin was small would be an understatement. There was only space for two small cots and a small crate in between them with a beat-up lantern that had been bolted to the crate.

Lord Julian lay down on one of the cots, folding his hands behind his head. "Get some sleep. We have a long way to go yet."

Mirra lay down on the other cot but couldn't make her body relax at all. She lay there stiff as a board, one arm near her side, the other close to the hidden weapons in her hair.

"I wouldn't reach for those pins if I were you," Lord Julian said.

Mirra turned toward him in surprise. His eyes were closed, and his pose looked relaxed, but she could nearly taste the undercurrent of tension that ran through his body. Why would he be nervous around her?

"How'd you know about it?"

He scoffed and turned his unnerving eyes on her. "Who do you think trained Nora?"

She silently cursed. "Do you blame me?"

"No, actually, I'm rather impressed at your forethought. Even masters have the potential to betray those who belong to them."

"So, should I just go ahead and stab you to get it over with?"

Lord Julian chuckled. "I think you might end up becoming my favorite. Given your assignment, it's for the best."

Mirra sat up. "What's my assignment?"

"All in due time."

Mirra groaned, flinging back onto the bed. She heard Lord Julian shift on his cot.

"We have a long sail ahead of us. We might as well get some sleep."

She turned her head. Lord Julian sat on his cot, holding a flask out for her. Slowly, she pushed herself to her elbows, turning to face him, but she didn't take the flask. He chuckled again before taking a long swig from the flask. She heard him swallow and saw a trickle of something red from the corner of his mouth. He held the flask out to her again. She looked at it as if it was a deadly serpent, and given who held it, it was just as good as one. The longer she refused to take it, the colder his eyes grew until they burned with icy fury. A sharp pain flared around her wrist. She snatched the flask, tipping it back to hide her own fury.

Brandy burned down her throat, filling her belly with warm fire. She tossed the flask back and stretched out on her cot. She turned her back to Lord Julian, even though every ounce of her instinct screamed that it was a bad idea. But so was showing her emotions. They both had the capacity to kill one another. The only thing that kept them from spilling each other's blood was their ability to swallow their true emotions. The moment that failed to be true would be the last day of her life. Mirra held no delusions about her abilities. She had killed in her past, but they were children, half-starved and untrained. She may be stronger now, but Lord Julian was a noble, trained in combat from birth with decades of experience at his disposal.

She must have been more tired than she realized because she suddenly found it hard to keep her eyes open. The brandy made her mouth feel dry and filled with cotton. She tried to swallow, but it only made her throat feel even drier. She tried to sit up to find a flask of water, but her head spun like it did when she had too much wine. But surely, the brandy wouldn't have hit her so hard already. The truth settled like a stone in the pit of her stomach.

"You bastard," Mirra slurred before the drugs took control.

She stood in the inner garden at Rosmanor. The corners of her vision were blurry and lacking in color. Her head throbbed slightly. She raised her hand and pressed the heel of her palm into her eye. The throbbing in her head didn't dissipate, but her mind cleared enough to register that not all was as it appeared. Thousands of flowers were in bloom around her, but she could not pick up a single scent. A bird flitted from branch to branch, but she could not hear their song nor the rustling of the branches. The tops of the trees swayed in a breeze that she could neither hear or feel.

This is not real. Maybe it's a dream or a memory.

"I hear that your studies are going well," Nora said. Her voice echoed unnaturally, causing Mirra to flinch. "But there is one lesson that I fear you may never grasp."

"What are you talking about?"

Mirra jumped as another version of herself came into view.

"You always talk about how you never had a choice when it came to serving Lord Julian."

"I didn't," the other Mirra said. "It was either him or the gallows."

Nora shook her head, the fake sun bouncing off her golden curls. "There's always a choice, but that's not what I mean."

The other Mirra cocked her head to the side. Nora sighed and walked forward, taking the other Mirra's hands in hers.

"You're a survivor. You had to be to make it as far as you did before crossing paths with him. Because of that, you will always choose the path that will keep you alive."

Mirra took a step forward, walking around the dream versions of herself and Nora. Her copy crossed her arms with a petulant look plastered on her face.

"I mean no offense by that. I am the same. We may be women. We may paint our faces, curl our hair, and dress up in pretty silks, but that doesn't change who we are on the inside."

"And how are we?"

"We are steel, fire, and stone. We will do whatever it takes."

Mirra smiled. She remembered the conversation now. It happened a few days before Lord Julian came to claim her. She now wondered if Nora had known and wanted to bestow some last-minute advice without his influence.

"When he presented me with the opportunity to escape the hell I was living in, I took it. And like you, I soon began to chafe under my leash." Mirra reached her original spot and stopped. The air in the dream garden had changed.

"Life is nothing but a series of crossroads. Every decision we make changes and reshapes our path. One day I was faced with a difficult decision that could have freed me from his clutches, but I had been too afraid to take it because it would have been the hardest road I had ever walked down." Nora's eyes shifted from the dream Mirra to the real Mirra.

Mirra took an involuntary step back. "You must be stronger than me. When you come to that crossroads, I pray that you will have the courage to take it, to take your freedom, no matter how hard the road will be."

The pounding in Mirra's head returned with a vengeance. Even in her dream, it drove her to her knees. The dream garden began to fade in a blinding white light, and all sounds came crashing down on her like a torrent wave. White turned to black, and the noise took on the familiar sounds of men shouting orders and footsteps on wooden planks.

Slowly, she opened her eyes and blinked against the pounding in her head and rolling of her stomach. It took more effort than she liked to turn her head toward the other cot. It was empty.

That bastard, she cursed before falling back into a dreamless sleep.

CHAPTER TWELVE

SEAGULLS SQUAWKED, TEARING MIRRA FREE FROM her drug-induced dreams. The men's footsteps and shouting made from the sailors on the deck above reverberated inside her head. Groaning, she swung her legs over the edge of her bed. Her stomach protested the movement, clenching to expel what it didn't have. *I need to get some air.* She stood up, swaying slightly on her feet for a few moments before plopping back on the bed.

A knock on the cabin door. "We are arriving at the docks if you wish to watch," said the person on the other side.

Mirra grunted something in reply, and the person left. She dug the heel of her palm into her burning eyes before dragging shoes on her feet. She missed the launch, all thanks to her benevolent master; she didn't want to miss the docking because of him too.

Sharp, cold briny air assaulted her senses the moment she emerged from the bowels of the ship. Mirra wrapped her arms around herself, wishing she had put on her cloak. The deck was a flurry of movement. Sailors dashed about their task to bring the great ship into the harbor without any mishap. For the briefest of moments, Mirra wondered if she would be able to hide on the ship long enough for it to set sail again, escaping whatever Lord Julian had planned for her. A familiar pain flared at her wrist, reminding her that it wasn't an option.

She turned her attention to finding the most unobtrusive location on deck for her to watch the docking. There wasn't one portion of the ship that wasn't occupied by a harried sailor. Determined, she walked to the bow of the ship and perched on top of the railing.

Mountains loomed on the horizon. They had already traded their green cloak for one made of vibrant gold, bloody red, and rich brown. The briny sea wind whipped strands of Mirra's hair from its braid, lashing her face. She paid it no mind. Instead, she leaned further into the wind, inhaling deeply, tasting salt and smoke on her tongue.

"Those mountains serve as a natural border between Undros, Nealet, and Lorcsea."

Mirra swallowed her disappointment to face her master.

"Is that so?"

"Yes, my estate is also nestled within those mountains. Winter never truly leaves them in case you were planning on running again."

Mirra turned back toward the shore. "I am loyal to you and your cause, my lord."

Lord Julian threw his head back and released a throaty laugh that sent a round of shivers down Mirra's spine. Mercifully, he left her alone, but the moment was already spoiled. Now that she knew her destination, it took every ounce of her will to live to keep herself from flinging herself over the edge of the ship into the icy waters below. Her trepidation only grew over the course of the three-day journey to reach Lord Julian's home. Her mind ran wild, imagining one horrible thing after another. When the tall stone walls finally rose from the horizon, she wasn't sure if she was relieved or disappointed.

Made of local stone and slightly taller than the walls of Rosmanor, the walls surrounding Lord Julian's home looked-normal. Sure, there were a *few* more spikes along the top, but nothing that would be out of place from a mountain estate.

The portcullis was down, but as the carriage grew closer, it opened with a great clacking and groaning. A feeling of dread took hold in her heart. Her fingers pressed through the lattice of the window of their own accord. She leaned forward, suddenly desperate for light and warmth from the sun. Something told Mirra that once she passed through the gate, both would be in short supply. The portcullis closed behind the carriage with a mighty clang, closing her into a world of shadows and suffering.

MIRRA STOOD SHIVERING ALONE IN THE COURTYARD. Lord Julian had strode into his home without a backward glance or guidance. Mirra scanned the courtyard. It lacked the warmth of Rosmanor, and that wasn't due to its northern local. Nothing grew in the courtyard, not even a single blade of grass. A quick glance up told her that not a single bird flew or roosted near the fortress. A cloud passed over the sun, casting the fortress in long, dark shadows that stretched out toward Mirra like a cat seeking caress. A part of her that hadn't been awake since that time in the woods stirred, reaching out to embrace the shadows in turn.

"Ready?"

Mirra suppressed a shudder and turned toward the servant that had spoken.

"Yes."

"Then follow me."

With no other option, Mirra followed the girl. Inside the fortress, the walls and hallways were bare. Nothing to indicate the owner's taste or to use as landmarks to help figure out how to traverse the seemingly endless labyrinth of darkened hallways and staircases.

"Your room."

"Thank you."

Her room turned out to be just a step up from a cell. The room was small and windowless. It already had her trunk and bags from the carriage and … "Dark Mother above!"

Someone had gone through her possessions. Her bags had been dumped on the floor and the contents of her trunk had been scattered across the small space. Mirra picked up her belongings and began the painstaking task of figuring out what, if anything, had been taken from her. By the time everything was back in its proper place, Mirra was ready to punch someone. Her books were gone! The one thing she had come to truly love. Her one solace in a hard world.

Another servant knocked and came in, bearing a tray with food. Seething, Mirra rounded onto the servant. "Who went through my things!"

Unbothered, the servant sat the tray on the bed. "You have no possessions. Everything within these walls belongs to The Viper—the food, the weapons, me, and you. Everything."

The servant bowed sharply before leaving Mirra alone with her rage. She sat on what was to be her new bed before picking up the chalice. She swirled the amber liquid once, twice, then tipped the contents into her mouth. The liquid was fiery, full-bodied, with just a hint of something bitter at the end.

Pain erupted into life in the pit of her stomach. She groaned, dropping the chalice as the fire spread from her gut to the rest of her body, boiling her blood. Coughing, Mirra fell to the floor. When she pulled her hand away from her mouth, it came away splashed with red. Spots danced across her vision as the edges of her sight grew dim. She had lost consciousness and fell hard onto the cold hard stones.

For the second time in her life, Mirra found herself chained in a dungeon. Still groggy from her latest bought of poisoning, she slowly eased onto her elbows. The iron around her wrist seared her flesh as long-forgotten memories drifted to the surface of her consciousness.

Why? Why am I here?

A snarky part of her mind snorted. *He's testing you to see if you've gone soft in the past five years.*

Well, he could have done it in a less painful way. She lay back down on the cold, hard floor and closed her eyes. She strained her hearing beyond the scope of her cell. The wooden door dampened most of the sound on the other side of the door. But if she couldn't hear anyone, then they wouldn't hear her if she was careful.

She sat up to fully take in her new situation. Her dress was gone, but at least they had left her in her shift. It wasn't much, but it was better than being completely naked. Her hair was in disarray, with several sections hurting, where some unknown person had ripped out the clips and jewels that held her hair back. She ran her fingers through the tangled bird's nest that was her hair. She pricked her finger against something sharp and smiled. Her secret lock pick. The same shade as her hair and braided discreetly against her scalp; someone would have to be extremely thorough to find it.

It took longer than she would like to admit to break free from her constraints, but she managed. She walked toward the door, crouching beneath the small open window near the top of her door.

No light at all. Not even the faint glow from a guard station. She stood taller. The air was dank and cold, but there was something else … *smoke*! If there was smoke, then nine times out of ten there were people somewhere close by.

Mirra managed to unlock her cell a bit faster than her chains. Her fingers slowly remembering the lessons they learned a lifetime ago. The door to her cell opened soundlessly on well-oiled hinges. She peered around the door, checking for guards or fellow prisoners. Spying neither, she ventured further into the open. The pick that gave her freedom became a weapon, albeit a minor one but better than nothing. She crept along the darkened hallway, her senses stretched to their fullest extent. Yet, try as she might, she couldn't discern a single living entity anywhere near her.

A chill ran down her spine. *Where were the guards? Where were the other prisoners? Hel, where were the* rats? Mirra came to a set of stairs without encountering a soul. She peered over her shoulder at the pitch-black corridor behind her. Mirra scoffed and left the hungry void behind her.

The stairwell spiraled up and up, no doubt some defensive structure to keep escaping prisoners from being able to attack. Soon enough, Mirra's breath became short, and her calves burned. *Just how deep are his dungeons?* She paused near a tapestry showcasing a knight slaying a mighty red dragon, attempting to catch her breath. Gasping for air, she went to brace herself against the tapestry to only fall right through it.

She landed hard on her hands and knees, muttering a string of curses in her head. She picked herself off and went to dust off, but there was nothing there. She squatted down and whipped her hand across the stone floor to make sure—nothing. From somewhere beyond her scope of sight, a breeze trickled through. Mirra inhaled deeply, her mouth watering over the scents of roasting meat and freshly baked bread.

Following her nose, Mirra navigated through the darkened passage, feeling at home in the darkness. She didn't have to walk for long before she found confirmation that she was, in fact, not alone. Scones along the wall bore small oil lanterns that pressed the darkness to the far corners of the passage. Mirra lingered in the dark, reluctant to leave its safety, but she had no choice. Keeping to the shadows as much as she could, she continued her trek. At long last, she came to a wooden door. She pressed her ear against the warm wood. She heard shouting, clanging, and bangs from the other side. Cautiously, she opened the door and peered through the crack.

The kitchen was a hub of life. Cooks, maids, and servants scurried about, paying little heed to the others around them unless they got in their way. It was the perfect cover. All she had to do now was to sneak out of the passageway without anyone noticing her. Mirra chewed on her thumb. If she walked out there as she was, dirty, haggard, and wearing only a shift, someone was bound to notice her, and then she'd find herself right back where she started.

Two scullery maids, each burdened with a large pot that blocked their vision, collided with a mighty crash. One of the maids screamed, holding her face as whatever hot liquid scorched her skin. The entire kitchen staff stopped what they were doing to watch the spectacle.

"Curse you, great galloping goons!" shouted a portly woman in a flour splattered dress, her hair wrapped up in a crimson scarf. "Canna you watch where you step?"

"I'm so sorry," sputtered the other scullery maid who, too, was wet but with soapy water. "Will she be all right?"

"What ... who ... oh, her ...well enough, but now I have to completely remake the soup for tonight's supper. It's not like I don't have enough to do around here." The portly woman scowled at the burned maid. "Get her outta here and BACK TO WORK!" Two men helped the burned maid to her feet and ushered her out of the kitchen, while the rest of the staff went back to their tasks. "You, wet one, go get a spare uniform and get to work!"

The soapy maid quickly curtsied. "Yes, mum." Mirra watched the maid make her way to a small door with a faded red tile on the door.

The portly woman continued to bark orders at the staff. Mirra used that to her advantage, slipping through the door, heading straight toward the room where the maid disappeared into. She crouched behind a collection of crates, waiting for the maid to exit. The moment she did, Mirra slipped in behind her.

Letting out the breath she had been holding, Mirra locked the door. She was safe for the moment. Rows of identical gray dresses hung from pegs along the length of the room. Small baskets sat in front of each dress. Inside, they held a head wrapping and apron. Mirra walked the length until she found one that would fit her. The fabric was coarse and scratchy in places, but she didn't mind. Anything was better than walking about the cold keep in her flimsy shift. Already, her hands and feet were numb from the cold. She would have to find shoes later, but for now, wrapping her feet in extra headscarves would have to suffice. It took her only a moment to pull her hair back into a braid, safely tucking her lockpick inside. Coiling her braid before hiding it under the pale headscarf, Mirra completed her look. Unlocking the door, she walked out of the room as if she belonged.

No one looked up from their stations as she strode straight toward the doorway where the injured scullery maid was taken through. As she passed the main cooking hearth, she snacked an empty bucket. *Just your average scullery maid on her way to tend to the fires.*

Mirra struggled to keep the smile off her face. It had been a lifetime since she last used the skills of her childhood. Though her heart hammered in her chest, she was calm and composed. She swiped a peering knife as well, dropping it into the bucket and walked into the rest of the keep.

In the servant corridor, she didn't see too many people. The few that she did passed her by without acknowledging her existence. Mirra rounded a corner, stopped, and quickly retreated to the shadows. A pair of guards strolled toward her. Servants may not pay attention to her, but guards might mark an unfamiliar face. Quietly retreating, she backtracked before taking a different route. She needed to make it to the upper levels if she was ever going to find a safe place to hide.

Three more times she was forced to backtrack due to roving guards. They always seemed to appear just as she was about to reach the eastern stairways. Once was fine, twice a coincidence, but three times ... they were herding her. She was left with only two choices. The next time she ran into the guards, attack and hope for the best or let them and see where they are trying to get her to go. Mirra knew that she was no match for two highly trained guards. They had light armor and short swords, while the only things she had was a peering knife and a bucket.

After two more herding attempts, she realized that they were trying to get her to go to the western wing of the keep. Once there, the guards and servants that plagued her steps disappeared like the morning fog. The hairs on the back of her neck stood on end. The air in this part of the keep was vastly different from the rest. The shadows had eyes that pierced her to her soul. Her breath came out in tiny puffs in front of her face.

She turned a corner and came face to face with a large door. The sight of it chilled her to the core. Her instincts screamed for her to turn around and flee in the opposite direction, yet she didn't. Her feet moved on their own accord, carrying her closer to the door. There was something about the door that was reminiscent of her tattoo. Instinctively, she raised her hand, reaching for the door. Something inside her recoiled, lashing out at the door. Whatever it was, it struck the door with enough force that the door swung open on itself.

"There you are, Mirra," the Viper said with the barest hint of amusement in his voice. "I was beginning to wonder if you had gotten lost."

"Did I pass your test?"

"With flying colors. I'm pleased to see the years have not fully erased the skills that initially drew my attention. That's one less thing to teach you before you get your assignment."

Mirra perked up. "I suppose you won't tell me what that is yet?"

"No. You have to survive the final stage of your training first."

Mirra swallowed. Lord Julian smiled, folding his hands under his chin. "You know how to maneuver in the lowest levels of society and in the highest. You have stolen for your dinner, tended to the land, and danced with nobles. Now you will learn the art of the shadows."

"And what is that?"

"The art of spying and assassinations. It's not *that* different from your early life, but there are some subtle differences. None of which I will get into now." The Viper looked over Mirra's shoulder. She turned and saw a bear of a man lumber out of the shadows. His face was made of granite and just as ragged, littered with scars and pockmarks. He crossed his impossibly thick arms across his barrel chest. Mirra noted that his forearms bore several serpent tattoos under, even more frightening.

"Everyone here works for me as you do. You will find no allies here. To survive this last stage, you will need to use every ounce of your skills." Lord Julian nodded to the beast standing behind Mirra before turning his back on her.

Mirra turned and was struck by a hammer. She careened to the floor, spots dancing before her eyes. For a man so large, he moved uncannily fast. He struck again. This time, Mirra was able to roll away. She felt the floor reverberate from the force of his blow.

In a heartbeat, she was on her feet, braced to either fight or run. She cursed herself for dropping the bucket with the knife outside. They would be no match on a foe this size, but they could give her enough to get out of the room, which gave her a better chance of survival.

The bear-man lunged forward, and Mirra attempted to dodge him, but he was faster than her. His meaty hand wrapped around her bicep. His grip was as hard as iron. There would be bruises later. He pulled Mirra back to him, balling his other hand into a fist.

Mirra heard the crack inside her skull. Thick, hot liquid ran down her face as pain blossomed from where her nose used to be. For surely, now it was just a crater on her face. Twice more, the bear-man struck her face before flinging her into the opposite wall.

The only thing that Mirra could do was cough and spit the blood from her mouth. Her vision swam as she struggled up onto her hands and knees. The bear-man stomped toward her, each step sending shockwaves throughout the floor. The acrid tang of panic coated Mirra's tongue. She tried to get to her feet but was too slow again. During the struggle, her head covering had fallen off, and her braid hung free down her back. He wrapped her long braid around his hand like a coil of rope and hoisted her up.

Mirra screamed, pressing her hands to her scalp as if she could keep him from ripping her hair out from its roots. The bear-man pulled harder. Mirra rose to the tips of her toes, but it wasn't enough.

"Be seeing you," he said, his voice just as hard as his fists. It was the last thing Mirra heard before another blow to her face caused her to blackout entirely.

CHAPTER THIRTEEN

FATHER, SAVE ME," MIRRA GROANED WHEN SHE regained consciousness. There was not a single part of her that didn't hurt in one fashion or another. She tried to open her eyes, but one was swollen shut. Her bottom lip felt swollen and sore too. A quick prod with her tongue confirmed her suspicions; a busted lip. A sharp pain at her side told her that she had a bruised rib, possibly even broken. "At least I'm alive … for now."

The smell of something pungent and slightly medicinal caught her attention. On top of a small crate sat a cup with some kind of tonic in it. She picked it up and gave it a sniff. It didn't smell any different than the other tonics she'd taken over the course of her life. She knocks it back in a single gulp, nearly gagging on the taste. Her pain did subside a bit afterward.

A slip of paper slide from under her door. With the utmost care, Mirra sat up. She counted to ten to keep herself from going under again. When she was sure that she wasn't going to blackout, she stood up from her bed, one arm holding her aching side. Crouching down, she picked the note up and shuffled back to her bed before opening it.

Mirra,

*Report to the kitchens as soon as you wake and report to
Ruby. Since you so carelessly ruined your last uniform, you may pick a
replacement from the others. Be sure to take your tonic every day.
Also, some thief has stolen a few of your possessions. If you want them
back, you will have to find them yourself.*

Your Humble Servant,

Lord Julian

King's Viper and Master of Spies

Mirra crumpled the note and threw it as hard as she
could across the room. It only went a foot before landing. A
knock came a short time later.

"I have your uniform."

"Come in."

Mirra recognized the girl from earlier as the maid who
accidentally dumped a pot of scalding soup on another maid.
She looked at Mirra with wide eyes, no doubt startled by the
remnants of Mirra's beating.

Mirra opened her mouth to assure the girl that she was
better than she looked. *You will find no allies here.* She shut her
mouth, keeping her thoughts to herself.

"I also brought some extra bandages."

Mirra only nodded and stood, gritting her teeth to keep
herself from flinching. The girl helped Mirra get out of her
bloodied clothing before she expertly wrapped Mirra's bruised
ribs. After that, she helped Mirra slid into the clean uniform
before leaving.

It took Mirra a long time to finish getting dressed. Simply tying the apron around her waist was an ordeal. She had to lay back down, gasping for air, after putting her shoes on. Once she caught her breath, she rose, gently holding her side. She could put it off no longer.

Soundlessly, she cracked her door open and listened. As far as she could tell, there was no one waiting outside her door. Mirra hesitated, chewing on her thumb. The people in this place were undoubtedly trained to be unobtrusive. Could she continue to trust the bare basic of her senses? She opened her door a bit more, going slow as to not make a sound. Pressing her body against the doorframe, she eased enough of her head out so she could see. Two quick scans confirmed that she was indeed alone. Sagging with relief, she fully stepped out into the hallway, closing the door gently behind her.

ALL SHE HAD TO DO TO FIND THE KITCHEN WAS FOLLOW her nose until she reached a familiar part of the keep. It was just as hectic as the first time she saw it. And like before, the large woman, undoubtedly the infamous Ruby, stood in the thick of it, directing the chaos like the goddess of the kitchens.

"I don't care what *he* told you," Ruby bellowed at the cowering maid in front of her. "*I* said that if that two-bit merchant tried to sell us half-rotten vegetables, then we would no longer buy from him. And just look at these potatoes!" She reached into a crate at her feet and pulled out a lumpy brown thing with a mass of tangled roots.

"Does this look fresh to you!"

"No, Ma'am."

The poor girl looked as if she were to break out into tears. Mirra chewed her bottom lip before walking up behind the looming Ruby. "Excuse me; are you Ruby?"

"NOT NOW!" Ruby turned around, face as red as her name. She frowned down at Mirra. "What do you want?"

Mirra drew herself as tall as she could and met the indomitable woman's gaze, showing no fear in her impossibly blue eyes. "Lord Julian said I was to report to you."

Ruby put her hands on her hips, her scowl deepening. "You're one of *his*, aren't you?"

"Aren't you?"

"Clean the hearths; restock wood and water. Stay out of way." Ruby scowled at the still cowering maid. "This one will show you the ropes since she's mostly useless."

Mirra glowered at Ruby's vast, retreating backside. The maid timidly walked up to her.

"Thank you."

"What are you talking about?"

"My name is Shallan."

"What needs to be done first?"

Shallan's shoulders curved inward. Mirra resisted the urge to reach out and comfort the young woman. She had no friends here.

THE KITCHEN BOASTED TWO MASSIVE HEARTHS LARGE enough for both Mirra and Shallan to stand in. In addition to that, there were two bread ovens and a moderate-sized hearth that served as a catchall for the rest. It took nearly the entire morning just to clean the ashes out of the hearths and rebuild their fires. By the time the last heart was cleaned, Mirra's stomach was ready to eat itself.

"Just grab one of the burnt rolls," Shallan said. Those were the first words she had spoken to Mirra since they started.

Mirra followed suit. Her brows furrowed as she beheld the hard, burnt, little reject of a loaf. It was a far cry from the delicate pastries she supped on back in Rosmanor. Even when she was an orphan living wild on the streets, she got better bread than this.

She nearly broke a tooth on the rock-hard crust. Once she got back the acrid taste, the inner loaf wasn't too bad. A little bland, but surprisingly fluffy. Using her soot-stained fingers, she picked out the more edible portions.

"Stop lazing about," Ruby thundered, appearing from thin air. Shallan leaped to her feet, dropping her pitiful meal on the ground. She opened her mouth to defend herself, but Ruby silenced her with a wave of her meaty hand. "Show the hatchling to the gardens. Emric needs some things from the garden."

Mirra arched her brow, wondering who in the Hel was Emric. Shallan led Mirra through a claustrophobic and dark hallway. Bright sunlight chased away the shadows when Shallan opened the only door. Mirra blinked against the sudden brightness, momentarily blinded. When her sight returned, she was greeted by a cluster of plants in neat little sections. Some she knew; many were a mystery.

"Here's the list," Shallan said, handing Mirra a slip of parchment. "Most of what you'll need is over there."

Mirra looked where the other girl pointed. A small section of the garden was sectioned off by rope with a warning sign. Before Mirra could ask about it, Shallan retreated back to the kitchen, leaving Mirra alone in the garden.

The hair on the back of her neck stood on end. There was something off about this garden, but she couldn't put her finger on it. Eager to get back inside, Mirra scuttled toward the garden, looking at the list. It was a strange one. Not a single word was written on it. Instead, there was a series of symbols and pictures.

"Odd …"

The meaning of the symbols didn't become clear until she reached the sectioned-off portion of the garden. In front of each little cluster of plants was a little sign with a symbol on it. Even more curious, a basket with a set of gloves already waiting for her. Nonplussed, Mirra picked up the basket and went about her tasks. The gloves were forgotten.

The first plant on her list was a bush with dusty purple leaves. She plucked a few of the tender offshoots and placed them into the basket. During this process, she accidentally bruised a leaf, releasing its juices.

"Gods in Hel!" Her fingertips turned bright red and burned. She went to put her finger in her mouth but stopped at the last moment. Instead, she whipped her stinging fingers with her apron, removing as much of the poison as possible. She slipped the gloves on and went back to her task with a little more respect for the plants around her.

"Haven't you finished yet, girl!" Ruby stood in the open doorway with her arms crossed, glaring.

"Just finished."

"Follow me."

Mirra followed Ruby's expansive backside down a short staircase to another part of the keep. The air had a muggier feel to it than the other areas. There was also a slight aroma of soap.

"The laundry is this way. You are responsible for keeping your own things clean. If you don't, I won't let you work in the kitchens, and then you'll have to answer to Him."

Mirra rolled her eyes behind Ruby's back. *Someone's gotta mighty high opinion about themselves.*

Ruby led Mirra past the laundry and down a small set of stairs that was barely wide enough for her massive backside. Once again, Mirra shivered against the damp and cold.

The stairs ended in a small antechamber with a single door with only a single green lantern to light the shadows. The pale green light cast a sinister light against the shadows. Mirra gripped the basket of poisonous herbs tighter, wondering what new horror she was about to face. She walked up to the door and raised her hand to knock, but it swung open before she got the chance.

A sickly thin man glowered at her. His skin was pale and clammy as if he never ventured above the subterranean levels of the keep. His hair, pulled tightly back into a horse tail, was so pale that Mirra had a hard time discerning his hairline from his skin. The man, most likely Emric, narrowed his already thin eyes at the sight of her.

"Took you long enough, slave."

Mirra recoiled. Her lips pulled back into a sneer. "I am *no* slave."

Emric snorted, eyeing her tattoo.

The denial bubbling in her throat died.

Emric snorted again. "I see you a bit smarter than the last one. Perhaps you'll survive a bit longer as well." He stepped back into his workshop, leaving Mirra standing alone with a single word raging through her head.

Slave. Slave. Slave. Slave. Slave.

She gripped the handle of the basket tighter, eyeing the toxic plants nestled inside. Could she do it? It wouldn't take much; just a handful of everything, and she'd be dead. It would probably hurt. She might even vomit or empty her bowels. Not exactly the way she wanted to go out.

"You coming, girl?"

I am a gutless coward. Mirra closed her eyes and entered into a world of darkness and pain.

EMRIC SAT AT A LONG TABLE, POURING OVER A BOOK bound in emerald green leather. His long nose was barely an inch from the pages as his tiny eyes scanned over the script. He continued to ignore Mirra, giving her the opportunity to study the space.

The room wasn't very large, barely above a closet, but what space there was had been taken up by long tables with simmering pots, long glass tubes, and an enormous bookcase littered with books, scrolls, herbs, and other strange things.

The fumes coming off the simmering pots assaulted her senses. Her eyes burned and watered. Her nose burned. Even her skin seemed to burn from the fumes.

"Put the basket over there and sit down."

Mirra placed the basket on the only open bit on the bookcase. When she walked past Emric, her eyes quickly scanned the page he studied. It looked like some sort of recipe, but the name *Waking Nightmare* sent a chill down her spine.

She took a seat at the farthest end of the bench, near the only door. Her frame tense and ready to run at a moment's notice.

Emric continued to study his malicious book. Mirra half turned, one ear cocked toward the door. She began to pick at her fingers, worrying away bits of cuticle. The seconds ticked by. Mirra could practically feel her bones humming with anticipation. If something didn't happen soon, she was going to punch someone.

"Best not take the same route twice."

"What?"

"Change up the paths you take around the keep."

Mirra arched her brow. "Why?"

Emric exhaled a frustrated sigh, pushing away from the book. "The entire staff were warned to give you a wide berth and to only interact with you when necessary because you're marked."

"Marked for what?"

Emric shrugged, turning back to his book. "I can't say for sure, but your master; it won't be pleasant."

"He's your master too," Mirra snipped.

Emric gave her an oily smile before ignoring her completely.

Mirra picked at her fingers. Her mind a swirling vortex of apprehension and fear. She didn't like that she had been marked, especially since not a single person would be willing to tell her. The longer she sat in Emric's workshop, the worse she felt. Her nerves had spoiled her stomach, and the continuous noxious fumes weren't helping either.

"You can leave now, slave."

Mirra was too grateful to finally have permission to leave that she didn't bother arguing Emric's use of the word "slave."

Her time spent with him must have affected her more than she thought. She struggled to walk upright. The only thing that kept her from falling flat on her face was the hand that she used to brace against the cold, slick walls. The stairs were torture. Mirra resorted to going up on all fours. Maids and other servants watched her with wary eyes, but none moved to help. Mirra didn't care. *To Hel with them all. I don't need them. I don't need anyone.*

If Mirra had been in the right frame of mind, she would have noticed the pair of gleaming eyes in the shadows that followed her from the bowels of the keep to her room. No mirth shone in those eyes, only a brutal promise of pain and blood.

"Sleep well, girl. I'll give you one night's rest, and then we begin."

CHAPTER FOURTEEN

THE SHADOWS HAD CLAWS. THEY RIPPED AND SLASHED AT Mirra. Her mouth was open, but no sound came out. She tried to defend against the onslaught, but her hands went right through them. The shadows didn't seem to have that problem. They wound around Mirra, binding her limbs to her body. The tang of fear coated her tongue. Something dark, deep in the core of her being, stirred. It uncoiled like a snake before lashing out at the shadows. Slowly, the shadows retreated, leaving Mirra gasping in her bed. The sheets were tangled around her body. With wild eyes, she scanned her cell for any signs of the creeping darkness.

"It was only a dream," she told herself, dragging a sweaty palm through her tangled locks. "Just a dream brought on from ... whatever I inhaled yesterday."

But she couldn't fully shake the effect the dream had over her. After braiding her long hair, she coiled it around her head, securing it with the dagger hairpins, the only artifact from her time spent at Rosmanor.

At least partially armed, Mirra felt marginally better. That still didn't stop her from listening through her door before opening it a sliver to check for assailants. The hallway appeared empty, but that didn't mean that someone wasn't hiding in the shadows.

The hairs on the back of her neck stood on end. The sixth sense that made her an excellent thief and kept her alive all those years living on the streets screamed that there was someone nearby. Only then did she remember the warning Emric issued the day before.

You are marked.

"Bastard," Mirra silently spat. She threw her door open. The resounding crash echoing in the silent hallway. *Don't let him get to you. He wants you to be careless. An angry mark is an easy mark.*

Mirra closed her eyes and took in a calming breath, pressing her back into the cold, hard stone of the wall. When she opened her eyes again, they were as cold and hard as frozen stone.

She wasn't familiar enough with her new home yet to stray from the known routes, so she went to the kitchen the same way she always did. Her ears strained for any sign of being followed while she reached out around her with her special sense to feel out the shadows that were always predominate. She marked corridors, doors, and windows, vowing to explore later— after she acquired some better weapons.

Once again, Mirra was tasked with clearing out the fireplaces and restocking the wood. Whether they meant to or not, they had given an edge. Clearing the fireplaces gave her a good excuse to wander around the keep. She drew a rough mental map of the locations that she went to, especially taking note of tapestries, paintings, and other landmarks. She would snatch a scrap of paper later and sketch it out until she had the whole place memorized.

Finally going on the defensive when it came to her twisted master, Mirra felt surer of herself. This is what she was used to, and as much as she hated to admit it, maybe Lord Julian was right. Living with Brian and Nora had made her soft, but she didn't think it was as bad as Lord Julian made it out to be.

She returned to the kitchen and swiped a sweat roll from a tray that had been set out to cool. Next to the door that led to the gardens, a slip of paper had been nailed to the door. On it were symbols similar to those that she saw yesterday.

Mirra used the gloves right away this time. As she collected the herbs, a wild thought ran through her head. *Take some and use them on The Viper.*

Searing pain erupted at her wrist, coiling up her arm like a burning brand.

"Son of a bitch!" Mirra glared at the serpent encircling her wrist. "It was just a fucking thought! I wouldn't have acted on it ... probably."

The burning subsided, but some of the pain lingered as a reminder. Grumbling under her breath, Mirra returned to her chore.

From the safety of a darkened window, a vast shadow smiled down at the girl cursing in the poison garden. She had spirit. He liked that. He would enjoy breaking it even more.

"Set the basket down over there and come here." Emric hadn't bothered to turn around.

Mirra stuck her tongue at his back but complied. When she walked up to the table where Emric was working, she noticed five small vials. A few of the vials held colorful liquid, but most were as clear as water.

Mirra got a sickening feeling in the pit of her stomach looking at those vials. No good could come from them, not if Emric made them.

He picked up one that was the color of blood and held it out to Mirra. "Tell me what you detect."

Mirra took the vial delicately. A heavy stone settled in the pit of her stomach. Her hands were wet for some reason. Her breath escaped her lips in panicked little bursts.

"Go on," Emric snapped, a quill poised over a scrap of paper.

Mirra gritted her teeth and removed the stopper. The smell of rotting fish poured out of the vial, causing her to gag.

"Strong physical reaction to smell."

Through watering eyes, Mirra saw him jot down her reaction.

"Now take it."

"You've got to be fucking joking!"

Emric looked up from his paper, arching his brow. "I am not, and you will drink it."

"The Hel I will!"

"You either drink this tonic voluntarily, or I will call your shadow in. He will hold you down while I pour it down your throat. Either way, you will drink it."

Mirra glared at Emric, cursing him, Lord Julian, and all the inhabitants of the keep. Though she desperately wanted to see the person who was charged with following her, she didn't like the idea of being vulnerable in front of strangers.

Curling her upper lip, Mirra tipped the vial up, emptying the contents into her mouth. It tasted just as bad as it smelled. Her stomach rolled, upsetting the stone in the process. The stone began to burn, rolling, turning her stomach into a tumultuous sea of bile and burning poison.

The liquid fire rose, burning her throat. Mirra held her body, folding over. When the liquid fire reached her mouth, she had no choice but to let it out. If she had been in the right frame of mind, she would have been slightly impressed by the distance the liquid traveled. Some part of her mind, however, wondered why it was yellow-green and not red.

"Interesting," Emric said, turning back to his notes.

Mirra spewed a few more times before Emric handed her another vial filled with a green liquid. She didn't hesitate this time, downing the contents as fast as she could. It was like drinking a cold, starry night. The liquid stars quelled the fires in her throat and stomach. A sigh escaped her stinging lips. She licked them with her icy tongue.

"Marrow root. Only found in the marshlands of Zallino. Smells of rotting fish and easily detectable. Causes intense gastric pain and vomiting. Only known cure, the night flower, the blossom of the marrow root during full moons."

"And did I have to take it if you already knew all that?"

"I knew it, but you didn't. Now you know how it looks prepared, how it smells and tastes. You have suffered under its influence and been healed."

"Is there a less painful way to learn?"

"Of course. Now take this one."

Numbly, she took the vial, this one crystal clear. *Bastard. Bastard. Bastard.* The word rang through her head, growing louder each time. She opened the vial, smelled nothing. She dipped the tip of her tongue inside. Sweetness.

Emric sighed heavily. Mirra stared at him with murder in her eyes. He motioned for her to continue. Mirra closed her eyes and offered up a silent prayer that she would survive this ordeal.

Mirra pushed the contents of her plate around. She had no stomach for the simple fair. Especially not after the afternoon she had. Her stomach, throat, and head had been assaulted again and again. The names of poisons, their symptoms and antidotes swam lazily through her mind.

Kelston, made from a gland in a puffer fish. Odorless, colorless. Caused paralysis. No known antidote, but the effects wear off in about an hour.

Syrux, made from black cane sugar stalks in Nealet. Clear but sweat and causes the victim's throat to swell. The only way to stop it is by drinking vinegar.

But the worst one was called Wraith. It looked like rose wine, tasted like nothing, and killed you in under half an hour unless you got the antidote in you. Emric had waited until the very last moment, asking Mirra all sorts of questions about what she felt, before giving her the antidote.

A bowl of simple broth appeared into Mirra's line of sight. Shallan smiled down at Mirra. "After spending all afternoon with the Poison Man, your poor stomach probably can't handle much."

Mirra stared down at the bowl. Slivers of vegetables floated on the top. Though no steam rose from the yellowish liquid, the bowl was quite warm. Mirra was hungry, but after her "lessons" in poisons, she couldn't trust the offering.

"No, thanks." Mirra stood, ignoring Shallan's crestfallen expression. She stumbled up to her room, taking a different route. She got lost a few times and had to double back, but she didn't mind. All the better to keep whoever tailed her confused. As she locked and barred her door, she wondered when, if ever, the person would strike. Not knowing was killing her.

Later that night, when all the keep was fast asleep besides the night watch, Mirra stole down into the kitchen. She breathed life into a small cluster of embers, enough to cook with but not enough to attract any attention. She grabbed a pot and filled it with water. She set the pot on the coals before delving into the trash heap. She pulled out bits of chopped vegetables and the undesirable cuts of meat. All that went into the pot.

Who would have thought I'd have to make trash soup again!

Mirra stirred the simmering soup, keeping an ear out for footsteps. Her mind drifted back to the numerous times she and Bao made it. The cold winters. The lean springs. She hated it then, but now, the soup would save her life. She could no longer trust any food she hadn't prepared herself.

"I never thought I would miss Ylanna," she said with a laugh.

CHAPTER FIFTEEN

DEMONS HUNTED MIRRA IN HER DREAMS. THEIR TALONS tore into her body, leaving tendrils of her soul streaming behind her as she ran. And all the while, Lord Julian loomed over her, laughing.

Gasping for air, Mirra sat in bed covered in a cold sweat. She pulled her knees into her chest and sobbed. How was she going to survive her time here? The growing cold only reminded her that winter was on the way, and she had no chance to survive the harsh mountain winters. She'd only been here a few days, but her mind and body were beaten to new low, she was making Heap Soup again, and hunted by someone. She was utterly alone, just like she's always been.

She couldn't face Emric and his toxic workroom. Nor did she have the strength to slave away in the kitchens. Instead of getting dressed, she lay back down, pulling the itchy wool blanket over her head, cocooning herself.

No one came to get her.

No one came barreling in to haul her out of bed. No one came knocking to see if she was alive. For all she knew, the rest of the keep could have died in the night, leaving her alone. She remained in her bed all day, watching the sunlight travel across the bare stone floor. She only stirred when night had fallen, cloaking her in darkness.

Like the night before, she silently made her way down to the kitchen. She made a bowl of Heap Soup and snatched a burnt heal of a loaf. The crust would be inedible, but the inside should be all right.

She wolfed the food down the moment she locked her door. The Heap Soup sat heavily on her stomach along with the slightly bitter bread. As soon as she swallowed the last bite, pain wracked her body.

Poison!

Panic took over. Stumbling, she threw her door open and fell face-first into the hallway. Through watering eyes, she spied a pair of dirty black boots. Weakly, she rolled onto her back. Emric towered over her, his arms folded across his chest. Though his face was twisted into a scowl, his eyes were bright with excitement.

"Don't do that again."

From a fold in his robes, Emric removed a tiny vial. He set it on the floor just beyond Mirra's fingertips. He left her there on the floor without another word.

Mirra studied the vial, blinking back burning tears. Her whole body was aflame, and her vision had started to darken. *What if it's more poison? But it could also be the antidote. He did warn me not to skip out. Is it worth it?*

Rolling onto her side, Mirra dragged her useless body toward the vial. It felt like she crawled miles through burning coals and broken glass. Once her fingers touched the vial, she rolled back onto her back, uncorking it as she rolled. The vial barely held enough liquid to coat her tongue, but as soon as it passed her lips, the effects of the poison faded away to a dull ache.

A sigh of relief escaped through Mirra's parted lips. She lingered on the floor, relishing the cool sensation of the antidote.

Another pair of boots came into her vision. Like before, she hadn't heard the person walk up. Mirra rotated her head to get a better look at the boots. They had been nice at one point, but now they were covered in wrinkles from wear. Dirt also clung to the seam where the boot met the sole. But it was the staining around the toe that caught her attention. Something about it felt familiar to her. Weakly, she extended her hand and rubbed the stain. Her fingers came away with rust-colored flakes. *Old blood.*

Without warning, the left boot moved, meeting her face with a swift kick.

A loud crack filled her ears, followed by a flood of warmth streaming down her face. The right boot followed suit. Each kick sent a fresh wave of pain coursing through her body. The kicks also moved her across the floor until her back nearly broke against the wall.

All she could do was curl up into a ball against the onslaught. He was going to kill her, and there was nothing she could do about it. She was going to die on the unforgiving stone floor without getting to see the world beyond Undros's boards. Without being free.

Is that so? What did you do before you sold yourself?

Mirra gritted her teeth and loosened her limbs, exposing her stomach. Her assailant kicked her in the stomach just like she expected him to. All breath left her body. She gasped like a fish on dry land, but that's where she wanted to be. When her assailant went to kick her again, she latched onto his ankle and pulled it toward her feet.

Unbraced and taken by surprise, her attacker fell to the floor with a grunt. Mirra scrambled to her feet, hurtling down the hallway as fast as her legs could carry her. Though her heart beat against her chest as frantic as a freshly caught sparrow, her mind was a still pond.

Left, straight, right, right, up and over.

Mirra vaulted over the railing of the walkway. Her stomach clenched as she fell. Her feet thudded against the hard ground of the garden. Her momentum carried her forward. Long forgotten instinct took over; she tucked her chin to her chest and rolled. When she regained her feet, she stumbled toward the poison garden, snatching a glove as she went. From her waistband, she pulled the knife she stole earlier. She ripped the leaves off one of the plants. She bunched the leaves in her gloved hand, slicing the blade across the purple leaves, coating the blade.

She turned, spying her attacker standing in the center of the walkway. It was the same man who had beat her before. She snarled, flinging the blade toward him. He moved faster than a man his size should. As it turned out, he hadn't needed to do anything. The handled struck a support beam, bouncing back to the garden below.

Mirra swore. She heard the man chuckle before disappearing down a darkened hallway. Mirra glared at the walkway for some time until Shallan entered the garden.

"Merciful Father! What happened to you?"

Mirra looked down. She was still in her nightgown. She was covered in blood and bruises. Her hair was matted and wild.

"Nothing."

Mirra limped across the garden and retrieved the poisoned blade. She then went to a plant that still bore pink flowers. She plucked a flower, folded it in half, then drew the blade across it, neutralizing the poison. Now the blade was safe to handle.

"Be back in a moment."

Shallan stared, mouth agape, as Mirra limped past her. Using the wall for support, Mirra slowly and painfully made her way back to her room. She heard footsteps behind her. It was Shallan.

"I don't need you," Mirra snapped.

Shallan rolled her eyes. "Sure, you don't." She gently wrapped her arm around Mirra's waist and gently threw Mirra's arm over her shoulders.

Mirra gritted her teeth and let Shallan lead her back to her room. Once inside, Shallan deposited Mirra on the bed before rekindling the fire. She then poured water from a pitcher into a small bowl. Pulling a spare rag from her pocket, Shallan turned to tend to Mirra's wounds.

"No," Mirra said, pushing herself to her feet. "I'll take care of it. You'd better get back to work before Ruby gets mad at you."

Wordlessly Shallan set the water and rag aside. "As you wish." She left the room stiff-backed.

Mirra sat back down, groaning. She didn't know what to make of Shallan. She didn't want to make more enemies than necessary, but when you live in a den of thieves and assassins, you can't trust anyone but yourself.

But she helped you.

Mirra eyed the water and rag suspiciously. Were they poisoned as well? Had Emric or the giant man tampered with the water while she was out? Was Shallan an agent?

The water went out of the window. The rag ended in the fire. Mirra tidied up as best she could. Using her spare apron, she wiped off as much of the blood as she could without water. At least most of the blood had stopped by now. Her nose still bled, but she pinched it and kept going.

She limped the whole way down to the gardens. The kitchen was mostly empty. But the few workers that were already there paid her no mind. In the middle of the garden sat the well that supplied water for the entire keep. Mirra bet that no matter how badly they wanted to hurt her, they wouldn't touch the only source of clean water for miles.

This deep into the mountains, the water was like ice. Mirra shivered in the garden but washed the blood from her face. She then plucked a few leaves of witch hazel, rolling them between her fingers to release their juices. She applied the leaves directly to her split lip. The juice stung and tasted bitter, but it would keep the cut from getting infected. She applied the leaves to a few more spots, leaving them where they stuck.

"Nice to finally see you," Ruby laughed from the kitchen doorway. "I see you learned your lesson."

Mirra scowled at Ruby. "Where's the list? I didn't see one."

Ruby laughed. "No list today. Head down to the workroom."

Ruby cackled as she went back to her domain. Mirra stuck her tongue out at the woman's back before heading down to work with Emric.

"Tell me what you notice," Emric said the moment Mirra entered the room. He made no comment about her two-day absence, nor the poison he slipped her, or the man who attacked her afterward.

If that's how you want to play it.

Mirra picked up the vial and inhaled.

THE WORLD HAD BEEN ROBBED OF ALL COLORS OTHER than black, gray, and white. Only on the mountains a few patches of green still lingered. Mirra stared out at the mountains. She did not feel the wind that leached away the warmth from her body. She did not hear the snow that crunched beneath her boots when she shifted her feet. The only thing that she was aware of was pain, her constant companion these past three months.

All the life and strength she gained was now gone. She couldn't pass for a farm hand, let alone a courtesan. Every day was a battle. When not suffering under the hands of Emric, she had the giant man to avoid. When she crossed his path, he would attack her. Sometimes she was able to get away, inflicting a few injuries herself. But more often than not, he beat her unconscious. A servant or guard would wake her, then leave her in a pool of her own blood and misery.

One of the few places that she was safe from both her tormentors was her room and along the roof. Emric rarely left his workroom, and the man was too heavy to traverse the sharp angles. A small smile tugged at the corners of Mirra's mouth as she remembered the day she discovered that. He had fallen and severely injured his leg. That earned her two weeks of peace. Of course, when he caught her the first day he returned, she had to have her nose reset.

An eagle flew overhead. Mirra watched it spiral over the barren woods surrounding the keep in search of prey. Perhaps seeing none, it gave a cry and flew off to search elsewhere. *I guess I should go too.*

As nimble as a mountain goat, Mirra trotted along the snowy slopes of the roof. The top beam, while narrow, created a path that was easy enough to follow. Reaching the end of the path, Mirra leaped onto a lower roof with a sharp slope. She landed with a thud before sliding down the shingles. She went over the edge, grabbing on the edge. She then shimmed along the edge until she reached a window. The tips of her toes could barely reach the ledge, but she had made this trip enough that it didn't bother her. She released her grip on the ledge, dropping onto the ledge.

For two breaths, she stood, poised on the narrow ledge one wrong move away from instant death below. Mirra closed her eyes, savoring the feeling of teetering on the edge. She often wondered what it would be like to let herself fall. To let her body break on the unforgiving stones in the courtyard below.

The thought passed through her head like leaves on a winter wind. Using a knife, she flipped the latch and entered into the keep. The hallway was dark, as it always was, and freezing. Just another aspect of living in the mountains.

Mirra made her way to the kitchens. They were the only part of the keep that had continuous heat, but that's not why Mirra went there. On one of the tables, food had been laid out. A simple soup and hearty black bread; a far cry from the rich meals served in the hall.

She sat and dove into the meal without saying a single word to the others. She couldn't remember the last time she spoke to someone that wasn't Emric. What was the point anyway? They were all agents of the Viper, and they would not help her gain ... She no longer remembered what she had once wanted with every fiber of her being. Her world had been reduced to one of toxins and blades in the dark.

"Excuse me, are you Mirra?"

A servant she'd never seen stood awkwardly behind her.

"The Master wishes to see you in the courtyard."

Mirra turned back to her lunch, sapping the dregs of the soup up with the heel of bread. She rose and followed the servant.

Though it snowed nearly every night, the stone footpaths in the courtyard were clear of snow and ice. Maids swept the footpaths daily and coated them in a special salt that prevented ice from forming. Most of the other trees were bare, their thin branches reaching toward the sky like boney fingers. But there were a few evergreens nestled amongst the skeletal trees. It made the space marginally less depressing. In the center stood Lord Julian, but he wasn't alone. Mirra's hand went for her blade. The giant man stood just behind Lord Julian. His face was stoic, but his eyes scanned everything, looking for threats.

"It's rather cold today, Mirra," Lord Julian said. "I'd like to continue this chat inside where it's warm if you don't mind."

From her wrist, Mirra felt a slight tug. She frowned down at it, stowing her knife before walking out into the light.

"You summoned me, my lord. If you wanted to stay warm, you could have summoned me inside."

Lord Julian frowned. Mirra doubted it had anything to do with her sass. His gaze roamed over her entire body, no doubt noting the weight she lost or the haggard shadows under her eyes.

"You look like Hel."

Mirra scoffed and curtsied. "My apologies, my lord. It is difficult to maintain one's appearance when subjugated to daily poisoning and while being hunted like a common animal."

Lord Julian's frown deepened. "You will continue to study under Emric, but you are not to take any more of his brews."

The giant man moved to stand next to Lord Julian. Mirra shifted into a stance where she could fight or flee.

"This is Tor, my captain of the guard. You will meet with him in the afternoons to improve your hand to hand combat."

Mirra starred at Lord Julian in disbelief. "This man has been trying to kill me!"

Tor shrugged his massive shoulders. "Nothing personal, just following orders." That did little to quell Mirra's apprehension over actively seeking the man who beat her nearly every day.

"Well, I'm off," Lord Julian announced with a clap of his hands. "See to your studies, Mirra."

She watched him stroll away with the swagger of a man with no fear or care. She found herself wondering why did she bind herself to a man like him.

"Oh, one more thing."

Inwardly, Mirra groaned.

"I'm surprised you haven't tried to retrieve your belongings."

Honestly, her missing bow and books hadn't even crossed her mind. Mirra had been too busy trying to stay alive. "They're just things."

"Good. Attachments will get you into trouble, but consider finding them an exercise in spying and thievery. I expect results the next time we meet."

Lord Julian walked away with a careless wave of his hand. Mirra eyed Tor with suspicion. He only sighed, hooking his sausage-like fingers in his belt.

"If you pull that blade on me, lass, you will suffer for it."

That was the only warning she received before Tor launched into the day's lesson.

You've got to be shitting me."

Shallan lingered in the doorway of Mirra's room, holding a maroon colored dress trimmed in gold velvet. Behind her stood at least three more maids, all carrying steaming pots of water.

"Orders from our master."

Mirra contemplated slamming the door in their faces. Instead, she sighed heavily and stood aside so they could invade her tiny sanctuary. A fourth maid entered, carrying a large washing tub. Mirra groaned and stripped. Only Shallan maintained her composure.

The water was barely warm, but it served its purpose all the same. Mirra sat in the tub and scrubbed. The soap was hard and left her skin tingling, but as the water turned from clear to murky gray, she was grateful for it. Afterward, she sat by the fire, wearing a simple shift, while Shallan detangled the bird's nest that was her hair. She then coiled the dark rope around Mirra's head, pinning it into a crown.

The dress was soft and warm. Mirra traced the velvet trimmings with her fingers. How long had it been since she wore something so fine, felt any comfort at all? Her throat constricted, and her eyes burned.

"Leave us," Shallan ordered the remaining maids.

Mirra hung her head in an attempt to mask the tears forming in her eyes.

"There's no shame in crying or in asking for help."

Yes, there is.

One breath. Two breaths. Three breaths.

Mirra swallowed her tears and slowly lifted her head. She willed her face into a mask of indifference. "If you are finished."

Shallan sighed and gathered her things. "If you don't bend, you will break."

Mirra continued to stare into the fire, saying nothing, but inside, she scoffed at Shallan's words. She was not a sapling struggling to take root. She was a mountain that cared not for the howling winds.

Filled with fire for the first time since entering the keep, Mirra squared her shoulders and went to have dinner with a snake.

FASTER!"

Mirra winced as the bow staff impacted against her side.

"See where your opponent is heading, not just where he is!"

Tor glared down the length of his staff at Mirra. Every morning, they met in the courtyard for training. They started off with fists, then quickly graduated to knives, and now Mirra was getting her butt kicked in staff fighting. The staff was long and heavy, completely foreign in her hands. She often ended up smacking herself instead of Tor.

In the distance, a bell tolled the hour. Tor relaxed his stance, shouldering his staff. "Best rush off and make yourself pretty for Master, little girl."

Mirra dropped her staff and took off running. In her head, she counted the seconds. She hit sixty just as she reached the door. Tingling along the back of her neck urged her to duck. Tor's staff hit the door like a spear, striking where Mirra's head had been only a few seconds before, leaving a small circular indention in the wood.

Swallowing back her fear, Mirra swung the door open and dashed through, making sure to bolt the door before running to the safety of her room.

A SECTION OF HAIR REFUSED TO STAY IN PLACE. MIRRA twisted the wayward strand and secured it with a pin. She was late. Lord Julian would undoubtedly poison her tonight. At least, Emric had finally started to teach her some stronger antidotes by now.

Upon reaching the massive doors that lead to the dining hall, Mirra took several calming breaths, checking to make sure that every piece of her clothing was in place before gesturing to the footman to open the door. Her dress this evening was a simple black dress with gray accents, far more muted than the others Lord Julian demanded she wears.

"You look as lovely as ever, my dear," Lord Julian said as he stood up from the table.

"You are too kind, my lord," Mirra said demurely with a deep curtsy. She kept her eyes low, studying the three men and a single woman seated around the table.

Two of the three men were clearly nobles. Their clothes were made of Nealetian fabric, bright and costly. Each man also boasted an assortment of jewelry around their neck and fingers. One man clearly never missed a meal with his midsection spilling over the arms of the chair.

The third man she guessed was a merchant. While he, too, was dressed in finery, there it was muted when compared to the other two. His eyes assessed every item on the table and on every person.

The woman smiled kindly at Mirra, though it didn't reach her eyes.

"No need to be so formal, niece. We are in simple company tonight."

Damnit! Mirra swore. *Another test night.*

Mirra rose, plastering a smile on her face. "Of course Uncle, forgive me. I am still getting used to being home again."

"Have you been abroad?" the woman asked with fainted interest.

Mirra folded her hands in front of her and looked down at her feet. "I've lived in Lorcea for the past five years."

"Good gods," the fat man exclaimed. "Why so long? What could have a young woman such as yourself learn from those barbaric clansmen? I hear they call themselves Horse 'Lords' as if they have noble blood running through their heathen veins."

"That's where my husband lived."

The room fell silent. The fat noble's face flushed crimson.

"It is customary amongst the lords of the Stone Clans to house their potential spouses within their walls for a time. This way, each person can see how their intended grew up. It helps to create a bond, especially for arranged marriages like mine."

The woman picked up her wine glass and smiled cruelly into the rim, thinking that Mirra wouldn't notice. "And where is your husband."

Mirra forced her eyes to water and clenched her hands tighter. "He died. Killed during raid. We had been married less than a moon."

"I'm sorry to hear that," said the merchant. He raised his glass. "To your husband, a man of honor and valor."

"Honor and Valor," the others echoed.

Mirra bowed her head in thanks before taking her place to the right of Lord Julian.

The conversation around the table turned to more pleasant topics, everyone ignoring Mirra—just like Lord Julian wanted. Mirra focused on her meal, listening to what wasn't being said.

For weeks, she had been grilled on Lord Julian's family history and the role she had to play in it. He *did* have a niece who married a lord of the Stone Clans. There had been a raid, but sadly, there were no survivors. Since no one outside the Keep had ever seen Lord Julian's niece, her parents long dead, and the fact that they shared a similar eye color, she had been able to slide right in with no problems.

At the end of the evening, the noble men and woman stumbled back into their carriage, disappearing to wherever they came from.

"Follow me," Lord Julian ordered.

Mirra suppressed a sigh. All she wanted to do was strip down and catch a few hours of sleep and tend to the multiple bruises on her body.

A small fire crackled merrily in the hearth. No sooner had Lord Julian sat down behind his massive mahogany desk than a serving girl entered, bearing a silver tray. As the serving girl passed, Mirra caught the bracing aroma of coffee. She quickly set it down before scampering out of the room as fast as her feet could carry her.

Lord Julian poured the steaming black liquid into a porcelain cup. "Report."

"The fat one is married to the woman. Though she isn't too happy about it; definitely an arranged marriage. The merchant is her lover and the fat one's business partner. She'll be pregnant within six months and clamoring for an abortion tonic."

"Is that all?"

Mirra shrugged. "If you wanted more, you should have spiked their drinks so they would have to stay the night."

Lord Julian smirked, adding cream and sugar to the cup. He dismissed her with a wave of a spoon.

Mirra curtsied and left. The hallways were littered with shadows. Mirra walked as quietly as she could, keeping an eye out for potential assailants. A yawn forced her mouth open. Her bed called for her.

Rounding a corner, Mirra came upon a pair of maids whispering excitedly about something. Mirra slowed her steps and blended into the shadows around her. The maids continued, unaware that they were no longer alone.

"I'm telling you, you have to read this book. It's the most amazing story I've ever read. There's this pirate, and he travels around the world, fighting other pirates, solving mysteries, and the romance ... gods above!"

Mirra froze. *That bitch has my books!* The sound of falling footsteps caused the maids to break apart and scamper off down the corridor. Mirra marked the maid that talked about her pirate. *See you later.*

TAMI WAS EXHAUSTED. ALL DAY LONG, SHE RAN UP AND down the stairs, carrying buckets of steaming water, buckets of ashes, clean and dirty laundry, and the worst ... trays to the lord of the house. He made her skin crawl with his oily smile and two-toned eyes. At least she didn't have to see him all the time, or that girl. Tami didn't know what to make of her. One time she saw her working in the kitchens, then the gardens, and she saw the girl every afternoon training with the captain of the guard. But last night, the same girl had been dressed like a noble, and according to Beth who served dinner that night, the girl had been introduced as the master's niece.

Tami shook her head. It just didn't make any sense. She dismissed the thought under "crazy nobles" and trudged up the last long flight of stairs to her attic room.

She swung the door open with a sigh. The room was dark with only the thin crescent moon barely skimming above the trees. Tami noted that her roommate was already asleep, her body nothing more than a mass of lumps under the covers.

Without warning, the door slammed behind Tami, causing her to jump. She spun, eyes wide. A dark mass grew and separated from the darkest corner and lurched for her. Tami screamed, stumbling over her feet toward her roommate's bed.

"Wake up!"

Tami's stomach dropped when her hand pushed through what she thought was a body, meeting only the hard mattress below.

"She's still in the kitchens scrubbin'."

Tami turned. The voice was soft, deadly, and somewhat familiar, but she couldn't place it. "What do you want?"

The shadow stepped into the thin light, revealing a figure clothed head to toe in black. A black cowl kept the face in shadows. The figure rested its hands on the hilts of long knives strapped to its waist. Tami gulped, backing up until she met the wall.

"What do you want?" she repeated, her voice quivering with fear.

The figure said nothing, lashing out as fast as a snake, striking Tami in the temples with the hilt of the blade. The last thing Tami saw before her world went completely black was the cruel smile under the cowl.

MIRRA TRIED TO NOT TAKE TOO MUCH SATISFACTION FROM the crumpled heap on the floor. It most likely wasn't the maid's fault. With more delicacy than their initial meeting, Mirra lifted the maid and set her on her bed. She unlaced her shoes, placing them under her bed. She then covered the maid with her too-thin blanket before leaving with a small collection of books under her arm.

YOUR STANCE IS ALL WRONG."

"No, it's not."

"Yes, it is," Tor growled. He stomped over to Mirra, slapping up her elbow and the arm that held a bow.

Mirra relaxed the string and turned with a growl of her own. "The damned bow's unbalanced and about to snap. My stance is fine. I hunted for years before I came here."

Pain exploded across her face, and Mirra found herself on the frozen ground. When the spots faded from her eyes, she saw Tor looming over her.

"Self-taught. I was trained in the king's army. I learned the right way."

With one giant stride, Tor walked over Mirra's prone body, snatching up her discarded bow and a handful of arrows. With a hand full of arrows, he pulled back the string in rapid succession, notching an arrow almost as fast as he released them.

Mirra rolled over onto her stomach and stared at the target in distance. Four arrows clustered neatly in the center of the bullseye. Surging to her feet, she resumed her stance, attempting to replicate Tor's.

With a grunt of approval, he made slight adjustments to her stance. "See the target in your mind, not with your eyes."

"But I have to see the target."

Tor shook his head. "Target in the mind, and the arrow will follow."

MIRRA'S ARM FELT LIKE IT WAS ABOUT TO FALL OFF. TOR had her firing arrows all afternoon. She had no idea how she was going to eat when a spoon was too much for her to bear. It took everything she had to unstring her practice bow.

A small group of guards entered the armory. They laughed and joked, jostling each other. Mirra ducked her head, turning her attention to the fletching on the arrows she used for any signs of damage.

"I can't believe you missed it!"

"Shut up; you try shooting a bow that isn't yours!"

"What happened to your bow?"

The guard shrugged. "I dunno. One day it was gone, and this one was in its place."

"How do you know it's not yours?"

"Look here, you see this weird symbol? My bow doesn't have that."

The arrows Mirra held fell to the ground, clattering. She dropped to her knees, scrambling to pick them up before the guards took too much notice of her. Just as she reached for the last arrow, a broad hand entered her field of vision.

"Here you go."

It was the guard that lost his bow. Mirra kept her eyes to the floor, mumbling a thank you before scurrying out of the armory. Behind her, she heard the guards laughing at her or the guard that tried to help her. She wasn't certain. But she was certain of one thing: he had her bow.

HE NEEDED A BETTER CLOAK. THE WINTRY WIND WAS barely tolerable during the day, but at night, up on the wall, it cut down to his bones. He wrapped his threadbare cloak tighter, hunching his shoulders. It was going to be a long night.

Snow and ice crunched underneath his boots as he walked back to his post. Maybe he could convince his watch buddy that they needed to stay close for warmth.

When he returned to the small covered watch station, his partner was in a better mood than when he left.

"Look at what I got!"

"What?" he asked, sitting down on a frozen bench. At least it was wood and not stone.

"I guess one of the kitchen maids finds me alluring and smuggled some warm, spiced cider out for us."

He scoffed. "Maybe she's just taking pity." His friend only shrugged, taking a long swallow from a skin.

"You want some or not?"

He held his hand out, and his friend tossed the other skin. The heat emanating from the skin burned his frozen fingers. With a sigh of relief, he uncorked the skin and took three long swallows. The cider was the perfect blend of sweet and spice. His friend smacked his lips in appreciation.

"Good stuff, isn't it?"

"Yeah," he replied.

It took only a matter of minutes for both skins to empty. The warmth from the cider spread throughout his body. He opened his mouth and yawned. Another quickly followed, and before either man realized, they were leaning up against each other in a deep sleep.

Mirra peered over the edging of the guard post. Behind her mask, she smiled. *Finally. My fingers were about to freeze off.*

She gripped the edge and gently rolled her body over, dropping silently into the snow-covered stones.

A tiny twinge of guilt caused her to pause before the two sleeping guards. When they woke, they would be in for a world of hurt. At least she was able to swipe another bow from the armory. She wasn't totally heartless after all.

Cradling her bow close to her chest, Mirra walked back to her room. As her fingers warmed and regained their senses, she reveled in the familiar weight and grain of the wood. At the tip, she lovingly traced her mark. A sudden longing tore through her. She missed Brian and the farm. Hel, she even missed Ylanna. Did they have a boy or a girl? What did it look like? Were they eating enough? Did Lord Julian release Brian, or was the poor man indebted to a monster for the rest of his days?

So, consumed by her thoughts, Mirra failed to notice the large black mass that peeled itself off a dark corner. A beam of moonlight illuminated Tor's face, completely lacking any human emotion. Mirra paused, stretching out with her senses. Slowly, she turned to look over her shoulder and barely managed to duck in time.

Startled, she dropped her bow, accidentally kicking it further down the hallway. Tor smiled cruelly, pulling out a billy club from his belt.

"I'm tired of this little game."

"Me too. So why don't you take it easy for the night?"

Tor shook his head. "Can't do that, girlie."

"Why, then? Why does he have you hunting me throughout the night?"

"That's for him to know."

Tor lunged, bringing the club down. Mirra spun out of the way again, drawing her blades, their keen edges glinting in the moonlight.

"Finally got yourself some claws, then."

Tor tossed the billy club behind him, drawing a wicked-looking blade of his own. "No more holding back, then."

He moved faster than a man his size should have. It took everything Mirra had to block and deflect his strikes. Back and back, he pushed her until cold hard stone pressed against her back. Mirra's eyes widened when she realized her mistake. Tor smiled and deftly broke through her guard, plunging his blade into her side.

Mirra screamed. Tor withdrew his blade, now painted scarlet, and watched as she slumped to the floor. Mirra placed her hand to her abdomen. Warm sticky liquid oozed out from her wound.

"Is that all you got?" Tor sneered. "I can't believe he thought you had it."

Mirra had no idea what Tor was talking about, and neither did she care. Her whole world consisted of the burning at her side and the blood pouring out of it. She tried to crawl away, but every movement stole her breath and threatened to push her into unconsciousness.

Mirra cried out again when Tor slashed her again, twisting his blade. Darkness crept into the corners of her vision. It whispered to her. Called out for her. A dark tendril snaked out for her, slithering between Tor's feet. Mirra reached out for it.

Let me in, the darkness whispered. *Let me in, and I'll take away your pain, your suffering, your sorrow. Join with me and become whole.*

Sounds good to me, Mirra thought as the tip of her finger met the dark finger reaching out for her.

Dark flowers blossomed along her bones, each flower beautiful and terrible to behold. As the petals opened for the world, black starlight rose to swim in her blood. Every part of her was touched by either the flowers or their glittering black pollen.

As promised, her pain went away. Her head cleared. She felt more of herself than ever before. It was as if some missing part of her finally clicked into place. She didn't even feel Tor's strikes.

Mirra opened her eyes and gasped. The world had been swallowed by shadows and smoke. She could still see the keep's structure around her, see the moonlight streaming in through the windows, but it was pale. Tor loomed over her like a nightmare come to life, blade poised to strike.

Mirra raised her arm to protect herself from a blow that never came.

"Where the hel are you!"

Tor's voice sounded muffled, as if she heard him through water or another room. He turned away from Mirra, scanning the hall.

"Where are you, you little freak!"

He can't see me, Mirra realized.

Of course not, said a voice inside her head. Mirra went to press her hands against her ears but stopped. Her arms were as black as shadows, leaving smoky trails in their wake. She opened her mouth to scream, but no sound came out.

Tor continued to swing his blade about, shouting for Mirra. "Your magic won't help you! That's what he wanted! He'll use your magic to hurt people like he uses my strength. And you'll end up liking it, like I will like making you scream tonight."

Dark fire blazed to life at Mirra's core. Darkness in all its various shades took over every part of her until there was nothing left. Mirra felt her body move, heard the screams, but it was nothing more than whispers in the dark.

The floor was cold. Mirra blinked and sat up, her hand going to her side. Her clothing was torn, but the skin underneath was whole, not even a scar remained. Her head thoughts were fuzzy, and her head pounded to the beat.

"What ... how ..."

She looked about the hall, recognizing it as one near her bedroom. Furrowing her brow, Mirra stood, swaying slightly. She took a few groggy steps, then tripped over something, landing sharply on the floor.

"Gods above! What did I ..."

Tangled in her feet was her bow. She picked it up with trembling fingers. Dark stains coated the bow. Mirra frantically tried to wipe them off, but they wouldn't fade. Her breath became ragged as her heart sped up, pounding against her ribs like a drum. Her vision blurred as strange images flashed in her mind.

The door to her room was slightly ajar, light spilling into the hallway. Mirra cursed herself for not thinking to grab at least a couple of arrows, but she had knives. Slinging the bow across her back, Mirra unsheathed her blades and crept toward her room.

"I trust you've had a productive evening." Lord Julian lounged in her chair by the fire, nonchalantly reading a letter. A small pile sat off to the side, teetering precariously on the arm.

"Yes."

She met his two-tone gaze unflinching.

"Good, here." He plucked a single letter from the pile, handing it to her.

She took it, flipping it over to inspect the seal, a crowned sea serpent. She let out a gasp. With quivering fingers, she broke the vibrant purple wax. Delicate sprawling script covered much of the paper. The queen requested the presence of Lord Julian Visser and his niece Mirra Ó Broin, previously Visser to the court, by the next full moon for the celebration of Princess Braelyn's eighteenth birthday.

"We leave in the morning," Lord Julian said, gathering his things. "I have spent years and a fortune molding you for this. Do not disappoint."

Mirra bowed her head, too stunned for words. Serving the Viper was one thing, but living in the court was something different altogether. Her stomach clenched, and the walls of her room closed in around her. She'd be dead by spring.

CHAPTER SIXTEEN

THE CASTLE WAS LARGER THAN SHE REMEMBERED. EVEN from the gates, it loomed, imposing on the hill, silently judging all who scraped out a living below it. Eight years ago, she was an orphan, thieving a ghost of life on the streets. And now ... now she reentered the city in a grand carriage dressed in a black silk dress with a dove gray velvet cloak trimmed in fox fur. Mirra snorted, leaning back in her seat. Not even the gods could have designed a more outrageous change in events.

A faceless guard waved her carriage through, and she is flooded with a thousand memories carried to her by sight, sound, and smell. She passed a corner where she and Em would tease the apprentice boys as they gathered for their morning meal. While Em would tease them, Mirra swiped their food and coins.

In the distance, she heard street musicians. She wondered if they were the same ones that Sorro danced with when he wanted to earn extra coin.

Mirra leaned forward, scanning the tops of the buildings, looking for the building that she and Bao sat on at the end of each day, planning their marks and schemes. *Bao*. Were he and the others still alive? Would they recognize her? What happened then? She picked at her thumbs.

"Relax," Lord Julian drawled from his seat in the opposite corner of the carriage. Mirra snapped the window shield shut, slumping back in her bench. "You're no longer a half-starved little girl. You're a noblewoman now. No one will look twice at you in the city."

"And in the castle?"

He shrugged. "They'll forget about you in a couple of weeks when your novelty has worn off." He went back to his papers, a seemingly never-ending pile started back at the keep and got larger the closer they got to the capital.

Mirra fixed nonexistent problems with her clothing. Her clothes benefited a woman of her rank in mourning. Not only did this align with what really happened to Lord Julian's niece, but it also kept the wolves of the court away. No man wanted to dance with a woman dressed in black.

Needing something to do other than worry over things beyond her control, Mirra pulled out a sheet of parchment from her pocket. It was heavily creased from multiple foldings and bore a small stain near the top right corner from where she spilled her tea the other morning.

Befriend the princess. She has a habit of trying to go where she should not, much like you. You are to keep an eye on her and perhaps to even temper her wild nature.

Use any means necessary.

"What do you mean by "any means necessary"?

Lord Julian sighed, stacking his papers before setting them aside. "Use your *training*, girl. Work your way through her defenses. She's highly perceptive for one so sheltered. Perhaps that is because she's had to dig for the truth her whole life."

Mirra arched a bow, not quite following.

"The court is often called a pit of vipers. You will meet people who say one thing to your face but another behind your back. People will stab you in the back for an inch of power."

Mirra snorted. "Then no different than navigating the criminal underworld. They just have more money and better clothes."

Lord Julian laughed. Mirra found his laugh pleasing. She fought against the smile that tugged at the corners of her mouth.

"And *that* is why I choose you. Your mind is sharp, and you see things that other people don't. Back in the temple, you knew, even before you made it inside, that you were going to fail. Then inside the temple, you knew that your little blonde friend was going to get caught. You took her place."

"So," Mirra said, her throat tightening, "look at where that got me."

Lord Julian studied her, his eyes cold and calculating. "Indeed." He turned back to his reports, ignoring Mirra completely.

Mirra opened the window screen and watched the city she once called home race past her. Through the Merchant's District, her nose was assaulted by a thousand odors. Spices from the farthest corners of the world, animals, baked goods; they all blended into something that was wholly Verance. Subconsciously, she leaned into the door, giving her nose better access to the smells of her childhood.

As they slowly made their way through the dense city traffic toward the castle, the scents and sounds outside the carriage changed. Spice gave way to incense and the songs of hundreds of holy men and women singing to various gods and goddesses. She wrinkled her nose. She was not overly fond of the smell. Then they entered a world she'd only glimpsed from the tops of buildings.

The streets thinned out. The people who walked by were dressed in brightly colored fabrics and jewels. A few noticed The Viper's carriage and whispered hotly behind gloved hands. Even servants, dressed simply in the colors of their house, stopped to stare.

Mirra leaned back to watch from the safety of the shadows. A number of people looked at the carriage with open unease, some downright afraid. Some looked on with intrigue as if they wanted what the carriage represented, and the rest—a manservant in a dark blue tunic trimmed in brown spat at the carriage as it passed him, hate burning brightly in his eyes.

THE CARRIAGE SLOWED. SHOUTS AND COMMANDS POURED in all around as a small team of guards surrounded the carriage.

Three sharp knocks on the carriage door caused Mirra to jump. A young man, not that much older than her, dressed in guards' uniform, peered into the carriage.

"Name and business."

Lord Julian leaned forward, making his face visible. The young guard swallowed and stepped back. Just before he waved them one, his eyes lingered on Mirra's face. She kept her face neutral, knowing that he was marking it for future reference. A brief stretch of darkness, and Mirra entered a foreign world.

They entered a massive courtyard ringed with open-air walkways. Stone paths divided the courtyard into sections, much like a herb garden. In one section, a group of youths stood in two lines facing each other. In between the lines, a hard-faced man bellowed instructions. In other sections, small groups of young men trained in archery, hand-to-hand, and swordplay.

A large hedge grove took up what space was left. There, gilded youths and distinguished nobles strolled without a care in the world. Though not a single person turned to watch the carriage, Mirra felt their calculating eyes.

The carriage pulled to a stop near a set of sweeping stairs. A small group of servants already stood, waiting. A middle-aged man with the royal emblem embroidered on his tunic opened the carriage door and bowed deeply.

"Welcome back, my lord. I trust your journey was unhindered?"

"It was," Lord Julian said. He turned, holding his hand out. Mirra grasped it and left all she was behind in the carriage. When her feet touched the cold stone, she was Mirra Ó Broin, niece to Lord Julian Visser, the King's Viper.

"My niece, recently widowed."

The man bowed. "My deepest condolences, my lady. Allow me to introduce myself. I am Arman, Head of House. If there is anything you need, do not hesitate to ask."

"My thanks, Arman."

Arman turned back to Lord Julian. "Baths have been drawn in preparation for your arrival. The new garments you requested have arrived just this morning. The seamstress is here as well for any final alterations before the ball tonight."

Lord Julian smiled. "As diligent as always. Please show my niece to her rooms. I have work to attend to."

Arman bowed. As he stood, a smirk of disgust flashed. It was gone when he turned and smiled at Mirra. It was an empty smile, one given purely out of expectations. "If you would please follow me, my lady."

Mirra gathered her skirts and flowed after. Dressed in black, she stood out like crow amongst a flock of songbirds. Whispers trailed after her like swarms of bees. Mirra clenched her teeth but kept her face a mask of cool detachment.

"Your rooms."

Mirra walked past Arman without a sound, closing the door firmly behind her. She leaned against the door and sighed. Her jaw hurt from clenching, and her skin felt raw. Absentmindedly, she rubbed her arms before turning her attention to her room.

Instead of a bed, a small but richly furnished sitting room greeted her. A fire flickered merrily in the hearth. A pair of wingback chairs framed the hearth. Vibrant rugs covered the floor, adding warmth to the room. A quick check revealed no hidden passageways or peek holes, so she turned her attention to the larger room in the back. There, most of the room was taken up by a large, four-poster bed with wine red drapes to guard against the cold. Again, she performed a cursitory check of the room, quickly followed by the bathroom tucked into another small chamber.

Mirra stretched her arms over her head, her spine popping. *Not a bad room. I don't think I'll be able to sleep until I go over every last inch, though.*

A timid series of knocks brought her back to the sitting room. *Bet that's the cleaning party.* A single maidservant curtsied when Mirra opened the door.

"My name is Daisy, m'lady. I am here to serve."

"Thank you, Daisy. I was just contemplating a bath."

Daisy entered the room, her eyes demurely on the floor. She quivered like a frightened rabbit in a snare. Mirra frowned but kept her thoughts to herself. "I saw that they had already brought up the water, but I don't see my trunks or the clothes my uncle commissioned for tonight."

Daisy clenched her hands together, white-knuckled. Her quivering became more pronounced. "I ... ah ... you see ..."

Daisy was saved from another knock on the door. A stern-looking old woman followed closely by two harried attendants strode into Mirra's room. "What's this! Why aren't you cleaned! How am I supposed to fit you when you're still in your traveling clothes and covered in road dust!"

Mirra rolled her eyes. She headed for the bath, summoning Daisy with a wave. While Mirra removed the pins that secured the veil that covered her hair, Daisy unbound ties of her dress. Mirra noted that the longer Daisy worked, the less afraid she seemed.

Once Mirra was stripped down to her shift, Daisy gathered the piles of clothes from the floor. "Should I take these to the laundry?"

"Thank you."

Daisy scurried out of the room as fast as her feet could carry her. Mirra smiled and pulled her shift over her head before stepping into the steaming tub. The water was the perfect temperature, just a smidgen on the hot side. The steam coiling up from the water carried with it the scent of lavender. Using a rag, Mirra scrubbed the road dust off her body, relishing pleasures she hadn't been able to experience the entire winter.

"Shall I wash your hair?" Daisy had returned, standing unsure in the doorway.

"Might as well."

Daisy approached and, like before, lost her fear while working. She gathered lengths of Mirra's hair, pouring scented water over it before dousing with soap. As she worked the soap into a rich lather, her fingers massaged Mirra's scalp.

"That's nice," Mirra said, her eyes closed. She tilted her head back, relaxing completely. She felt Daisy smile.

"Thank you, my lady."

"Mirra."

"What?"

"My name is Mirra. You don't have to call me 'my lady' when it's just the two of us."

Daisy's fingers stilled. "Yes, I do."

Mirra bit her lip, holding back her retort. After bathing, Daisy towel-dried Mirra's hair, turning a small towel into a headwrap before helping her slip into a thin shift.

The shift felt like nothing against Mirra's skin, with the exception of where water lingered on her skin. The shift stuck in those spots turning sheer. Daisy helped her into a corset, stockings, and underskirt, all dove gray and equally fine.

"Finally," the seamstress said, clapping her hands together. "Let's begin if you want to wear more than your underthings tonight."

An assistant took Mirra's hand and helped her get into the dress. It was a fine dress made of crushed velvet the color of the night sky and trimmed in shimmering black silk. Small dark stones were sewn along the bodice, twinkling like dark stars.

The seamstress and her assistants bustled around like chickens, squawking away. They poked and prodded the dress, occasionally sticking Mirra with a pin. But by the time the hour chimed, the seamstress stood back, a look of pride on her face.

"Mourning dresses are always a challenge, but you're young enough to not look completely dreadful. Send word when you're ready for colors again."

Mirra studied her reflection in a long mirror. The seamstress was brilliant. Overall, the dress was black, but upon closer inspection, the subtle differences in color and texture turned what could have been a boring dress into something worthy of court. Over her shoulder, Daisy appeared, holding a headpiece. It was flat black-crested hairband trimmed in the same way as the black jewels on her bodice. Attached to the headband was a long black veil with black pearls stitched along the edges to ensure that it laid correctly.

Mirra turned away from her reflection and sat down in front of a vanity. Daisy brushed and braided her hair, coiling it around her head. The headband was secured with pins.

A knock at the door pulled Daisy away. Mirra wished she had some makeup or something to put on her face. All the black made her face look near white.

"Your things have arrived, my lady."

"Excellent."

Four trunks took up most of the sitting room. Mirra threw one open, then turned to the others, digging through them until she found a small chest. She took it back to the vanity. Opening the lid, she smiled at the brand-new cosmetics Lord Julian purchased for her before they left.

In mourning, her face was supposed to be bare, but she looked washed out. A devilish smirk broke out across her face. Her husband was of the Stone Clans of Lorcea; their mourning traditions were slightly different. And if she had lived with them for a time, wouldn't she have adopted some of their customs?

Lord Julian was lounging in a chaise when Mirra entered the Announcement Chamber. He frowned slightly when he saw what Mirra had done to her face. However, he kept his opinions to himself, standing and offering Mirra his arm. He nodded to a dumpy man with an absurdly large collar.

The man bowed, making a motion with his hand. Unseen attendants drew the curtains back. The small chamber was flooded with light and the sounds of laughter, talking, and music. Mirra swallowed, stealing her spine against the hoard below.

"Lord Julian Visser, Master of Shadows. Lady Mirra Ó Broin Visser."

A sea of colorful faces turned as one toward the man. The music still and was replaced by a stream of whispers. With slow, deliberate steps, Lord Julian led Mirra down the grand staircase. When they reached the bottom, the sea of people parted, leaving a clear path.

Even though her eyes were focused on the far end of the hall, Mirra saw the courtiers whispering behind their hands with cruel intent in their eyes. Mirra raised her chin and continued her march toward the end of the ballroom, where a dais stood.

Lord Julian stopped and bowed before the dais. Mirra curtsied. The king stood and walked down the three steps of the dais. The tips of his finely made boots entered Mirra's field of vision. He made a motion with his hand, giving Lord Julian and Mirra leave to stand. Mirra looked onto the ruler of Undros for the first time.

Fine silver strands streaked through the King's coppery hair. His beard was entirely silver, only adding to the wisdom that radiated from his weathered face. His eyes were dark brown and cold, much like frozen mud. Mirra swallowed.

"Lord Julian," the king said, his voice echoing throughout the hall. "Welcome back." The king's dark eyes shifted to Mirra. His icy gaze melted, warming his eyes, turning the frozen mud into hot cocoa. "And We see that you've brought us a new jewel for Our court."

The king reached for Mirra's hand, placing a ghost of a kiss on the back of her palm. Up close he was even more imposing, his aura threatening to swallow her whole.

"Darling, you are frightening the poor child."

Mirra cut her eyes over the King's shoulder. The queen placed a hand on her husband's shoulder. The king chuckled, relaxing his stance. "She always ruins my fun."

His words sounded harsh, but the light and love in his eyes when he looked at his wife told another story. He took the queen's hand and placed a loving kiss on her knuckles, running his thumb over them.

"We welcome you to our home," the queen said, giving Mirra a motherly smile. "I am sorry to hear about your husband."

Mirra bowed again. "Thank you, Your Majesties. He fought well and is feasting in the halls of his fathers."

A ripple went the watching courtiers. Mirra started to pick at her thumbs. The king and queen didn't seem to notice. The queen turned and waved toward the dais. The prince and princess rose from their seats as one to join their parents.

Mirra and Lord Julian bowed again.

"Allow me to introduce my children. This is my son Gaitlan and my daughter Braelyn." The royal siblings bowed. "They will help you get settled. In the meantime, please enjoy the ball."

"With me, Viper," the king said. "We have much to discuss."

Mirra bowed again and rose to face not only royals but her target. The prince favored his father with his coppery hair and dark eyes. His stance told Mirra that he was overconfident in his abilities.

The princess' golden hair curled around her face, framing its delicate features. Her eyes, a warm brown like the queen's, were carefully empty of all emotions. She stood a step behind her brother, watching Mirra's every move.

Prince Gaitlan studied Mirra from head to toe. Whatever he saw held no interest for him. "Well, I leave you to it, dear sister."

"Mother wanted us *both* to help her get acquainted with the courts."

The prince paid his sister no heed, disappearing into the crowd with a careless wave. "But you have more experience than me, dear sister."

"Prat."

Mirra snickered. She couldn't help it. Clearly, the stress of the evening was getting to her. "Sorry, Your Highness."

Princess Braelyn smiled. "There's nothing to apologize for." She looked out at the sea of glittering people and sighed. "Let's get this over with."

Mirra trailed behind the princess like a shadow. She was introduced to nearly every noble person in the hall. Their names and titles swam around Mirra's head until her head pounded like a drum. The king and queen had retired hours ago. Mirra envied them; all she wanted to do was crawl into her new bed and sleep until noon the next day.

Her jaw cracked and popped when another large yawn forced its way out. Mirra heard the princess chuckle.

"Don't stay up on my account. I have years of practice lasting with balls. You've been on the road for months. Please retire for the evening."

"Thank you, Your Highness."

Mirra watched the princess disappear into the crowd that showed no sign of stopping anytime soon. Shaking her head at the spectacle, she turned and exited the hall. She woke a half-asleep footman to lead her back to her room.

Daisy, blurry-eyed and yawning, helped Mirra out of her ballgown and get ready for bed.

"You don't have to wait for me," Mirra said.

Daisy smiled. "Thank you, my lady. Peaceful sleep."

“And to you.”

Alone for the first time in weeks, Mirra shuffled to her bed, massaging her sore scalp. The bed was as warm and plush as she hoped it was. The soft mattress cradled her tired body, carrying her off to sleep before she had time to process everything she noticed and heard at the ball.

CHAPTER SEVENTEEN

THE EARLY MORNING AIR BURNED THE INSIDES OF MIRRA'S nose. Dawn had yet to reach the inner courtyard of the palace, allowing shadows and the frigid night air to linger a while longer. There were only five other souls strolling through the courtyard, mostly guards with a few servants. They had their tasks, and Mirra had hers.

It would take her a while to memorize the castle grounds. The castle and its grounds took up nearly the same amount of space as one of the districts below. It had taken her years to learn only a fraction of the streets and alleyways when she was a thief. She highly doubted that Lord Julian would let her take that long with the castle.

A flash of gold caught Mirra's eye. Princess Braelyn walked alone in one of the covered walkways. Her face was full of grim determination, looking none the worse for a late night of revelry.

"Good morning, Your Highness!"

Princess Braelyn paused, ire flashing across her face quickly before settling into a bland mask of politeness.

"And you, lady Mirra. I trust you slept well?"

Mirra bowed, smiling brightly. "Yes, thank you. I don't think I've ever had a more comfortable bed. Where are you off to this morning, if I may be so bold as to ask?"

Princess Braelyn's mask sharply fell. "Look, it's too early for me to pretend this morning. I don't care what your uncle wants you to do. You're not fooling anyone, so don't even try."

The princess turned on her heel and walked away, her shoulders tight and her head held high.

Well, fuck. I'm screwed.

Mirra turned when she heard a small cough behind her. A servant stood behind her, shifting on uneasy feet.

"Beggin' your pardons, my lady, but your uncle demands your presence in his study. I'm to take you there right away."

Mirra closed her eyes. *Oh gods above, kill me now!*

THE LAST TIME MIRRA HAD BEEN IN LORD JULIAN'S STUDY, she was nothing more than a twelve-year-old thief, plucked from the gallows. Now, she was a woman of eighteen, and she wasn't sure what she was anymore.

First, she'd been a farmer and hunter. There, she grew strong and learned the first shocking truth about her tattoo. The man with the scar, she'd forgotten his name, flashed briefly across her mind. She wondered if he was still alive or had the Viper finally gotten his prey.

Then she was transformed into a courtesan where she learned the art of observing, listening, and becoming someone else. And lastly, at the Keep, she learned how to dole out death by means of poisons, avoid death herself, and hone everything down to a fine point.

She may have been given an assignment, to look after the princess, but what did that make her? A hidden bodyguard? A spy? Or was she something else entirely?

"Your uncle's study is atop the stairs. I trust you can find your way?"

Mirra smiled at the servant and nodded. The servant fled, not bothering to hide his fear. Shaking her head, she began her ascent toward her master. Her knock on the door went unanswered. Cautiously, she jostled the handle. The door swung open without a sound.

"Hello?" She poked her head through the door.

The room looked much like she remembered it. It wasn't a bad room, especially with the fire crackling merrily in the hearth. What made the room even more inviting was that Lord Julian wasn't in it.

Mirra entered the room and carelessly walked around. She trailed her fingers over the numerous spines, reading their titles. *Histories of the Ancients, The Fall of the Mystics, The Purge years.* She frowned, nothing interesting.

She then turned her attention to his desk, coming to stand behind it. The papers scattered across the desk looked like nothing but reports from his agents in other countries. In Zallino, many volcanoes once thought to be dormant have started to erupt or partially erupted. Unusually, high amounts of rain in Nealet had turned the savannas to swamps. Storm's Pass was nearly impassable. Mirra returned the papers to their original placement before moving on. She attempted to open the drawers of the desk, but they were all locked. Footsteps coming up the stairs sent her scurrying to the bookcase.

Lord Julian breezed into the study, saying nothing to Mirra. A coy smile splayed across his face. "Greetings, niece. I trust your first night in the castle went well."

Mirra turned and took the seat in front of his desk. "Well enough, Uncle."

"I must admit, I am surprised you're not accompanying the princess."

Mirra began to pick at her thumbs. "She does not want me around her."

Lord Julian frowned. "Failure already. Perhaps I was wrong to choose you. Perhaps you are nothing more than a slightly intelligent thief. If you cannot handle one princess, then maybe you're better suited for other work."

Mirra's face flushed with anger. "You haven't made my job any easier. Your reputation has ruined mine. Already, I am surrounded with suspicion if not outright hatred. Perhaps you should stop being a manipulative cunt."

For three tense heartbeats, Lord Julian stared at Mirra. She swallowed but refused to break eye contact. Then, much to her surprise, Lord Julian threw his head back and laughed.

"Now there's that fire I saw in you all those years ago." He wiped his eyes. "Go and try again."

Mirra rose, still stunned that she wasn't going to be thrown in the dungeons. As she opened the door, Lord Julian spoke again. "I like you, Mirra, but fail me again, and there will be no crawling out of the hell I have planned for you."

With as much dignity as she could muster, Mirra closed the door and walked down a few flights of stairs before breaking out into a run.

MISTRESS?" DAISY STOOD AT THE FOOT OF MIRRA'S BED, a concerned look on her face. "Are you ill? Should I fetch a healer?"

Mirra stirred, rubbing her burning eyes. She only got to bed an hour before dawn. "No, I'm fine."

Daisy pursed her lips, clearly not buying it.

"I have nightmares …"

Daisy's expression softened. "About your husband?"

Mirra nodded.

"Forgive me, my lady. I'll leave you to rest."

"No, don't. I'm up now, might as well get familiar with my new home."

Daisy smiled and set out a change of undergarments for Mirra to change into. "Now what do people do for entertainment around here?"

"The Dragonian Library, my lady."

Mirra walked past the footman with a small nod in thanks. Daisy had listed several things while helping her dress, most of which Mirra had no desire to do. But the moment she mentioned the libraries, Mirra perked up.

"There are libraries in the castle?"

"Yes, several, in fact. There is a large one open for everyone, at least three smaller academic libraries specializing in alchemy, history, and lore. The royal family has one for their personal use, and a few other nobles have personal libraries as well."

Mirra shook her head. Libraries were places that one went to; she couldn't imagine having one all to herself. They were meant to be large things, like what lay behind the massive, intricately carved doors in front of her.

The footman pushed the door open for her. Walking over the threshold, all other thoughts flew from her mind like sparrows, stealing her breath with it. *This is no library; this is a treasure room!*

Every window she could see was a work of art. The light that filtered through the stained glass cast warm pools of light on the white marble floor as well as the three levels of shelving. Each ebony bookcase held more books than Mirra even realized was in the world.

Overstuff chairs and chaises were scattered strategically everywhere, tempting her to never leave.

"I looked the same way when I first came here."

Startled, Mirra turned, her hand shifting the hidden blade strapped to her side.

"I'm sorry," the speaker said. "I thought you heard me walk up. My name is Munin, fifth Binder in Resident.

It was then that Mirra registered Munin's simple garb, brown robe trimmed in cerulean bands. Her golden hair was in a long braid down her back, and her face held no signs of suffering or hardship.

Munin smiled. "Yes, I know that I'm younger than most masters. I grew up on the Isle of Mist after my mother died giving birth to me."

"I'm sorry, and your father?"

Munin shrugged. "The Abbot was the only father I ever knew. The other masters were my family."

Mirra felt a twinge of jealousy that she quickly squashed. "Thank the gods for small mercies."

Again, Munin smiled.

"Is there anything I can help you find today?"

Mirra's strange encounter her last night in Lord Julian's keep flashed through her mind. As much as she initially denied it, the truth was that she had used magic. From her tutelage under Nora, she knew the only beings in existence that used magic were the Mystics, but they were all dead now. Mirra secretly smiled.

"My late husband's people kept rich histories about their ancestors and people. It made me realized that my knowledge of my own people's history is lacking. Do you happen to have any histories from before the Great Purging?"

Munin's brow furrowed. "We do have some, but you will need to ask for permission to see them."

"Why?"

Munin hid her hands inside the sleeves of her robe. "For one, they are extremely delicate. And king Arshen the Bloody ..."

"Wasn't he kind during the Great Purging?" Mirra asked.

Munin nodded. "He put down ordinances restricting access to everything after the Purging."

"Why?"

"Because my ancestor did want future generations to see him for what he was, a warmonger and betrayer."

Mirra and Munin bowed as Princess Braelyn walked up. She studied Mirra with a thinly veiled distaste for a moment before turning her emerald eyes to Munin.

"I've finished my readings; the books are on my table."

Munin bowed again before quickly walking away from an awkward situation. Mirra wished she could do the same. She hadn't gotten enough sleep for a battle of wits.

"Are you following me."

"No."

The princess snorted. "For some reason, I find that hard to believe. Tell your uncle …"

"Tell him yourself." The words flew out of Mirra's mouth before she could stop them. Her lack of sleep the night before and the looming threat on her life hanging over her head made her a little snippy.

Braelyn blinked rapidly, the only outward sign that Mirra's words had any effect on the princess.

"I'm sorry, Your Highness," Mirra said quickly, curtsying low. "I didn't sleep well last night … everyone here … I know better …"

Mirra heard the princess chuckle. She dared to look up.

Princess Braelyn's cheeks were flushed, and her lips were pressed into a thin line. "Don't fret," she said. "I'm not going to have you thrown into the dungeons or anything." The princess studied Mirra's stunned expression for a few moments before turning to leave. "I'll leave word with the Head Binder that I gave you permission to the archives. Enjoy your research, Lady Mirra."

What the hell was that about?

Mirra's pondering was interrupted by another footman bearing a lavender envelope.

"Her Majesty wishes for you to join her tomorrow morning for breakfast."

Mirra accepted the envelope. "I am honored to accept."

I CAN'T WAIT TO GET OUT OF THESE MOURNING DRESSES, Mirra thought as she ran a finger underneath the too-tight collar of her dress. Knowing Lord Julian, he would probably demand she stay in them indefinitely, just to make her suffer. It wasn't that she wanted to wear the bright colors of the other courtiers; she just wanted a dress that wasn't made of itchy hot fabric that made her look like a demon from the Night Realm.

"Lady Mirra Ó Broin."

Mirra entered a small room and bowed. The queen, as well as the prince and princess, was already seated around a cherry wood table ladened with food.

"No need for such formalities, my dear. You're practically family; come and sit."

Mirra sat and served herself, seeing food already in front of the royal family.

"How are you finding my home?"

"Very well, Your Majesty. The libraries are especially impressive."

Prince Gaitlan snorted and proceeded to stuff food in his mouth. The queen frowned slightly before plastering a smile back on her face.

"You must see more than just the libraries, my dear. We are a world unto ourselves here, and outside the palace gates, there are shops, museums, and all other delightful places."

"I'm sure she knows that already, Mother, given who her family is."

The queen's composure cracked again, this time with the princess earning a scowl.

"Our family name does not define us. I'm sure Mirra has heard dozens of horrid things about our family."

"No, not really," Mirra said, unheard by the people around the table.

"A pale shadow in comparison to the rest of the court," Braelyn shot back. "Honestly, Mother, there's so much more to this world than you know."

"I believe I know a fair deal more than you, child. Besides, this is not the time or place for this discussion. We are not here to bicker amongst ourselves like common fishwives. We are here to help Mirra become accustomed to life here."

The three royals turned their gaze toward Mirra, causing her to choke on the bit of fruit she had started eating when it became clear that no one was paying any attention to her.

The queen beamed at Mirra before continuing. "My son is often busy with his ... friends. But I am sure that my daughter will be more than willing to spend the day with you."

Like hell she is. "You are too kind, Your Majesty."

The queen dismissed Mirra's thanks. "Thank you for joining us for breakfast. I hope to see you around the castle soon."

Mirra was the only one to jump to their feet when the queen rose and left the table.

"Thanks for backing me up, brother."

"You handled Mother well enough." The prince threw his silverware down, rising from his seat. "As always, dear sister; I leave this to you."

Prince Gailtan mockingly bowed to his sister before flashing a wink in Mirra's direction. Princess Braelyn scowled at her brother's retreating.

"Prat."

She turned her fiery gaze toward Mirra. A small sneer marred her face. Mirra felt her own face flush in response. Perhaps it was being so close to her old home, or the stress of the past few days, but the look on the princess's face sent her blood boiling.

"Don't bother," she told the princess. "I rather face my uncle at his worse than be where I'm not wanted. Don't worry your pretty little royal head over me. I can take care of myself."

Without waiting to be dismissed or even a bow, Mirra stood and walked away from the princess. "Tell your mother thanks for the meal."

Tucked away within the safety of darkness and hidden places, a shadow frowned at the retreating noble woman's back. If she wasn't too careful, her mourning garb would become her funeral dress.

Later that evening, Mirra's head swam with long-forgotten rulers, battles, and kingdoms. None of which held the answer as to why she had access to magic. She rubbed her burning eyes and rose from her seat by the fire to answer the knock at her door. Daisy stood on the other side, bearing a tray with a slightly steaming pot and a cup.

"I saw that you were still up. Perhaps some calming tea will help you sleep?"

Mirra smiled. "Thank you, Daisy. Just set it on the table."

"Do you need help getting ready for bed?"

"No, I can manage; go to bed, Daisy."

Clothed in a warm nightgown, Mirra massaged her scalp. Wearing her hair up all the time in tight braids was killing her scalp. She was half tempted to sleep with it loose but dismissed the idea, knowing she would have a mass of tangles in the morning.

Mirra was just about to crawl into her bed when she spied the teapot. She had intended on going right to sleep, but perhaps she could wrestle out the dilemma that was the princess over a cup.

She filled her cup, savoring its light flora scent and warm amber color. Holding the cup with both hands, Mirra stared out her window. The moon was only a thin sliver in the velvet sky.

Mirra sighed. From her window, she couldn't see the sloping city below.

She turned away from the window. Perhaps that was a good thing. If she saw the lights of her childhood, the temptation to run would be too strong to resist. Lamenting over what can never be, Mirra took a sip of her tea and immediately started to cough.

She stared at her cup in disbelief. There was no way in hell that Daisy would intentionally poison her. As her coughing grew more intense, Mirra scrambled toward the only trunk not unpacked. She had told Daisy not to touch it because, in the bottom, the trunk was a hidden compartment filled with poisons and their antidotes.

Mirra flung open the lid, throwing bits of fabric, clothing, and what not over her shoulder. Delicate bottles of perfume shattered behind her, releasing cloying scents of lavender, rose, and jasmine into the air.

Reaching the bottom, she dug her nails into the near-invisible seam that held the false bottom. Struggling for air, Mirra clawed at it like a wild cat. The more her throat closed, the more frantic her attempts became.

I'm going to die ... again ...

Must we always be so dramatic? a familiar voice in her head said. The darkness that lived inside her uncoiled from its slumber, reaching out for her. This time, Mirra didn't hesitate snatching the dark tendril and slamming it down on the false bottom.

Her hand became living shadow, passing through the wood like it wasn't even there. Mirra curled her hand into a fist and pulled back. Her hand, turning solid once more, ripped the false bottom out. Using her other hand, Mirra snatched up a blue tin and stuffed its contents in her mouth. She frantically chewed, racing against the encroaching darkness at the corners of her vision.

Mirra collapsed on the floor, gasping like a fish out of water. She stopped her throat from closing all the way, but it was still swollen, and using her magic intentionally left her feeling weaker than a newborn kitten.

A pair of shiny black boots entered into her field of vision. Weakly, Mirra rolled over to meet a pair of eyes: one black and cold like the depths of the Night Realm; the other glowing white and cold as the steeps of Cemont.

"I have her, you bastard," Mirra ground out before the darkness took over her, yet again.

CHAPTER EIGHTEEN

MIRRA MUMBLED IN HER SLEEP INCOHERENT THREATS TO the person who nearly took her life.

"Shush now," said a gentle voice. "You're going to be all right. Just a bout of something nasty."

Mirra's eyes fluttered open, revealing Princess Braelyn sitting at her bedside. She frowned, looking around her room. The destruction she caused in her frantic attempt to save her life was gone. Instead, her room was neat with a large fire crackling merrily in the hearth. Her heart stopped spying Lord Julian sitting in the very chair she sat in ...*just how long was I out for?*

"You've been asleep for three days," the princess said, seeing the question in Mirra's eyes. "Your maid found you in the morning." She followed Mirra's gaze toward Lord Julian. "Your uncle has been by your side nearly the entire time."

Lord Julian rose, coming over to the other side of Mirra's bed. "When you weren't taken care of by the princess, that is. I do not know how I will ever repay you for your kindness, Your Highness."

He reached across Mirra and took the princess's hand. She recoiled, pulling away and tucking her hands into the folds of her dress. From the corner of her eye, Mirra saw a ghost of a smile break out across his face.

With a small nod, Lord Julian retreated, leaving Mirra alone with the princess.

"I know he's your uncle, but he creeps me out."

Mirra shrugged. "He's a creepy guy. I guess it comes with the territory."

"What do you mean?"

"He's a spymaster. He deals with the dregs of society to lie, cheat, and steal information for your father. Sometimes he even has to remove foreign spies without causing too much fuss. He does his job well and gets scorned for it. If he failed, the outcome would be the same, so can you blame him for intentionally making you uncomfortable?"

Princess Braelyn chewed her bottom lip, guilt all over her face. Mirra swallowed back her own because the princess was right to want to keep Lord Julian as far away from her as possible.

"You're right," Princess Braelyn relented. "And I have treated you terribly too. I have not acted the way a princess is supposed to, especially to one of her subjects."

Mirra swallowed and looked down and her hands, letting her hair mask her face. "I'm not even sure I am Undrosian anymore."

"Pardon?"

"I've lived with my late husband's family for two years before marrying him. I learned to walk like them, talk like them, even worshiping their gods. After a while, it stopped being an act and became who I was."

"At least you got to see something new."

Mirra picked up her head. Princess Braelyn stared off into the distance with a look of longing on her face that cut Mirra to her core. How many times had she worn that same face staring out at the horizon with Bao?

"Princess …?"

And just like that, the look was gone. "Please call me Braelyn."

"If you insist, Braelyn."

Braelyn smiled. "I do, Mirra. Now I leave you to rest, and when you're ready, we'll visit the temple to your husband's people and make an offering."

Mirra kept the smile on her face until Braelyn left. After waiting to make sure that no one else was coming to visit her, Mirra threw the blankets back and rolled out of bed. Her legs buckled when she tried to stand, but they held her up. As shaky as a newborn foal, she tottered over to the trunk that she ripped apart. Underneath the piles of clothing and books, the shattered remains of the false bottom confirmed that she did what she remembered.

How much did he see? Did I use magic in front of him? Mirra felt sick again. With the utmost care, she went through her stash of ingredients, making sure that no one had tampered with them. As for the solutions she already made, they went straight into the toilet. She would have to replace them later.

Daisy entered after knocking gently. Her face clenched as she saw Mirra shuffle out of the bathroom. "Oh, mistress, I am so sorry!"

"What for?"

"I didn't notice you were ill!"

Mirra laughed. "I didn't even know I was ill."

That earned her a smile from her faithful maid. "Well, I'm here to remedy it all the same. Back into bed with you, and let's get some broth in you."

Mirra blanched. Her most recent poisoning made her a bit reluctant to eat something she hadn't prepared herself. She wracked her mind for a solution.

Daisy went about, completely unaware of Mirra's distress. She prattled on about what happened while Mirra was out. How the court went into a small panic thinking someone had poisoned her and then panicking again when someone mentioned that Mirra might have contracted the Sweating Sickness.

Mirra stared at the bowl of broth on her lap. She couldn't dump it beside her bed; that would be too noticeable, and Daisy would raise a fuss if she got out of bed to pour it out the window. Her panic started to rise, but so did something else, magic.

It had saved her life twice now, and she had an inclination that she'd been using it her entire life without realizing it. All the times that she was able to stay hidden, knew where things were even in complete darkness.

Mirra held her hand over the broth. Her fingers trembled. She closed her eyes, took a deep breath, and then reached inside. The dark pit of her magic curled into her touch like a cat, easing some of her fears. Keeping what she wanted in her mind, she cast a haze of billowing shadows over the bowl. Every ingredient in the broth flew into her mind, none of which were deadly in any way. Mirra released her magic, relieved.

"Best eat that before it grows cold."

Mirra picked up the bowl and slowly slurped the contents down. Daisy was shocked for a moment over Mirra's lack of decorum but quickly got over it, laughing at her mistress.

After eating, a healer came in to check on her, declaring that all Mirra needed was another day or two of rest to be back to full health. Daisy tucked Mirra into bed, wishing Mirra a good sleep before closing the door behind her.

Mirra tossed and turned for an hour before finally falling asleep. Her dreams were filled with fire and smoke so strong, so clear that when she woke the next morning, she tasted them both on her tongue.

THE STREETS WERE CROWDED AS USUAL. THRONGS OF richly dressed nobles milled around from shop to shop, spending only a fraction of their vast wealth, how he hated them.

Every day he sat on the border of the Divine District and Noble District begging for coin. Once, he had been a soldier in the king's army. He fought and bled for a cause not his own, and when he was injured too badly to continue fighting, they dismissed him. Sure, they gave him severance pay, but the doctors took that for themselves. Left with no coin and too broken to work, he lost everything.

Now those pompous, overstuffed pigeons passed by him all day without a second glance as if he was nothing. If he had the strength, he would lay waste to them all.

"Here you go."

A pretty young thing with golden hair and a kind smile put a small bag into his bowl before walking away. Her companion, a dark shadow with glowing eyes, grimaced.

"If you keep doing that, Braelyn, you're going to be mugged."

The golden one, Braelyn, laughed. "If they can make it past my mother's guards, then they've earned it."

It was then that the veteran noticed the quartet of guards in royal livery walking in the crowd. They formed a diamond of protection around the two girls.

He opened the bag. His mouth fell open at the sight of the largest amount of gold coins he'd ever seen. Braelyn should listen to her dark friend. Once word got out about her, she'd never be safe.

From the moment they left the castle, Braelyn's face glowed as brightly as the sun above. She smiled and waved at every person they passed, earning strange looks. It drove Mirra crazy. Her lips were pressed into a thin white line, and her fingers itched to hold one of her hidden blades.

"Let's not rush back to the castle after the temple," Braelyn said.

"Why?"

"I rarely get to go beyond the castle grounds. When I do, I'm usually with my mother or with a gaggle of courtiers I loathe. I want to actually enjoy the city this time."

Mirra chewed her lip. The longer they stayed out in the open, the more dangerous it was. Her job was to protect the princess. *Pretty hard to do that if she hates you.*

"Sure, know any good places?"

She was rewarded by Braelyn smiling even wider before she gave Mirra a bone-crushing hug.

I am royally fucked.

Never in a thousand lifetimes did Mirra ever think that she would ever smell the heavenly aroma that wafted out of the capital's infamous bakery, Cros Buns. *He's going to kill me tonight.*

"The court practically buzzes about this place," Braelyn said. "Let's stuff our faces."

The inside was packed, as always, so Braelyn and Mirra were forced to sit outside, next to one of the braziers. Mirra was nearly catatonic. Inside, she ran the risk of being recognized by the owner, but outside ... outside anyone could see her. She cursed the court for making her have to wear her hair up and Lord Julian for making her wear black all the time. She stood out like a sore thumb.

"What shall we get? My treat." Braelyn paused, finally noting Mirra's unease. "Is it too much?"

Mirra blinked a couple of times until she registered the princess's meaning. "There are many cities of the Stone Clans, but I don't think that even Eddany, the Capital, is as busy as Verance."

Braelyn frowned. "I'm sorry. I was so occupied by my own selfish wants that I didn't notice that."

"You aren't selfish," Mirra said, cutting her off. "If I was watched as much as you, I would probably act the same if given the smallest taste of freedom."

"Things aren't the same in Lorseca?"

"It depends. Women of Lorseca do have more freedom than most. In the Stone Clans, women are still somewhat protected; however, due to raids from the Horse Lords, all women know how to fight, ride, and survive. The freest women, I think, belong to the Horse Lords. They can be war chiefs, shamans, and ride in raids."

Braelyn's eyes were wide with envy. "You've seen so much more of the world than me. I can't imagine all the interesting people you've spoken to, foods tasted, music heard. I'd give anything to be like you."

"What's stopping you? There's plenty of interesting people here in the capital. Foreign dignitaries that stay at the palace or just outside."

Braelyn sighed. "I tried that, but my mother quickly deemed it improper." Mirra arched a brow. "She claimed I was too *impressionable* to be left to my own devices. I mean, who does she think she is! As if I am completely incapable of formulating my *own* thoughts and opinions!"

Mirra was saved by further rantings by a server coming to their table.

"Good afternoon ladies. Our specials for today are," she stopped speaking and stared at Mirra as if she were a spectator.

Mirra picked up the menu, pretending to read it. She was going to vomit. She recognized the server and she was damn sure that she recognized Mirra.

"I'll have a fruit tart. What about you, Mirra?"

Mirra swallowed her rising panic, willing her face into neutral amusement. "I think the apple fritter sounds delightful. Could we also get two spiced teas as well?"

The server recovered from her shock with a shake of her head. "Yes, of course, right away."

The rest of the afternoon went well, Mirra supposed. She listened to the princess prattle on about her life, the trappings of the court, how petty and shallow everyone was. But she was only half-listening. The majority of her focus was on the server that recognized her. Much to Mirra's dismay, she kept casting fleeting glances at their table, surety growing in her eyes each time.

Mirra was just about to rise and go after the server when Braelyn said something that caused warning bells to go off in her head.

"That's why I want to go to the lower districts, to really see where the people are hurting so we can actually help them."

"That's not a good idea."

Braelyn frowned at Mirra who quickly back-peddled. "I'm not saying they don't need help, but they won't take it. They may not have much, but they have their pride. Some, if not most, will not take a government hand out because they hate you. Let's not even start with the crime bosses and gangs."

"Those men and organizations only succeed because good people are too afraid to do something about it."

Mirra snorted. "People who think like you often end up missing or dead."

Now Braelyn's face flushed scarlet. "You seem to know quite a bit about the underworld and its workings."

"My uncle *is* the King's spymaster. You don't think I've seen the reports or heard the stories?"

"I suppose." Braelyn went back to her tart, sullen and silent.

Mirra sighed, scanning the crowd for the server. She spied her walking around the side of the shop, heading to the water pump in the back. It was now or never.

"And speaking of my uncle, he loves apple fritters too. I think I'll order another to take back."

Braelyn said nothing as Mirra rose from their table and wove through the crowd. Thankfully, her back was turned toward the front of the shop, giving Mirra the freedom to do what she needed.

The server vigorously pumped water from below into a large barrel. When full, she would have to wiggle it back near the back of the shop, reattaching a secondary pump for inside.

She paused, shaking out her arms before reaching into her pocket and pulling out a rolled cigarette.

Acrid smoke drifted through the air when the server exhaled. Silently, Mirra walked up behind the girl, releasing one of her hidden blades with a flick of her wrist.

"Scream, and you're dead," Mirra said, pressing the blade against the girl's throat.

"I don't have any money."

"I don't want your money." Mirra spun the girl around so that they faced each other.

The girl's eyes widened. "You're supposed to be dead."

Mirra clenched her jaw. "That girl did die."

The girl shook her head. "No, I remember you. You used to come in with that other boy, Bao."

Mirra quickly slashed the blade across the girl's cheek, leaving a thin red line, no more than a scratch.

"She is dead. Keep saying otherwise, and so will you and everyone you love or ever talked to." Mirra shifted her arm, letting the sleeve fall back enough to display the snake encircling her wrist.

The girl's eyes turned into saucers, wide and afraid. "I'm sorry; I was mistaken."

Mirra smiled cruelly, sheathing her blade before patting the girl on the same cheek she scratched. "Have a nice day."

"Are you ready to go, Braelyn?" Mirra asked as she walked up with a second apple fritter wrapped up in a pretty box.

Braelyn sighed. "If we must."

"We can always come out again."

"Don't hold your breath."

They picked up a royal carriage in the Divine District. The ride back more subdued than their ride out. Braelyn watched the city roll past her window with a pained expression. The longer Mirra watched her, the more diminished the princess became. Her heart ached for the princess with a fiery spirit who was forced to live in a gilded prison.

"You should be more discreet when coming to me. The princess will surely suspect something if you come to me after being with her."

Mirra frowned at her master who hadn't even bothered to look up from his work. She flung the box at him, scattering his papers. He then glanced up, ire flashing briefly in his two-toned eyes.

"I had a good excuse."

Lord Julian fingered the binding of the box. "Indeed. Anything interesting happened on your outing?"

Mirra stood straighter, meeting his gaze dead on. "Nothing interesting at all."

CHAPTER NINETEEN

Did you know that in Bardon they have schools that are open for everyone, regardless of their station?"

Mirra grunted from behind her pile of histories, maps, scrolls, and other bits of her research. Nearly every day since heading to the temples, Braelyn and Mirra were consumed by the library. Braelyn gobbled up book after book about countries and cultures her mother deemed too strong for a princess. Mirra continued to search for any explanation about her magic and how to use it.

Braelyn glanced at Mirra over the book in her hands with a mischievous smirk. "They also have flying dragons that they use to build their great halls."

"That's nice."

Braelyn laughed, bringing Mirra to the present.

"What?"

"Did you even hear a word I said?"

Mirra smiled. "Not really."

Braelyn shook her head, walking over to Mirra's horde of information. "What are you looking for?"

Mirra shuffled the pages with half scratched sigils underneath some long-dead priest's journal entries. "Mystics lived in this land for thousands of years before we landed. They had a rich culture and magic. Where did they go?"

Braelyn leaned against the desk and trailed her finger over an illuminated page. "If you believe the histories, they were all killed during the Purging." Mirra slumped back into her chair. "But," Braelyn went on, "there are stories about how small groups managed to make it through the mountains to safety. Legend has it that the descendants of those survivors travel the continent in nomadic bands, only staying in one place long enough to get back at the humans that took everything from them."

Mirra snorted, rubbing her burning eyes. It was time for a break.

"Or at least that's what my nurse would always read to me."

All exhaustion and pain dropped like a stone into still water. "Your who did what?"

"She would read to all the children. Her favorite book was *Tales of the Ice Hunter*. It was all about this knight that dedicated his life to hunting down and killing the Mystics that escaped. It was full of him finding them causing trouble, then defeating them."

"Could I borrow it?"

Braelyn shrugged. "I don't see why not. It's somewhere in the nursery, I think. I'll have a servant bring it to you later.

Mirra thanked the young maid, closing the door behind her. The book was smaller than she hoped, barely a hundred pages long. Its brown leather cover was well worn as if handled roughly and often for many years.

She flipped through the pages, stopping to read a random passage.

Sir Thomas the Just saw the markings carved in the tree and knew that the devilish Mystics were nearby. They always carved the runes near their camps to shield themselves from sharp eyes. Sir Thomas pricked his finger with his dagger, drawing a rune of his own over the one he found. It flashed briefly before the blood vanished as if it never was. They would never see him coming.

She groaned. The book was nothing more than Purging propaganda. Mirra tossed the book onto her bed before slumping into her chair by the fire. Her mind drifted back to her parents for the first time in years. Just who were they and why did they abandon her?

Her eyes fell on the book lying on her bed. It might be a steaming load of horseshit, but under it all just might be a few kernels of truth.

"My lady, were you up all night?"

Mirra blinked up at Daisy from her position on the floor. "Not quite."

Daisy slowly walked further into the room, careful for the field of papers scattered around Mirra. She didn't recognize any of the symbols sketched on the pages, but whatever they were, they made her feel uneasy.

"Sorry, just got caught up in research. Could you maybe draw up a hot bath?"

Daisy bowed, grateful for a bit of normalcy and rushed off.

Mirra placed her hands against the small of her back and stretched. Her back popped, releasing the small ball of pressure that had been building all night. Her mind was brimming with everything she'd discovered. A hot bath was just the thing to help her put it all into place.

Fragrant steamed curled from the milky tub. Mirra leaned her head back and closed her eyes. The warm water helped to ease the small bits of tension still lingering in her joints. She let her mind wander.

Mystic blood.

The only explanation for her ability to cast magic was that she had Mystic blood flowing through her veins. Only the Mystics and those who carry their bloodline have the ability to channel the magic of the world. There were cases of Mystic and humans mating and passing the traits on their offspring. Although its appearance was unpredictable in later generations.

Though the mages and teachers were long gone, their teachings remained.

Three books out of millions; that's all she had to learn about her heritage and her abilities. *The Book of the Moon, Song of Mist, The Chronicles of Caltharis.* Hopefully, the Draconian Library or any library in the castle had at least one of them. Unfortunately, Mirra didn't have time to search for them. It would take her years to possibly even find one. But she had the next best thing; a small journal.

During one of her outings with the princess, Mirra purchased a small black traveling journal. In it, she jotted down the few runes and spells she gleaned from the histories and from legends. Now all she needed was a safe place to practice.

CEMETERIES TRULY ARE AMAZING THINGS, SILENT FORESTS of stones and sorrow. Many secrets were buried under the earth and spoken aloud to those who no longer have a voice. The perfect place for a budding mage to practice without certain people finding out.

"How ya doing, Jacob?" Mirra said, dropping her things unceremoniously on top of a sarcophagus. Some people would have urged her to respect the dead. Why? She had no idea. The dead were dead; what did they care about the living anyways?

Mirra pulled out a stick of charcoal. On the door, she sketched a wide diamond with a large x running through it. At the top and bottom of the diamond, she added simple eyes before adding crescents topped but dots. This was one of the first runes she learned to cast—the rune for protection against discovery. After sketching the rune, Mirra placed her hand on the rune and pushed a bit of her magic into it, activating the rune. Now no one could hear her or enter the mausoleum until she washed away the rune.

Safely guarded against discovery, Mirra stood in the center of the space and summoned her personal darkness. It swirled and coiled around her like smoke, stopping only when it covered her entire body. Using a finger, she traced another rune in the air. A broken piece of marble rose into the air. A fine shine of sweat glistened across her brow. Keeping her focus on the floating marble, she drew another rune, and the marble was consumed by fire.

Beads of sweat now poured down her face. Her eyes burned with the need to blink. She framed the burning marble with two hands, her world zeroing in on keeping both spells active. Both her arms shook with effort until she dropped them by her side, exhaling.

The fire extinguished instantly and the broken marble fell to the floor in a blackened heap. Mirra smiled; that was the first time she'd ever used two spells at once. She leaned back against Jacob's sarcophagus, utterly exhausted.

"Did you see that, Jacob? Two runes at once. Well, three if you count the one on the door." She rubbed the heel of her palm into her eyes. "Might not see me for a few days. That tired me out something fierce."

Mirra stood up, swaying slightly. "See ya around."

The night air was sharp and sweet. Mirra's breath came out as little clouds from her lips. She wrapped her cloak tighter around her body, grateful for its warmth. A massive yawn pushed its way from her mouth. *Time to go to bed.*

As she walked along the icy stone path, Mirra heard something that made her cringe, a rowdy group of noble men. From their loud and rambunctious voices and given the time of night, they were clearly drunk. Mirra swore, lingering in the shadows until they passed. She could have taken an alternative route, but she wanted to get to bed as humanly soon as possible.

Her frustration grew when she recognized one of the men in the group, Prince Gaitlan.

"Come on," one of the youths goaded. "Just one bag; it doesn't even have to be a large one."

The prince swayed on his feet, laughing and frowning in random intervals. "Why do we need it? I'm the prince! They give me credit everywhere."

Another youth, not quite as drunk as the others, threw his arm around the prince's shoulder. "You don't want your name attached to where we're going. What's the problem? Isn't all the coin in the treasury yours by default?"

Prince Gaitlan's face contorted with drunken thoughts. "Not really. Where are we going again?"

The not so drunk noble sighed. "The Den. Now, go fetch us some spending money like a good little princeling."

Mirra scowled in the darkness. The Den was bonedust den with the reputation for robbing its patrons.

"No," the prince said a tad bit more assertive. "I'm going to bed."

The prince turned his back on the group. The one that had tried to get the prince to steal from the crown pulled a dagger from his side, its blade shimmering in the firelight. He lunged toward the prince. Mirra dropped her bag, springing into action using her magic in a surprisingly new way.

She momentarily became a shadow herself. The darkness she'd hid in swallowed her whole, depositing her clear across the open space right behind the group of young nobles. When fully corporeal again, she drew the hidden daggers from her sleeves, slashing at the two closest youths. Her blades slashed across their backs, doling just enough damage to incapacitate without killing, sending them to the ground with twin thuds.

The noble with the dagger spun as did the prince, their eyes widening at the sight of Mirra with bloody daggers and the two fallen youths at her feet.

"Mirra, what?" the prince managed to get out before his friend launched himself at Mirra.

Their daggers meet with a clang, forcing Mirra to spin away or risk the larger youth gaining the upper hand. They circle each other until the youth lashes out again. Mirra deftly dodged his attack, catching the hilt of his dagger, twisting it out of his grip.

"If you leave now, I'll let it go," Mirra swore, her blades still at the ready.

"Who are you to tell me what to do?" The noble drew a short sword from under his tunic.

Mirra swore again, crouching into a fighting position, wishing she was in pants instead of a dress.

The courtyard was filled with the sound of clashing metal. In the distance, Mirra could hear the palace guard rousing. She needed to finish the fight soon or risk everything. In her distracted state, the young noble managed to get past her guard, cutting her arm.

Mirra cried out, dropping on her blades. Pressing his advantage, the noble jabbed at her legs, causing her to fall.

"Women are weak," the noble sneered as he loomed over her. "You are a pretty thing; shame we hadn't met sooner. I think I would have enjoyed taking a tumble with you."

He raised his blade for a killing blow. Mirra flung out her uninjured hand, sending a wave of blackness out. The noble flew across the courtyard, striking a pillar. Even from halfway across the courtyard, Mirra heard his spine snap. A terrible crunching sound magnified by the silence that followed.

Mirra and the prince stared at the fallen noble in mutual shocked silence. Heedless of the encroaching palace guard. It was the prince who broke the spell.

"Who, what are you?"

His face was a mixture of horror and fear. Mirra shakily got to her feet and calmly walked over the prince who stumbled away from her. Mirra paused for a brief moment, hurt by his reaction. She picked up her blades, resheathing them before reaching out for the prince again. He scurried backward, catching the heel of his boot against an uneven bit of stone. He windmilled his arms to no avail. He hit his head on the unforgiving stone, losing all consciousness.

A cry of alarm rings out before she can help. Alarm bells chime, destroying the calm of the evening as guards start to pour into the courtyard. Mirra turned and ran for the nearest shadow, willing it to take her somewhere away from all the commotion. She emerged near her room, crashing into the wall, knocking down a painting in the process. Fortunately, no one was around to see or hear. She quickly hung the painting back up, not caring if it was crooked or not. The only thing that mattered was getting to the safety of her room.

Mirra kicked open the trunk at the foot of her bed, ripping her incriminating dress off and stuffing it inside. Her blades followed suit before burying them all under a mass of blankets. Luckily, the wound on her arm was superficial. She treated it with a mild healing salve before wrapping a bandage around it. Then, she unbound her hair, tossing it before slipping into a nightgown.

She had just grabbed a shawl to throw around her shoulders, further hiding her wound, when a fist pounded on her door. Quickly rubbing her eyes for good measure, Mirra opened the door wide enough for her to peek out.

The palace guard on the other side quickly registered her garb, messy hair, and sleep-rimmed eyes. "Pardon the intrusion, my lady, but I need to inspect your chambers."

Mirra clutched her shawl closer to her body. "Why?"

The guard's eyes softened a fraction. "Just routine. There has been a disturbance."

Mirra made a show of chewing her lip, still uneasy, but let the guard in. He took three steps in the room, eyes scanning for anything he deemed out of the ordinary.

"Best keep your windows and doors locked tonight."

Mirra nodded, willing her face to pale. She locked her door behind the guard, falling into her chair by the fire.

Gods above, how am I going to get myself out of this mess?

MARTIN OF GRASHON; THAT WAS THE NAME OF THE NOBLE that Mirra killed with her magic. The healers said that his spine had been fractured in three places, causing him to die almost instantly. They said he died without pain, a small blessing for his grieving mother.

Hundreds of the city's best and visiting dignitaries turned out for the funeral. For once, Mirra blended into the crowd, just another face in a sea of black.

The priest and priestesses of the Yulla, the Dark Mother, sang the song of the dead, beseeching her to judge the youth kindly, allowing him to enter the waters of rebirth to walk the earth again.

Prince Gaitlan served as a bearer for the man who would have killed him if Mirra hadn't intervened. Perhaps he remembered nothing from that night. He hadn't treated Mirra any differently.

"You did well," Lord Julian said.

Mirra scowled, keeping her eyes on the funeral procession.

"How ever did you manage to break his spine so thoroughly?"

"Leverage."

Lord Julian softly chuckled. "Don't tell me you're feeling guilty?"

"Bastard had it coming."

Mirra could see Lord Julian studying her from the corner of her eye. "Does he remember?"

"No." *I don't think so.*

Later that evening, Mirra sat in front of a fire, reading a book that had nothing to do with lost lineages, magic, or anything. It had been so long since she read anything simply for the joy of reading.

Her pleasant evening was destroyed by Prince Gaitlan walking into her room as if it were his own.

"What the hell?"

"I still don't know how you did it," he said. Dread building in her stomach. "That night's still a little hazy. But I know it was you who killed him."

Mirra said nothing, swallowing the words that threatened to spill from her mouth.

"I guess I should thank you for that."

That shocked a response out of her. "Why are you even friends with people like that?"

Prince Gaitlan frowned. "What else is there? It's not like you're any better. There's more to you than you let on. My sister likes you, so there's nothing I can do to stop you from being near her. But let me warn you now; you hurt her, and there will be no place that is safe."

The prince turned to leave, pausing in the doorway. "You may have saved my life, but I know your secret, and if you want me to keep it, you'll do a favor."

"No, I won't," Mirra spat. "We're even."

The prince laughed coldly. "Not even close. You'll do the favor, or you can find out just how hard the hammer falls on those who dare to kill a noble."

CHAPTER TWENTY

For two weeks, the prince "mourned" his friend.

He and the rest of his little group of friends drank, fought, and whored their way through the districts. While his escapades were brushed off initially as grief, now, there were whispers about his rumored depravity, with a few wondering if that is as truly killed young Martin.

Mirra watched his antics with growing resentment. Whenever the prince came around, he would smile and wink at her. She, however, fought the urge to smash her fist against his face.

If Braelyn noticed, she kept her opinions to herself. Like her brother, the princess had been causing waves of discontent but for a very different reason. In retaliation for the death of one of their own, the noble class descended from their homes on high, administering their own brand of justice. Crossed blades rang out from the Divine District all the way down to the docks. Innocent people were caught between enraged nobles and those brave enough to push back. It had gotten so bad that the king issued a curfew for all his citizens. The fighting stopped, but the resentment lingered, festering like a wound. In response to all the needless violence, Braelyn stood before the council of elders and shamed them all.

"It was nobles who stirred the pot, not the people," Braelyn said, scowling at the gathered old men like petulant children.

Lord Yennic, Martin's father, leaned forward in his chair, his knuckles white. "You are mistaken, princess. Those miscreants stole into our home and killed my son. They would have killed your brother, too, if not for the guard."

Braelyn shook her head. "We do not know who sent the assassin. They got away. For all we know, it could have been another court."

The old men laughed, but Braelyn persisted. "I understand your hurt, Lord Yennic, but hurting the innocent will not bring your son back."

The oldest of the elders folded his hands under his chin and spoke. His voice soft with age, with an undertone that hinted at a warrior's past. "What do you want from us, princess?"

Braelyn inclined her head at the man. "To bring those responsible for the first attacks forward. Present them to the court so they may answer for the suffering they have caused."

"And why should we do that?" an elder scoffed.

"To show the rest of the kingdom that no one is above the law, especially those at the pinnacle of society."

The room fell silent. Mirra shifted in her seat at the far end of the chamber. Only the princess was allowed to stand before the council without summons. For a single heartbeat, Mirra thought that the lords would do as Braelyn laughed. But that hope was shattered when every member of the council started to laugh.

To her credit, the only emotion Braelyn showed was a slight raise in her chin and the hard glint in her eyes.

"Little girl," one of the men said with a laugh. "You may be the princess, but you know nothing about the intricacies of justice. Why don't you go back to what you're good at and leave the rest to us?"

Mirra stood from her seat, striding across the hall to stand by her friend. *Friend.* The word wracked through her. Until that moment, she'd never even considered the fierce and kind-hearted princess a friend.

The room fell silent when she stood next to the princess, taking her hand in hers. Mirra turned her ice blue eyes on the council, calling on her magic for the first time in weeks, making her eye shimmer slightly with power.

"Enjoy your seats while you can, my lords, because if you continue to carry on this way, the people will rise."

"We have the gods' favor," Lord Yennic sneered.

"And yet your son died."

Lord Yennic sprung from his seat, his face crimson. "What do you know of it? My son was taken from me! I am owed my vengeance!"

It was Mirra's turn to chuckle. "Life isn't easy. It's hard, cruel, and doesn't owe you a gods' damned thing. Not good fortune, a peaceful life, or the life of those you love."

"Get out!"

Mirra opened her mouth to argue, but Braelyn gently squeezed her hand, warning her not to push further. Braelyn bowed to the council. Mirra did not. She turned heel and walked away. She heard the grumbling behind her and didn't care. *Dark Mother, take those pompous bastards. Braelyn is the only noble that actually gives a damn about the rest of us. Shame her brother came first; otherwise, she would have actually made a difference.*

"Thank you," Braelyn said, breaking Mirra out of her thoughts.

She waved Braelyn's thanks off. "Someone needed to put those bastards in their place."

Braelyn chuckled. "You should have seen their faces when you walked away. I thought Lord Tannerwen was going to burst into flames."

"Who's that?"

"The really old guy."

"I'm surprised I didn't give him a heart attack."

Braelyn threw her head back and laughed. Mirra smiled. It had been a long time since she had a friend.

LORD JULIAN WAS PISSED.

Mirra schooled her face into an empty mask as he paced behind his desk, ripping into her for her action in the council chambers.

"Your assignment was to temper the princess, not join her! The moment you left, the lords bombarded me in my office, demanding I do something about my disrespectful niece."

A pleased sort of smirk broke through her mask. Lord Julian moved around his desk faster than she'd anticipated. His eyes burned with rage and something else. As quick as a viper, he lashed out, but Mirra was faster.

Pushing with her feet, she caused her chair to topple backward. Using the momentum, she rolled backward, landing in a crouch near the door. She felt her magic rising in her defense. *No, he can't know.* Her magic settled back into the core of her being, just like a sullen child told they couldn't go play.

"Don't you dare mock me, girl," Lord Julian snapped. "I haven't worked this hard for some *slave* to ruin it all."

"What?"

Lord Julian fell back into a relaxed pose, straightening his tunic before running his hand through his hair. "Certain people need to be steered into their appropriate place for the betterment of the kingdom. Rein her in, or I will get someone else to do it for you."

Mirra stood, placing the chair upright again. "As you wish, *master*." Her voice quivered with simmering rage. She flung the door wide and stomped down the stairs.

Prick, prick, prick. The same word flashed through her with each step down the winding staircase. She shouldn't have reined in her magic. She should have released it, sending him crashing into the wall.

The sickening crack of a spine against stone echoed in her mind, followed by the image of a lifeless body falling to the ground. But it wasn't Lord Martin; it was Braelyn, with her golden hair cascading around her bloody face, her green eyes wide and empty. In the shadows behind the pillar, Lord Julian smiled viciously.

"No," Mirra cried out, shaking her head to dispel the vision. She would never let that happen. She would swallow her pride and suffer instead of giving The Viper a new deadly weapon that had already claimed a life and got away with it.

There you are."

Mirra rolled her eyes. Prince Gaitlan swaggered toward her, linking an arm in hers.

"At least you've showered and changed."

"Very funny, my little assassin."

Mirra jerked her arm out of his. "I'm your nothing. What do you want?"

The prince smiled over Mirra's objection. "I'm calling in the favor."

Mirra blinked three times before responding. "No."

She brushed past the prince, wanting a bottle of wine to drown herself in. When did her life become so fucked!

"I heard you managed to piss off Lord Yennic quite thoroughly today. If he knew who *really* caused the death of his beloved son …"

Mirra glared at the prince over her shoulder. "Fine, bastard. What do you want?"

"I need you, in disguise, to accompany me to a tavern tonight."

"That's all?"

The prince nodded. "It's in a seedy part of town, and I don't want a repeat of before. You come, keep us from getting killed, and we're even."

Mirra chewed the inside of her mouth, thinking. "Fine, what's the tavern?"

"The Gilded Lily."

Can this day get any worse?

It was just as she remembered. Even the air smelled the same. Mirra closed her eyes and breathed in the air of her youth, letting the familiar sounds and smells transport her back through the years to when her biggest concern was stealing enough for the tithe. A high-pitched giggle broke the spell. Mirra frowned at the woman responsible, just one of three women purchased for the night.

The women—two brunettes, one blonde—flashed empty smiles at the young noblemen they were paired with. Their dresses were a tad bit nicer than common streetwalkers but still left little to the imagination, giving away their true identities, no matter what lies they spewed from crimson painted lips.

"Smile," Prince Gaitlan ordered her. "You're on the arm of the Crown Prince of Undros, accompanied by sons from *all* the most important families of the noble class. Stop looking like you're heading for the gallows."

"What do you know?"

The prince frowned down at Mirra. "You sound like you've been to the lower districts before. I thought you'd never seen the city before."

Mirra silently berated herself. "I've heard the rumors," she quickly lied.

Prince Gaitlan laughed, throwing his head back. "So have I; that's why I've brought you, my dear Lady Savage."

He tried to pull her in close, possibly to plant a kiss on Mirra's cheek. She jabbed him in the stomach, stomping away to cool her temper.

He doesn't know. He doesn't know. Mirra repeated the phrase over and over in her head to prevent her from killing the heir to the throne. She paused near an empty shop, it's windows black and empty, and took a deep breath. She had taken precautions before going out. Her hair flowed loosely around her face. Her dress, while simple in appearance, held a special feature. If a fight broke out, or Mirra needed more mobility, all she needed to do was pull at a thread along the sides of her dress, and it would fall away. The final precaution was her eyes. Using the special dye Nora gave her, she darkened her eyes to a more natural shade.

Hopefully, if someone thought they recognized her face, her company, darker eyes, and the fact that she was supposed to be dead would convince them otherwise.

"Just where do you think you're going?" Prince Gaitlan grabbed Mirra, his fingers painfully digging into her arm. She looked up at him, fire blazing in both their eyes. "You do not walk away from me."

Mirra swung her arm around, breaking his grip and opened her mouth to speak, but someone beat her to it.

"She does whatever she pleases."

Ice ran down Mirra's spine. There was something familiar about the voice. Something that tugged on her memory, stirring up feelings too complex for her to cess out fully. She turned, her hands going for hidden blades and quick releases.

But when she saw who stood behind her, all plans flew out of her head.

Bao, whole and strong, scowled at the prince. "I don't care what you paid for her; if you damage the merchandise, there will be consequences." Bao's once familiar eyes shifted to Mirra. If he recognized her, his face gave away nothing. He looked at the prince and his party, plastering a merchant's smile on his face. "Come and have a drink on me, my friends."

Bao linked his arm through Mirra's, steering her toward the Gilded Lily. Numbly, she heard the bemused murmur of the prince and his party at her back, but it meant nothing to her. She was a tiny fishing boat caught on the sea during a storm. If not for the steady pressure of Bao's arm under her hand, she would have been lost to storm inside her.

The epitome of a gracious host, Bao sat the prince and his party at one of the tables closest to the fire. Mirra noted the absence of the bossman's throne. Perhaps he only brought it out on tithe night.

"Not you, girl." Mirra arched a brow. Bao wrapped his hand around her arm, though not as hard as the prince, and steered her to a table across the room. Tucked into a small shadowy corner, the table could only sit two people. Bao took the seat facing the room, forcing Mirra to sit with her back to it.

"Don't even think about going for your knives, Mirra. That would cause a fuss, and we have a bit to talk about."

Mirra's stomach dropped. She opened her mouth to lie, but Bao cut her off.

"You were my best friend, even though you were a bitch. There's no way in this world that I would ever forget your face, no matter what you do to mask it."

Bao's eyes blazed with anger, confusion, and hurt. Mirra looked down at her lap in guilt.

"Don't say anything. If word gets back to Jax, he'll have me killed."

Bao snorted. "You don't have to worry about the bossman."

"Why not?"

"Because I'm the bossman now."

"Wait … what?"

Bao leaned back in his seat, a bemused light in his eyes. Mirra's breath hitched, seeing a familiar expression on a face different from the one in her memories.

"Tell me yours, and I'll tell you mine."

Mirra raised her left hand toward the bar, signaling for two pints. The hem of her sleeve fell back, revealing the serpent encircling her wrist. She felt Bao's gaze narrowed on her mark.

"That explains it all right."

Mirra flashed him a small half-smile. When the pints arrived, Bao chucked his in three large gulps and handed it back to the barmaid. "Keep them coming."

He chucked half of his second before diving into his tale.

"When you got caught, we asked Jax if he was going to try and get you out. We told him that you were integral to our success, and we were only there because he asked for us. He, of course, laughed, saying that he wouldn't waste time and men on freeing a blade that got taken. That's when I realized he didn't give a shit about any of us. That we were slaves to him."

"I decided right then and there to take him down. We had to play nice. If he thought for a second that we were trying to move against him, each of us would find ourselves dead. It took three years. Three years of secret meetings, planning, and gathering allies. But in the end, he fell as did most of his supporters. The rest are either laying low or left the city." Bao shrugged, taking another sip of his pint.

"Where are the others?"

"After things settled, Em left. She'd met this nice farm boy and got married. She lives a quiet life somewhere in the country. She sends letters from time to time."

Mirra closed her eyes and smiled. She could picture Em, her hair shining in sunlight surrounded by squawking birds finally at peace.

"Sorro ran away with that girl that he fancied from the brothel. Last letter I got from him was from a small town near Noble Lake. I'm pretty sure he went back to his people."

"I thought he said he would never go back?"

"She ran away the night of her auction. Leaving the kingdom was the only way they would be able to live in peace."

"What about Tull and Kril?"

Bao's face softened, causing Mirra's stomach to sour. "They stayed with me. Tull is my second, and Kril—he was killed last year."

"What happened?"

"Some John had been going around, beating the prostitutes nearly to death. Kril tracked the guy, found him, and the two duked it out. Kril killed the guy, some brute from Cemont, but later died from his wounds."

Mirra tried to swallow her rising grief, but it got stuck in her throat. She chugged the rest of her pint, washing it down.

"So ... The Viper? That's got to be an interesting story."

Mirra absentmindedly traced the tattoo with her finger. "I'm not sure how much I can actually tell you."

"Try me."

She opened her mouth, but nothing came out. The tattoo flashed, sending sharp needles of pain up her arm. She hissed, covering it, lest the flash draw unwanted attention."

Bao cursed in his mother tongue. He wrapped his hand around hers, sliding in close to speak between clenched teeth. "Why do you have a magic tattoo?"

"I didn't know what it was when I got it," Mirra hotly whispered back. "That's how he's able to control us. I don't know where he learned it."

"But humans can't."

"I know," Mirra said. She placed her hand on top of her friend's.

"You should have died." Mirra jerked away. Bao's eyes simmered. "You should have died than let that, that *monster* put his unnatural brand on you."

"You don't get to judge me, Bao. I was twelve, facing the gallows. You don't get to make me feel bad for surviving. I'm not the one who waged war for revenge or turned my back on everything I knew."

Bao opened his mouth to retort, but something over Mirra's shoulder caught his eye. "Looks like one of your masters is leaving. Wouldn't want to get left behind."

Mirra rose and fell instep behind the prince and his companions. Prince Gaitlan scowled at Mirra, but his gaze softened when he noticed the pain on her face. He looked at the man still sitting half-cloaked in shadows. He sucked on a tooth, running through the complexities and contradictions of the woman who saved his life.

THE WHOLE CASTLE WAS BUZZING WITH EXCITEMENT. Midwinter was fast approaching. Not only was there going to be a ball, but it also was the prince's twenty-first birthday. On the night of the ball, the king could proclaim his son the new ruler of Undros and step down, staying on as part of the new king's council until he found his feet.

If Prince Gaitlan was a prat before, he was a total ass now. He tempered his drinking and whoring slightly but not enough to quell the worried whispering that he was too wild, too self-indulgent to successfully run a country. Not everyone was bothered by the prince's antics. Many held firm to the belief that once the crown sat on his head, he would settle, taking on the responsibilities and duties of his father.

Mirra was firmly in the first category. The more she watched the prince and his band of miscreant nobles, the worse she felt about the future of the country. Not that she had an overbearing sense of national pride or anything like that. She lived in Undros and couldn't leave, thanks to the man who held her life in thrall by magic. If the country went tits up, there was nothing she could do about it.

What the king thought about his son or the whispers of the court, he kept to himself. In every public setting, he presented himself as nothing but calm and pleasant. However, Mirra's keen eyes picked up on the faintest hint of a frown whenever the king watched his son swaying about the castle, face flushed and eyes glazed. If the prince was crowned on his birthday like he'd expected, Mirra would be highly surprised.

"I do hope everything goes smoothly tonight." Braelyn smoothed imaginary wrinkles off her dress. Her hands flew to her hair, patting it apprehensively.

Mirra swatted her hands down. "You'll mess it up if you keep at it. Everything will be fine, you'll see."

Braelyn mumbled, still not convinced. Mirra just smiled brighter, hoping to bring her friend's mood around.

"I'm happy I'm out of mourning in time for the ball," she said, switching subjects. "I didn't think I would miss colors so much."

Braelyn genuinely smiled. "Yes, that green suits you nicely."

"As is yours." And she meant it.

Braelyn's dress reminded Mirra of snow. It wasn't a true white but close. Hundreds if not thousands of crystals had been stitched into intricate swirls along the sleeves, bodice, and hem. Her golden hair was pinned up in an elaborate braid, with a few strands left strategically out to frame her face. To Mirra, the princess looked like a walking snow sprite, bright, shimmering, and beautiful.

As bright as Braelyn's dress was, Mirra's was dark, though not black. Her dress was a deep green, similar to the evergreens of the northern mountains. Her dress's accents were bright green holly leaves with blood-red berries at her collar, bodice, and hem. Mirra's hair fell free in dark waves, with the sides pinned back by rubies.

"You two are a vision," the queen said, clasping her hands together. "You look like you were meant for each other."

Braelyn and Mirra curtsied, both preening over her praise.

"Thank you, Mother."

"Your Majesty is too kind."

The queen waved them off before ushering them toward the nearest, and presumably single, men at ball. Despite herself, Mirra had fun. The ballroom was a sight, decked out in silver, green, and red. For once, she blended in with the crowd, although a few people opted for black attire. The band played one jaunty tune after another. Couples spun about the dance floor like fairy, bright and shimmering underneath the warm glow of a thousand candles and tinted lanterns. Laughter rang out from every corner as people toasted and celebrated their successes from the year and the promises of the next.

The night was so pleasant that Mirra forgot who she was supposed to pretend to be and simply was.

"And then I saw this eight-point buck," said Carron, one of the young noblemen in their group. "I wanted to bag him, but he was about 100 yards out, too far to shoot."

Mirra snorted. The group turned and stared at her, even Braelyn. "Most bows have an accurate range of 200 yards."

Carron's face flushed with embarrassment. "What would *you* know about hunting with bows?"

The other youths chuckled, rallying behind their comrade. Braelyn frowned.

"Mirra lived amongst the Stone Clans of Lorseca. Their women fight and hunt alongside their men."

"Prove it."

Mirra studied Carron from his expensive boots to the top of his dark curly locks. Although his face and posture said that he didn't think much of Mirra's archery abilities, the truth behind his eyes told a different story. He desperately wanted people to think well of him. Mirra had challenged his ability and so his manhood. To save face, he had to meet the challenge but act like he thought it was beneath him. *I could use that*, she thought, already forming a plan to lose but in such a way that only Carron would know and hold that over his head.

Her stomach soured. *I'm not like that. I'm not* him.

The dread of what she was about to do settled like a stone in the pit of her stomach. She plastered a vacant smile on her face. "Another time. Let's just enjoy the evening."

Carron smiled arrogantly. "If you say so." Pride appeased, the group fell back into easy conversation, drifting off toward the banquet table for food and drink. Braelyn fell instep next to Mirra.

"You could have destroyed his pride."

Mirra shrugged. "Not worth it. Not tonight anyways. Why ruin a perfectly good party?"

Braelyn laughed, shaking her head. "Just when I think I have you figured out."

Mirra laughed as well, looping her arm through Braelyn's. It was going to be a great night.

"Prince Gaitlan."

The entire ballroom turned to stare. Prince Gaitlan stood atop the grand staircase, smiling down at the hundreds of faces gathered below. Even from where she stood, Mirra could see the way the prince swayed on his feet, the flush across his cheeks. And when he spoke, she noted a slight slurring. *He's roaring drunk …*

"Thank you all for coming to celebrate my birthday!"

A small pattering of applause filled the awkward silence. The prince was too drunk to notice that the applause was only polite, not enthusiastic. He also failed to notice the growing concern on the courtier's faces as he stumbled down the stairs and across the ballroom toward his father.

"Father, I have arrived!"

The king frowned. "So you have." Prince Gaitlan beamed drunkenly at his father, swaying slightly on his feet. "You also seem to have started celebrating earlier than the rest of the court."

The prince hiccuped. "Why shouldn't I? It's my day, and now I've come to claim what's mine."

The king frowned at his son. "And just what may that be?"

Prince Gaitlan failed to hear the warning tone in his father's question. Beside Mirra, Braelyn clenched her hand so hard that it hurt.

"Quiet, you fool," she whispered hotly.

The whole court held its breath.

"For my crown," Prince Gaitlan bellowed.

The king's face tightened. "We will discuss this tomorrow, with sober heads."

"What do you mean?" Prince Gaitlan demanded, his face screwing up.

"We will discuss this tomorrow," the king said, turning his back on his son.

Prince Gaitlan's face flushed when the reality of his father's words broke through his drunken haze. "The crown belongs to me now, Father! I am of age! It is my right!"

A collective gasp echoed throughout the gathered nobles. The king's spine steeled. When he turned, he was no longer the prince's father but a king in all his righteous fury.

"The crown *may* pass to an heir on their twenty-first birthday if and only if the *current king* deems them ready. And you, my son, are not ready for the responsibilities that this office demands. Maybe in another year, once you've proven yourself."

The prince stared at his father's retreating, mouth open wide. A nervous cough from the crowd urged him into action.

"You cannot do this to me! It is my right! I demand …"

"You demand!" The king spun on his heel, storming toward his son. "You are nothing more than a petulant child; spoiled and soft. Perhaps a few years traveling as a diplomat will force you to grow up."

"You're going to exile me? Me! Your firstborn!"

Prince Gaitlan surged forward, clenched fist flying. Braelyn released Mirra's hand, rushing toward her warring family before Mirra could stop her. She got in between her father and brother, arms extended.

"Please stop," she pleaded. But she was too late. Her brother's fist connected to her jaw, sending her careening into her father.

Outrage roared through the collective court. Prince Gaitlan backed away from the crumpled form of his sister, eyes wide with horror.

"I didn't ... he made ... Brae ..."

Prince Gaitlan turned on his heels and ran out of the ballroom before anyone could stop him. It was only when he reached the doors that someone attempted to stop him. The prince shoved the man aside, causing another cry of alarm to rise.

Mirra rushed to her friend's side, helping Braelyn to her feet.

"I'm all right," she said weakly. She held a hand to her face, eyes filled with sorrow.

"Find the prince and bring him to me!"

Men surged into action. Small bands formed to hunt the prince, their rising cries demanding justice. Even Mirra felt the tug of the mob, taking a single step forward. Her magic swelled, sinking its fangs into her consciousness, breaking her free.

Mirra peered over her shoulder. Behind the scattering crowd, cloaked in dancing shadows, Lord Julian watched the growing chaos with a wicked smile and eyes the color of sin.

CHAPTER TWENTY-ONE

Keep the compress on for a bit, Princess." The healer smiled kindly, giving Braelyn a gentle pat before going to speak to the king and queen, setting a small bowl with thick, black wiggling worms on a table.

"The leeches will help reduce some of the swelling and bruising but not all. The compress will help with the rest. She should use a warm for the pain, and a cold for the swelling. Time will take care of the rest."

"Thank you."

The healer bowed, making a discrete exit. Mirra lingered, not wanting to leave the princess alone after what she witnessed in the hall. *That bastard caused all this. I know it. But why? What game is he playing?*

"When we find your brother," the king growled, "he will answer for tonight."

Braelyn dropped the compress, taking her father's hands. "Please, Father; let it go. He was drunk and embarrassed."

"And that's why he has to be punished. If you hadn't gotten in the middle, he would have struck me. You saved him from facing the executioner's block."

Braelyn blanched, recoiling from her father. "I need to rest." Her voice was tight and chipped. Neither the king nor queen noticed the change in their daughter's tone, nodding with tight-lipped smiles.

"Mirra, will you walk with me?"

"Of course."

Braelyn walked out of the healer's office, straight-backed, leaving the compress forgotten on the floor. She said nothing to Mirra as they made their way toward the princess's rooms. People bowed as they passed before whispering behind their hands as soon as Braelyn passed. Mirra scowled at them all.

They reached Braelyn's rooms without incident. Mirra curtsied and turned to leave, but Braelyn stopped her.

"Please stay; I could really use a friend, and you're the only one I have."

Mirra gave Braelyn a sad smile. "I can say the same thing, Princess."

Braelyn's rooms were easily twice the size of Mirra's and far more elegantly furnished. She sat in front of a vanity and proceeded to yank out the pins that kept her hair in place. Mirra watched from a distance, unsure what to do until she saw Braelyn's face crumble in the mirror.

Mirra walked up behind her friend and gently pushed her hands aside. One by one, she removed the pins from Braelyn's hair, setting them in a pile on the vanity. Braelyn's hair fell in golden waves down her back. Mirra picked up a brush and gently released any tangles before putting Braelyn's hair into a simple braid.

"He'll never recover from tonight," Braelyn whispered before succumbing to tears.

Mirra wrapped her arms around her friend's shaking frame, offering nothing but support. The events of the night were beyond words.

After some time, Braelyn's tears ran out. She straightened, going over to the washbowl, splashing cold water on her face. When she faced Mirra again, determination shone through every pore.

"Teach me to fight."

Mirra was taken aback. "I don't know how."

Braelyn's eyes narrowed. "Don't lie to me, Mirra. You told me yourself that you learned the ways of your husband's people. And I've seen the way you walk, the way you watch everything and everyone. You know who else does that? Fighters. So, don't you dare sit there and lie to me."

Everyone underestimates you too much, Princess. Maybe you should be the one to sit on the throne instead.

"Basic moves, nothing else," Mirra said. "No blades at all."

A ghost of a smile flashed across Braelyn's face before determination took over. "Agreed."

I DON'T THINK I'VE EVER BEEN IN A MAUSOLEUM."

Mirra chuckled. "Unless you're dead, not much reason for anyone to be in one."

"But you do?"

Mirra mentally made a face. She kept forgetting herself around the princess. If she wasn't too careful, she'd end up giving away something that would put her in danger.

"My uncle told me to hide the fact that I hunt, fight, and ride."

"Why?"

"He wanted me to transition to court life as smoothly as possible. Or as smooth as I could with him as a relative."

Braelyn clasped Mirra on the shoulder. "I'm sorry for my part in that. No one should feel like they have to hide who they are."

Mirra smiled at her friend, disgusted with herself.

"Let's get to it, shall we?"

Now, what are the softest points on a person?"

Laying on the cold stone floor, sweaty and sore, Braelyn recited the litany Mirra had drilled into her head for the past hour.

"Solar plexus, nose, instep, groin, and eyes."

"Good. Let's head back before your mother sends an army out to look for you."

Braelyn groaned but extended her hand in the air. Mirra laughed, clasping it and hoisting the princess to her feet.

"Next time we do this, we're wearing britches," Braelyn said, dusting off her skirt.

Mirra shook her head. "Dresses are better." Braelyn arched a brow. "What do you normally wear?"

"Dresses."

"Exactly. You need to know how to maneuver in what you wear day to day. Training in men's clothes would be more comfortable but not practical."

Braelyn laughed. "Who would have thought dresses would ever be *practical?*"

Mirra joined in, throwing her arm around Braelyn's shoulders. "You and me both."

After a quick trip to the baths, Mirra returned to her room, only to find Lord Julian waiting for her. She froze like a deer when they spotted a predator, and without a doubt, he was a predator.

"What do you want?"

He smiled, folding his hands in his lap. "Is that any way to talk to family?"

"Yes."

Lord Julian's smile fell. "Close the door and sit. You're overdue for an update."

Mirra complied, keeping ire on her face to mask her other emotions. "The princess asked me to teach her hand to hand."

"Are you?"

"She left me no choice, but it's just some simple things, nothing that would hurt her."

Lord Julian frowned. "You must delight in making things harder for me."

"What do you mean? You put me here to watch over and protect the princess. She's got a wild streak a mile long with no sense of self-preservation at all. Knowing how to block a punch and get out of a hold would make my job easier."

"Things have changed."

Mirra sat straighter in her chair. "How so?"

Lord Julian looked into the fire. "Last night brought certain things into light. The prince has always been a wild card, but now it is clear he can never be allowed to rule. The king and queen are at odds with each other over what to do with him."

You caused the discourse yourself, you manipulative prick.

"Do you want me to find him and bring him back?"

"I already have people working on it."

Mirra frowned. "Then what do you want of me?"

Lord Julian turned his eyes on Mirra, sending a chill coursing down her spine. "I'm getting to that. My agents abroad are reporting some disturbing whispers from the other kingdoms. Whispers of war."

Mirra surged to her feet. War was the last thing that anyone wanted or needed. Thousands of people would suffer, in cities and rural villages. "What can I do to help?"

"I'd hoped you say that."

"Well?"

"Are you sure that you want this new assignment?"

Warning bells rang in the back of Mirra's mind, urging her to be careful with her next words.

"Tell me."

Evil, that was the only way to describe the look on Lord Julian's face. Cold dread uncoiled in the depth of Mirra's heart, turning to blood to ice. She watched in horror as the black of Lord Julian's eyes grew, swallowing all color until they were nothing more than twin pools of ink.

"Kill the royal family."

Mirra's legs gave out, sending her tumbling back into her chair. "Why?" she asked, not bothering to hide the horror in her voice.

"*I'm hungry*," Lord Julian answered in a voice that wasn't his own.

Mirra's fingers inched toward her hidden blades. "What did you say?"

The blackness retreated until his eyes returned to their normal colors. "Why? The entire royal family is weak. And I am tired of serving a ruler who is beneath me."

Mirra quickly swallowed back her panic, schooling her face into just the right amount of shock. "How are we supposed to pull this off?"

"You only have to worry about the princess. The rest will be taken care of. Prepare yourself and wait for my signal."

Lord Julian rose from his seat, carelessly strolling toward the door as if they had talked about the weather, not starting a coupe. He stopped next to Mirra, who still sat, clenching the arms of her chair as if they were the only things keeping her rooted in the world.

"Should anyone find out about our little conversation this afternoon."

"They won't," Mirra promised.

He left without another word, leaving Mirra reeling in her chair.

Something *else* answered her question. Something dark, unnatural, and apparently hungry inhabited Lord Julian's body. What was it; a demon from the Dark Realm? Had he invited it in, or was he just as much a slave as she was? Is that where he got his magic from?

"My lady, are you all right?"

Mirra jumped from her chair, drawing her blades as she spun, pressing them against a shocked Daisy. "Gods above," she said, dropping her blades. "I didn't mean to. I'm so sorry."

Daisy retreated a couple of steps, a hand wrapped around her throat. "It's all right," she said shakily.

Mirra shook her head. "No, it's not. I am terribly sorry. I guess I'm a little jumpy with everything that's happened these last few weeks."

Daisy's face was still pale, but she managed a weak smile. "I think we all are. It's nearly time for the banquet. I thought that the sky-blue dress would be nice tonight."

"Yes, of course."

Mirra submitted to her maid's capable if not somewhat shaky hands. Mirra made sure to sit perfectly still as to not further startle her. Daisy prattled on about one mindless topic after another using her voice to fill in the awkward space around them.

As always, Daisy transformed Mirra into the perfect image of a woman of the court. The brightness of her sky-blue dress contrasted nicely with Mirra's raven hair and dark blue trimmings. Her hair was half up, curly gently down her back;

nice and simple. Her makeup was also simple, with just a hint of rouge on her cheeks and lips.

Mirra thanked Daisy, giving her the rest of the evening off to apologize for scaring her so thoroughly. The rest of the night passed in a haze. That night, when she crawled into bed, Mirra had no recollection of what she ate, who she talked to, or any conversation happening around her. The only thing she could say for certain was that Braelyn was the only one to notice that something was off about Mirra but not enough for her to probe deeper.

There was no moon in the sky to chase away the shadows, leaving Mirra alone in the dark. For the first time in her life, she found herself wanting to light a candle against the darkness. But she didn't because she knew that in the flickering light, monsters would come for her. Instead, she buried under her blankets, curled up as tight as she could get, with her hand firmly wrapped around a freshly sharpened stiletto.

She was in a world completely made of fire, smoke, and screams. Dark masses of people ran around her, screaming incoherently as massive chunks of burning debris fell from the sky. Mirra ran forward blindly, searching for a safe place away from the inferno around her. The smoke burned her eyes, making it hard for her to see the path ahead. Something crashed into her, sending her to the ground, knocking the air from her lungs. Mirra gasped for air, only drawing in acrid smoke that burned her throat and lungs. Coughing, she pushed herself up. Her hand slipped in a pool of thick, dark liquid. She fell face-first into the liquid, getting some inside her mouth. She recognized the coppery taste; blood.

Horrified, Mirra pushed herself up, scrambling away, spitting the vile liquid from her mouth and wiping her hands on her clothing.

A cloud of smoke shifted, revealing a temple bathed in moonlight. Mirra ran toward the temple for all she was worth. The great doors were carved with strange symbols that tugged on the recesses of her memory, but in her panic, she only cared about getting inside. Inside, she would be safe. Inside, she would find sanctuary. But the doors wouldn't budge.

Mirra pounded on the doors until her fists bled, screaming, "Let me in!"

The doors swung open just as flames began to lick at Mirra's heels. Blindly, she stumbled into the darkness, slamming the doors closed behind her. All sounds of destruction and chaos were shut off, making Mirra rub her ears against the silence.

"Hello? Anyone here?"

There was nothing inside the temple. No priest or priestess. No benches, alters, or source of light, except for the circle of moonlight streaming in from above. Mirra wrapped her arms around her quivering body and walked toward the light. The floor, she realized, was a massive mosaic, but she could only see vague images of five people standing with objects in their hands.

Mirra entered into the circle of moonlight, looking down at the only clear piece of the mosaic, an orb swirling with darkness. She squatted to have a closer look. Perhaps it was a trick of the moonlight or maybe the after-effects of smoke inhalation, but the swirls within the orb appeared to move. Mirra reached out to touch the swirling shadows but was stopped by the sound whispering.

"Hello?"

The whispering grew louder.

Mirra shivered. "Show yourself!"

Hundreds of shadowy masses came out of the darkness. They stayed well away from the circle of light Mirra had claimed.

"Why?" the masses collectively asked. Their voices hurt, forcing Mirra to cover her ears with her hands.

"Why did you do it?"

"What?"

"Why did you do nothing?"

Their accusations spurred Mirra into speaking, even though she had no idea what they were referring to.

"I had no choice."

"You've always had a choice, Mirra."

Mirra fell to her knees as Bao walked forward, covered in blood with the mark of a hangman's noose around his throat.

"You've always had a choice."

Again and again, the specters spoke, revealing the king and queen, Braelyn and Gaitlan, Nora, Em, Sorro, Tull, and Brian; each one bloody, beaten, and dead. Mirra wept, her tears leaving streaks down her soot-stained face. Ylanna was the last to emerge from the darkness, leading a small boy no more than five by the hand.

She looked down at Mirra, her eyes blazing with fire from the pits of hell. "Choose."

Mirra woke, drenched in sweat with the bitter tastes of smoke and blood in her mouth. Her room is even darker, swirling like the contents of the orb from her dream. The voices of the dead echo around her one last time before fading away into the night.

Choose.

CHAPTER TWENTY-TWO

HE MUST HAVE ROYALLY PISSED OFF THE CAPTAIN OF THE Watch to pull patrol on a day like this. Icy wind tore through his uniform, sending rivets of cold water down his body. Yes, he was going to be frozen solid by dinner time.

A woman in a massive dove gray cloak slipped on the practically frozen cobblestones. The young city watchman caught her before she fell.

"Are you all right, Ma'am?"

The woman's hood fell back, revealing a mass of brown curls. Her amber eyes widened as she hastily regained her footing.

"Oh yes," she said. Her accent was unfamiliar to the watchman. She raised her hood, shielding her head from the freezing rain.

"Not quite the best day to be outdoors, eh?"

"Yes, but today is the only day my companion can see me."

The watchman tipped his hat to the woman. "Have a good day, then, Ma'am."

"To you as well." She flashed a brilliant smile before trudging along to her destination.

The wind picked up again, sending stinging rain into the watchman's face. He wondered how much of his shift was left before he froze to death.

Mirra felt bad for the poor watchman. Today was not a day to be away from the fire. She wouldn't be out if not for her meeting in an hour.

The bell of Cros Buns jingled merrily. Behind the counter, Mr. Cros called out a greeting. Mirra lowered her hood.

"Could I please have a medium pot of spiced tea with an order of mini jelly tarts?"

"Right away, Madam. Please sit wherever you like."

Mirra had no problem finding a place to sit. The table was small, built for two. She took the seat facing the door, quickly scanning the crowd. Not the usually throng, but still enough to fill the air with conversations. As long as she and her friend talked in low tones, no one should overhear them.

The tea and tarts had just been brought to her table when the bell jingled again. A Zallino merchant entered to shop. He waved when Mr. Cros greeted him. He scanned the crowd, smiling when his eyes landed on Mirra in her corner.

"Does your little eye trick work on darker eyes?" Bao asked, taking the opposite seat. He didn't seem at all bothered by having his back exposed to the room.

Mirra shook her head. "No idea. Thanks for coming. I wasn't sure if you would."

Bao poured a steaming cup of tea with one hand, tossing a tart into his mouth with the other. "Neither was I."

Mirra pressed her lips together. She started to pick her nails under the table.

"So, spit it out already."

Mirra took in their surroundings with a trained eye one last time before drawing a steady breath.

"I know you think I betrayed you. But right now, I need you to trust me. Can you do that?"

Bao studied her, cocking his head to one side. After three tense heartbeats, he nodded, motioning her to continue.

Mirra nearly sobbed but held back the wave of relief and happiness. There was important work to be done first.

"Don't react."

Bao arched a bow, skepticism written across his face. Mirra placed her ungloved hand on the table behind the teapot. In the center of her palm, a black mass of swirling darkness blossomed, slowly coiling around her fingers like a snake.

Bao's white-knuckled grip was the only emotion that he allowed to show. Mirra clenched her hand into a fist, and the darkness dissipated.

"The Viper isn't the only one with magic." She slipped on her gloves and hid her hands under the table. "I don't know why, but I do too."

Bao took a large gulp of tea. "You know, it actually explains a lot about you."

"What?"

Bao waved his hand. "A thousand little things that aren't all that important right now. What's the real reason you called me here?"

"I just showed you that I have magic!"

"As a way to earn my trust. I know you, Mirra. Now spill."

Mirra wanted to scowl, but he was right. Bao flashed her a crooked grin, and the years between them fell away. She felt like she did when she ran wild in the streets as a child.

She reached into the pocket of her cloak and pulled out a thick envelope and handed it to Bao. Confused, he took it, broke the seal and started to read. Mirra poured herself a cup of tea. She sipped it silently, watching Bao as he read her letter.

Wording is a funny thing. A simple phrase could have a thousand other meanings. Lord Julian warned her not to speak of his plans, and she promised, and she kept that promise. After her nightmare, Mirra hadn't been able to fall back asleep. The ghosts demanded she choose a side, and she did.

Writing everything down hadn't sparked a response from her brand. Pleased at finding a loophole around her magical bindings, Mirra quickly hashed out a plan.

Bao folded the letter up, tucking it into his pocket. His face was pale from alarm, but his eyes were filled with resolute determination. "I will do what I can. It might take a week or so."

"We don't have that luxury."

"I understand."

Bao stood, placing his hand over his heart before bowing slightly. Mirra stood as well, confused by the gesture. He then pulled her into a tight embrace, burying his face into the crook of her neck.

"You died and came back once. I don't think we'll get that miracle a second time. Be careful, my friend."

Mirra blinked back tears, wrapping her arms around him as well. "Same to you. I thought about you and the others every day that I was away."

They pulled away, smiling at one another. A single tear ran down Mirra's face, leaving a streak of brown in its wake. Bao gently wiped it away.

"Best hurry back before you cry away your disguise."

Mirra blinked back her tears, dabbing the damning liquid with her gloved finger. "Before you go, I want to tell you I'm sorry."

"For what?"

"For being so broken that I failed to see my family around me."

Bao blinked twice before throwing his arm across her shoulder. "It's all right. We all knew you were a little thick."

Mirra laughed, poking him in the ribs. They walked out of the bakery, spirits high despite the chaos looming on the horizon.

Mirra sat by the fire, curled up in her favorite reading chair. A book sat open in her lap, but she wasn't reading. Her mind was picking over her half-cocked plan. Bao would secure horses, clothing, food, and coin to get the royal family out of the capital fast. Mirra would be with them, guiding them to

Em's farm where they could lay low for a few days until they could come up with a plan for what came next.

She groaned, ranking her fingers through her hair. *So much can go wrong. What if the king doesn't believe me? What if no one does? What about the tattoo? This is why I left the planning to Bao.*

Daisy entered, carrying a large wooden box wrapped up with red ribbon. "This just arrived for you, my lady."

Mirra walked over to Daisy, taking the box from her. The box was beautifully crafted from cherry wood with little bits of silver inlaid around the edges. "Who is it from?"

Daisy shrugged. "There wasn't a note." She left Mirra with her mystery present, pulling out a dress for the night's banquet.

Mirra set the box on her bed. She unbound the ribbon, revealing an engraved serpent twisting its body into a complicated knot. She pulled her hand back as if the snake had bitten her. She shoved the box, ribbon and all, under her pillows, sick to her stomach. She had a sinking suspicion of what the contents of the box meant.

"Are you all right?"

Braelyn's face was full of concern. Mirra looked down at her plate, realizing that she hadn't taken a single bite from the first course. Servants were clearing away the plates to make way for the main meal.

"I'm sorry," Mirra said. "It's the weather. It has me all fuddled."

Braelyn didn't look convinced. "Are you sure?"

Mirra plastered a smile on her face and nodded. To prove her point, she dug into the roast beef with vegetables. They tasted like ashes in her mouth.

Mirra dismissed Daisy for the evening so she could open Lord Julian's present alone. She pulled it out from underneath the pillows, setting it neatly down. She watched it as if the box would lash out.

"Stop being childish," she said out loud. "You're a trained spy, thief, and apparently assassin. Get it over with!"

The lid came off easily with hardly a sound. Mirra set it aside and peered inside.

Six silver darts shine against black velvet along with a long silver tube with parchment wrapped around it. Though there was no signature on the note, she recognized the script.

These darts have been dipped in poison from the deadly Nealetian moon vipers. There is no antidote, so take care not to prick yourself. Be ready.

Mirra stared at the note, rereading the words over and over, searching for any hidden meanings. Finding none, she went to throw it into the fire. Just as she was about to fling it into the dancing flames, new words blossomed around the edges in the same neat hand as the rest of the note.

Fail, and you will experience the effects of the poison yourself.

Mirra crumpled the note, tossing it into the fire. She remained there, staring into the fire long after the words had turned to ash and were carried away on the biting winter winds.

CHAPTER TWENTY-THREE

THE SKY CHANGED FROM DARK BLUES AND PURPLES TO vibrant oranges and pinks. Dawn had come. Mirra rubbed her burning eyes with the heel of her palms. She hadn't been able to sleep a single wink the night before. Her mind whorled all night about the events to come while her stomach twisted itself into one knot after another with each new worry.

Today was the day; she knew that down to her bones and there were so many things that she still hadn't figured out yet. She flexed her fingers on her left hand. Trying to figure out how to defy the magical bindings caused them to go off. She spent half the night biting back screams, and she was no closer to finding out how to set herself free and not commit treason.

Not wanting to face the very people she was about to betray because she couldn't get her shit together fast enough to have a fully-thought-out plan, Mirra crawled into bed. She pulled the covers tight under her chin and finally drifted off to sleep as the sun crested over the walls of the castle.

"My lady?"

Mirra cracked open a single bloodshot eye. Daisy stood at the foot of the bed with the day's dress folded over her arm.

"Are you ill?"

In so many ways. "I'm afraid so."

"I will make your excuses. Shall I fetch a healer? Perhaps some tea?"

Mirra pushed up into a seated position. "Tea, yes; healer, no. I just need to rest."

"As you wish, my lady."

Only in the assured safety that comes from bathing oneself in the light of the sun, Mirra slept the day away. She woke only to eat the food Daisy brought her and to relieve herself. As the sun shone its last rays of protection, Mirra rose from her nest and dressed. She didn't dress herself in the brightly colored gowns that had become her usual attire but in an all-black suit that hugged her body close enough not to snag on anything but loose enough to provide a wide range in movement.

At her waist, she attached numerous knives of varying lengths. Around one thigh, she strapped a small band of throwing knives, and around the other, she strapped the life-ending darts. To complete her ensemble, she braided her hair back. Once completed, there was nothing left for her to do but wait.

She threw a robe around her body, concealing her damning attire, and settled in her favorite chair. She must have zoned out while looking into the flames because her room was full of shadows when Daisy returned carrying Mirra's dinner.

"You look well-rested, my lady," Daisy said, setting the tray down on a small table.

"A little," Mirra replied. Though she didn't have any appetite, her body demanded nourishment. "Thank you for everything."

Daisy flushed with pride. "It's my honor, my lady. I enjoy serving you."

Mirra picked up a cup of steaming tea. "Did you always want to work in the palace?"

Daisy folded her hand in front of her apron. "We don't always get to do the things we dream. Sometimes we have to do what's needed."

Mirra gave her maid a quizzical look.

Daisy sighed. "When I was little, I wanted to be a seamstress. I wanted to make beautiful pieces of clothing and not just for nobles. But when my father got sick, I had to take what jobs I could get. He died, and I became the sole provider for my family."

"I'm sorry about your father."

"I miss him every day. But I don't regret my choices. I would do anything for my family. If that will be all, I'll head down to the kitchens for my own supper."

Mirra dismissed Daisy with a smile of thanks. Picking up the roll next to her stew, Mirra leaned back in her chair, still pondering the conundrum of circumventing Lord Julian's magic.

Can't think on an empty stomach. Mirra bit into the roll and shouted. "Dark mother curses!"

Something hard and metal, by the lingering taste in her mouth, had been baked inside the roll. Tearing it open, Mirra discovered a small cylinder. "What the hell?"

She spied a seam near one end, and using her nails, she pried it open, revealing a tiny roll of paper. Dread coursed through her veins. *This is it. This is the order to move. I'm not ready yet.*

She unfurled the scroll with trembling fingers to only sigh with relief when she saw the strange series of symbols sketched on the inside.

Shaking her head over the dramatic flair Bao possessed, Mirra studied the marks.

Back when she was a member of the Shadow Guild, Bao had insisted that they develop a secret code to communicate. Since no one but Bao knew how to read, they settled for symbols. Each member of the guild created their own mark. Mirra spotted Bao's mark, a Zallino coin, and Em's, a feather. Mirra smiled, tracing her fingers over the images, piecing them together until she unraveled the message.

I reached out to Em, and she's ready. Still working on means out. No sign of the prince in the city. Don't worry. We have a few tricks up our sleeves. Especially you, Mirra.

Mirra cursed, slapping her forehead. *I'm such an idiot. Lord Julian isn't the only one who has magic.*

Three sharp knocks reverberate through her bedroom door. Mirra quickly tosses Bao's note into the fire, cylinder included, rising slowly to her feet. The knocks were too heavy to be made by Daisy. On silent feet, Mirra positioned herself just to the left of the door and listened.

Three more heavy knocks came, this time with more force. Mirra pulled a small dagger free, palming it so that it remained hidden. She carefully opened her door, leaping back as two giants pushed their way into her room.

Mirra still kept her blade hidden, assessing the situation. Both men were dressed in all black with a small arsenal of weapons strapped to them. If not for the slight differences in their faces and hair color, the men could have been twins.

The blond man took half a step forward, extending his left wrist. He pulled back his sleeve to reveal a tattoo of a serpent coiling around his thick wrist. She felt a throb of familiarly around her own wrist.

Resheathing her dagger, Mirra released the ties of her robe, letting it drop to the floor behind her.

"Shall we?"

Using servant's passageways and a healthy measure of stealth, Mirra and her deadly entourage never crossed paths with another living soul. Her spine itches from having two large threats at her back, but there's nothing she can do about it. As soon as she stepped out into the hallway, they fell instep behind her. Whether to back her up or take her out, she couldn't be sure.

At this time of day, there was only one place that Braelyn would be. Worn out from the political battlefield that was her evening meal, Braelyn would retreat to the Draconian Library to lose herself in a literary world for a few hours.

The massive doors to the library were open, a sign that the princess was still inside. She was always the last patron of the library. Mirra slipped between one of the bookcases, keeping to the shadows as she headed toward the area where she and Braelyn spent a large portion of their days.

"Mirra, what are you ... who are these men?"

Muinn emerged from the shadows, clutching a small stack of books to her chest. Mirra lashed out before the two goons at her back could, drawing a dagger. Muinn gasped, dropping the stack of books and turning to flee. She never got the chance.

Using her arm, Mirra cut off Muinn's air supply. "I'm sorry," she whispered, striking the priestess in the temple with the hilt of the dagger. Muinn crumpled to the floor just like her beloved books.

"Double time, boys," Mirra said, plastering a cruel smile on her face. "We don't want anyone else to disturb our fun."

Braelyn was exactly where Mirra knew she would be, curled up in her favorite window seat. Mirra took three breaths to steel herself for what needed to be done before she stepped out into the light.

Braelyn looked up from her book, frowning as she took in Mirra's appearance and weapon. Her frown deepened when Mirra was joined by the two goons.

"So, this is who you truly are?"

Mirra said nothing, could say nothing.

"I guess I should have trusted my instincts after all."

"Let's go, Princess," Mirra growled, gesturing with her dagger.

As calm as a summer's evening, Braelyn closed her book, setting it aside before standing up.

The blond goon strode forward, crossing the distance in three strides, taking the princess roughly by the arm. "No fussing," he spat, shoving her forward.

The other goon took the lead, followed by Braelyn. Mirra tried to position herself at the princess's back, but the blond goon beat her to it. Silently cursing, Mirra had no choice but to follow, hoping that she hadn't lost the opening she needed to save her friend.

They are taken down another passageway. A narrow spiral staircase, barely large enough for the men between Mirra and Braelyn. Mirra smiled. It was the right place to make her move. Unfortunately, Braelyn thought the same thing.

Just as the first goon rounded the corner, Braelyn shoved him for everything she was worth, sending him stumbling into the stars. She spun around, coming face to face with the blond goon. She attempted to use one of the defensive moves Mirra taught her, but her attacker was faster than she was.

The blond goon struck Braelyn in the face, sending her crashing into the opposite wall. Mirra watched in horror as her friend slid down the wall, blood spilling from her lips, and her eyes glazed over.

The first goon recovered, snarling. He kicked Braelyn in the stomach, forcing her to cough and gasp for air.

Mirra surged forward in defense of her friend. Pain consumed her entire body, forcing her to drop her blades as she fell painfully onto the steps below. The goons' full attention was on Braelyn. They repeatedly kicked her with savage delight, utterly unaware of Mirra's suffering.

Mirra tried to call on her magic but couldn't. The pain was too much. She was going to fail.

Through the shifting feet of the goons, Mirra caught Braelyn's eye. Whether the princess actually saw Mirra or not, she couldn't be sure. The only thing she was sure of was that Braelyn had already accepted her death. Accepted all the things that she wasn't going to be able to do, all the changes that weren't going to be made. She closed her eyes and accepted her death.

Mirra screamed, lurching to her feet, drawing her daggers and summoning her magic. It burst forth, coiling around her body and her daggers, eager for blood. The two goons halted their assault on the princess, turning their attention toward Mirra.

She lurched forward, burying her daggers into the blond goon's neck. He tried to throw Mirra down the stairs, only to have his hands move right through her. Mercilessly, Mirra dragged her blades across his neck, feeling the sudden flood of warmth as his life force spilled onto her.

The blond goon fell to the steps with blood bubbling from his lips. Mirra stood on his dying body before launching herself at the other goon. This time, she buried her daggers just below his collar bone, twisting to cause the most pain. Mirra's momentum carried the first goon back onto the stairs, pinning him under her. Black tendrils of her power streamed out, keeping him pinned down.

"Where's the prince?" Mirra asked.

"Got to hell, you bitch," the man spat.

Mirra gave her blades another twist, causing the goon to cry out in pain. "Where is he!"

"Near the throne room."

"Thanks." Mirra slashed the goon's throat before he even realized it. He stared up at her in disbelief with his last breaths gurgling out of him like a man drowning.

A small noise from behind drew Mirra's attention. Braelyn stared up at her with eyes full of fear.

Mirra extended her hand toward Braelyn. "There's still time to save your family."

Braelyn looked at the dead bodies of the men who meant to kill her. Shakily, she got to her feet.

"How can I trust you?"

"You don't really have much of a choice now, do you?"

"I guess I really don't," Braelyn said, taking Mirra's bloody hand into her own.

CHAPTER TWENTY-FOUR

THE ENTIRE PALACE HAD BEEN TAKEN OVER. EVERYWHERE they went, the sounds of fighting rang out.

"Just a little further, Braelyn," Mirra shouted over her shoulder.

Braelyn remained silent, more focused on keeping up with Mirra, hampered by her skirts than anything else.

On and on, they ran up and down one set of stairs after another. Dashing through servant and hidden passages, hoping to reach the prince before anything permanent happened.

"Where are you taking me?" Braelyn gasped when Mirra paused to peer around a corner.

"To save your brother."

"What's going on?"

Mirra turned around. "Lord Julian is throwing a coupe. These are his men who are storming the castle, taking down nobles. He ordered me to kill you."

Braelyn's face blanched. "But you didn't."

Mirra shook her head. "No, I didn't."

"Since you're in a sharing mood, care to explain what all that black stuff was back there?"

"That's a bit trickier, but in a nutshell ... I have magic."

It was as if a final puzzle piece fell into place. Braelyn's eyes widened as her mouth formed a tiny o. "That's why you wanted to know everything from before the Great Purging. What are you?"

"Right now, I'm the reason you're still alive. We need to move faster if you want to save your family."

The same iron will that helped Braelyn navigate the trappings of the court settled around her shoulders. She held her hand out for one of Mirra's daggers.

Mirra handed one over without a second thought. They were well past the time for over-caution. Braelyn cut the ties to her gown, ripping it off until she stood in nothing but her shift. "Lead the way, Mirra."

A fierce wave of pride rushed over Mirra. "I grew up hating nobles, thinking you were all a bunch of indulgent pricks. But you're different. You could actually do some good for this world. Don't let anyone ever tell you otherwise."

Braelyn's face softened a fraction before slipping back into a mask of stone. "Sentiments after victory, Mirra." She motioned for Mirra to lead on.

Mirra smirked, turning back to the hallway to recheck. "Thank you for being my friend," Braelyn whispered.

"Anytime, Princess."

There were several entrances to the throne room. Most visitors entered through the main doors that were guarded day and night. The king and queen entered from another set at the back of the chamber that, too, was heavily guarded. But there was a third, less secure way. It was a place where visiting dignitaries could wait for their turn to meet with the king and queen without mixing with the common day man. If the goon had spoken the truth, then that is where the prince was being held.

It made sense to Mirra. Unless the king held open court, no one ever used the rooms. Servants cleaned the rooms once a month at most. No one thought to look for the prince inside the castle because he always ran to the city to escape.

Mirra peered out into the wide hallway, looking for any potential signs of danger. At one end, she spied four lifeless bodies. From where she stood, she couldn't tell if they were the king's men or Lord Julian's.

"This way, Braelyn."

Together, they scampered across the open space to the door that would grant them entrance to where the prince was being kept. Mirra tested the handle, not surprised in the slightest to find it unlocked. She motioned for Braelyn to wait for a moment. She cracked the door open slowly, poised for an attack that never came.

There was nothing but darkness on the other side of the door. Mirra stepped through, taking Braelyn's free hand in hers. She blinked against the pressing darkness and walked forward. As her eyes became adjusted to the darkness, Mirra began to make out the doors on either side of the narrow corridor.

At the far end, a light shone from under a single door. Mirra pressed a finger to her lips, warning Braelyn to remain quiet and hidden. Mirra drew another dagger, taking a steady breath before kicking the door in.

Surging into the room half-blind, Mirra swung her blades around. A single lantern sat on a small table. From the multiple dishes and half-eaten food, it was clear that someone had been living in the space for some time. And even though Mirra couldn't see anyone, the tingling at the back of her neck warned her that she wasn't alone.

"I see you've made your choice, then."

Horrified, Mirra spun around. Nora stood in the open doorway with the dagger she'd given Braelyn at the princess's throat.

Mirra sheathed her daggers, holding her hands up. "Yes, and so can you."

Nora laughed. "My chance came and went, remember?"

"Maybe this is your second chance."

Nora shook her head. "You know I can't defy him."

"No," Mirra agreed, "but I thought you were smarter. Who is he but another man? Aren't you the best when it comes to handling men, figuring out what they really want, even when they *say* something entirely different?"

Confusion blossomed across Nora's face but was quickly replaced by delight. Laughing, she released Braelyn from her hold, giving back the dagger to her.

"Well played, little one. You'd best hurry along before it's too late. They're in the throne room"

Mirra hugged her former mentor. "I could try," she started to say, but Nora cut her off.

"Don't! Save whatever strength you have for facing him. If you win, then you can free me. If not, then you have an ally."

Mirra embraced Nora one last time before racing off to the throne room with Braelyn at her heels. They burst into the throne room, but nothing could have prepared them for what they saw.

Braelyn's heartbroken screams ripped through the silence. She fell to her knees, wailing behind Mirra, her dagger clattering to the cold marble floor.

In the very center of the room, the king and queen lay dead, their blood spilling out beneath them like wine. Swaying over the dead monarchs with a bloody sword, Prince Gaitlan stood, swaying on unsteady feet. Mirra spared the prince only a passing glance before turning them on the true danger in the room, Lord Julian.

Lord Julian stared at Mirra in shock for a fraction of a heartbeat before schooling his face into his usually bemused expression.

"It's a rare feat for someone to surprise me," he said. "How did you?"

Lord Julian's unmatched eyes lit up like a child receiving a gift. He clapped his hands together in wicked glee. "You *do* have magic. Delightful! You've managed to surprise me twice. Bravo, my dear."

He bowed to Mirra mockingly, and when he rose, both his eyes were completely black. When he spoke again, it was with the same strange voice she'd heard only once before.

"It has been an age since I'd seen one of your kind; longer, in fact. Come here, little one, and let me have a taste."

Black serpents coiled around his body. They were darker than anything Mirra had ever witnessed, and they seemed to drink in all surrounding light.

Mirra summoned her magic again; she took comfort in the fact that her magic, while black, was more reminiscent of smoke and shadows than all-consuming darkness.

She surged forward, pouring her magic into her blades. The thing possessing Lord Julian laughed, holding his hand out. One tendril divided into dozens, dropping to the floor, morphing into ink-black snakes.

One snake slithered toward the prince and opened its maw to strike. Mirra shouted, pointing a dagger at the serpent. A single black arrow struck the snake. It hissed, flailing about until it disappeared in a whiff of smoke.

Mirra stumbled, breathing hard. Using a dagger, she started to scratch a rune of protection into the floor.

"I don't think so," the thing said, sending hundreds more serpents into the room.

Mirra abandoned the rune, slashing and striking down as many serpents as she could.

"Mirra!"

Braelyn had jumped onto a wooden bench as three serpents rushed for her. Mirra gathered her strength, sending three bolts toward the snakes. The bolts struck true, as each snake disappeared, hissing as if angry they were unable to reach their prey.

Mirra drew the rune of protection in the air. "Braelyn and Gaitlan," she shouted, causing the rune to duplicate, speeding toward the remaining royals. When the twin runes reached their targets, they blended into their bodies, creating a halo of shadow around them.

Mirra fell hard to the floor. When the snakes slithered near, she slashed at them weakly. She was reaching the end of her strength.

The thing inside Lord Julian laughed. "You are a delight. Do try and learn a bit more before we meet again." The remaining serpents returned to their master, swarming over him until he was nothing more than a writhing mass of night. Pressure built inside the throne room, making Mirra's ears pop and ache. It continued to build and build until it drove her further into the floor, covering her ears.

Without warning, the pressure released, causing Mirra, Braelyn, and Gaitlan to fall to the floor.

"Mirra! Mirra! Wake up."

Braelyn shook Mirra's shoulders, desperately trying to wake her friend.

"Dark Mother curses," Mirra groaned, easing herself up. "Are you all right?"

"Physically."

A weak chuckled forced its way out of Mirra. "That will have to do for now."

Using each other for support, Mirra and Braelyn shuffled to where Prince Gaitlan still lay in the cooling pool of his parents' blood. Braelyn swallowed a sob when she saw her parents' vacant eyes, turning all her focus on her remaining family member. She shook and called his name until he woke, blinking heavily dilated eyes.

"Drugged," Mirra commented.

Together, they were able to get Gaitlan back onto his feet.

"Brae?" His voice was slow and slurred. "What are you?" He looked down at his blood-soaked clothing and sword which he had managed to hold onto. "What happened?" Swaying and looking a bit green, Gaitlan took a single step forward and tripped over his father's corpse.

Braelyn rushed forward, slipping on blood. Instinctively, Gaitlan latched onto his sister, halting her fall. And that was what the team of nobles saw when they came crashing through the doors of the throne room.

For a moment, everyone was too stunned to move or speak. But not for long.

"The prince has murdered the king and queen!"

Mirra pushed Braelyn toward the entrance they came through. She grabbed Gaitlan by his still extended arm and dragged him after her. She heard the clang of his sword falling to the floor and the rush as the nobles surged after them.

It hadn't taken them long to lose their pursuers, but they weren't out of the woods yet.

"Head for the kitchens," Mirra shouted. If they could make it to the kitchens, there was a small chance they could make it out of the castle.

She followed Braelyn's lead, trusting the princess to know the fastest route to the kitchens. They passed by dozens of fights during their wild dash through the palace. Mirra hoped that the raging chaos would mask their escape, perhaps even giving them a head start. *Bao better be ready.*

So caught up trying to come up with a plan to get out of the capital, Mirra failed to warn Braelyn to not run into the open courtyard. By the time she realized her mistake, Braelyn barreled right into a group of nobles, including several members of the palace guard looking to make their own escape.

The sharp-eyed guards took in Braelyn's blood-stained shift, Mirra's attire, and the dried blood on both Mirra's and Gaitlan's hands. To further complicate matters, one of their pursuers finally caught up with them, gasping his damning accusation.

"The prince murdered his parents."

The guards shove Braelyn behind them, drawing their blades.

Seeing no other way out, Mirra dragged the last morsel of her magic up from the depths of her soul. A collective gasp rang out from the gathered nobles as Mirra turned into a living shadow. She latched onto the prince and dragged him with her through the closest dark corner.

They emerged into a thankfully empty kitchen, both retching. Mirra was the first to her feet, grunting as she pulled Gaitlan to his feet.

"We gotta keep moving, Your Highness," she told him, half carrying, half dragging him toward the door that led outside the palace's walls.

Once they reached the loading area outside the castle walls, Mirra let the prince go. He fell to the ground like a stone, dry, heaving and covered in sweat.

"Just stay down and let me think."

Mirra paced back and forth, mindlessly checking her weapons. She was in no condition to carry the prince all the way to the *Gilded Lily*. They would be caught before they made it to the Divine District. She needed to come up with a plan and fast.

"State your name and intention!"

Could this night get any worse? she thought, turning to face yet another obstacle.

A single archer stood behind her, his bow notched. "Keep your hands in the air and step forward." Mirra complied. "Remove your weapons."

With slow, deliberate movements, Mirra removed every weapon strapped to her body. When her fingers touched the cold metal dart gun, she knew what to do.

She brought the dart gun to her lips and blew at the same time the archer released his arrow. Mirra dodged the arrow, but the archer wasn't as lucky.

Dark purple veins emanated from where the dart struck. The poor archer's eyes went wide as he struggled to get air. It took only a matter of seconds for him to collapse to the ground, convulsing. Mirra forced herself to watch the archer's last moments, offering a prayer to the dead when his body went still.

Prince Gaitlan groaned, bringing Mirra back to the present. Throwing his arm over her shoulders, she continued her trek toward safety. Down one street after another, Mirra scanned each house. The streets were filling fast with members of the city watch and curious spectators. Behind her, portions of the palace were up in flames. From every tower, alarm bells rang, urging more people into the streets. The longer she and the prince stayed out in the open, the higher the risk of getting caught.

"Where are you?"

She nearly wept for joy when she spied a soft green glow coming from the back window of a tavern. She made a short series of knocks on the door.

A wide-eyed scullery maid cracked open the door. Mirra shoved through, kicking the door closed behind her. The scullery maid backed up against the wall, mouth opening to call for help.

"Do it and die," Mirra growled. She pulled back her sleeve, exposing the now mostly useless tattoo. "No questions, no talking."

The maid's face paled, but she shut her mouth and waited for Mirra's orders. "Get me whatever healing herbs you have. You know what else needs to be done."

The maid scurried away, returning a few moments later with a small box containing common healing herbs and tinctures. Mirra tore through everything until she came across a small pouch of white flowers, a powerful detoxifier. She forced them into Gaitlan's mouth.

"Chew this, and you'll feel better. I hope."

The maid returned for a second time, bearing two small, nondescript traveling bags.

"Thanks. I can take care of things from here."

Looking like she was about to faint, the maid curtsied sharply before fleeing to safer rooms.

Mirra dumped the contents of the bags onto the floor. Clean modest clothing, two pouches of coins, a day's worth of provisions for the road, and the name of two different towns. Mirra shredded the slips of paper before throwing them into a bucket of kitchen scraps.

She threw the clean clothes over her black suit. She turned to the prince who was still dutifully chewing away. "Put these on over your clothes."

"Why?" His eyes were clearer than they were earlier.

Mirra pinched the bridge of her nose. "You're in danger. I need to get you to safety. Please, Your Highness, trust me."

"Mirra?"

"I don't have time for this." Taking the hilt of a dagger, she struck the prince hard, knocking him out.

Grunting and cursing, she managed to get the clothes over Gaitlan's blood-splattered clothing. Panting and sweating, Mirra glowered at the prince with her hands on her hips. *Now what?*

Through a crack in the window, Mirra heard a horse's whinny. For the first time that evening, a smile broke out across her face.

THE MOMENT THE BELLS STARTED RINGING, EVERY GATE was bolted shut. But a coin in the right hand can open anything. Pushing their stolen mounts as fast as she dared, Mirra with the prince, in two, fled Verance. She spared the city one last glance over her shoulder. The castle glowed like a beacon in the dark.

Be safe, Braelyn.

Thousands of people crowded into the throne room, every last one dressed in black or gray. At the far end of the room, two identical raised platforms. Cleaned and dressed in funeral garb, the king and queen lay side by in death as they had in life. Behind them, both thrones were covered by black veils as tradition demanded. In between the dead monarchs, Princess

Braelyn stood straight-backed and pale. Her eyes were rimmed in red by tears shed for all that had been taken from her.

"They were taken too soon," Lord Julian commented.

Braelyn clenched her fists, turning on the man responsible for the death around her. "You did this, you bastard."

Lord Julian ticked his tongue. "Such language. Your poor mother would be ashamed." He stepped closer to Braelyn, taking her into his arms. "Remember, sweet princess, raise too much fuss, and I will kill every last man, woman, and child in Verance."

Braelyn shuddered, remembering the soulless serpents that very nearly took her life.

Lord Julian released her, turning to address the mourners gathered. "Angered over his lack of ascension to the throne, Prince Gaitlan gathered dark forces and turned on the very people he was supposed to protect. With his own hands, he slew his mother and father, our beloved king and queen."

The crowd cried out for blood and justice.

"Justice will be served, I swear this to you! Let this message be carried to every corner of the known world. By order of the crown, Prince Gaitlan and Mirra Ó Broin are declared traitors, and their lives forfeit. Any person or persons caught giving the rebel prince aid will suffer the same fate."

Near the back of the crowd, a small group of mourners didn't take part in the mob's lust for blood. Bao crossed his arms, scowling.

"Can you believe this horse shit!" Tull whispered hotly.

"It doesn't matter what I think," Bao replied.

"What do we do now?"

Bao had no answer for Tull. Before he turned to leave, he scanned the crowd one last time, pausing when they landed on the grieving princess whose rage-filled eyes bore into Lord Julian's back. A small smile tugged at his mouth. Looks like not everyone in the palace was so easily swayed.

Acknowledgments

As always, to my partner in crime, Dmitry, thank you for resigning yourself to those long nights playing video games while I pounded the keyboard. Your supper tin all my crazy endeavors is the reason why I keep you around. JK, love you babe.

A huge thank you to all the people who agreed to suffer through my early drafts. Thank you for all your input and for keeping me straight. Especially Christina and Gayles. Your absolute love of this story from the get go and throughout everything really kept me going.

And I can't leave without thanking Shelby of letting me create a writing club at school. You didn't know it, but I was thinking about giving up writing. But working with those kiddos, helping them create their stories, rekindled the same fire that I used to have. Thank you soul sister!

K. N. Timofeev has been a lover of stories for as long as she could remember. Some of her earliest memories consist of consuming every book she could get her hands on and making up elaborate stories to play with her friends and often unwilling brothers. When not writing, she can be found curled up with a new book (even though she has a literal to read mountain), in her garden, or out on the water with her husband trying desperately to not fall off the paddle board.

You can find out more information by going to www.timofeevbooks.com or by scanning the code below.

Please don't forget to leave a review on whatever platform you choose. Reviews are like bread and butter for poor little authors.